The Guest Who Stayed

by

Roger Penfound

Published in 2013 by FeedARead.com Publishing – Arts Council funded

Copyright © Roger Penfound

First Edition

The author has asserted their moral right under the Copyright, Designs and Patents Act, 1988, to be identified as the author of this work.

All Rights reserved. No part of this publication may be reproduced, copied, stored in a retrieval system, or transmitted, in any form or by any means, without the prior written consent of the copyright holder, nor be otherwise circulated in any form of binding or cover other than that in which it is published and without a similar condition being imposed on the subsequent purchaser.

This book is a work of fiction and, except in the case of historical fact, any resemblance to actual persons, living or dead, is purely coincidental.

A CIP catalogue record for this title is available from the British Library.

Contents		Page
Prologue		5
Chapter 1	1915–1917	9
Chapter 2	Autumn 1919	23
Chapter 3	Winter 1919	41
Chapter 4	Spring 1920	53
Chapter 5	Summer 1920	63
Chapter 6	September 1920	77
Chapter 7	Late 1920	89
Chapter 8	Spring 1921	103
Chapter 9	Summer 1921	123
Chapter 10	August Bank Holiday 1921	145
Chapter 11	August 1921	165
Chapter 12	August 1921	181
Chapter 13	August 1921	201
Chapter 14	August 1921	219
Chapter 15	October 1921	231
Chapter 16	Winter 1921–Autumn 1922	247
Chapter 17	Christmas 1927	269
Chapter 18	Spring 1928	291
Chapter 19	July 1940	315
Chapter 20	Summer 1942	345
Chapter 21	February 1946	365
Chapter 22	1947	389
Chapter 23	August 1960	401

The Guest Who Stayed: Prologue

As consciousness penetrated the black infinity in which he was immersed, Jed's first impression was of pain. It felt as if a hammer was striking the inside of his forehead with relentless ferocity, whilst a more acute sense of agony gripped the back of his head – as if someone was trying to burrow their way in through his scalp.

He recognised the first pain as merely that of an excruciating hangover. The rancid taste in his mouth confirmed the presence of stale alcohol coating his teeth and gums. But it was the pain at the back of his head that confused him. Had he fallen? Had he been attacked?

Up till now, he had not subjected any part of his body to the test of movement. Now, slowly, he tried to connect with his limbs. He felt his legs move across some sort of dirt or gravel surface. His fingers responded but he felt new pain lacerate his shoulders and arms.

He paused, trying to recollect where he was. Eventually he tried opening his eyes. The pain in his forehead increased immediately forcing him to clamp his eyes shut again. Gingerly, he squinted from behind half closed lids. The place was in semi–darkness. He could make out a door in a wall from under which shards of light reached into the room.

He closed his eyes again and tried to remember. There had been a fight. Alice was there. She had been naked, screaming and hitting him. He remembered entering the house. He was holding his shotgun. He had wanted to teach them both a lesson.

Before that, he could remember sitting in his shed, watching them through the half pulled curtains as he eased his pain with whisky, seeing them as they laughed together and crying as he saw them kiss.

He carried the gun up the stairs. Was he just going to frighten them or kill them? He couldn't remember. Bursting into her room, he had faltered. Then she was there – upon him – screaming. A hand jerked him from behind, wheeling his body round. He came face to face with Jack whose fist made splintering contact with Jed's chin. As he spun round again and fell, Alice pinned him to the floor, spreading her naked body across his. He remembered briefly inhaling her perfume and thinking how beautiful she looked. She reached for his gun. He tried to pull it away. Then the shot; a deafening crack; more screaming; another blow to his head and a vague vision of snow falling from the sky across his aching body.

As memories of the previous night filtered slowly into his brain, he was filled with a deep sense of fear and misgiving. Had the shot hurt anyone? Alice had been on top of him. Had the shot killed her? If it had, he couldn't live. His own death would be the only way out. Perhaps he had killed Jack. If he had, he was glad. No man could suffer what he had been made to endure without taking revenge. Would a jury exonerate him? Was there mitigation for a crime of passion? He doubted it. He would probably swing from the gallows.

He redoubled his efforts to move only to discover that his hands were bound together with cord. He managed to pull himself into a sitting position in spite of the pain.

Slowly he began to recognise where he was. His bike was leant against the opposite wall. Coal was piled in one corner. They had bundled him into the coal house at Hope Cottage – the very house that he'd built for him and Alice to spend their lives in together.

He began to sob silently, tears mixing with the coal dust that lightly coated his face.

It was hard to recall the journey that had brought him here, a journey that had begun with tragedy back in 1917.

He heard footsteps approaching outside. He would know the truth soon enough.

The Guest Who Stayed: Chapter 1 – 1915 – 1917

Jed: August 1917

Clouds were blowing in from the North Sea and temperatures had begun to dip. Jed was walking back from Frampton where he was apprenticed to a local handyman. At sixteen, he was still too young to be fighting in the war like his eldest brother, Matthew, who had left triumphantly two years earlier to join the Norfolk Regiment.

As he turned the bend in the drive leading to the farmhouse, his attention was drawn to the unfamiliar sound of an engine making its way along the road from Frampton. There were still not many petrol vehicles in this part of the country. Some of the better off farmers had begun to purchase diesel tractors but in the main the fields were still worked by the faithful shire horses which had trodden the loamy Norfolk soil for generations.

He saw a motor bike turn off the main road and onto the farm track. As it made its way towards him, he could see that it was painted khaki and the rider seemed to be in uniform. The bike growled onwards, throwing up clouds of dust from the unmade track. Jed expected the rider would stop to ask directions but he continued on past, with just the slightest inclination of his head.

Jed stopped where he was, gripped by a sense of unease. The bike stopped on the gravel outside the front door. He watched as the rider kicked down the stand and took an envelope from a pouch strapped to the back of the bike. Then he appeared to glance from side to side as if expecting someone else to join him. Having decided that he was on his own, he made his way to the front door and banged with his fist.

Jed's heart began to race as he waited. The door opened to reveal his mother. She was wearing her baking apron over a brown woollen dress. Strands of black hair had broken away from the bun on the back of her head and hung casually across her face. Jed saw the rider hand over the envelope. He couldn't see his mother's expression but he saw her rip the envelope open.

She let out a penetrating scream. He raced towards the house, tripping, stumbling, thorns tearing at his legs. His mother was now crumpled on the floor. The man stood motionless on the same spot. As he reached the garden fence, he saw that his father and his elder brother Tom were already at the scene. He vaulted the fence and arrived by the door as his father was lifting his mother from the step. His father's face was ashen and blank. His mother sobbed uncontrollably as she was carried into the parlour. The door was slammed in Jed's face and he was left listening to the sounds of despair – his father's voice as he'd never heard him before, braying, gasping, breathless yelps.

Jed realised that he was shaking uncontrollably. He heard the engine of the bike start up and the wheels move away over the gravel. He banged on the door.

"Ma, Pa, let me in, please let me in."

Moments later the door opened and Tom came out. Tears rolled down his cheek. He took Jed by the shoulder and led him away from the parlour.

After the news of Matt's death at the Somme, life for Jed began to change. When the official period of grieving was over, a steel shutter seemed to slam closed in the household. Photos of Matt disappeared and his name was not mentioned. Jed yearned to talk about the brother he had idolised and sometimes tried to draw his mother into conversation.

"Ma, I was thinking earlier about that time that me and Matt went fishin' over the ponds on the heath. And do you remember, Matt goes chasin' a puppy an' falls in the water and you's right mad with 'im 'cos 'e's lost a shoe in the water and ..." She interrupted him.

"Jed, let it lie. What the Lord giveth, the Lord taketh and we can't interfere. We just have to accept what comes our way and hope death takes us from this miserable life quick."

The impact on Jed's mother had been particularly severe. In a dour family of farm labourers who seldom smiled or celebrated, Matt had stood out like a shining beacon. He represented all that Jed's mother would have liked for herself but never had the slightest chance of achieving. Through Matt and the stories he told her, she had begun to live a little. Though she scolded him for his cheek and misbehaviour, inside she had rejoiced in his irreverence, self–confidence and appetite for life.

Whilst Jed's father and Tom took refuge in their work and seldom left the outbuildings where some job always made demands, his mother became increasingly depressed and dependant on Jed. It wasn't long before he had to take time off work to care for her as her health was declining rapidly.

Almost a year after Matt's death she was diagnosed with consumption and took to her bed. There was no money to pay for nurses so Jed had to take on the role of full time carer. It was a job he hated but it was made plain to him that he had no choice. As his mother's health deteriorated and she became bedridden, he found himself having to care for her very private needs – helping her wash and deal with toilet pans. As she declined further, his mother lost her sense of modesty and Jed often saw her withered body exposed to him as he struggled to cope with her daily care.

This was his initiation into the world of women. Whilst other young lads his age were becoming sexually active and their minds were beginning to fill with erotic fantasies, Jed was witnessing his mother's physical decline, hating the sight of her wrinkled skin and the stale smell of urine that constantly filled his nostrils.

Alice: September 1917

The rain fell in sheets across the flat Norfolk country permeating every item of their clothing. They had been walking for three days now along tracks and unmade roads, running away from the scene of their father's latest drunken exploits.

"Father, can we stop for a few minutes? Polly needs a rest. Look, she's exhausted."

He had been warned by the local police constable that unless they packed their bags and left, he would be arrested and thrown into Norwich gaol.

"Only a few more miles now and then we're at Frampton. We're sure to find somewhere warm to sleep tonight. Just keep going a while longer."

With that, he picked up the kit bag that contained their sole belongings and slung it over his shoulder. He strode forward without looking back to where Alice and Polly were huddled under a tree.

Seeing him disappear into the mist and rain, Alice had no alternative but to gather Polly up into her arms and follow him.

It had been so very different until five years ago when Alice's mother gave birth to young Polly. Their father had been a respected metal smith, mending agricultural machinery and making simple farming implements. They had lived comfortably, feeding themselves from the cottage garden and using what little money their father made for occasional luxuries. Alice, who was ten when Polly was born, attended the local village school and had surprised her teachers with her tenacity and determination to succeed in her subjects.

Then, when her mother died a year after Polly's birth, their world fell apart. Their father found consolation in drink and was prone to outbursts of violence which could be directed equally at his daughters or to other drinkers in the ale houses he frequented. When money became scarce, he thought nothing of stealing from shops or from friends. At first, neighbours rallied round to help Alice care for Polly but, as they were met with drunken abuse and insults, the help soon evaporated. Alice was able to attend school less and her father began to treat her as a substitute wife, demanding that she carry out chores and occasionally beating her if she failed. Alice lived in fear of him hurting Polly whose health was beginning to deteriorate. From once having been a plump and boisterous baby, she now had a sallow complexion and was nervous with people.

"Look, this is it. This is Frampton," he announced.

"But where are we going to stay? Where's the cottage you spoke of?"

Alice guessed the truth. There was no cottage. Her father had heard of fruit picking work in the area with accommodation provided, but there was no specific offer of a place to stay. It was only gossip passed on by drinkers in an ale house somewhere.

"I'll go to find it. I know it's not far from here. I want you to stay put whilst I go looking. I'll be back before long and I'll bring some food too. Mind you stay here."

With that he was gone, striding into the evening gloom. Alice held Polly close to her and stared at the bleak surroundings. The road they were following wound through a wood and the foliage seemed to offer some protection. Alice dragged the kit bag that her father had left behind into the wood and felt inside for an old army tarpaulin, the prize for some bet her father had wagered. Still damp from the previous night, she hung it over an overhanging branch and placed stones on the extended sides to form a basic shelter. Then she gathered Polly into her arms and they both huddled together, listening to the monotonous patter of drizzle on the tarpaulin.

Peering out into the grey gloom, Alice felt heavy with fatigue and depression. She seemed trapped in this spiral of decline which got worse with each day. She had to find a way to escape yet leaving Polly to her fate with a drunken father was not an option. She feared each day for Polly's safety as well as her own. Soon she would be sixteen and was already experiencing some sexual harassment from her father – comments about her breasts, unwanted touching and lewd language. She shuddered with her private memories.

Dusk turned into night and still he didn't return. Alice and Polly slept fitfully, being awoken by strange unseen sounds in the dark.

Then a different noise roused Alice. In the distance she could hear the faint sound of someone singing – a tuneless, flat dirge. She knew at once that it was her father returning. He had spent their remaining money on drink. There would be no food and no proper shelter. They would spend the rest of the night like wild and hungry animals.

Flora: October 1915

Flora and her mother and father were made to wait outside the small chapel which had been created from one of the cottages. The Brotherhood owned a dozen of these rundown premises which were situated in a working district of Frampton. They cast their eyes down as latecomers made their way past them into the chapel. Flora's father was dressed in a black suit with a starched white shirt buttoned tightly to his neck. Her mother wore a long black dress with white cuffs and a black bonnet. Flora was dressed in her usual chapel attire, a black cotton dress over which she wore a white apron, a sign that she was a virgin.

The door of the chapel opened and a lean, white haired, old man spoke to them.

"The congregation is ready. You must answer to the people in the sight of our Lord."

He stood aside and Flora's father led the way into the chapel. Her mother followed with her head bowed low and Flora walked behind.

Inside, the chapel was dimly lit and meagrely furnished. Six rows of seats were positioned either side of an aisle. They were filled with Brotherhood members, most of whom directed their gaze at the floor. A few looked with curiosity at the strange procession. At the end of the aisle, and below a large wooden crucifix, were three seats set out for Flora and her parents. To the right of these and facing the congregation were six seats, five of which were occupied by elders. The sixth was taken by the senior elder who had brought Flora and her family into the chapel. He remained standing and spoke.

"It is the tradition of our church that those who deviate from our laws be judged by the congregation in the eyes of our Lord and that those who are found guilty of transgressions shall be banished from our midst. Today, we are called to pass judgement on the Fulton family: Harold Fulton, his wife, Henrietta Fulton, and their thirteen year old daughter, Flora Fulton. It is in respect of the activities and behaviour of Flora Fulton and the refusal of her parents to curb her sinful ways that we are gathered here. Let me first remind you of the rules of the Brotherhood which have been passed down to us since the founding of our church in 1778 by the Venerable Thomas Aitchison. In the sacred words of Psalm 1, 'Blessed is the man that walketh not in the counsel of the ungodly'."

Flora sat rigidly on her chair gripping the sides till her knuckles were white. She wished she could be anywhere but here, part of this terrible stifling institution that infiltrated all aspects of their lives. The doctrine ordained that they had to be pure; they had to avoid contact with all other sinners, which in practice meant everyone else except church members. They were expected to marry within the church and avoid all forms of entertainment. The church provided them with work and basic sustenance so that they became dependant for everything.

"Wherefore come out from among them, and be ye separate, saith the Lord, and touch not the unclean thing; and I will receive you."

Flora had heard this quotation from Corinthians and many like it used to justify the teachings of the church. Since her earliest memories, she had been encouraged to learn and chant passages from the bible. Learning a new passage was one of the few ways she knew to please her parents.

"And so it is," she heard the elder saying, "that in spite of much counselling and warning, the Fulton child has been permitted to break our sacred rules."

He proceeded to read a list of alleged transgressions, some of which Flora recognised and some of which were pure fabrications. It was common within the Brotherhood to gain favour with the elders by telling them about the supposed wrong doing of your neighbours.

"Spending time with sinners and taking part in impure activities."

She had to attend the village school because the community was too small to have its own school. She had been told by her parents to remain separate from the other children and read her bible during breaks. But their constant teasing and taunting made this difficult in practice.

"Reading forbidden and impure literature."

Her teacher at school had loaned her great novels to read because she showed promise. Is this what he meant?

"Going into the homes of non believers and taking sustenance therein."

On a cold winter's day last Christmas, Flora had been invited into the home of a fellow pupil whose mother had taken pity on her. She had accepted a mince pie yet somehow word had got back to the elders. All her life it seemed she had been controlled and manipulated by others in the name of faith, respect or fear. How she longed to be rid of these shackles yet she knew that once she left the Brotherhood she would be ostracised for the rest of her life. The Brotherhood was not forgiving. They would forbid her from ever seeing her own family again.

Now it was the turn of her father to address the congregation and plead for forgiveness in the name of his daughter. How she hated his demeaning and obsequious manner. His tall and gaunt figure was bent from the shoulders down and he wrung his hands in a gesture of piety as he addressed his audience.

"Dearest neighbours and fellow worshippers, in the name of Christ we have always sought to provide a strict and righteous way of life to protect ourselves and our daughter from the evils of the world. We have sought to remain exclusive and reject the ways of the devil in line with the teachings of our leader. But the devil has exploited our weakness and found his way into our lives through the frailties of our daughter."

Flora remembered a time when they had first come to Frampton. Then, her parents were full of hope and welcomed the friendship of the Brotherhood who helped them find accommodation and even provided work for her father. In those early days, there were frequent feasts and days of rejoicing when the church would be decorated with flowers and bunting would be strung across the small square around which the cottages were arranged. Then new people arrived and there was a change of direction. All frivolity was forbidden and the doctrine of 'separation' from non church members came into being.

"You have heard the views of the elders and you have heard the views of Harold Fulton speaking on behalf of his daughter."

The senior elder was standing and addressing the congregation. Flora fixed her gaze on the floor in front. She felt the eyes of the congregation drilling into her very being.

"It is the view of the elders that the Fulton family must be punished for permitting blatant acts of defiance against the rules of our church. We have heard the pleas of Harold Fulton and believe that he truly repents of his daughter's sins. However, he was negligent in permitting the sins to occur in the first place. It is, therefore, the recommendation of the elders that the Fulton Family be 'isolated' for a period of thirty days. During this period, no member of the Church will speak to them or participate in any activity that includes them. They will be banned from eating in the presence of other members of our congregation and will be required to repent publicly once a week of their sins. Are you in agreement with the verdict of the elders?"

A low murmur of ascent rose up from the congregation.

"Then it is decided. 'Depart ye, depart ye, go ye out from thence, touch no unclean thing; go ye out of the midst of her; be ye clean, that bear the vessels of the Lord'."

The congregation dispersed, leaving Flora, her mother and her father sitting on their seats with their eyes cast downward. In the silence of the empty chapel, only the whimpering of her mother could be heard. Then, with a roar that seemed as though it came from the depths of hell itself, her father delivered a savage blow to Flora's face which threw her from her chair and sent her spinning across the stone floor until she hit the opposite wall. As she felt a searing pain engulf her head, she knew that she could no longer live like a trapped animal in this perverse community. Somehow she had to find the strength to leave.

Jack: November 1917

He lay still in the rickety bed, trying not to wake the other three members of his unit. His army issue tunic itched across his back and he had an overwhelming desire to scratch vigorously. He contemplated turning to his right to face the damp wall, but the smell of mildew deterred him. If he turned to his left he would come face to face with Bill's boots, still encrusted with cow dung from the yard outside. So he remained on his back and shifted his body back and forth against the rough mattress to achieve some measure of relief.

Intermittent snoring from the other bed where Greg and Fred slept told him that he was the only one awake. If he listened carefully, he could hear guns booming from the distant front line. How lucky he was to be in the relative safety of this French farmhouse rather than the squalid hell of the trenches. It was less than six weeks since he had been pulled from his unit on the front line and told to report to HQ some two miles back from the fighting. It was in a bombed and half ruined French chateau that he was introduced to his three unit members. Jack had been chosen for his fluent French, Greg for his pyrotechnic skills, Bill for his combat skills and Fred for his way with the carrier pigeons. They were to form a unique unit in the British army and try something that had seldom been attempted before – to go behind enemy lines and collect intelligence.

As trench warfare became increasingly futile, pressure had grown on the British Government to inject new life into the war initiative. The voices of younger officers began to be heard, considered heretics by the older brigade who had learnt their fighting skills confronting Zulu warriors in Africa. The new voices talked of intelligence, sabotage and espionage. And so Jack led his squad of three men across no man's land one dark night in April to acquire intelligence and feed false information to the Germans through a network of French collaborators.

Chief amongst these collaborators were two sisters in their mid twenties, Yvette and Simone. Their parents had died before the war and left the sisters to run the small farm consisting of a few milking cows and goats plus numerous hens. Jack had met Yvette in a café and, using his impeccable French, had recruited her and her sister. Now the unit lived in the farmhouse with the two girls – the four men sharing two single beds in one room.

Lying on his back with the first light of dawn filtering through the tattered curtains, Jack knew that their position here was precarious and they would need to move on. As the network of collaborators increased, so the opportunity grew for someone to inform the Germans in return for favours. Outside the window, he could hear the cooing of the carrier pigeons in their basket, waiting for their turn to carry messages back to the British front line.

He thought he heard a rustle, a scrape of a boot – something out of the ordinary. His body froze and his right hand gripped the knife that was strapped to his leg above his right boot.

With explosive force, the door to the room splintered from its hinges and the air filled with shrieking German voices. Guns fired. Bullets ricocheted off stone walls and a smell of cordite invaded the room.

He leapt from the bed, brandishing his knife and lashing out wildly. In the smoke and confusion it was impossible to make out what was happening. The room was full of enemy. Through the smoke, he could just make out their silhouettes. The sound of Germans yelling was now joined by the agonised screams of his comrades as rifle butts pounded their prostate bodies. Jack let out a primal roar and leapt with his knife outstretched towards one of the attacking figures. In full flight he was caught on the back of his head by a leaden instrument and his body crashed heavily onto the stone floor.

When he awoke, he was aware of being trussed with his hands tied to his feet. His head was on the floor and a sticky red substance flowed from his nose. His line of vision was limited but he could see Greg and Bill on the stone slabs bound and bleeding. A black boot was landing heavy kicks into Bill's groin, each strike causing further agonised screams. By moving his head slightly, he could see Yvette. Her night clothes had been ripped from her body and she was kneeling on the floor with her hands bound behind her. Outside of his line of vision, he could hear the sounds of another woman screaming. He felt a pistol pushed against his temple and heard the click of the trigger being cocked.

The Guest Who Stayed: Chapter 2 – Autumn 1919

Jed

Jed sat disconsolately on the top of Offa's Mount, a large outcrop of rock in an otherwise flat landscape. It had been a favourite place to visit with his elder brother Matt when he was younger. From here, you could see for miles across the flat and featureless Norfolk country. To the east, it was just possible to catch glimpses of the sea sparkling on the horizon. The origins of the rock were hotly debated, some claiming it was a meteorite from outer space, others arguing that it had been deposited there by an ancient glacier. Human remains had been found at the bottom of the steepest face suggesting that it had once been used as a sacrificial site.

He came here to think. Since his mother's death less than a year ago, he'd tried to become involved in running the farm with his father and Tom. But the daily ritual bored him. Walking behind the two Shire horses as they ploughed the ground ready for winter barley, his sense of isolation only grew. He sometimes wondered whether he truly existed or whether he was just a figment of someone's imagination. When he was with people they didn't really seem to notice him.

It had been so different with Matt. People had been drawn to him, even from an early age. If he was naughty, people said he was mischievous and laughed. When Jed was naughty, people shouted at him and he was punished. It seemed so wrong that it was Matt who had been killed. Matt had already achieved so much and would have succeeded at whatever he did, bringing great joy to his mother. Jed had achieved so little and had no idea where he was going. His life seemed to stretch ahead of him like a void.

Looking out across the fields below him dotted with newly stacked hay bales, Jed realised it was time to confront this demon. At eighteen, he felt unprepared and ill equipped for what lay ahead but he knew for certain that his destiny lay somewhere down there in the real world – not suffocating up here on the family farm.

Alice

The cottage was cold and cramped. Water dripped from the broken thatch and formed puddles on the clay floor. Alice was struggling to cook a meal on the stove but the meagre flame from the coals was failing to heat the rabbit stew. Polly was seated close to the stove to warm her thin body. She had developed a chesty cough and Alice feared for her health.

Her father was readying himself to go out. As soon as he'd eaten, he'd be off to the Fox and Hounds in Frampton to join his drinking friends. Since they'd arrived in Frampton he'd managed to secure occasional employment and this tumbledown cottage was at least better than sleeping under a tarpaulin.

But money was still in scarce supply. Sometimes there was no money for days on end yet still he managed to drink. Alice feared he was stealing again and if he was found out, they'd be forced back on the road. That was why Alice had been enquiring about part time work. She'd also been corresponding secretly with an aunt in London, collecting letters from the post office rather than let them be delivered.

She needed to speak to her father before he engaged in another bout of drinking.

"Father, I've got something I need to tell you," began Alice as she doled his stew onto a plate. "I've got a little job lined up, nothing much but it'll help out a bit and bring in a little money."

"What sort of job?" he enquired slurping stew into his mouth.

"Working in the baker's shop in the mornings – seven till eleven. I'll be home in plenty of time to get your lunch."

"What do you need to work for? Your place is at home looking after me."

"But, Father, we need the extra money. We need clothes for Polly and she needs feeding regular like. Sometimes she only has one meal a day."

"So what are you saying? Are you tellin' me I ain't providing for my little girl, because if that's what you're saying you can shut your bleedin' trap – Bitch."

With this he leant forward to hit her, but the weight of his body tipped the wooden table and sent the contents crashing to the floor where they formed a sludge of broken earthenware and rabbit stew. Alice rushed to the scullery and tried to close the door, knowing what would follow. But before she could slide the bolt he had his shoulder pinned to the door. Desperately, she pushed against the weight of his body.

"Father, please, I'll still be here to look after you. It's just a little job, that's all."

He heaved at the door and pushed it further open. Alice braced herself against a work table, using all her strength to keep him out. But he managed to squeeze his unshaven head around the door and Alice found her face inches away from his, breathing in the stench from his stale mouth. His toothless grin sent shudders down her spine.

"You see, you can never get away from me our little Alice," he called in a taunting voice. "Your place is here with me and if you don't understand that I'm going to teach you a lesson so you'll never forget."

She heard him trying to undo the belt to his trousers and knew what to expect. Feeling his weight still pressing against the door, she adjusted her own position with her back to the table. Then stepping quickly sideways, she pulled the door open which had the effect of propelling her father forward in an uncontrolled stumble, crashing headlong into a clothes mangle and crumpling into a heap on the stone floor.

Seizing a knife from a drawer, she held it in front of her, expecting the next attack. Her main thought was to prevent him getting to Polly in this state. She braced herself, prepared to use the knife if necessary. But instead of an attack, she heard crying. Her father was holding his head and crying loudly.

Alice was rooted to the ground, completely unprepared for this. She had only ever seen aggression and rage burning in his eyes. But something had snapped. His misery was so deep that finally it had engulfed him.

"Father, stop that at once," Alice heard herself saying with an authority she didn't recognise. "I'll be here for you but there are going to be changes. I am going to work because we need the money. And though it breaks my heart, I've arranged for Polly to go and stay with

Mother's sister in London. She's ill, Father, and she can't stay here any longer. It's killing her."

Tears were spilling down Alice's own cheeks now as she leant down to place a hand on her father's shoulder.

"Things has got to change now and you must accept that, Father, because with Polly gone, there's nothing holding me here anymore."

Flora

They had told her to expect a visitor but they hadn't said who it would be. Visitors seldom came to their cottage so Flora knew it must be important. She had been told to wear her black church dress with the white apron. Her father wore a black suit with a starched white collar. Her mother was dressed in her black gown and grey bonnet trimmed with white lace.

There was a light knock at the door. Flora's father heaved his bent body from the chair and shuffled to the entrance. The door opened to reveal a man who Flora knew was one of the church elders, Eli Krautz. He was in his early sixties but looked older. His head was bald except for a fringe of white tufts which circumnavigated the perimeter of his crown. His lack of growth on top was compensated for by the abundance of hair sprouting from his ears and his nose.

"Brother Eli, what an honour to welcome you to our humble home. Please come in and be at peace," grovelled Flora's father as Eli Krautz made his way into the living room.

Flora couldn't understand why a church elder was paying them a visit. Had she been involved in some 'transgression'? She couldn't recollect anything. For months now she had hardly left the community, spending most of her time sewing in the work shop.

"Brother Eli, this is my wife Henrietta and, of course, this is my daughter, Flora."

Eli observed them impassively but said nothing.

"Such an honour deserves a celebration. Would you care to take a little wine?"

Eli inclined his head slightly forward and this was taken by Flora's father to signal consent. He reached up to a high shelf and took down a dusty bottle. This was the only alcoholic drink in the house and to Flora's knowledge it had lain there untouched for two years. Her father blew the dust from the bottle and poured out two glasses. He gave one to Eli and took one for himself. The women received nothing.

"Please be seated, Brother Eli. Flora, this is indeed a great honour for our family."

She was immediately alerted to danger. Her father never addressed her directly in the presence of other people.

"Brother Eli is being spoken about as the next leader of our congregation – a very great honour. Therefore, the news that he brings is even more wonderful for our family."

Flora's father inclined his head towards Eli in the expectation that he would deliver the news, but Eli continued to stare impassively ahead.

"Well, the wonderful news, daughter, is that Brother Eli, in spite of your past indiscretions and er frailties, would like to take you for his wife."

Flora felt a sudden sickness well up in her stomach and she had a great desire to retch. The thought of physical contact with this man left her feeling faint. She knew he was a widower. His sickly and browbeaten wife had died childless nearly two years previously. In their church, it was considered shameful not to provide children for the next generation of the Brotherhood and Flora could see clearly what Eli's intentions were. She realised that her father was still speaking to her.

"You know, daughter, that in our congregation it is considered a great honour for an older man to wed a younger woman. He can then instruct her in the ways of our Lord and curb her excesses."

Flora knew that there had been talk of beatings and punishments in his household. Normally, what went on behind closed doors was of no concern to anyone else, but the crying and shouting that had disturbed the tranquillity of the community's life had led to murmurings and quiet words of 'advice'.

"We are going to leave you and Eli to talk alone now, daughter." Flora pleaded with her eyes as her mother and father rose from the table, but her anguished looks were ignored.

"Listen carefully to what Brother Eli has to say and be guided by his wisdom and experience."

Her parents left the room and Flora found herself alone in the chilling presence of Eli Krautz. He played with his wine glass, his stubby white hands gliding up and down the glass stem. When he spoke, it was to the opposite wall.

"You are young and I imagine you are fertile. That is good. If I am to be leader of this community – and I will be – I need children to follow in my name. It will be an honour for you to be my wife but I will expect you to perform your duties as a wife with the utmost diligence."

Flora felt a shudder run down her spine and she fought to stifle a scream.

"You will obey me at all times. Especially, you will obey me in the bedroom. Being a virgin and being naive, you will encounter some things that may not be to your liking and may seem, how shall I say, unholy."

Flora noticed that he was speaking more quickly now and his breathing was getting deeper.

"Within marriage, everything is acceptable and it is ordained that you will accommodate the desires of your husband – whatever they may be."

Now he had turned towards her and was leaning forward. She could see that his eyes were opaque and bloodshot.

"When I penetrate you it will be for the glory of our church. When I sow my seed, it will be for the honour of our founding fathers."

Now he had raised himself from the table and was lurching forward. Flora leapt to her feet and grabbed hold of one of the rickety wood chairs, letting out a stifled scream as she tried to create a barrier between herself and the advancing spectre. He didn't seem to notice. His eyes were distant and unseeing.

"When I take you …"

Suddenly, he was clutching at his chest and emitting a croaking sound from his throat. Froth started to bubble from the sides of his mouth. Flora was transfixed and unable to move. He clutched at the table with one hand and stretched out his other arm towards her. She made no move. Their eyes met briefly and she saw panic and fear within his. She felt suddenly removed and calm, as if she was disembodied from the scene that was playing out before her. He fell to the floor still gripping his chest. Flora knew that she should call for help but a stronger force held her back. She had been told all her life that God had ordained our lives to be led as he wished. Then this was his will. She would place her trust in him and not intervene.

She watched his final jerking movements as he lay on the floor. Instead of feeling weak and vulnerable, she felt a new strength invade her body. It was time to take control of her life and stop being the eternal victim. She had to leave this place and soon.

She took a deep breath and then let out a scream, shouting loudly for help as she rushed to the door of the next door room where her parents were waiting to offer their congratulations to the happy couple.

Jed

It was a bright morning with a hint of frost on the ground as Jed set off on the two mile walk from Mount Farm to Frampton. He had travelled the distance many times before when he had attended the town school, but since his mother's illness his visits had been far less frequent. He had also lost contact with many of his friends there. When his mother was first diagnosed with consumption, neighbours and friends would call by to offer help, but the curt greeting they received from Jed's father soon reduced this flow to a trickle and finally it dried up altogether. For over a year Jed hardly left the house, bound by his mother's need for constant attention.

Now, as he made his way between hedgerows and smelt the familiar pungency of freshly ploughed Norfolk loam, he felt as if he was entering the town for the first time, seeing it with new eyes. As he reached the outskirts, low roofed workers cottages lined the road, each with evidence of some form of toil. Smoke billowed from the furnace of a smithy and across the road milk churns littered the path outside a small dairy. Washing billowed in the wind by a laundry and a tethered cow lowed mournfully as it patiently waited its turn to enter the slaughterhouse.

Further into the town, the buildings were more substantial and imposing, housing the co operative bank, the doctor's surgery and the police station. All roads led to the market square. The buildings surrounding this were gothic in style and looked onto a central pavilion which had once served as the food market. Now, long since abandoned as a market, it housed a few benches which were usually occupied by the elderly men of the town, sitting and observing life unfold as it had done for centuries.

Today was market day and, as Jed entered the square, stall holders were busy selling a range of produce brought in from neighbouring farms and fresh fish from nearby Cromer. As he weaved his way through shoppers and stall holders, he recognised the faces of people he'd known from before his mother's illness but no one seemed to recognise him. He had the strangest feeling of being invisible.

He had to stop to get his bearings. At the far end of the market square, tucked in between two buildings was a narrow alley, known locally as Thresher's Cut. He made his way down this path until it opened out onto a small courtyard surrounded by stone buildings. The taller buildings were used as store houses and rope pulleys swung from first floor landings. Between the taller buildings were a few single story thatched workshops which predated the store houses. Jed made his way towards one of these.

Inside, he felt immediately at ease as he recognised a scene which hadn't changed in the years he'd been absent. By the window which overlooked the courtyard, was a large work bench made from rough hewn oak. Its many indentations and gouged scars were evidence of years of creative toil. On wooden racks attached to the wall by the side of the table were artisans' tools – chisels, files, wood planes and numerous hand saws. From the wooden rafters hung a profusion of additional tools and implements, some of which looked as if they'd last seen service in the Middle Ages.

Jed picked up one of the chisels and ran his fingers down the metal shaft. It brought him pleasure to handle an instrument with which he could create something useful and lasting. Jed's deliberations were halted by a gravelly voice calling out from the back room.

"Who's that out there? Is you wantin' somethin'?"

Jed recognised the voice of Daniel.

"It's me, Jed Carter."

"Who?"

"Jed Carter. I used to help out here."

Daniel came into sight, emerging from the gloom of the backroom. He looked older than Jed recollected. He was small and very slightly hunched. His body showed signs of having once been powerful but the muscles had long since given way to a fat belly which gave him a rounded and benign appearance.

"Well, blow me – Jed Carter. I thought you'd gone – left the village. Folks said there was trouble up at your place and you'd all left."

"No, it weren't like that."

Jed placed the chisel on the work bench and struggled to find words to explain his situation.

"You see, my Ma got very ill and I had to look after her. There was no one else to do it. Pa and Tom were busy on the farm and looking after Ma was left to me. I tried to get word to you."

"I heard nothin'," replied Dan, with a hint of indignation. "One day you was here and the next you was gone. I would 'ave come looking but folks said you'd left."

"I'm real sorry, Dan, but they wouldn't let me out. Ma needed seeing to all the time – you know, bed pans and all that."

"That doesn't seem right, a youngster like you having to nurse his mother."

"It wasn't good. I seen things and had to do things I don't care to talk about.

"Weren't there no one to help you, neighbours, that sort of thing?"

"You know what it's like round here. Mind your own business and keep yourself to yourself. And my Pa and Tom didn't help. Anyone come a knockin' at the door and they'd send 'em packin'."

There was a prolonged silence as Dan digested this news. Jed allowed his eyes to scan the workshop shelves, taking in boxes of rusty nails, assorted chair legs and misshapen knives. He felt his spirits begin to rise, surrounded by these implements which enabled people like Dan to create order and structure from simple raw materials.

"So what's brought you back then?" enquired Dan at last.

"My Ma died a year ago and since then I've just been left to myself."

"Why aren't you helping out on the farm then?"

"I tried but it just ain't working out. I don't fit in."

"Why's that?"

"The place is dead since Ma and Matt has gone. Matt were the life and soul of the place. You should have seen my Ma's eyes light up when he was around. He told her stories that made her laugh and got up to pranks that took her breath away. An' you could see Pa loved him too. He didn't say much but you could see it in his eyes. Now they've gone the place is like a morgue. Pa and Tom work together and no one seems to know I exist – or even cares."

Dan sat down heavily on an old sea chest that served as a seat.

"Well, I care young Jed. I done my fair share of being alone and I know it ain't good. We all need to belong and we all need some purpose. Have you had any thoughts about what you want to do?"

"I was brought up to do farming and I ain't trained for anything else. But I love this place, all them tools and that lathe over there. I like making things. I think I'd like to build things, houses, cabinets, chairs – anything."

Dan rubbed his beard thoughtfully and scratched his ample stomach as he pondered Jed's situation.

"Well, it seems to me, young Jed, there ain't no choice. How about you come and work for me again and learn yourself a proper trade. My arthritis stops me doing all the things I need to do an' I need a pair of young hands to help me."

Jed's face was transformed from desolation to ecstasy. It was the outcome he'd hoped for but hardly dared believe might happen.

"I don't know what to say. I mean yes – yes. It's what I want. You're a real friend, Dan."

"I can only pay you a small wage, mind. If you wants you can sleep overnight in the loft. Saves you having to go back each night when we're working late."

"I'll work for a pittance and I'll work real hard and learn from you and …"

"So be it," said Dan, interrupting Jed's torrent of gratitude.

"Just you mind you don't go runnin' off again like last time. Now, how about you beginning by fetching me a mug of tea. I like it real dark, mind, with five big spoons of sugar."

Jack

Jack rearranged the papers on his desk once more. Behind him, the factory was visible on the other side of the glass panelled door. The low hum of machinery provided a constant background to any conversation. The volume rose suddenly as the office door opened.

"Good news, Jack. We'll meet the target this week. Ten machines completed by the end of today."

The young factory manager was in his mid twenties, conventional save for the wooden peg leg that replaced the one he had been born with.

"Thanks, Adam. That's good work. Have they all been tested?"

"All but the last one. That's just going on the test rig now."

"Good. I'd like that to be on the rig when I show this fellow round. He should be here shortly. I'll have a chat to him, then give him a brief tour."

"Right. We'd better get the place tidied up a bit."

The factory manager left, leaving Jack waiting for the visitor. A sudden fit of coughing forced him to sit down at his desk and hold onto his chair for support. The words of his doctor were still ringing in head. It was only two days since he'd been summoned to the surgery to receive the results of hospital tests.

"The news isn't good, Jack," announced his doctor, reclining into a deep leather chair. "It's the mustard gas that's really done the harm to your lungs and it's damaged the linings of your bronchial tubes too. All this coughing and straining is putting huge pressure on your heart and it's getting weak. Then that beating you took has weakened you too. Basically, your body is showing signs of giving up."

"So what are you saying?" enquired Jack, nervously. "What treatment are you suggesting?"

"There isn't any treatment. Your condition is chronic. I'm afraid you've got five years at the most – three if you stay here in London. You need to get out of the city, away from the smog. Find somewhere near the seaside and enjoy what time's left to you."

Sitting at his office desk, Jack tried to compose himself before his visitor arrived. He had returned to the family business at the end of the war making sewing machines for the tailoring trade in the east end of London. His father had started the company in 1883 after he and his French wife had arrived in London as refugees from Russia. It had been modestly successful and Jack's brother had been destined to inherit the factory on his return from war, but like so many other young men he became another victim of the slaughter in the trenches of northern France and the business passed to Jack.

Jack's war had ended in late November 1917 when he was rescued, half dead, from a German interrogation centre. It took six months for him to convalesce and though the physical scars healed, the mental scars would trouble him for the rest of his life. Determined to put the war behind him, he put all his efforts into rescuing what had by then become a failing business. Using skills learned in the army, he experimented with attaching electric motors to sewing machines instead of the traditional foot pedal. The idea proved successful and their fortunes began to revive but Jack soon realised he needed investment to make the business secure. Other rival companies were offering similar innovations and scale was the answer to keeping prices competitive.

Now, with the news that his life expectancy was five years at the most, carrying on with the business seemed futile. He had to get away – do something different for these final years. That's why this meeting was so important. He unfolded the letter again and re read the contents. It was from a Mr. Grant P. Hoester, Chief Executive Officer of Deltic Sewing Machines of Chicago. It read:

Dear Mr. Malikov,

Deltic Sewing Machines of Chicago intends to launch a new range of electric driven models into the UK. Having researched the market in your country, we have decided that our preferred policy would be to buy a British company and develop an existing product. We have conducted exhaustive tests on the S104 model made by your company and are very impressed with the performance and durability. We would like to arrange a convenient date for our agent in the UK, Mr. Alec Morgan, to meet with you and discuss the potential for a sale.

Jack knew the rest of the letter by heart – he had read it many times. He stood up from the desk and looked out of the soot–stained window. A dank mist clung to the buildings and pavements, making it difficult to determine exact shapes – 'five years at the most, three if he stayed in London'.

He would do as the doctor had suggested, go to the coast, maybe buy a small place with the proceeds of the sale. The sea air would be good. Perhaps he could even cheat death a little longer.

The Guest Who Stayed: Chapter 3 – Winter 1919

Winter began early in 1919. There were extensive snow falls in mid November and the Norfolk country side was buried beneath an icy white blanket. Work in the fields ceased and animals were brought back into the barns to protect them from the plummeting winter temperatures.

In Frampton people hurried about their tasks with shawls pulled across their faces to protect them from the biting wind that drifted in from the North Sea. No one stopped to chat or pass the time of day. Many carried logs or kindling wood, desperate to keep their fires well stocked against the penetrating cold.

The bad weather brought plenty of work for Dan and Jed. Pipes were bursting and roofs collapsing under the weight of snow. Together they worked from dawn to dusk, wrapped in layers of old clothing with thick hoods pulled over their heads. They spent much of their time up ladders exposed to the full fury of the wintry weather. In the evenings they would sit by a wood fire in Dan's back room, cooking a meal on the hot embers. Jed enjoyed these quiet evening together. It gave him a chance for the first time in his life to discuss things that were on his mind.

"I been thinking, Dan."

"Thinking what?"

"The future. I'm thinking about my future. Is it good thing to have ambition, you know, to want things?" Dan raised his gaze slowly from the fire where he had been quietly contemplating the dancing embers.

"Well, that's a big question. What makes you ask that?"

"Perhaps I could make something of myself, you know, earn some real money – become successful. And I was just wondering, what's it down to? Is it luck or is it down to me? I mean – does what I do make any difference?"

"You mean can you control your destiny? It's a big question – one that wiser men than me have considered."

Dan drew heavily on the clay pipe, emitting a plume of acrid grey smoke. He had no formal education but he made up for this with a life spent travelling and observing many different cultures. Brought up in a farming community on the east coast, he tired of working on the land and at the age of nineteen he signed up with the British army and was shipped out to the Transvaal where he saw action in the Anglo Zulu war of 1875. He travelled widely across Africa as an infantryman and took part in many bloodbaths as the boundaries of the Empire were extended across the continent.

When he came home in 1880, he suffered a breakdown and lived an isolated life in the woods and forests of eastern England, eking out a meagre living by making simple pieces of furniture from fallen wood. In fact, so good did he become at crafting wood, that his services were sought by increasing numbers of people, leading him eventually to this simple work shop in the centre of Frampton, which also served as his home.

"Let me tell you about a wise man I met in North Africa," he said eventually, tapping the remnants of tobacco from his pipe onto the stone hearth. "Sort of priest he was. He'd travelled right across Africa and knew about lots of things. I was in charge of him. He was my prisoner. We got on well together, talking through the hot nights about this and that. I asked him that same question, 'Do we all have a destiny and if so, how do we reach it?'"

"What did he say?"

"He told me that there's two sorts of people in this world, those that follows their dream and those that follows their star."

"What does that mean?" enquired Jed, not quite seeing the point.

"It means this. Those that follows their dream has an idea of what they want and where they want to get to – call it ambition if you like. They shut their eyes to everything else because they're busy chasin' that dream. If they achieve that dream, then they're happy and contented. Trouble is most people don't realise their dream and end up miserable. And they also miss a lot of chances on the way 'cos they've had their eyes shut."

"What about them that follows their star?"

"Well, them's different, you see. They don't have a dream. They go where life takes them – following all manner of twists and turns on their way. They let fate decide for them."

"Like they're not in control?"

"Well, this wise man told me that some of the greatest people he'd met followed their star. They never set out to be special, they just went where life took them and did what they had to do. But somehow they succeeded. Maybe because their eyes were open and they could see things that others couldn't."

"So what do you think, Dan, follow your dream or follow your star?"

Dan relit the pipe with a smouldering taper pulled from the embers.

"It seems to me you've got to do a bit of both. We all need a dream, something that we want to reach out for – something that drives us on. But you'd be foolish to close your eyes to other opportunities. So I think you've got to be open. Head off down your path but if you see a good opportunity, don't be afraid to make a turn and take a chance. Life's a gamble alright but if you don't join in the game you'll never get the winnings."

There was a pause whilst Jed reflected on Dan's story. He was beginning to feel the stirrings of ambition within him where before there had only been dull acceptance of the inevitable. He had never dared to dream before but now he was excited by the possibilities that began to flood though his mind.

"Well, I've got a dream."

"What's that?"

"Be successful, have people look up to me and respect me – maybe even run my own business."

Dan tapped his pipe on the hearth again with apparent agitation.

"What about friends, lovers, family? What about travel, learning, and wisdom – don't they have any place in your dream?"

"Maybe," answered Jed, slightly taken aback. "But they'll have to fit in with that dream. I ain't going to compromise, Dan."

They both returned their gaze to the fiery embers which seemed to conjure up in Jed's mind tantalising yet intangible images of a future he couldn't yet visualise.

"What happened to that prisoner of yours – the wise man?"

"We shot him dead a few days later. He was a trouble maker."

It took Alice half an hour to trudge through the snow to the bakers shop. The contrast between the freezing streets and the warm shop smelling of freshly baked bread was blissful. She had settled in well to her work and the little extra money she earned had made a big difference. For the first time she had some independence and the taste of this made her yearn for more.

One morning in early December, a new customer came into the shop. She was a girl about Alice's age, with a rounded figure, a pretty face and shoulder length black hair. Her name was Flora and she told Alice that she'd just moved out of her parents' house into a room in the centre of Frampton. She was housekeeping for an old lady in the afternoon and working at the drapers store in the morning. The two girls soon became firm friends, meeting during their lunch breaks and occasionally visiting the tea shop together after work. They discovered that their lives shared common themes. Both had oppressive fathers and both had suffered physical abuse. Flora told Alice about the 'Brotherhood' and how it controlled the lives of its congregation and about her near forced marriage to an ageing elder. Alice recounted the story of her flight from their former home after her father had been caught stealing; how her sister Polly had become ill and how she had to arrange for her to be sent away to stay with an aunt in London. Over many long conversations, they slowly helped to build each other's confidence, daring to talk about their hopes for a different type of future.

"What chance is there for women like us?" asked Flora one evening as they slowly walked home together through the gas lit streets of Frampton. "I mean, it seems like men have all the power and the best we can hope for is to marry someone who treats us nice."

"I don't think like that," replied Alice. "I think you've got to treat marriage just as you would any other deal. You've got to see what both sides offer and if it makes good sense – take your chance."

"How do you mean? What about loving the man?"

"It's not all about love, Flora. It's about power and position too. That church elder they tried to make you marry – that wasn't love. That was control – him controlling you. Well, women have power too – it's just different to men. Men need a home, they need a companion, they need a woman in their bed. They need someone to encourage them and sometimes to comfort them. That's a lot of power a woman has. All I'm saying is that you've got to use that power. Don't be a victim, Flora. You've got to be a bit cunning."

"So you're not going to fall in love, Alice?"

"Some things are more important than love, Flora."

As Christmas 1919 approached, Jed felt himself becoming more reclusive again. Decorations were beginning to appear around the town and this added to his sense of detachment. The continued bleak winter meant that he and Dan were either battling the elements on a windswept rooftop or else toiling in the workshop late into the evening. Although ostensibly they continued to work together well, Jed had begun to notice that Dan was slowing down. His 'after lunch' snooze was extending from one hour to almost two hours and he increasingly left the heavy work to Jed, complaining of attacks of 'lumbago'.

Jed spent Christmas Day with his father and Tom. They ate in silence around the large table in the farmhouse kitchen. After lunch his father retired to their little used sitting room, and sank into his late wife's favourite chair where he drank half a bottle of brandy before slipping into a coma from which he didn't recover until the next morning.

Early on Boxing Day, Jed returned to the workshop, unable to stand the atmosphere at Mount Farm any longer.

"What you doing back here then?" asked Dan in surprise as Jed walked in.

"Come back to work. Ain't nothin' of interest to me at home."

"You should be off with the other youngsters, not working on your holiday."

"Doing what?"

"Well, I don't know. In my day we went skating in the winter."

"I've no time for sliding around on ice, Dan. We've got jobs to get done so we gets paid on time. A bit more work and a bit less snoozing would make all the difference."

Dan felt a wave of dismay wash over him.

In February the winter turned icy. There were storms in the North Sea and fishermen were reported lost in the freezing waters around the coast. People no longer lingered to chat in Frampton's town square and Jed found himself becoming morose and uncommunicative.

"Somethin' wrong with you then, lad?" enquired Dan one afternoon. "Hardly said a word to me in days. Somethin' I've done is it?"

"There's nothin' wrong with me."

"Well, if it's not me, it's gotta be somethin' else. I reckon you need to get out a bit and meet some people your own age – time you found yourself a young woman. That's what most lads your age would do."

"Then why ain't you ever married, Dan?" demanded Jed more aggressively than he had intended. "Maybe we're not so different after all."

There was an uncomfortable silence during which Jed regretted his outburst.

"There was a girl, many years ago," replied Dan in a quiet and reflective voice. "Her name was Mary – lived in Little Marcham, about twenty mile from here. We were due to be wed. Her parents had agreed and it was all set."

"What happened?" asked Jed, putting down a chisel and listening more attentively.

"It were after I came back from Africa, fighting them Zulus. I'd been living rough in the woods for over a year. My head had been done in and I needed time alone. One cold winter, her father found me, frozen and half dead. They took me in and brought me back to life. That's how I met Mary – she nursed me. They treated me like their own son and when Mary and me announced our engagement, they were delighted. But then it all started to go wrong. Lots of arrangements, a wedding service, a new job and talk of babies. My head still weren't right. On the day of the marriage, I just couldn't do it. I went back into the woods. I heard the bell tolling in the distance. I knew it was for our wedding and I should have been there. But I couldn't do it. I deserted her."

"You deserted her?"

Dan's head drooped and he placed a hand over his eyes.

"That weren't good, deserting a girl on her wedding day."

"Worst decision of my life – never forgiven myself."

"So what did you do?"

"I went back to living in the woods. I was there for another two year before I eventually found my way to Frampton."

"And Mary?"

"She found someone else – at least her parents did. A local lad – simple but OK. They had children and still live in Little Marcham, I believe."

"Did you ever see her again?"

"Once I met her. I wanted to say sorry – to explain that it wasn't her – it was me. But she didn't want to know. It was over. She had moved on. And that's it, I suppose. You've got to seize your opportunity. 'Cos if you don't you may not get another chance."

In early March the winter weather finally broke and spring invaded the Norfolk countryside. Hedgerows burst into life and bird song filled the air. Heavy Shire horses moved out from their winter barns and once again worked the fields and meadows, side by side with spluttering tractors which were an increasingly common sight on the land now.

The spring brought with it news that the traditional May Fair was going to be revived. During the war years it had been cancelled but now the town council had decreed that Frampton needed an injection of merriment to counter post war gloom and the first weekend in May was designated for the event.

As May Fair fever began to grip the small town, Dan and Jed found their time increasingly taken up with making stalls and sideshows. Jed had to visit the site to help plan the position of stalls that he and Dan had been commissioned to build. The fairground was situated on common land to the east of the town. In earlier times it had been grazing land, given to the village by the local land owners. Now, it had mostly reverted to gorse and grass with small pockets of stunted trees, their branches bent towards the west by the powerful winds blowing inland from the east coast. It was a place where town's people walked in the summer with their families and where young lovers would linger in the evenings, slipping in and out of cover provided by wooded thickets. Jed thought how pleasant it would be to walk with a girl up here amidst the freshness of the spring flowers.

In the final weeks leading up to the fair, Dan and Jed were kept frantically busy producing a range of items that seemed essential to the success of the event – latrine seats, a magician's screen, a maypole, staves for the Morris dancers and flagpoles.

On the few occasions that he was able to venture into the town, Jed noticed strangers beginning to arrive – tinkers, traders, horse dealers, fortune tellers and beggars. They gathered around the Fox and Hounds which began to take on a distinctly decadent aura. Two constables were drafted in from neighbouring North Walsham to help the local policeman who found himself accommodating extra 'guests' each night in a gaol designed for two inmates. The day before the fair, crowds gathered in the square to watch a massive steam engine trundling slowly through on its way to the fairground. It was towing a trailer emblazoned with the words 'Famous Flying Horses Carousel'. Joining the cheering crowds by the roadside, even Jed felt his spirits lift briefly.

Jack was seated in the opulent surroundings of a private dining suite in London's Mayfair Hotel. The table was laden with wine and cigars. Opposite him sat the imposing figure of Grant P. Hoester, Chief Executive Officer of Deltic Sewing Machines. He was flanked by two aides who had accompanied him on his trip from Chicago. Alec Morgan sat next to Jack, sucking on a large Havana cigar.

Through the fog of cigar smoke, Grant P. Hoester addressed Jack.

"So, Jack, I deliberately haven't told you how much we'll pay. For me that's not an issue. If I want something I'll pay for it and you'd be stupid to refuse my offer. In here, Jack, is my offer price. It's non negotiable."

Grant P. Hoester passed an expensive looking envelope across the table. Jack opened the gold embossed flap and pulled out a folded piece of note paper. Across the table, all eyes were trained on him. Jack unfolded the paper – twenty five thousand pounds. It was much more than Jack had imagined. This was a fortune to him, an East End boy brought up on charity in hard times.

"There's one thing though, Jack. I need you to stay with us for one year from today to help us get established in the UK."

"One year?" echoed Jack.

"Yes, one year – it's non negotiable."

Jack calculated that left him with four years at the most. Twenty five thousand pounds to spend in four years. Then he would be dead.

The wine and the cigar smoke began to play tricks on his mind. Banished memories came flooding back. A cellar, stinking of sweat and urine. Ropes cutting deep into his flesh. A whip lashing mercilessly into his back. The sound of his own screams. Yvette nearby, calling out in pain. How he longed for death then. Now he wanted to live. But he knew he was going to die.

"Jack, Jack – are you ready to sign?" Hoester was standing over him, a document clutched in his hand.

"Sign here, Jack. Then we're done."

The pen felt leaden as Jack lifted it to sign his name. Four years to live the rest of his life. What could he do in that time? Where could he go?

"That's it, Jack. You're going to be a rich man."

They clapped him politely. It felt like he'd just signed his death warrant.

The Guest Who Stayed: Chapter 4 – Spring 1920

The fair opened on Friday, 30th April, but for most towns folk this was still a working day with Saturday and Sunday set aside for the main celebrations. Jed was occupied in the workshop, angered by the absence of Dan who had met former cronies amongst the travellers and itinerants who had flooded into Frampton and was spending increasing time drinking with them in the Fox and Hounds. He relied on Dan for conversation and normality. Now, working alone in the cluttered workshop, he began to feel himself drifting back towards that feeling of isolation that he'd tried hard to put behind him.

Saturday morning dawned bright and warm. Everywhere there was evidence that the long cold winter was now a distant memory. Cherry trees were in full blossom and Frampton had taken on a distinctly pink hue.

At midday he stopped his work to go and fetch some bread from the bakers. The town square was surprisingly empty. Jed assumed that most people had already gone to the fair. He felt a morose apathy start to take hold of him. Back in the workshop, he tore with his teeth at the bread loaf, bit chunks from a lump of cheese, belched loudly and passed wind – regressing in minutes to a primitive state that evolution had taken countless generations to eradicate.

Jed's meal was interrupted by the door of the workshop bursting open and Dan tumbling into the room, his legs giving way beneath him. Jed stayed seated.

"You been drinkin' again? Seems all you been doing the last few days, is drinkin'," observed Jed, tetchily.

He tore another chunk of bread from the loaf with his teeth as Dan pulled himself up from the floor and dusted down his clothes.

"Don't you go insinuatin' nothin'," Dan slurred as he grabbed at the work bench for support. "These people I'm 'avin a drink with are my friends. Known 'em on and off for years I 'ave. But I suppose you don't know nothin' about friends on account of the fact you ain't got none."

Dan let out a growl from deep within his stomach and crashed onto a chair.

"Anyway, what you doin' workin' 'ere when everyone else is up the fair? I don't want folks thinkin' I'm treatin' you as some sort of a slave."

There was silence as Jed tried to swallow the bread that he had forced into his mouth and Dan searched for a rag to wipe saliva from his beard.

"I ain't interested in fairs," retorted Jed. "Can't see what all the fuss is about. All them silly side shows and people gettin' drunk and pukin' all over the place."

"Your problem is you ain't got no guts. You're so bleedin' sorry for yerself you don't act normal."

"I been working, runnin' your bloody business whilst you drink with them gypsies."

"What you been doing boy is hiding 'cos you ain't got the nerve. You idolise your dead brother, but d'you think he'd be sittin' round with the fair in town? No, he'd be up there with the others, drinkin' and womanising like the best of 'em. That's what you should be doin'."

Goaded by the mention of Matt, which struck to the core of Jed's insecurity, he leapt from his seat and grabbed Dan's collar, spitting his words into the old man's face.

"You bastard, Dan. That's what I get for all the help an' work I been doin' for you. I thought we was goin' to be partners, build this business together. But what chance of that now, eh? No way I'm going to work with a nasty old bastard who turns on 'is partner. So keep your bloody workshop, I don't want none of it anymore."

With that, Jed pushed open the stable door and rushed into the street beyond.

Dan remained sitting. He chuckled nervously to himself. Jed had it coming. It was a risk but he had to do it. He'd seen it in the army when a young recruit first went into action and was filled with fear. There was no use being kind to the fella because he would cry like a baby. He'd seen the sergeant major shout and bellow at the recruit in front of all his comrades till he was broken. Then he didn't care what happened. He didn't care whether he lived or died. Sometimes it worked and sometimes it didn't.

Out in Thresher's Cut, Jed propped himself against a wall, breathing heavily as tension gripped his body. He looked back at the workshop, half expecting Dan to call out and apologise, saying that it was the drink talking, not him. But the door remained shut. Jed made his way to the end of the cut and into Market Square. It was now empty, only a few stragglers hurried through on their way to the fairground. He stood there, not knowing where to turn next. Returning to Mount Farm was not an option. His life was here in Frampton with Dan, or it had been up till five minutes ago.

The empty square seemed like a metaphor for his life. There was an eerie silence except for the distant sound of fairground music carried on the breeze. Unthinkingly, he turned to the direction of the music and began walking. As he reached the outskirts of the town, he caught up with small groups still making their way to the fair – families with small children clutching at a parent's hand and older couples, arm in arm, all drawn towards this unlikely Utopia.

Arriving at the fair, his senses were attacked by a raucous mix of sound, sight and smell. The thumping rhythm of a steam organ provided the background beat, and the discordant noise of each stall as he passed provided a constantly changing chorus. His ears were accosted by the wailings of unseen apparitions as he made his way past the ghost house and he was nearly knocked over by a small child being ejected at speed from the bottom of the helter skelter.

Jed pushed his way further into the throng of people. There were many he recognised – shopkeepers, traders, farmers, even the minister was there. The air was full of laughter and shouting. Men swilled beer from pewter flagons and puffed at clay pipes. Women drank cider and scolded 'out of control' children.

Elbowing his way past the swing boats and the funicular ride, Jed found himself at the heart of the fair. The prize position was taken by the carousel. Finely sculpted horses were set in rows of three around a central spine and each horse was festooned with feather plumes.

Jed stepped back into the crowd to watch the scene. Children and adults alike were clambering on, searching for a vacant horse. Ordinarily taciturn faces were now lit with smiles as they clambered into saddles.

With a hiss of steam the organ in the centre burst into life. A strident tune began to play as the horses strained forward and the carousel turned. A cheer went up from the onlookers and the riders waved back or gripped on for their lives. As it picked up speed, the horses and their riders began to rise up and drop, faster and faster as the music rose in tempo. Men laughed and shouted to friends who were watching. Ladies clung to their hats with one hand and to their horses with the other. The crowd roared its greetings as friends or family sped past.

Jed felt himself pulling back. The noise, the shouting and the music was starting to echo again in his head and mock him. He wasn't part of this. He felt his chest tighten and his breathing become shorter. He looked for an exit but he was locked in by the crowd. Pushing his way through, he ignored angry shouts in his haste to escape.

Away from the carousel he felt calmer. There was more air to breathe and the throbbing in his head subsided. After a few moments rest, he started to retrace his route back to Frampton. But his progress was interrupted by raucous screaming from a ride just ahead. Unable to resist the urge to find out what causing the commotion, he slipped in amongst the watching crowd. The ride was just stopping and disorientated passengers were staggering or falling from six small cars that appeared to run on an oval track. Jed looked up to the banner flying over the ride. It was called 'The Whip'. Not having been to a fair before, that meant nothing to him. He watched as the crowd surged forward to fill the empty cars. Just in front of him, two girls about his own age were taking their place in the nearest car. Jed had noticed them before in Frampton. One was small and neat with shoulder length auburn hair. The other had a fuller figure with long dark hair tumbling in ringlets down her back.

A bell sounded, indicating the ride was about start.

"Last few seats. Take your places quick," yelled a young attendant.

Jed watched the two girls in front of him gripping the sides of the car tightly, anticipation etched across their faces. Suddenly, he felt a strong arm on his shoulder propelling him forward.

"Here y'are, mate. Do us a favour and sit in that one. Them girls 'll need a fella."

Taken by surprise, Jed found himself bundled into the car before he could protest. He sat in the empty seat between the two girls, completely unsure of what to say. His discomfort was evident.

"I'm Alice," said the girl to his left.

"And I'm Flora," said the girl to his right.

Suddenly, the car moved forward with a sickening lurch. Both girls screamed loudly. Jed looked around frantically, trying to work out where they were going. The cars were being propelled around the oval track at increasing speed. As they came to the first bend, the car seemed to hold back momentarily before being whipped forward as is it shot around the curve. Jed was deafened by the screams of the two girls either side of him. Still the car picked up speed. When it reached the second bend, Jed felt his stomach grip in anticipation of what was to follow. A violent movement lurched the car forward, throwing Flora sideways across his lap. He glimpsed fear in her eyes as she struggled to extricate herself. Onto the first straight again. From the corner of his eyes, Jed could see people in the crowd waving and laughing. As they approached the next bend, he braced himself with his feet pressed up hard against the front panel. A momentary pause and then the car was swept around, the centrifugal forces pinning him to his seat. As the car came out of the turn, Alice was tossed across the seat with such force that she collided with Jed and temporarily winded him. Briefly they exchanged bemused glances. Jed now felt more in control. He knew what to expect next. To his right, Flora had stopped shouting and had turned ghostly pale. At the next turn he braced himself. Flora had let go of the side of the car and the swinging motion shot her straight into Jed's arms. This time, he held onto her, thrusting his arm around her waist and pulling her tight against him. Down the next straight now, still gathering speed. A violent swing and Alice was thrown hard against him. He seized her with his free arm and clung on. Both girls willingly succumbed, placing their own arms around Jed and gripping tightly. At the next turn, screaming turned to laughter as the forces fused the three of them into one writhing mass.

Momentarily, Jed seemed to be looking back at himself on the ride. He saw himself laughing, shouting and holding the two girls tightly to him as the cars ricocheted around the track. Never before in his life would he have imagined he could do this. This was the sort of thing other boys did as he would look on from the shadows. He had a strange feeling that Matt was there with him – enjoying it hugely – laughing and urging him on.

He was dragged quickly back to reality as a new sensation gripped the car. A juddering squealing wail replaced the chatter of the wheels as brakes were applied somewhere on the ride. With ferocity their speed was reduced and the forces pinning their bodies together subsided. Jed felt a huge sadness engulf him as the girls self consciously retrieved their limbs. As the cars pulled into the disembarkation platform, the three found themselves smiling nervously at each other.

"What did you say your name was?" enquired Alice.

"I didn't. I mean, it's Jed. Jed Carter."

"I think we've seen you around in Frampton. Do you work there?" asked Flora.

"Yes, I work with the joiner down Thresher's Cut. He's got a workshop there. I help him."

They pushed their way through the throng of people waiting their turn to ride the Whip.

"I'm really glad you joined us," ventured Flora. "I think I would have died if you hadn't been there."

"Well, to be honest with you, it was the fairground bloke who pushed me onto the ride."

"Then I'm glad he did."

Jed felt inwardly relieved that their forced introduction on the Whip had been met with approval.

"So now we have met, why not join us," suggested Alice. "You never know, we might need saving again."

The three of them made their way round the fair, stopping at the coconut shy where Jed's precise aim won him the largest coconut. They retired to the shade of some trees where they prised open the fruit and laughed uproariously as they tried to pour the sweet milk into their mouths, ending up with torrents of white liquid drenching their clothes. Jed felt overwhelmed with the heady euphoria of knowing that he belonged.

First it was gunfire, short rounds of automatic fire outside the interrogation room. It was enough to stop the German soldiers in the midst of their brutal acts. Then an explosion and the door of the interrogation room flies back, crushing two soldiers to the wall. After that, pandemonium. More gunfire and smoke. Hooded men in black pouring into the room. The Germans grab their weapons and fire back. In the small confines of the room, blood spurts from punctured bodies and forms patterns on the wall behind. Someone is shouting at him.

"Malikov, Malikov. Are you Malikov?" He has been drifting in and out of delirium and manages only a gasped, "Yes."

A searing pain pulses through is leg. He must have been hit. Then he is being untied, his naked body pulled away from the pipe to which it had been chained. The gunfire is incessant. There is screaming and broken bodies lying on the floor. He recognises Bill's prone body. Someone grabs his legs and somebody else grabs his arms – he is being moved out of the room. Then he sees Yvette. She's still alive, chained like him to a pipe – naked and bloodied. He summons his strength to shout.

"Take her, take her too."

"Only the Brits mate – them's the orders."

"Please."

Suddenly cold air bites at his body. He is outside and wrapped in blankets. He hears barked orders.

"How many have we got?"

"Two, sir, the others are dead."

"What about our boys?"

"Two gone, sir, Mckenzie and Burgess."

"Right, finish them off in there with grenades then get these two to the airstrip. Move!"

Lying on his bed in the dark of the night, Jack revisits the scene as he does most nights. Two of his unit lost as well as Yvette. What about Simone? Was she there? He can't remember. He tries to blank out the image but it becomes sharper, the screaming, the lash of whips and the shouting of the interrogators. His men knew the mission was dangerous but did he betray Simone and Yvette? Did he cause their deaths in that most brutal and horrible way? Or did someone else betray them? The question gnaws at him relentlessly and gives him no peace.

The Guest Who Stayed: Chapter 5 – Summer 1920

As late spring turned into early summer and the weather settled into a cycle of hot days and warm, sultry evenings, Jed's friendship with Alice and Flora began to blossom. They would meet up two or three evenings a week to walk along the farm lanes surrounding Frampton and occasionally to picnic on the heath where the fair had been held. For Jed, these were happy times. He had very little experience of being in female company and found himself relaxing and enjoying the gentle banter and innuendo that was part of their emerging sexuality.

"So do you have feelings about girls then, Jed?" asked Flora one evening as they lay sprawled on a blanket beneath the shade of an old elm tree.

"What sort of feelings?"

"What makes you want a girl?"

Jed paused, realising that he was rapidly leaving his comfort zone.

"I dunno really. How she looks, how she smiles, how she talks to me."

"But what things turn you on?" persisted Alice. "Do you ever have thoughts about what it's like to lay with a girl?"

"Course I have thoughts about it, yes. It's only natural? I imagine things like any man."

"Do you imagine things about us?" asked Flora, trying hard to suppress an embarrassed grin.

"I suppose I do, yes."

"What sort of things?"

"I'm embarrassed to say. You're friends."

"But we're women too, Jed. Don't forget that," added Alice.

Jed pondered Alice's words and turned them over in his mind for some days after that. He knew he was attracted to both girls in different ways. Alice was self assured and confident. Her neat good looks gave her an aura of efficiency. When he was with her, he felt safe and at ease. With Flora it was different. She lacked Alice's simple sophistication but she radiated warmth. Her looks were often dishevelled but her face was illuminated by a broad smile which highlighted her full red lips. Her contours were more rounded than Alice's and Jed began to realise that his 'imaginings' were mostly centred on Flora.

"It's the same old routine, day after day," complained Alice one evening as they strolled along country lanes bathed in the warm glow of an evening sun. "We work all day then boast each evening about how we're going to change everything, then we go back to work the next day and do exactly the same. Nothing changes – ever. We're trapped in this endless cycle of grind. It's like the world only consists of Frampton. What goes on outside of here? Don't you two ever wonder?"

"Hey, what's got into you then?" demanded Jed, grabbing Alice playfully by the wrists and trying to look her straight in the eyes. Alice grumpily shook herself free.

"It's the difference between saying you're going to do something and meaning it," replied Alice in a quiet but assertive voice that reduced the other two to silence. "Are we just like everyone else – like the old men in the market square, like the old women in the wash house, like the drunks in the Fox and Hounds – full of big ideas but not the slightest chance of doing any thing about them. Will that be us in thirty years time?" Alice visibly shook at the thought. The three of them walked along in silence for the next few minutes, unable to decide how best to break the awkward impasse. Flora took the plunge.

"We could have an outing."

"An outing?" shrieked Alice, incomprehension emblazoned across her face. "I'm talking about changing our lives and you suggest an outing."

"Don't be hard on her," replied Jed, coming quickly to Flora's help. "Every journey's got to start somewhere. You just said nothing ever changes. Well, an outing's a first step. Let's do that. Let's make a little change then we can move on to bigger ones." Alice sighed with resignation but reluctantly agreed.

They decided to take the train to the Norfolk Broads, a picturesque network of inland water ways which were popular with boating enthusiasts. They had been formed by people extracting peat in the middle ages but had long since been filled with water diverted from nearby rivers.

Sunday, 6th June dawned bright with a low lying mist that would soon burn off in the heat of the promised sun. They caught the early train to Wroxham which lay at the heart of the Broads. As they pulled into the station, the opposite platform was full with people arriving for the day from Norwich or coming from as far away as London to begin a boating holiday. Since the end of the war, people were again beginning to take a summer break and a week boating on these popular waterways was becoming a fashionable choice.

The three of them followed the throng of people out of the station and into the high street. The road was like a scene from a picture postcard. Tea rooms and eating places adorned with colourful canopies stretched along both sides of the street, interspersed with curiosity shops and stalls selling flags and souvenirs.

They made their way to the bridge in the centre of Wroxham which crosses the River Bure. Here was a scene of nautical frenzy. Boats of all sizes jostled for mooring places against the congested bank. Sailing boats with their sheets half hoisted foundered in the middle of the waterway as inexperienced sailors struggled to control their vessels. Gleaming new motor boats with 'throaty' engines wove their way through the chaos. Couples and young families in hired rowing boats steered random courses through the congestion.

After twenty minutes of enjoying the colourful chaos, they followed a footpath which wound along the river bank and away from the town. The path took them past busy boathouses with people engaged in all the paraphernalia of launching boats into the water. Beyond the boat houses were small holiday cottages scattered amongst the trees and, further still, the path crossed through meadows with cows ambling slowly to the waterside to drink from the cool water.

After an hour of walking and talking, the heat of the sun was making it uncomfortable to continue.

"Let's just sit by the water's edge," suggested Alice. "I'll be content just watching for a while."

"I'll join you," added Flora. "I've done enough walking for now."

The two girls rested on a grassy bank by the water's edge whilst Jed explored reed beds nearby. Alice and Flora dozed as the warmth induced a pleasant drowsiness. Dragonflies flitted through the grass, the gentle humming of their wings providing a mellow backdrop to the tranquillity of the surroundings. Suddenly, they were woken by excited calls from Jed.

"Hey, Alice, Flora, look what I've found!"

"Are you alright? Mind you don't go falling in now," replied Alice, sleepily.

"I've found a boat hidden in the reeds here. I think it's some sort of punt."

Flora got up from the bank and wandered over to where Jed was busy removing reeds from a narrow inlet.

"See here, Flora, I reckon it's still floating."

Flora stared at the punt, still half hidden. It was low in the water but the inside appeared to be dry. Flaking green paint covered the hull and the rotting remnants of once plush cushions were attached to the back rest of the seat. The punt had clearly seen better days and had probably been consigned to this watery grave before the outbreak of war.

"How about a ride?"

"What are you two planning over there?" shouted Alice as she reluctantly picked herself up from the grassy embankment.

"We're going for a boat ride. Are you coming?" called back Jed.

By now he had pulled the punt from the reeds and placed it by the bank where it lay bobbing gently in the shallow waters.

"We can't take it without asking," said Alice. "It must belong to someone."

"I doubt it does now. Someone's just left it here – probably someone who never came back from the war."

"Just a short ride then – and close to the bank," replied Alice, not wanting to appear a killjoy.

Jed clambered into the punt and picked up a long pole which was stowed on the floor. Alice and Flora followed gingerly behind, positioning themselves on the remnants of the seat. The punt moved slowly forward as Jed thrust the pole into the mud. Alice held tight to her seat and kept her eyes on the bank to make sure it stayed within grasping distance. After some faltering manoeuvres, Jed got the hang of the pole and the boat glided forward. Alice began to relax and Flora hummed a tune. The water was calm and the sun's rays reflected off the shallow bottom. As they continued along the bank, the broad began to narrow as it joined again with the main river. Jed felt a current begin to pull at the boat and found it more difficult to control.

"Jed, stay closer to the bank," said Alice nervously as the front of the punt begun to swing away from the shore.

"I'm trying," replied Jed, struggling with the pole. The front of the punt was now pointing into the centre of the broad and the boat was beginning to turn in an arc.

"Jed, stop messing about," said Flora anxiously. "Get us back to the bank."

Jed pushed hard with the pole but the water was deepening now and the punt failed to respond. As the boat surged forward, Jed almost fell from the back as the pole failed to make contact with the bottom.

"Try paddling," yelled Jed as he crouched at the back and flailed his hands in the water. Alice and Flora both splashed ineffectively as the punt moved rapidly away from the bank.

"What are we going to do?" yelled Flora.

"It'll be OK, just hold on," shouted Jed. "The current will carry us to the end of the broad. There's sure to be someone there."

"Oh my God, look!" shrieked Alice. "Look what's happening to the floor."

The wooden planks that formed the bottom were no longer lying flat. Instead they were breaking up and water was gushing into the punt.

"We're sinking!" cried Flora. "I can't swim. We're going to die."

"Shut up, Flora," snapped Alice. "You're not going to die. Someone will see us."

By now the water was pouring into the front of the punt and the decking was perilously close to the water level.

"Get someone's attention," shouted Jed. "It's our only chance." He stood on the rear decking waving his arms. "Help, help, we're sinking! Over here, somebody help us!"

There were boats in the distance and others moored by the bank, but nobody appeared to respond to the call. Suddenly, the front end of the punt dipped under the surface. Flora screamed as water swirled around her. Then the boat began to cartwheel, slowly lifting Jed above the two girls until he lost his grip and plunged into the broad. As the punt slipped away from beneath them, Flora began to scream and thrash around.

"You swim for the shore, Alice. I'll help Flora."

Jed grabbed Flora. He was a strong swimmer. Flora, however, had never swum and was panicking – tugging at Jed's shirt. Jed tried to swim on his side, holding Flora in front of him with her head above the water. But she struggled, gasped for air and pushed him beneath her. Jed found himself fighting for breath – his lungs bursting from lack of oxygen. Only his nose and mouth were above the surface as the whole weight of Flora bore down on him. He took a deep breath so he could hold his head below water. As the air became exhausted he felt himself slowly becoming disconnected from what was going on above him. His head dropped back and he felt himself losing touch with Flora. The surface seemed to be receding and there was an eerie silence around him. *Is this it? Is this how it's all going to end? Is this how it feels to die?*

Suddenly, he felt a hand grab his collar. Uncomprehendingly, he gasped and took in a gulp of water. He felt himself being dragged upwards until suddenly sunlight dazzled his eyes. He was assaulted by a confusion of noise. Someone was calling his name. He heard the sound of an engine close by and the words of an unseen person.

"You'll be OK. We got here just in time. Thought we'd lost you."

He found himself being hauled onto the deck of a cruiser and laid on the polished wood decking. He heard Flora coughing and the barely intelligible sound of Alice shouting.

"That was a bloody stupid thing to do. You nearly killed us. Thank God for this man. He saved our lives."

As Jed recovered and coughed water from his lungs, he slowly took in his surroundings. He was on a modern motor launch, bedecked with brass fittings and teak inlay. An older man dressed in white slacks and a blue peaked cap was tending to him whilst a young woman wearing shorts and a blue striped shirt was clutching the boat's steering wheel.

"We heard your shouts before you went in but we were too far away. By the time we got here you were already under the water."

"A stupid, stupid thing to do," he heard Alice repeat over and over in the background. Pushing himself up from the floor, he looked to see what had happened to Flora. She was propped up at the other end of the boat, apparently unharmed.

"We've hired this boat for a week. The best we can do is take you to Wroxham."

"But all our things are on the shore," he heard Alice saying. "We need to go back there."

Back on the shore, they sat by their belongings, wet and exhausted. There was an embarrassed silence which was eventually broken by Alice's strained voice.

"You should have known better. You should have known it would be rotten. You nearly killed Flora and me."

"I'm sorry."

"It's no good being sorry now, Jed. I've changed my opinion of you."

Jed knew the prank had been stupid. What started out as an innocent adventure could have been fatal.

"But he saved my life, Alice," spluttered Flora as she regained her composure. "Without Jed, I'd have drowned. He kept my head above water till that boat arrived. It wasn't his fault. We all agreed to the trip. I owe you my life, Jed."

Jed raised his head from his chest and smiled weakly at Flora.

"It's OK, Flora, it's OK."

"Well, maybe I was a bit harsh," said Alice, sensing that she didn't have an ally in Flora. "I blame myself for agreeing to it. I don't go along with pranks and that sort of thing. But Flora's right, Jed. You did save her life. That was brave."

Jed struggled to find suitably contrite words but none came. A light wind rustled through the grass and made them suddenly aware that their clothes were soaking wet.

"I don't know how we're going to get home like this," bemoaned Alice. "They won't let us on the train looking like drowned rats."

'Special Motor Show of Austin Cars' stated the leaflet that Jack held in his hand. 'For one week only W. Vincent of Castle Street, Reading will be displaying a fleet of Austin cars and offering trial runs'.

Jack checked the name above the showroom he had come to visit. He could see a flurry of activity around twenty or so cars which were parked on the forecourt opposite. A slight feeling of unease still troubled him. He had never in his life before spent money unnecessarily. It had been drummed into him as a child that any spare money had to be saved for the inevitable rainy day. But now it was different. Soon he would have more money than he had ever dreamed of and only three years, five at the most, to enjoy it. When he was freed from his contract with Deltic, he would take off and see where fate led him. But he needed transport. He needed a car. Deltic had advanced him a small sum of money and here at these show rooms he would make his first ever luxury purchase.

He walked along the lines of cars, knowing little about what to look for. An Austin Twenty Coupe, priced at eight hundred and fifty pounds. An Austin Twenty Landaulette priced at eight hundred and seventy five pounds. To Jack's eyes, most of the cars looked very posh and a little conservative. But at the end of the line his attention was drawn to a car finished in bright yellow. It had a black fold back roof and large chrome headlamps. He ran his fingers over the bonnet and smiled at the graceful lines. The sales literature stated that it was an Austin Twenty Tourer priced at six hundred and ninety five pounds – which Jack considered more reasonable.

"Can I interest you in a test drive, sir?" It was the ubiquitous car salesman. Usually Jack would have made his excuses and left, but this time he bit his tongue and politely accepted the offer. He had learned to drive in the army and most of his experience had been behind the wheel of a three ton truck.

Jack sat in the driving seat whilst the salesman cranked the engine into life. It let out a gutsy roar and the accelerator responded briskly to Jack's first tentative contact.

"When you're ready, sir," advised the salesman, who was now seated in the passenger seat.

Jack depressed his right food hard and released the brake with his left hand, just as he had the three ton army lorries. With a squeal of tyres, the Austin leapt from the forecourt like a pouncing tiger, scattering onlookers and salesmen alike. Jack hauled on the brake causing the car to spin in the road and startle a horse which set off down the street at a gallop with its cart still attached. Now he was in the road, he decided that the best option was to continue.

"Learn to drive in the army did we, sir?" said the salesman, clinging to the edge of his seat. Gradually gaining control, Jack headed down the leafy suburban street with his speedometer indicating fifty miles per hour.

"Goes well, doesn't she?" Jack observed enthusiastically to the salesman.

"Yes, sir, but people normally keep their speed down to about twenty miles an hour in residential areas."

As the suburban roads gave way to country lanes, Jack asked for the hood to be folded back. Then with the sun on his face and the wind grabbing at his hair, he felt more happy and free than he'd felt in a long time. His darker memories were forced into the recesses of his mind and for a while he looked forward to the future.

"Only one thing we can do," said Alice. We'll just have to let them dry on us. It's still hot so they should be dry in a couple of hours."

"You mean sit in wet clothes for two hours?" protested Flora. "I can't do that. I'll catch me death. Why don't we take them off to dry?"

"Don't be daft, we can't just sit here naked. We'll be arrested," protested Jed.

"I don't mean we walk around naked. See that meadow over there? We make our way carefully so as not to leave a trail and lay in the long grass so no one can see us. Then we take our clothes off to dry and have a sleep in the sun whilst they're doing."

"You've forgotten something," protested Jed. "I can't strip off in front of the two of you, it wouldn't be proper."

"Don't see why not," replied Flora with a suppressed giggle. "We're friends."

They collected their belongings and made their way into the meadow. The wetland reed grew as high as their chests. Moving in single file, they managed to leave virtually no evidence of their trail. They selected a patch of ground with shade provided by overhanging trees and proceeded to flatten out a small area. Jed tried to busy himself by removing twigs from the ground in order to avoid being the first to undress.

"No one'll see us here," announced Flora. And with that, she proceeded to pull off her dress and remove her underclothes. Jed was unable to stop himself looking with admiration at her body, her full rounded breasts, her olive skin and her contoured thighs. Alice undressed too and lay down beside Flora, revealing an athletic body, slim and white as porcelain.

"Come on, Jed, get them clothes off," demanded Flora. "Alice and me's got our eyes closed. We're not going to see anything."

Jed pulled off his clothes and felt the warmth of the afternoon sun embrace his body. He felt more alive than ever in his life before. He looked at the two naked girls lying on the grass in front of him, Alice with her eyes screwed tight shut and Flora peeping through half closed lids. He lay on the grass next to Flora, squinting at the blue summer sky dotted with wisps of white cloud. A feeling of supreme happiness seemed to take hold of his body and he sighed with the intensity of the emotion he felt.

"I hope you're not having any of them imaginings," he heard Flora whisper with a giggle.

The Guest Who Stayed: Chapter 6 – September 1920

It was against everything he'd been taught – to get emotionally involved with informants. The rules were precise. The informants knew the risks and they volunteered their services. You didn't ask why, you just did your job. So why had he allowed himself to get involved with Yvette and potentially risk the operation?

He looked at her sleeping now beside him. For a short while the tension under which they constantly lived had gone. She looked peaceful, her long black hair spread across the pillow. He knew she had lovers in the past – she was skilled at making love. But they didn't speak of this or of their past. They lived only for the moment. They both knew this time would come – the looks, the touches, the innuendo. In peace time there would have been flirting, laughter, banter – perhaps talk of love. But in war you seize what you can quickly. So whilst Simone was out visiting newly recruited informants, they had taken the opportunity. There were few words spoken – just greedy and passionate sex. He had sensed past pain in the way she made love. There was anger. She bit and clawed at his back. She made it clear what she wanted him to do. When she reached a climax, it was intense and private. He was there as a means to an end – not as her lover. Yet somehow he was excited and exhilarated by their lovemaking. It was free of commitment and took place in a vacuum suspended somewhere between life and death.

In her dreams he could see that she was elsewhere. Her face was relaxed and happy now. Perhaps it was her childhood on this small farm. Perhaps she was with a former lover. Once a whispered name slipped from her lips; was it Gilbert or Pierre? It didn't matter. It was another world – a different universe.

She stirred and her eyes opened. Their eyes met briefly.

"Ma cherie," he whispered.

She smiled, kissed him briefly on the lips then rose quickly from the bed. He watched her silhouetted against the window. Her body was contoured with firm muscles developed from working on the farm but the roundness of her hips and breasts endowed her with a simple beauty. Her olive skin suggested a Mediterranean link somewhere in her ancestry.

She dressed quickly in a shirt and trousers, then with just a fleeting look that conveyed both longing and regret, she was gone from the room leaving Jack to his own confused thoughts.

The hot summer of 1920 ended early in Norfolk. In the first week of September, cold winds blew inland from the North Sea and rain squalls sprinted across the flat autumnal countryside.

For Alice, Flora and Jed, leisurely country walks were now a distant memory and the three of them took to meeting in Dan's parlour after work. The parlour was a dark room lit by one small window. It was full of various trophies that Dan had collected through his life, including a Zulu warrior's spear and the severed head of an African gazelle. The room was dominated by a huge open range which served as a means to cook food and boil water. Hanging from the grey stone mantle were an assortment of copper pans, ladles and cooking implements which provided all the hardware required by Dan and Jed to cook their simple meals.

It was early evening. Jed stoked the fire ready for Alice and Flora to join him. At precisely six thirty, the door opened and Alice came in, her head covered by a thick grey shawl which extended over her shoulders.

"Evening, Jed, let me close to that fire fast. There's a fierce wind out there tonight."

"You warm yourself, Alice, I'll get you a mug of tea. Have you seen Flora today?"

"I saw her briefly at lunch time. She called into the bakers for bread. Must say, she seemed a bit odd, not her normal bright self."

"Maybe she's not well."

"I'm not sure. She'd normally say if she was ill. It was more like she was embarrassed to see me."

Alice and Jed were joined by Dan and the ritual of toasting muffins began. By seven o'clock there was still no sign of Flora.

"She's never been this late before," said Alice. "And she'd always say if she wasn't going to come."

"I wonder if anything's happened to those parents of hers?" suggested Dan. "You know how she worries about them even though they treat her like a slave."

"I'd better go to her lodgings and see if she's there," volunteered Jed. "It'll only take a couple of minutes."

Fifteen minutes later Jed was back, drenched through by the torrential rain.

"Come and get dry by the fire," called Alice. Did you see her? What's the matter with her?"

"I didn't see her. She wasn't there."

"Did you find out where she's gone?"

"I spoke to her landlady, old Mrs. Potts, and it seems two of them members of her church came to see her this afternoon. Mrs. Potts refused to let them in at first but when she called Flora she agreed to see them. They went into her sitting room and shut the door. Mrs. Potts says there was raised voices and she could hear Flora shouting out something about 'sacrifice' but she couldn't make out the rest of it. When they came out she could see Flora had been crying. She told Mrs. Potts that she had to go because her parents needed her. Then one of them elders paid the outstanding rent from his own pocket and they went away."

"It's what I thought," said Dan. "The parents is putting pressure on her. They're making her feel bad about going away – making out they're ill."

"But Flora's not stupid," said Alice. "She'd soon see through that."

"Maybe she's got no choice," replied Dan. "Why do you think they sent two people to fetch her? Sounds more like they kidnapped her."

"We must find out," demanded Jed. "I'm going to go to her parents' place. I'll get her back."

"Supposing she don't want to come back?" said Dan.

"Course she'll want to come back."

"Don't go tonight, Jed" pleaded Alice. "It's terrible out there and you'll never find your way round in the dark. It's a mass of unlit alleyways in that part of town."

"Then if Dan don't mind, I'm going first thing tomorrow morning," replied Jed, slumping heavily into a fireside chair.

The next morning was grey but dry. Heavy clouds hung above Frampton, promising rain later in the day.

Jed set off from Dan's workshop after breakfast. He passed through the square where a vegetable market was already in full swing. Then he took the road to the west of the town, a direction he seldom followed. He soon noticed that the buildings here were shabby and unkempt. Many occupants seemed to keep animals around their dwellings and there were numerous hens, goats and cows penned in behind makeshift barricades.

As he moved further towards the edge of the town, the buildings became less substantial. They were mostly constructed from wattle and daub. The roofs were made of rough thatch and most had smoke pouring from makeshift chimneys.

He stopped to ask an old man pulling a cart full of potatoes if he knew where the Fultons lived.

"Fulton? Can't say I know that name," he said removing a cloth cap and scratching his head.

"Flora Fulton. She lived here with her parents. I think they belong to some kind of religious sect."

"Oh, it's the Brotherhood you'll be talkin' about. I won't be knowing anything about them. They keep themselves to themselves. But I knows where they live alright."

"Could you tell me then?" pleaded Jed.

"You got to follow that path," he said pointing to a muddy track that led off between two derelict shacks. "Follow that path till you gets to a square. They all live round there. Ask someone and they'll be sure to know."

Jed set off along the path, his feet squelching in the soft mud that lay underfoot. Either side of him were old workshops where smithies repaired broken farm machinery. The smoke from their braziers swirled around him and hindered his view. Eventually the path opened out onto a square surrounded by eight simple cottages. The square was empty and Jed searched in vain for someone to ask. Then he spied an old woman wearing a white peaked skull cap rounding the corner of a building carrying a bucket of water.

"Excuse me, I'm looking for Flora Fulton. I think she lives here."

The old women froze in her tracks and stared intently at the cobbles in front of her.

"Flora Fulton, does she live here?"

Still the woman made no move. Jed felt anger rising.

"What's the matter with you, woman? Can't you speak? Where does Flora Fulton live?"

The woman turned her head towards Jed. She was pale with gaunt skin and eyes that receded deep into their sockets. With the merest inclination of her head, she appeared to indicate a house to Jed's right. As he turned to look at it she shuffled quickly away.

The house was a simple single story building with two small windows positioned either side of a door covered in peeling grey paint. Jed made his way to the door and hammered with his fist. There was no sound from within so he hammered on the door again and then stepped back to watch for signs of life. A thin wisp of grey smoke was escaping from a chimney perched on the ancient thatch. The windows were covered on the inside by greying fabric which hung limply from sagging cords.

Suddenly, Jed heard the sounds of a lock being turned. He went to the door again and waited in anticipation. A second lock was slowly drawn back. Then to the accompanying noise of groaning hinges, the door was hauled open.

Standing in the gloom of the unlit interior was an elderly man. He was tall and immensely thin. White strands of hair framed a haggard face and his pallid complexion gave him a ghostly appearance. He wore an old fashioned dark waistcoat and breeches which were tucked into battered boots.

"Who are you and what do you want?"

"My name's Jed Carter. I'm a friend of Flora's."

"Flora don't have friends. Now go away."

Angered by this response, Jed moved closer and placed his shoulder by the door post, preventing the door from being closed.

"I said I'm Flora's friend. I want to see her."

"The Lord says, 'Remove the wicked person from amongst yourselves', Corinthians chapter five, verse thirteen."

"I don't care about that. I'm interested in Flora and how she is. She should have been with us last night but she didn't turn up. Is anything wrong with her?"

"'The Lord knoweth them that are his. And let everyone that nameth the name of Christ depart from iniquity'. The book of Timothy, chapter two, verse nineteen."

"Will you stop all that and just answer my question?" said Jed, feeling the anger well up inside him again. "Is Flora alright?"

"Flora has broken the rules of our church and brought great sadness and shame upon us. She should never have gone to visit that place of entertainment with you."

"What are you on about? Do you mean Wroxham?" exclaimed Jed incredulously. "It's a pretty little place on the broads where people go to enjoy a day out by the river."

"Our church doesn't allow frivolous outings. Everything we need is provided by the church. We don't need outsiders and we don't mix with those who seek idle amusement. 'If any man that is called a brother be a fornicator, or covetous, or an idolator, or a railer, or a drunkard, or an extortioner; with such a one, no, not to eat', Corinthians five, verse eleven."

"Look, we just had a day out. Flora needed to get way from all this mumbo jumbo. She'd already decided to leave your church and if you've taken her back by force then you've got me to deal with."

Jed wedged his body closer into the doorway.

"Flora has been made to see the error of her ways. She is going to repent and will be accepted back into the blessed church and once again be clean in the eyes of God."

"What have you done to her?" asked Jed anxiously, his voice rising now.

"We have given her guidance and helped her to see the truth which is based on the teachings of the true Christians. On the next Sabbath, our congregation will gather and Flora will make a full confession. If the elders believe her confession to be complete and heartfelt, she will be welcomed back into the arms of the congregation."

"Let me see her, I need to see her," shouted Jed, his anger now spilling over. He lunged at the old man and tried to push him away from the door. Momentarily, he resisted but his wasted body was no match for Jed's power. Jed pushed by him and into the darkened room. It took a few seconds for his eyes to adjust to the gloom. As the old man ranted behind him, he took in the scene. There was a single wooden table in the centre of the room with three chairs placed around it. A small range glowed dimly at one end. On the wall opposite the door was a large wooden crucifix with a roughly carved figure of Christ. Other than that the room was bare.

"Where's Flora? I need to see her," he yelled at the old man. He saw a door at the far end of the room and made to open it. The old man screamed at him.

"Sinner, sinner, you'll be damned for this!"

Jed pushed the door with one hand, fending the old man off with his other. What he saw brought him to a sudden halt. There was a large bed in the middle of the room and to one side was a small wooden cot. Kneeling by this and clutching a bible was Flora. Her dress had been torn from her back and red weals across her exposed flesh showed that she'd been recently beaten. Her wrists were bound and she was tied to the frame of the bed.

"You bastard, you bastard!" screamed Jed as he flung himself to the floor beside her.

"Don't worry, Flora. Come with me and leave all of this."

"You don't understand," sobbed Flora, "I can't leave. They own me. Without the church we have nothing. We gave everything to the church. I have to come back. I have no choice. Please go away. Just forget me."

"I can't do that, Flora," cried Jed as he tried to take hold of her and pull her away from the cot.

"We're your friends. We won't let you go."

"You must, Jed, it's my decision. You have no right to do this. Go now!"

There was a commotion at the door and three young men appeared, led by Flora's father.

"There he is, a sinner, a viper, an evil doer. God damn his soul! Throw him out of my house."

The three men seized Jed from behind and in spite of his struggles, dragged him from the house and out into the square. They threw him roughly onto the cobbled ground and stood barring his way back into the house.

Jed picked himself up from the ground and brushed the dirt from his clothes.

"You're freaks, all of you," he screamed at them. "Call yourselves godly? You ain't got a caring thought between you. We'll get Flora out. I'll be back, you'll see."

The four brethren stood implacably, arms folded across their chests as Jed ranted at them. Eventually, he was forced to leave the house and make his way back into the town.

Later that evening, Jed met with Alice and Dan in the parlour to discuss what they should do.

"We can't just leave her there," demanded Jed. "They'd beaten her, I know they had. They're holding her captive."

"But from what you told us, Flora said it was her wish to stay," argued Dan. "Even if she don't mean it you can't go takin' a person away from their family without their consent. You got to leave some things to run their natural course."

"But there must be someone we can tell. How about Constable Barker?"

"Like Dan said, unless Flora's willing to come there's nothing the police can do," added Alice. "And remember what people are like round here. What goes on in the home behind closed doors is nobody else's business. It's a family matter and you got to let Flora sort it out."

"But she's only doing it for her parents. She told me they've given everything to their church. They don't own anything. The church owns them."

"They sounds like desperate people to me then, Jed," said Dan. "And you can't reason with desperate people. You got to trust Flora to see sense and leave when she's ready. She knows she's got friends and we'll be waiting for her."

Sleep eluded Jed as he lay in bed that night. He couldn't put the image of Flora out of his mind, lying crumpled by the bed with her dress ripped. Should he have been stronger? Should he have tried harder to take her away? Was Dan right that some things couldn't be changed – you had to let fate take its course? His mind drifted back to an earlier conversation with Dan – something about 'follow your dream' or 'follow your star'. It seemed to Jed that you needed more than a dream. You needed ambition. You needed a plan. Perhaps you had to be ruthless. If you left it to fate, you'd get blown about like a leaf in a storm – like poor Flora, battered and damaged. It was becoming clearer to him now. He needed to take control of his destiny. But just as he was filled with enthusiasm and excitement by this idea, it was replaced by an empty realisation that he had very little in the way of skills or ability. He was not bright. He could just read. He didn't communicate well. But he could work hard. No one ever disputed that. He could work till he dropped. What he didn't have was money or knowledge. He fell into a troubled sleep.

The Guest Who Stayed: Chapter 7 – Late 1920

The loss of Flora cast a shadow across the days that followed. Without her infectious laughter and her incessant questions, meetings in Dan's parlour became less enjoyable. Alice seemed to be taking a greater interest in Jed's future and would frequently goad him about his lack of ambition.

"You can't always just be Dan's assistant, you know," said Alice as they sat alone by the fire in Dan's parlour one evening. "What about starting your own business and being your own boss? People know you well enough round these parts now and you've got a reputation for working hard."

"Are you asking me to go against Dan?" said Jed indignantly. "After all he's done for me, taking me in when I arrived here from the farm and giving me work. He's become like a father to me, like my own father should have been. He talks to me, hears me out when I got something troubling me, tells me about his life and how it's led him to see things in a certain way. You can't put a price on that sort of friendship so there's no way I'm walking out on him. Besides, he's beginning to need me more now. He can't do nearly as much as he did when I first arrived, so we make a good pair. He's got the knowhow and I've got the muscle."

"I'm not saying you should be disloyal, just that you got to look after yourself because there's nobody else going to do it for you. It's because Dan needs you that you got to make sure he pays what you're worth. Don't forget he's your boss and you've got rights, you know."

"Don't go fillin' your head up with all that modern political talk. This ain't Russia. I'm not planning to start a revolution."

"You may scoff, Jed, but you've got to be sharp these days. It's no good just carrying on doing things the way we always have – just being the victim. You've got to ask questions, stand up for yourself, recognise what you're worth. Times are changing. You just got to look around to see that; women have the vote now, more cars on the roads, fancy clothes in the shops, people building themselves modern houses to live in with bathrooms and all that."

"But that's only a few people, Alice. For the likes of us life don't change very much."

"That's the point, Jed, it is only for the few but you got to make sure you're one of them. There's opportunities out there for those who's prepared to take them."

There was a pause whilst Jed digested Alice's words. Staring into the spitting embers, both of them had a sense that they were ill equipped to break free from the servitude that life had assigned to them.

"I'm not sure I've got the strength to do what you're saying, Alice. I never thought of myself as being different. All I really wanted to do was fit in."

"Let me help you then, Jed, you know, be your friend. I can see you've got talents and sometimes it takes a woman to bring them out in a man. Let me be a special friend."

"How do you mean?"

"You and me want the same things, Jed, to improve ourselves and make a better life. Sometimes it's easier if two of you do it together. That's all I mean, being close and helping one another out."

The next morning Jed went with Dan to repair a damaged barn on an outlying farm. Jed sawed vigorously, cutting new planks to size whilst Dan removed the rotten wood. After two hours of working in silence, Dan suggested they stop for a break. He produced a flask of tea which they took turns to drink from as they rested on a fallen trunk.

"Alice and me was talking last night, Dan, when you was down the pub. She's got me thinking a bit about my future and what I needs to be doing to get on."

"She was talking to you about that was she?" replied Dan with a laugh. "In that case, she's got her sights on you and there's no mistake."

"Oh, I don't think she meant it like that. We're like brother and sister, me and Alice."

"In my experience, Jed, once a woman starts talkin' to man about his future he better watch out. She's got her sights on 'im."

Jed was slightly taken aback by Dan's comments and he lapsed into silence as he pondered their meaning. If Dan was right and she had 'her sights on him' then he had certainly missed the signs. What did Alice want? Was marriage on her mind? Jed hadn't thought seriously about marrying. He felt completely unprepared for any commitment to anybody other than himself. And if he was to marry, he'd always felt that Flora was his more likely partner, with her easy ways and fatalistic approach to life more easily matching his own style.

"And why do you reckon I'm in her sights, Dan? It's not as if I've got much. Alice is an ambitious woman and I don't see her thinking I've got a lot to offer."

"You ain't got much at the moment but I'd say you got prospects. That's what a woman wants Jed – a man with prospects."

"It's my prospects that I wanted to talk to you about, Dan. I think we're a very good team and you taught me all that I know. But I don't earn much and if I'm going to better myself I've got to be thinking about how I can earn a bit more."

"Well, you know I ain't making a lot of money. People round here don't have much. Sometimes it takes them months to pay me and some never do. So I can't do much in the way of paying you an extra wage. But there is somethin' I've been thinking about a while now which might make you want to stick with me."

"What've you got in mind?" asked Jed, his interest suddenly aroused.

"If you don't mind, I'll leave it till this evening and tell you over supper, otherwise it'll be dark and we still won't have this job done."

Simone slipped into the barn where her bike was kept, using her feet to disperse the hens which gathered round her looking for food. She had brought a small box of eggs and some potatoes which she placed in the front basket strapped to the handlebars. If the Germans stopped her, they would think that she was indulging in a bit of black market trading and turn a blind eye as they normally did. She felt around the waist of her shirt, just to make sure that the documents were safely strapped to her body.

Pulling the bike away from the barn wall, it was only then that she noticed the flat tyre. She cursed quietly and tried to think where the puncture repair kit was kept. Already she was running late and agents were instructed not to wait more than five minutes at a rendezvous in case something had gone wrong. She knew that if the English found out she was late they would try to stop her. She didn't much like the English. They were superior and treated the French as if they had already lost the war. Unlike Yvette who seemed to attract the attention of the English, Simone was regarded merely as a courier.

Seizing a pump which was hanging from a nail on the wall, she prayed it was a slow puncture that would get her to her destination about two kilometres away. By the time the tyre was inflated, she was running seven minutes late. She would have to pedal fast to make up time.

Gloom was setting in as she wheeled the bike out of the barn. To avoid being seen she ducked down under the parlour window as she passed along the wall. The bedroom window was her last hurdle and then she was free to go. Bending low, she passed underneath the open window pane. Suddenly she froze. Goose pimples erupted along her arms. She could hear sighing, gasping. Crawling past the window, she stood up at the far side. From here, she could just glance past the tattered curtains and see into the room. There, on the bed that she shared with Yvette, were two naked bodies fused together in a hungry embrace.

Simone felt sick in the pit of her stomach. Her sister was breaking the rules they had agreed – no fraternising with the English. They were here to fight and die. Relationships were no part of this. Simone had not wanted to get involved in this espionage in the first place but Yvette had persuaded her. Yvette had wanted revenge – revenge for a deep hurt that she harboured inside her. Simone was drawn unwillingly into Yvette's vendetta, not realising how high were the stakes in this deceit.

She listened as the love making reached a climax and then subsided into quietly murmured endearments. She was jealous, angry, hurt. She had feelings too – but no one ever noticed. Instead she had to endure his furtive glances towards Yvette and whispered exchanges.

She had to focus. She had to make the rendezvous. With her head spinning she mounted the bike and pedalled out of the yard and into the lane beyond. But inside, her heart burned with a smouldering fury.

After returning late from work, Dan and Jed both scrubbed up and ate a simple meal by the fireside. As usual, neither spoke whilst they concentrated on the important task of satisfying their hunger. It wasn't until Dan had wiped his plate clean with a chunk of bread that conversation resumed.

"I said I had an idea that might make you decide to stay with me."

"Don't get me wrong, Dan, it's not that I want to ..."

"Just hear me out, lad, will you? You know that I'm getting a bit old and stiff and I can't work like I used to. And there's only one thing that happens to old people like me with no money and no one to look after them – they end up in the workhouse. Now, that would kill me so I need you to carry on working with me and I'm prepared to slowly let you take over the running of the business till you eventually own it – if that's what you want. But the trouble is, Jed, there's no rich pickings in this trade so you ain't going to make lots of money. But there is one thing I can do which might change your mind."

"You got me all ears now, Dan, what is it then?"

"Well, they say an Englishman's home is his castle, that's if you got a home in the first place. Most youngsters like you finds it very difficult to rent a place let alone have their own home. So here's where I can help you. Twenty year ago, I think it was, I did a big favour for a local farmer here – Grimes, his name was, Herbert Grimes. There was bad floods that year and the water from the brook overflowed and washed away two of his barns. Well, I worked with 'im for two days – day and night without sleep to save those barns and get them put up again. At the end of it I presented my bill to 'im and full of apologies he told me he hadn't any money to pay. When he'd called me out he didn't give a thought to how he was goin' to settle the bill. Well, there wasn't much I could do about it. But he'd heard me talkin' about building' a house, 'cos in those days it was still in my mind to marry and bring up a family somewhere. So what he done, he give me a bit of a field he owned right on the edge of the town. It was all done legally so I have the deeds as proof I own that land. Now, as it happens, I never did meet that wife or have that family so my little plot of land just turned into a wilderness. People walk past it now and think it's just a rough bit of meadow that belongs to no one. But they're wrong. It belongs to me and I'd be happy to give it to you to build your own house for you and maybe that family of yours."

"You mean you'd give it to me for nothing?"

"On one condition, you stay with me and gradually take over the business."

"Dan, I don't know what to say. That's a right generous offer. To have a bit of land and build me own house, it's – well, it's a dream."

"Of course, you've got to build the house but I'll give you a hand and we can always call on a bit of help when it's needed. You'll have to borrow some money to buy the bricks and all the other stuff you need but I think I know someone who'll loan you that and you can pay a bit off each month."

"Where is it, Dan, where's the land? I've got to see it."

"It's about half a mile from here down a little road called Duck Lane. Why don't you go and take a look? Take Alice with you. She'll certainly think you've got prospects then."

Jed arranged to meet Alice the next day during their lunch break. They sat together on a wall in the market square, eating pies that Alice had bought from the bakers.

"You're going to build your own house? How can you do that? You've never built a house before. How are you going to know where to start?"

"Dan'll help me and there'll be plenty of others to give advice. Folks have been doing it for hundreds of years round here so it can't be that difficult."

"It's incredible, Jed, you owning a house at your age. You're really going to be someone round here."

"Why don't we go and see the land tomorrow?" suggested Jed, "Both of us, together."

"Are you sure you want me to come too?"

"I don't see why not. You said about us being partners, you know, special friends. I'd like you to come and tell me what you think."

At which point Alice leant across and kissed Jed lightly on the lips.

"It's OK, Jed. We're special friends. Kissing's OK between special friends."

The next day was a Saturday and Alice finished working at lunchtime. Jed met her outside the bakers shop and the two set off to find Duck Lane. Walking south of the market square, they followed the main road out of the town in the direction of North Walsham and Norwich. The houses here were solid brick built structures with their first floors overhanging the street to offer some measure of protection to pedestrians below. Professional people and artisans lived here. There were brass plaques on the walls of houses proclaiming various services such as 'dress making', 'tooth extraction' and 'herbal medication'.

Jed spied a landmark ahead which Dan had told him to look out for – an old Methodist church sat at the intersection of the main road and a small track. Jed and Alice turned down this track which soon led them away from the main road.

"It's a funny name, Duck Lane," said Alice.

"Dan said there used to be a duck farm down here and the ducks were always wandering all over the place. I think it went many years ago. Look just there," said Jed, pointing to a small cottage with a well in the garden. "Dan said to look out for that cottage and the plot is just beyond it."

They were now in a narrow part of the lane with high hedges growing either side. There was no apparent way into the fields beyond and no obvious plot of land. Jed peered into the hedge on the left of the lane to find some sign of access.

"Look, Alice, there's an old gate here. It must be years since this gate were last opened."

They both pulled and pushed at the gate which creaked noisily on ancient hinges. This action gradually created a gap in the hedge and revealed a first glimpse of the plot beyond. Jed crawled through the hole first and then helped Alice through, taking care not to cut her on the razor edge thorns.

They found themselves standing on a plot of land waist high in meadow grass and ringed by trees. Birds sang noisily and flitted between strands of tall grass which swayed gently in the breeze. The scene had a timeless quality about it, as if it had been waiting since the beginning of time to be discovered. They both stood in silence, taking in the peace and serenity of this secret place.

"It's beautiful," ventured Alice at last. "It's a like private world. Can you imagine a little house right there in the middle?"

"It's much better than I thought," replied Jed. "I'd imagined a bit of waste land at the end of the village, sort of derelict."

"It's so private," whispered Alice as if her words might be overheard.

They walked through the long grass into the middle of the plot. The perfume from wild flowers filled their nostrils.

"I would be very happy here, Jed," said Alice, almost in a whisper. "I can't think I'd want for much else. Except, of course, a husband to look after and make happy."

Jed turned to her, comprehension slowly dawning.

"What are you saying, Alice? Are you meaning me and you together – married like?"

"Why not, Jed? We make a good team and we get on well. I reckon we'd make a good husband and wife."

"But what about being in love?"

"Who's to say we're not? Sometimes you can be in love and not realise it. It takes something to happen, like a big change in your life, to make you see the people in your life differently. Like I'm seeing you differently now, Jed. Before I saw you as a nice enough young man – perhaps a bit naive."

"And now?"

"Now, I'm seeing a man emerge, a man with a future, a man who seems to know where he's going. That's what a woman looks for in a man, someone who'll provide."

"What about us, Alice? You know, being intimate and all that?"

"That'll come with time, Jed. We'll learn together. You'll see."

"Well, I don't know much about romance and loving, Alice, there's not been much of that in my life to tell the truth. I might not be any good at it."

"Then I'll teach you. Take your jacket off and lay it on the ground."

"Now?"

"Just do what I say."

Alice slipped Jed's jacket from his shoulders and laid it in the long grass. Then she pulled him down by her side.

"The first thing you got to learn, Jed, is kissing. That's where it starts."

She took his head in her hands and kissed him fully on the lips. Jed closed his eyes and let his body respond. He felt goose pimples on his back and a stirring in his loins as Alice pressed her body firmly against his. He felt her tongue slip into his mouth and make contact with his own tongue. Still he remained passive as Alice took control, kissing, nibbling and biting. His hands which had lain limply by his side now took hold of Alice as she lay across him. He held her waist then ran his hands down to her thighs. He'd never before held a woman and the sensation enthralled him. He felt the softness of her body and the roundness of her curves. His kissing became more passionate and he pulled Alice tighter towards him, locking their mouths together. He felt his hands touch the bare flesh on the back of her legs and started to move them further upwards.

"See, Jed," said Alice, brushing his hands away and pulling her lips from his mouth, "it isn't difficult and you're getting the hang of it just fine. But to do it properly you really got to be married. A little bit of kissing and cuddling is OK beforehand but the marriage bed is the proper place for this type of thing."

"Does this mean we're engaged to be married?"

"Not till you ask me, Jed, and I accepts. That's when we're engaged."

"Well, you got me thinkin', Alice, that marrying you would be something I'd like a lot. I mean, I don't want to live in this house on my own and I don't know any other lass I want to marry. I mean, there was poor Flora and I did sometimes think that she and I would be a good match."

"I'd forget about Flora," said Alice, hastily. "Flora's never going to marry outside of her church. If she does marry, her husband's going to be chosen for her by the elders. It's sad, Jed, but there's nothing you can do about it now."

"Well, don't you think I should discuss it with Dan? He's like a father to me and I like to get his advice, especially on something as important as this."

"You could do but you're a proper man now and deciding on the woman you're going to marry is something only you can do. Dan'll know that and he'll respect you all the more for it."

"So do you want to marry me, Alice? Do you really love me?"

"We'll grow to love each other, Jed. That's how it works. We'll be strong and we'll be a good couple. We'll support each other and we'll make our way so that people respect us and look up to us. Why don't you ask me to marry you?"

"You mean now, here?"

"Why not? It's the place where our future home's going to be and the place where we'll bring up or children. Say it nice now, Jed. Ask me to marry you."

They were both on their knees in the grass facing each other. Jed studied Alice's face. He saw the urgency and intensity in her look. She smiled nervously at him. He felt the breeze on his face and he looked up to the sky above, noting briefly that dark clouds were racing in from the North Sea. He felt Alice's grip tighten on his hands and he looked her straight in the eyes.

"Alice, Alice, my love. Will you marry me and be my wife?"

"Yes, Jed, I will."

And she leant forward and kissed him again.

The Guest Who Stayed: Chapter 8 – Spring 1921

By early March of 1921, the worst of the winter weather had passed and spring flowers were beginning to push their way through the softening ground and brighten the dormant countryside. Buds were appearing on the trees and early blossom was beginning to bloom in the cherry and plum orchards around Frampton.

Alice and Jed visited the plot again and made final preparations for the building work to begin. They decided to position the house in the middle of the site where it would be surrounded by garden. Another area was designated as the site of a workshop for Jed as they had already decided that when Dan retired, he would run the business from home and save on the cost of renting the workshop. They hadn't considered what would happen to Dan who lived above the workshop but Alice persuaded Jed that this could be dealt with at a later time.

It was a sunny Monday in mid March when a small party gathered to witness the first sod being turned. Dan had been invited to attend and also two of his drinking friends from The Fox and Hounds. Alice brought a flagon of cider and five cups so that they could toast the occasion properly. Jed stood poised with a heavy duty spade as Dan prepared to make a speech. He cleared his throat and puffed out his chest in a gesture befitting the solemn occasion.

"We are gathered here today," began Dan.

"You're not marrying us, Dan," interrupted Jed, "just do something brief and to the point."

"That's just what I'm trying to do if you'll shut up and give me a chance."

Dan adjusted his posture and began again.

"It were many years ago when I acquired this land, and when I did so I had in mind to marry and raise a family. But sad for me, it never turned out that way. I let my opportunities slip by and then it were too late. So it gives me real pleasure to pass this land on to Jed and Alice. 'Cos unlike me, Jed has done what a young man should do and ask a beautiful lass to marry him and she's had the sense to say yes. And I reckon they'll be raising a lot of little ones here too. So raise your cups and drink to Jed and Alice and their new home."

A chorus of congratulations rang out and Jed seized the shovel, plunging it deep into the rich black loam. The small audience clapped and downed the remnants of their cider before making their way home.

Jed and Alice were left alone on the plot as the setting sun met the horizon, bathing the site in a warm pink glow. Jed slipped his arm around Alice's waist and they watched in silence as the sun dropped out of sight. A sudden chill in the air caused them to cling to each other more tightly.

"You know, Jed," said Alice softly, "we need a name – a name for our house. What do you think?"

"I don't know. I haven't given it any thought."

"Well, it seems to me, Jed, that this place is full of hope – hope for our future, hope for your work and hope for us being together. So why don't we just call our home 'Hope Cottage'?"

"Hope Cottage. I like the sound of it. It's everything we hoped for isn't it? Our own place, being a couple, being accepted."

"That's it then, Hope Cottage," repeated Alice, sinking contentedly into Jed's arms.

"You don't think we're tempting fate, do you?" asked Jed, looking suddenly concerned.

"I don't believe in fate, I told you that. Whatever you want, you got to make it happen. That's what we're going to do, Jed, me and you together."

Jack coughed and spluttered as the doctor moved the stethoscope across his back

"It's no better, Jack. There's still fluid on your lungs and I see you're bringing up blood. That means something's ruptured. You should really go into hospital and undergo observation and tests."

"Can't do that."

"Why not?"

"I've given my word to this American company that I'd work for them for a year."

"How much longer have you got?"

"Six months. Come the end of July I'll be a rich man and I'm off."

"You may be a rich dead man the way you're overdoing things."

"You said I had between three and five years."

"I'm downgrading that to between two and four years. You're not looking after yourself. What's the point in being rich if you're dead?"

"I've given my word now. How would you spend twenty five thousand pounds in two years, Doctor, if you knew you were going to die at the end of it?"

"It's not my problem, Jack. I'm going to live a lot longer than that," replied the doctor as he washed his hands. "But if you do really have that money to spend, I'd advise you to go and do something entirely different. Get away – meet new people – spend the money. Don't keep it all to yourself. It'll only bring misery."

Jack lay on the sofa in the darkened living room. Across the road he could see a Christmas tree lit with candles framed in a downstairs window. In the distance, he could make out the sound of carols floating across the frozen evening air.

It was Christmas Eve. Perhaps he would only live to see two more before his lungs finally gave way. He felt a deep melancholy taking him over. He tried to fight it. *Think of good times, happy times* – when he was a boy. The table at Christmas; a goose in the middle; his father wielding a carving knife with the precision of a surgeon; he and his brother eagerly anticipating juicy goose meat and sniffing the aroma of thick gravy on the stove.

His was the generation that went to war – most of them slain on battlefields in France – boys like him who, just a few years earlier, had been sitting round tables feasting on goose and plum pudding. What terrible force had picked them up from the comfort of those homes and deposited them within just a few years into stinking water logged trenches?

He tried to think of Yvette but his mind delivered him cruelly to the wrong memory. He is being carried out of the interrogation room by the snatch squad. Three of his comrades are already dead. He sees Yvette, bloodied and chained to a pipe. But he doesn't see Simone. Did they get her?

"Take her – the woman. Take her too." He uses all his strength to gasp the words out.

"Only the Brits, mate."

He knows the Germans will torture her again.

"Finish them off in there with grenades."

A deafening explosion and they're racing through the undergrowth to the airstrip. He lapses back into unconsciousness.

Could he have done more to prevent her death? Was he responsible for her last terrible moments? Or did somebody else betray them?

He forces himself to think of their last time together, her body arched over his, bearing down on him with uninhibited fervour. Then in his mind he watches her rising naked from the bed, her body silhouetted by the window. And there it is again, something that's troubled him. A brief memory – a recollection of a face by the window. He's seen that face in his mind before but never dwelt on it. Now he forces himself to think. Could it have been ... ? Panic wells up inside him.

Jed plunged the spade into the damp soil and tossed the contents out of the trench. He swung the spade back down into the void and, with a squelch of muddy water, ejected another shovel full of black earth.

He paused and wiped the perspiration from his forehead, leaving streaks of black mud across his face. Sweat dripped down his naked torso and soaked into the waistband of his trousers. It was late March and this was the second week that he'd been working in the evenings on the construction of Hope Cottage. Already the shape of the house was visible with the foundations tracing out the lines of the ground floor rooms.

As he worked, often alone, he couldn't help wondering about the course his life was taking. It seemed to him sometimes that getting married was part of a bigger package that he'd been unwittingly drawn into, including taking over Dan's business and building a new house. Any one of these was a big step in its own right but doing all three together was like jumping off a cliff into the unknown.

By the end of April the walls were up to the top of the ground floor. Spaces for windows and doors were visible and it was possible to walk around the inside and imagine what the finished rooms would look like. As the weather improved, Alice joined Jed more frequently to discuss plans for the forthcoming wedding.

"I want it to be in the church, Jed, people will expect it. Not that I want lots of people, just a small affair, you know."

"I was thinking September would be a good time to get married, Alice, when all this building work is finished."

"No, why wait that long? I think June. Let's make it June."

"I'm going to have to work doubly hard to get it ready for then."

"You'll do it, Jed, I know you will."

She leant forward to kiss him, her body pressing against his. Jed felt desire growing inside him and he reached out to take hold of her body but she pulled away.

"Later, there's work to be done now."

Early May saw the final slate hammered into place on the roof and work begin on the interior fittings. Alice busied herself making arrangements for the wedding day which was set to take place on Saturday, 11th June in St. Martin's Church. Alice was keen to have

Flora as her bridesmaid as she was the only real friend she had in Frampton. Dan undertook the delicate task of negotiating with Flora's parents and after much discussion it was agreed that she could attend the wedding but not the reception.

Saturday, 11th June 1921 dawned bright and sunny. Outside the church, a small band of people gathered. There were three assistants from the baker's shop where Alice worked and a small number of junior staff from Frampton Hall where she sometimes helped out at formal functions.

Standing back from the younger people was Jed's father, looking from the bulges in his grey suit as if he had been sewn into the outfit. A white collar held in place with a stud was clasped tightly round his neck and his bright red face gave the appearance of being about to burst. Tom, by comparison, had the appearance of a coat hanger draped with oversized garments as his clothes hung limply on his slight frame.

There was a ripple of applause from the group as Jed and Dan joined them. Dan bore a passing resemblance to Charles Dickens' character, Samuel Pickwick, with a grey suit bulging around his mid rift and pince–nez perched precariously on his nose.

Jed looked smart though not quite co–ordinated. He wore a mustard yellow jacket over brown checked trousers and sported a large white rose in his lapel.

The double doors of the church giving access to the chancel were pulled open revealing the Reverend Charles Bowman. The minister had been in residence in Frampton for as long as most people in the town could remember, making him somewhere in his mid seventies. He was unmarried and was attended to by a group of well meaning church ladies who cooked and cleaned for him. On this occasion they had not paid too much attention to cleaning his vestments as his white cassock displayed vivid evidence of recent meals.

"Welcome, everyone, please enter the Lord's House." With this he turned and led the small procession into the church and up the aisle to the altar. The guests hardly filled the first two rows of the knave and a deep quiet settled on the group as they waited for Alice's arrival.

Suddenly, the organ burst into life and a thinly disguised version of the Trumpet Voluntary spluttered from ageing pipes. The congregation turned to see Alice walk up the empty aisle. She wore a simple white ankle length dress that she had made herself and a white veil covered her face. In her hands was a bunch of white roses.

By her side, and looking most uncomfortable, was Alice's father. His gait was unsteady and he stumbled twice as he progressed up the aisle. He wore the expression of a man who had been transported out of his own dimension and had entered some parallel universe where nothing made sense.

Behind Alice came Flora in a pink dress and clutching a single red rose. She had lost weight and her clothes hung limply on her. Her eyes were cast down and she wore a nervous expression on her face.

"Dearly Beloved, we are gathered together in the sight of God, and in the face of this congregation to join together this man and this woman in holy matrimony," began the Reverend Bowman.

Jed kept his eyes on Alice, her veil now lifted to reveal her face. To the side of Alice he was aware of her father casting hostile glances in his direction.

"Holy Matrimony is an honourable estate instituted of God in the time of man's innocency, signifying unto us the mystical union that is betwixt Christ and his church."

Jed wondered about his own 'mystical union with Alice'. Were they really bound together by love or was it more likely a common desire to escape their oppressive pasts?

"First, it was ordained for the procreation of children, to be brought up in the fear and nurture of the Lord."

Alice felt a shiver run through her body. She had tried to put the idea of children out of her mind. The truth was that she didn't feel a strong attraction to Jed physically. She loved him as a person and she admired his honesty, his hard work and his loyalty but she couldn't get excited about going to bed with him. She hoped that Jed had not realised and that over time her passion would grow.

"Secondly, it was ordained for a remedy against sin and to avoid fornication ..."

But if that passion didn't come, didn't grow – could she maintain the lie in the face of Jed's persistence?

"Thirdly, it was ordained for mutual society, help and comfort that one ought to have of the other, both in prosperity and adversity."

Jed knew well enough that Alice wanted to be prosperous, craved status and success. But how would it be if it all went wrong? Would she stand by him if times were hard? He had his doubts.

"No one should enter into it lightly or selfishly but reverently and responsibly in the sight of almighty God."

Alice heard the wheeze of her father's breathing behind her. She caught sight of Flora to one side, hunched and frightened, and she looked again at Jed, confident and solid. She had to make this work. However much effort or pretence it took, this was the only way forward.

"Therefore if any man can show any just cause why they shall not be lawfully joined together, let him speak now or else hereafter forever hold his peace."

There was a tense silence in the church. Alice heard her father's breathing stop short as if caught by surprise. Jed's father looked nervously at Tom, and Flora raised her head to stare briefly at Jed.

"I require and charge you both, as ye will answer at the dreadful day of judgement when the secrets of all hearts shall be disclosed, that if either of you know any impediment why ye may not lawfully be joined together in Matrimony, ye do now confess it."

Alice's heart began to pound. If God really knew the secrets held within her heart, she was already doomed.

"Jed, wilt thou have this woman to be thy wedded wife, to live together after God's ordinance in the holy estate of Matrimony? Wilt thou love her, comfort her, honour and keep her in sickness and in health; and forsaking all other, keep thee only unto her, so long as ye both shall live?"

Jed turned to Alice. She looked very desirable and he wanted her as a wife and lover. But how could he promise it would be forever? He looked into her eyes, searching for answers.

"I will."

Alice felt Jed's eyes penetrating her own. His face looked anxious.

"And will you, Alice, take this man to thy wedded husband, to live together after God's ordinance in the holy estate of Matrimony? Wilt thou obey him and serve him, love, honour and keep him in sickness and in health; and forsaking all other, keep thee only unto him, so long as ye both shall live?"

She had been so sure. A way out of poverty. Status as a married woman in the community. Her own house to live in. It had all been so clear. But now? She heard a nervous cough from Reverend Bowman and realised that the whole church was waiting in expectant silence.

"I will."

The small congregation watched in silence as Alice and Jed made their vows, committing each other to a future which was steeped in uncertainty in both their minds.

"For as much as Alice and Jed have consented together in holy wedlock, and have witnessed the same before God and this company, and thereto have given and pledged their troth either to other, and have declared the same by giving and receiving of a ring and by joining of hands, I pronounce that they be man and wife together, in the name of the Father and of the Son, and of the Holy Ghost. Amen."

After the service Alice, Jed and the small group of well wishers made their way back through the centre of Frampton to Dan's premises. Alice and Flora had prepared a buffet of sandwiches and cold meat. The girls from the bakery had produced a single tier wedding cake with bells etched in white icing on the top whilst Dan provided flagons of beer and cider which the men quickly consumed.

The conversation was polite and muted as they began eating. Alice's father tore hungrily at pieces of meat as if he hadn't eaten in days. Jed's father and Tom held back from the main crowd, rolling their food slowly round their mouths, observing the others present with suspicion.

Alice and Jed stood close by each other, hardly believing that they were now married – Mr. and Mrs. Jed Carter. Jed felt for Alice's hand and held it gently. Alice relaxed and leaned closer to Jed.

Dan rose to his feet and banged on his glass with a knife.

"Ehem. Excuse me. I just wanted to say a few words. As you all knows, this Jed is a very special person to me. He's helped me build this business and he says he's going to stay to help me run it, maybe even take over from me. So this young man deserves the best and he's got the best. Since I got to know young Alice here, I see that she's got her head screwed on right. She don't let the grass grow under her feet and she's got big ideas, so I reckon the two of them together are going to go a long way. But it ain't just about the money you make or the things you buy, is it? We all know it's about a bit more than that. Now I can't give you advice about marriage, Jed and Alice, 'cos you all knows I ain't been married and that's a sadness for me – but that's another story. But I have done a bit of travelling in the course of fighting for this country of ours and I seen a few funny things. I seen men who have more than one wife, sometimes many wives. I seen men marry women they've never even met 'cos their families make an arrangement. I seen old men engaged to girls no more than five years old and I seen men who prefer the company of other men to their own wives.

So why am I tellin' you all this? Well, I think that the way we do it, one man and one woman making a lifelong commitment to each other, is probably the most difficult of the lot. It takes a lot of hard work and patience and love to make it work. But when it does work it seems to me there ain't anything better. So, Jed and young Alice, keep working at it and all of us here wishes you lots of happiness. Ladies and Gentleman, Alice and Jed."

They raised their glasses to Alice and Jed, then soon after began to leave. Alice's father was first to go. He held Alice by the arms and seemed to be searching for words that never came. Then he grunted and departed quickly.

Jed's father and Tom were next to go. They muttered something about 'fetching in the cattle' and thanked Alice for the 'spread'.

Finally, just Dan was left with Jed and Alice amidst an array of plates and remnants of food.

"You two leave this to me," suggested Dan. "I reckon you'll want to be getting back to your own place now."

"Oh no, Dan, let us help, there's no hurry," argued Alice.

"I'll be hearing no more about it. Off you two go now."

Alice and Jed walked back through Frampton as husband and wife with a sense of elation and optimism about the future. Already they had achieved much more than was usual for young people of their age and a whole lifetime lay ahead.

"Tell me, Alice," said Jed, "where do you see us in ten years time? How do you picture us then?"

"In ten years time? That's a difficult one. I suppose I'd like to see the house all finished and furnished. I'd like to see you doing well with the business and I'd like you and me to be getting older happily."

The conversation paused for a while as they walked on towards Duck Lane.

"But haven't you forgotten something?"

"Have I? What's that?"

"Isn't there something missing from what you just said? What about a family? What about children?"

"Well, yes, of course, children," answered Alice, slightly nervously. "I'm sure they'll come all in good time."

As they walked along Duck Lane and rounded a bend, Hope Cottage suddenly came into view. The trees obscuring the plot had been felled and a neat white fence erected in their place. The front garden was still full of rubble but beyond that Hope Cottage stood gleaming and new. Alice and Jed arrived at the front door.

"I think I got to lift you over the threshold, Alice, isn't that the custom?" said Jed, grinning broadly.

"You mind how you go then. Remember, there's no step there yet and I don't want you killing me on our wedding day."

With a powerful sweep of his arms, Jed lifted Alice up to his chest and clasped her to his body as he climbed into the house. The entrance hall was bare and Alice and Jed made their way through to the parlour which was furnished simply. A wood burning cooking range had been installed and took up most of one wall. In the centre of the room stood a simple oak table and two matching chairs that Dan had given them as a wedding present. A wooden dresser completed the furniture, resplendent with a bunch of red roses that Alice had put there earlier.

They stood looking out towards what would become the garden, now a tangle of thorns and nettles. Birds chirped their evening song and an owl hooted in a distant field. They sat on the floor in silence, Jed with his arm around Alice. Jed felt at peace with the world and himself. Alice was beginning to worry about what would happen in the bedroom shortly.

By ten o'clock the sun was setting and they made their way upstairs. Only one bedroom had been furnished and the bathroom was operational. It was Alice's pride and joy with its large white porcelain tub, matching wash basin and imposing WC.

As they mounted the stairs, Jed felt an almost imperceptible change of mood, a sense of anxiousness coming between them. As they entered the room, Jed took Alice in his arms and kissed her.

"You once said, Alice, that marriage was made here in the bedroom and now it's our chance to make our marriage real."

Alice was strangely quiet and excused herself to go to the bathroom. Jed sat on the side of the bed, rubbing his hands over the new eiderdown. He'd always expected that this would be the difficult part but he trusted Alice to make it work as she had made so many other things work.

Jed went to a drawer and pulled out a white and blue night shirt. He'd given some thought as to what he should wear on this first night. His father and Tom had always worn nightshirts and so he had followed suit.

He looked up as Alice came back into the bedroom dressed in a plain cotton nightgown which reached down to her calves. It clung to her body revealing the shape of her breasts, stomach and thighs in more detail than Jed had ever seen before. Her thick auburn hair lay like a curtain over her shoulders and a sweet perfume filled the air. Their eyes met and for a moment they stared nervously at each other wondering what lay ahead.

Jed made his excuses and went to the bathroom. He splashed water onto his face and relieved himself in the WC, trying hard to pee on the side of the bowl so as not to make too much noise.

He stripped his clothes off and struggled into his nightshirt. As he was about to leave the bathroom, he caught sight of a strange figure in the mirror – an apparition enveloped in a large white shroud.

"Oh my God," Jed thought to himself. "I can't go to her like this. She'll fall out of bed laughing."

There was only one course of action open to him. He pulled off the nightshirt and stood naked in front of the mirror. The apparition had now gone to be replaced by a young man with a well developed torso and strong muscular thighs. He felt much more confident that this was the image Alice would prefer on their first night. He also noticed with pride that his male member was now noticeably bigger than usual, surely a good sign.

As Jed made his way back into the bedroom, his arrival was greeted by an audible gasp from Alice who had settled herself in bed under the sheets. At the sight of a totally naked Jed she hauled the sheets further up under her chin until only her eyes and forehead were visible peeping over the crisp white bed linen.

"It's alright, Alice," said Jed moving towards her and causing the sheet to be hauled even higher. "It's alright now 'cos we're married. We belong to each other and it's OK to be naked."

"But it's a bit soon," replied Alice in a faltering voice. "I thought we'd take our time, you know, get to know each other slowly."

Jed felt his erection shrinking rapidly so he moved towards the bed to hide his body beneath the sheets.

"I think you're supposed to do it on the first night, you know, Alice. It's what they call 'consummating the marriage'. If you don't do it I've heard it said that you're not considered married."

Alice looked shocked and released her grip slightly on the sheet that she was clutching to her face.

"Are you sure that's true, Jed? Can't we wait a few days?"

"I'm only tellin' you what I hears, Alice."

Alice took in the room around her. Blue drapes hung in the open window. A wooden dresser stood opposite, decorated with lavender. The bed was large and the mattress was soft. It was the first time she had slept in a bed of this size. All this was hers now. She had worked so hard to get here. She couldn't possibly let it all go now.

"Alright, Jed, my love, let's give it a try. You do what you has to do."

This wasn't quite how Jed had expected it to be. In most other areas of life, Alice took the lead and he was happy to follow. Now, in this matter where he had the least experience of all, he was suddenly expected to be dominant.

"If you prefers me to take the initiative, my love, that's fine. But I think we got to get closer and I've got to get on top of you."

Alice looked momentarily startled but she obliged by letting go of the sheets and moving closer to him. Jed felt passion rise inside himself again as he took in her slender and inviting body. Pulling her to him, he began to kiss her, moving from her mouth to her breasts. He was relieved to feel his erection responding immediately. He levered himself over Alice's left leg and found himself lying between her thighs, his face level with her breasts. He heaved himself further up her body, ignoring her indignant grunts.

"I think we're getting somewhere now, my love."

He started to wrestle with her night dress which had somehow become entangled with the sheets. He tugged hard at a piece of bedding which had wrapped itself around her leg but his hand slipped and he elbowed Alice in the ribs. She shouted with pain and pushed Jed's head away.

"I'm sorry, my love, but you'll have to help me. We've got to do this together."

He lay once more between her thighs and tried to lift the night dress. This time Alice obliged by lifting herself off the mattress and allowing the nightdress to slip up. Jed now felt the warmth of her flesh on his. Moving his trunk between her thighs, he attempted to make love, but his unfamiliarity with the terrain in which he now found himself made it difficult to judge what was actually happening.

"Are we doing it, Alice? Am I doing it right my love?

"I think so. Maybe if I move my back down the bed a bit ..."

By now, the urgency being felt by Jed was uncontrollable. Suddenly, he had an overwhelming sense of release and he gripped Alice hard as he lost control of his body. She shouted with surprise and

Jed gasped as he climaxed. Then he collapsed onto the bed, breathing heavily.

"Have we consumed the marriage now, Jed, my love. Are we properly married?"

"We've *consummated* it, Alice, I'm pretty certain we have. So yes, we're properly man and wife." They lay together for a short while until the need to remake the bed caused them to move.

Later, when Alice had put on her night dress and Jed had found some underwear to replace his nightgown, they lay in bed talking quietly. This was how they functioned well together, talking like close friends, sharing ideas and enjoying each other's company. As Jed turned to look at Alice with the moonlight casting a soft glow over the whiteness of her body, a nagging worry began to form in his mind that the bedroom might not be the bedrock of their marriage in the way that he had hoped.

The Guest Who Stayed: Chapter 9 – Summer 1921

Jack motored into the centre of London in the Austin Tourer. It was a sunny day so he had lowered the canvas hood. As he made his way down Piccadilly to the Mayfair Hotel where Hoester had established his UK base, he felt more alive than he had done for almost a year. Working for Hoester and Deltic Sewing Machines had been hard. There were production targets to meet, new facilities to be installed and a succession of American executives passing through who had to be entertained. But today, Friday, 22nd July 1921, he was finished – done. In just a short while he would be receiving a bankers draft from Hoester for twenty three thousand pounds – the balance of his promised payment.

Jack tried to stifle a coughing fit that threatened to grip his body but it exploded into choking paroxysms which caused him to pull the car to an emergency stop by the curb. He fought to regain his breath. He was determined to survive the two or three years that his doctor had promised him – perhaps even cheat death and live a few years longer. He had given himself a week to clear up his affairs in London and then he would take off on the open road to 'who knows where'. But first he had to get as far as the Mayfair Hotel and lay his hands on that money.

After the wedding, life for Jed and Alice returned surprisingly quickly to a familiar routine. Alice continued to work in the bakery during the day but spent most evenings making furnishings and fitments for rooms that were still little more than shells. Though not taught to be practical, Alice had a natural ability to fathom out how things worked and to produce competent, if not always artistic, household items. Curtains were created from old parachute fabric that Jed had seen on sale in Frampton market. Cushions were sewn in a patchwork using discarded clothing and rugs were cut from old sacking.

Jed was working longer and longer hours in Dan's business and often when he returned home in the evening would complain to Alice at length about Dan's absence.

"Seems to me, Alice, that Dan's leaving me to pick up more and more of the work. I had to have words with him 'cos he'd gone off early yesterday to meet some cronies down the Fox and Hounds and left me to finish off a job that was needed for this morning. I think now we got this house he seems to think he owns us. Like he's done us this big favour and we're supposed to tug our forelock and be grateful to 'im."

"Well, in that case, Jed, you got to make a move to take over the business. If Dan's not pullin' his weight then you got to take over the reins and no more messin' about. The sooner you take control the better and then you can start paying yourself a bigger wage too."

At bedtime Alice and Jed would lay in each other's arms talking and drifting in and out of sleep. Making love seemed to require more effort than either of them could muster. But by some unspoken agreement Friday was designated the night when they would try again to consummate their union.

From the moment they opened their eyes on a Friday morning, palpable tension was in the air.

"What time are you back this evening, Alice?"

"Why are you asking? You know what time I'm back. It ain't no different because it's Friday."

"I know it makes no difference, my love. I was just wondering if you might be doing anything else after work, that's all."

"Like what?"

"No need to be like that," growled Jed grumpily as he cleared his plate from the table. "I was only trying to be a bit civil with you, that's all."

Friday evenings were even more tense. Neither Alice nor Jed had the vocabulary or the depth of understanding to discuss the problems openly. Instead, after various diversionary tactics such as rinsing clothes or preparing the next day's meal, they would end up in bed together facing the same dilemma.

"Alice, my love, shall we do it?"

Jed was still haunted by the experience of looking after his dying mother. When other boys in their adolescence were beginning to discover the excitement of their own sexuality, Jed was attending to the physical needs of a dying woman. And when his contemporaries began to hone their dating skills and learn the art of sexual negotiation, Jed was locked into a joyless existence from which the death of his mother would be the only release. Jed's perception of making love was therefore based on technical competence as opposed to emotional warmth.

"I got an idea, my love. Let's try putting a pillow underneath you."

Jed's approach to love making was like an incendiary device to someone like Alice who battled low self esteem. Raised in a household with a drunken father she was used to frequent verbal abuse and to disparaging remarks about her appearance. Now, in bed with Jed, she craved some sign of adoration. Did he like her breasts? Were they too large or too small? Did she turn him on? He had never told her. Instead, the Friday night ritual was more like being measured for a coffin.

"Just lift your knees up a bit and then I think it'll be OK."

Alice had not given much thought to the idea of 'being in love'. Her objective had been to escape from the shackles which bound her to a life she so despised and in this one objective she had been singularly successful. But now as she lay in bed watching Jed making final technical adjustments, Alice began to wonder if there was another dimension to this whole business of relationships which she had overlooked.

The dullness of the daily routine was broken early in July by one surprising event. Blue skies had been replaced by low cloud which hung over the countryside like a grey blanket depositing a fine coating of misty rain over the landscape. Alice was serving as usual in the bakery when the door of the shop was flung open by an unusually exuberant Flora.

"Alice, Alice, I got something to tell you; something that'll amaze you."

Other customers looked on with eager anticipation, keen to share in the news that would amaze them but Alice guessed that the news was not something that Flora would wish to share with the entire town.

"Come to my place tonight, Flora. Will it wait till then?"

"Yes, yes. I'll be there about sixish. See you then."

And with that and hardly a glance at the other shoppers, Flora turned and rushed from the shop.

That night at just gone six, there was a light tap at the door of Hope Cottage. Alice opened the door to let in a severely drenched Flora.

"Oh, Alice, I'm sorry about this morning but I just couldn't stop myself. I was bursting to tell someone."

"Come into the parlour and sit by the fire. Tell me what's brought this on."

Alice led Flora into the parlour and sat her by the fire then poured a large mug of tea from a pot that was gently sizzling on the range.

"Well, you'll never believe it, Alice, but the Brotherhood that Ma and Pa belongs to and what I was forced to join, well, it's broken up. It doesn't exist in Frampton no more. It seems there was some big disagreement over meaning of the scriptures, something to do with being 'separate'."

"What's all that about then?" inquired Alice.

"It's about not having anything to do with outsiders – people like you and Jed – 'cos you're bound to be evil. Not that I'm saying you and Jed is evil. But it's what the elders think. If you don't belong to the brotherhood then you've got to be evil."

"Well, that's crazy and nasty. What's happened to these elders?

They've closed the church down and gone to Norwich to start a new ministry. They reckoned the church was too small here to stay separate. They couldn't avoid talking to sinners."

"Well, good riddance to them is what I say. You're much better off without them. What about your ma and pa – have they gone too?"

"Ma and Pa were always considered a bit on the outside ever since we were cast out for a while and, of course, that was all my fault. So no, they weren't invited to join the elders. Them and a small group of others have been left behind. They're leaderless, like lost sheep. They don't know what to do."

"So what about you, Flora? How do you feel?"

"It means I'm free – free at last of all that bigotry and them controlling every aspect of my life."

Alice threw her arms around Flora who began to sob quietly as the magnitude of the change fully dawned upon her.

"You know what this means, Flora? I've got my friend back again. You and me, it'll be like old times."

"But you've got Jed now. You'll be wanting to spend your time with him."

"Oh, Jed's busy. He loves his work and besides he's got to do long hours to earn the money. He won't mind if you and me spend some time together."

Jack drove into the bay outside the Mayfair Hotel and reluctantly vacated his seat to a uniformed doorman to park the Austin. He didn't like people driving his car but felt on balance it was safer being parked at the Mayfair than being left on a London street.

He made his way into the lofty lobby and paused for a moment to take in his surroundings. All around him were signs of affluence and wealth – portraits of the great and good, statues of Greek goddesses, their modesty cleverly protected by marble fig leaves or a well placed hand. Distinguished looking men in morning suits accompanied by ladies carrying parasols clustered in small groups and talked in hushed voices. It was everything he hated, the pretence, the vanity, the hypocrisy and the greed. Faced with only a few years to live, he became more certain by the day that his short future lay outside of this unforgiving city in some small community where values were more honest and uncomplicated.

Entering Hoest's suite on the third floor, Jack was met with an explosion of well-rehearsed warmth as he was seized by the arm and embraced.

"Jack, my dear, dear, fellow. Welcome to our little gathering. Sit down and I'll fetch you a drink – bourbon alright?"

Jack sat and listened to the back slapping and self congratulatory oratory.

"Deltic Sewing Machines are now well established in the UK domestic market," announced Hoest as he addressed his small audience. "The Deltic Speed Stitch, which is, of course, based on Jack's S104, is being produced at a rate of fifty five machines each day at our new plant in Wembley. And in just two months, we'll be introducing our own Deltic Promaster X5 into the commercial tailoring market. Gentlemen, I think we can raise our glasses to a job well done."

Jack sensed his mind was drifting away from the proceedings. He didn't belong to this world of mass production and tight margins. He had been trained by his father as a craftsman. He took pride in the machines that he built and he knew the people he sold them to.

July 1921 was an unusually wet month. Grey cloud hung low over the countryside and a permanent dampness seemed to permeate all aspects of life. Shire horses were brought out of retirement on the farms to work the sodden ground as modern tractors failed to cope with the quagmire. Finally, in the last days of July the sun began to break through the cloud cover and temperatures began to climb. By early August people were throwing off their clothes and struggling to stay cool as temperatures reached 30 degrees and above.

It was the 6th August – the beginning of a bank holiday weekend. As Jack set off from London he could sense a holiday mood, with traffic heading out of the capital and children playing in the small parks that he passed on his way through the suburbs. He had settled his affairs and spent the last few days in a hotel as he prepared to begin his new life. As he motored through the outskirts of London, he felt a strange mix of emotions. He was free from the responsibility and routine of his job. He was well off – in fact, rich. He could please himself. But he was dying. How could he embrace the future and whatever opportunities came his way with this cloud hanging over him?

Jack had decided to head for the east coast, to enjoy the sea air, to feel the warmth of the sun on his body and to experience being part of a holiday crowd. For so long his life had been driven by business targets and also the dark memories that still resurfaced in his mind each night. He desperately sought to throw these off and hoped that by escaping his past he would discover some peace in his final years.

At Hope Cottage, Alice was up early working in the vegetable garden. Amongst the weeds and overgrown vegetation, small oases of cultivation were now beginning to emerge as she slowly imposed her will on the fertile soil.

"I'm off then, Alice," shouted Jed as he pulled his builders cart from its resting place at the side of the house.

"Are you sure you won't stay at home just for today, Jed. It is meant to be a holiday weekend after all."

"I told you I got to get that fence fixed for Mrs. Walters. We needs the money, Alice. We've got that loan to be paid each month."

"Surely a day won't make a difference. I thought we could take a picnic up to the heath. That's what lots of other folk do round here on a holiday."

"I'll be back about sixish." And with that he wheeled his cart out onto the road and made his way into Frampton.

Alice stopped her work and listened to the noise of the wheels grinding on the road as the cart slowly disappeared along Duck Lane. She felt suddenly despondent. She'd only been married for seven weeks but it seemed like seven years. Already her day was governed by routine. Up at six to get Jed's breakfast; start work at the bakery at eight; get home at four; tidy the house; prepare Jed's evening meal; listen to Jed moaning about Dan; go to bed and feign sleep. It wasn't what she had expected. Somehow, she thought that marriage would liberate her, that people would see her differently, seek her out and want to make friends with her. But she seemed trapped – locked into a lifetime of monotony with a man who seemed to thrive on convention and routine. She felt suddenly frightened and alone.

Jack had chosen Cromer on the east coast as his first destination. He knew little about it except that it was a popular seaside resort and it had a much admired pier built in 1901. So here he was, strolling at last along the promenade in the warm sun. The sea to his right sparkled and glinted like diamonds. Children dressed in bathing costumes played noisily on the beach and family groups gathered in clusters, unwrapping picnics and laughing loudly at private jokes.

Jack felt uplifted. It was what he needed. He had wanted to see people enjoying themselves and throwing off the gloom of the post war years. He hoped that somehow their good humour would transfer to him and that by being in their presence he would absorb some of the tonic.

He spotted a small pub with a terrace overlooking the sea and bought himself a scotch. For a while, he sat pondering the scene around him, listening to snatches of other people's conversations and laughing at jokes directed to others. Then it slowly dawned on him that he wasn't part of this scene at all. In fact, he was invisible to everyone else – just a man sitting by himself on the terrace of a small pub. No one knew that he had just become very rich – or cared. No one knew that he had a beautiful yellow Austin Tourer. No one knew that he had only a few years to live. These things only mattered if there was somebody else to share them with. They only mattered if you could tell someone about them.

He felt his spirits drop and decided to go in search of accommodation. He needed to be alone. Signs on the seafront directed him to the tourist information office. A young girl in her mid twenties smiled broadly at him as he entered.

"I need accommodation for the night, maybe two nights. Could you recommend a small hotel?"

"I'm sorry, sir, but everything's completely booked up. We've no vacancies at all. It's because it's a holiday and it's so hot. People have been flocking here from London. Our last vacancy went half an hour ago."

"There must be somewhere. I can't believe there's nothing."

"The vicar's planning to make beds available in the church hall, sir. We might be able to get you in there."

"I am not sleeping in the church hall. I haven't come all this way to spend the night like a refugee. I'm not well. I need somewhere decent to sleep." Jack felt immediately annoyed that he had resorted to his health problems to gain the girl's sympathy. Should he also tell her he was dying?

"I'm sorry to hear that, sir. There is one possibility. I've heard that the WI ..."

"The W what?"

"The WI. It's the Women's Institute. The Cromer WI is contacting groups in outlying villages to see if any of their members can put up visitors as it's an emergency. Do you want me to see if I can get you a place with one of the WI ladies?"

Jack had visions of a comely matron showing him into a small chintzy bedroom with floral cushions scattered across the bed. She would invite him to take cocoa with her and chat about the vicar's tea party and the state of the village flower beds.

"Sir, would you like me to investigate that option for you?"

"Oh, er, yes. I suppose I have no option. It sounds marginally better than the church hall."

Alice was still working in the garden of Hope Cottage, perspiring under the hot sun as she coaxed new life into the dry soil. Being a bank holiday weekend many townsfolk were heading for the coast and Alice felt distinctly detached from the festive mood. Suddenly, her attention was caught by a shrill voice calling out her name.

"Alice, Alice Carter, is that you?"

The caller was an unexpected visitor – Mrs. Burns, a stalwart of conservative gentle society and also chairwoman of the local Women's Institute. Alice gave people such as her a wide berth as she knew that she was considered by some of her kind to be below them socially.

"Hello, Mrs. Burns. How nice to see you. You're not often in this part of town."

"Just passing by and I've heard so much about your dear little cottage I thought I'd just catch a glimpse for myself. So very pretty. I gather your husband actually built it himself."

"That's right, Mrs. Burns. Jed's a builder so it seemed a good idea."

"Oh yes, I know Jed and Daniel. They've done jobs for me in the past. Cleared the drains last time, I think. Did it very well too. But listen, there was another matter I wanted to raise with you. I had the head of the WI in Cromer on to me this morning in a bit of a state. It seems that this hot weather is bringing thousands of trippers out to the coast. Well, given the terrible weather we've had I suppose you can understand that. Anyway, they've all been arriving in Cromer by train and charabanc and motor car expecting to be put up. But they've run out of accommodation. They're simply full up. So the word has gone out to find bed and breakfast accommodation in the surrounding villages. Well, of course, they'll pay, so I thought of you. I expect a little bit extra will help and all you have to do is provide a bedroom and give them breakfast. What do you say? Are you interested?"

"Well, I'm not sure. I'd have to see what Jed says. I mean, who will we have to stay? Do we have a choice?"

"No, luck of the draw. You'll just have who the WI in Cromer send and we've all agreed the rate will be twelve shillings a night."

"Twelve shillings? That's quite a lot. When do you need to know, Mrs. Burns? Can I think about it?"

"I need to know now, Alice. I've got to go to the post office and put through a call by two this afternoon."

Alice was in two minds. On the one hand, she knew that she should discuss this with Jed first. He wouldn't take well to having a visitor in the house and she would have to do a bit of persuading. On the other hand, she knew Jed was worried about money and especially about paying this month's loan instalment on the house. Twelve shillings would almost cover the payment and take the pressure off Jed having to work such long hours.

"Alright, Mrs. Burns, we'll do it. I'm sure Jed won't mind. We'll say yes."

Alice spent the rest of Saturday morning preparing a guest room. Jed had already requisitioned a bed, one of many pieces of furniture that he and Dan had been asked to mend but for which no payment was forthcoming. By cleverly juggling their existing furniture and liberally decorating the room with flowers, Alice managed to create a pleasant, though simple, environment.

She began to feel nervous about Jed's reaction. If the guest arrived before he got home, it would be difficult explaining the presence of someone else in the house. Alice hoped it would be a woman, perhaps an elderly spinster taking a short break from London.

Suddenly, her attention was drawn to the sound of a car engine outside. Cars seldom ventured down Duck Lane so their presence was unusual. Standing close to the window but taking care not to be seen, Alice observed a large yellow open top sedan navigating its way slowly through the pot holes. She could see that the car contained only a driver and on the back seat was a large leather trunk. She wondered why such a car would come this way. Beyond Hope Cottage there were only a couple of smallholdings before the lane petered out into a marshy meadow.

The driver appeared to be searching for something and was consulting a piece of paper that he held in his hand. Alice's heart began to race as she realised that this could be the paying guest. She pulled the old apron that she was wearing from her waist and patted energetically at her hair with no discernable result.

The car had now drawn to a halt outside Hope Cottage and the driver was staring intently at the front door. Alice suddenly had a great sense of foreboding. How insane to invite an unknown stranger to stay with you in your house. He could be anyone, a murderer, a rapist, a thief, and she was going to open the door and let him walk in.

He was out of the car now and making his way hesitantly to the door. She could see that he was a broad shouldered man, probably in his early forties. He had thick dark hair protruding from under a sporty driver's cap and he wore a blue checked open neck shirt with light coloured trousers.

A loud knock at the door sent a shock wave through her body. Momentarily she found herself rooted to the spot but a second knock drew her down the stairs and into the hall. Taking a deep breath she opened the door to reveal the stranger. He was tall, about six foot one. His face was clean shaven and when he lifted his cap a shiny head of thick black hair was revealed.

"Mrs. Carter, Mrs. Alice Carter?" he enquired, a broad smile spreading across his face.

"Yes, that's me."

"I'm Jack, Jack Malikov. I understand that you've very kindly offered to take in a paying guest." He paused, confused by the blank expression on Alice's face. "I'm your paying guest."

Alice was speechless. The man had an imposing presence. His frame filled the small porch and she found she had to look up to make eye contact with him. He extended his arm and she felt her hand engulfed by the hugeness of his.

"Is it still alright? I mean, you were expecting me?"

"Oh yes, yes, of course it's alright," stammered Alice. "We're very happy to be having you as our guest, that's me and my husband, Jed. We're both very happy to be having you to stay. You must excuse our place, it's very simple but we've only just built it."

"You mean you built this house yourselves?"

"Well, it was mostly Jed, he's the one with an eye for that sort of thing."

"He must be a very talented man, your husband. I look forward to meeting him."

"Well, he's working at the moment but I dare say you'll see him later. Look, please come in and I'll show you to your room."

Alice took him upstairs into the room that had been designated as his. Although simply furnished, the room looked fresh and inviting and Jack seemed pleased with the arrangement. She left him to unpack his case and retreated into the parlour, unsure about what was required of her next. It seemed strange to hear someone she didn't know moving around in the room above. She heard him opening drawers and moving his trunk across the floor then walk out of his room and into the bathroom. It hadn't occurred to her that someone would be sharing her prized bathroom and she felt uneasy about it. The toilet flushed and she heard him making his way back to the bedroom. She tried to get on with some jobs but found herself obsessively listening out for his next move. The bedroom door opened again. Then came the sound of him walking slowly down the stairs. She busied herself by the sink, hoping that he would go straight out.

"Mrs. Carter, can I have a quick word?"

She turned to see him standing in the doorway, smiling.

"Are you off then?"

"Yes, I thought I might take a drive into the country – just to get my bearings."

"Would you care for a cup of tea before you go?" Alice hadn't meant to ask him and regretted it the moment the words slipped out.

"Well, if it's no trouble, a quick cup before I go out would be very welcome."

As Alice prepared the tea, Jack sat at the parlour table talking.

"I've been really looking forward to this break. I haven't stopped working for nearly three years. This is the first holiday I've had in all that time."

Alice tried to place the accent. His voice was warm and resonant with a clear London twang, but beneath that lay another suppressed accent, possibly foreign, which occasionally surfaced and caused some words to be pronounced in unexpected ways.

"I had to get away. I can hardly breathe when I'm in London so I thought I'd head out to the coast and get some sea air. Thought I'd book into a little guest house with no problem but they were all full up. So I went to the tourist office and they suggested I sleep on the church floor like a refugee. Well, I must have looked dumbfounded because the next minute the young lady's telling me the local WI's providing bed and breakfast in the outlying villages. So here I am in a pretty little cottage being served tea by a very pleasant Mrs. Carter."

Alice blushed. "Call me Alice, please."

"Only if you call me Jack."

Alice poured tea for Jack into a cup from her best set.

"I hope you're going to join me. I've got plenty I want to ask you."

Alice chose a matching cup and poured tea for herself. She listened whilst Jack told her a little more about himself. He was careful not to mention his illness but was happy to talk about his business and how he had just sold it for a large amount of money.

"So you're not doing too badly, Mr. Malikov – I'm sorry, I mean, Jack. That's a very posh car you got sitting outside there."

"Ah, do you like her?" A broad grin spread across Jack's face. "I've only had her a week. I promised myself that when this deal was agreed I'd treat myself to a car. It's an Austin Twenty Tourer. I bought her new for six hundred and ninety five pounds."

Alice gasped. It seemed a huge amount of money. She and Jed had borrowed less than that to build Hope Cottage.

"Perhaps you'd let me take you out in her, Alice, and your husband too, of course. We could go for a drive tomorrow – to the sea."

"I don't think Jed would like to do that. He's planning to work tomorrow."

"Well, I can't blame a man for having to work. I've been doing that myself for too long." Then he added rather tentatively, "Perhaps Jed would still allow me to take you for a drive?"

"I don't think Jed would think that was very proper."

"How about if you brought a friend? Can you think of anyone who would like to go for a drive in my beautiful car?"

"Well, there is Flora, of course. She's my best friend. She could do with a day out," said Alice, beginning to warm to the idea. "I can't say for certain just now but I'll talk to my Jed tonight and see if I can persuade him. I would love to go for a drive. Thank you so much for asking."

"It would be my pleasure," he said, rising from the table and taking hold of his driving cap. "I'm going to keep my fingers crossed that Jed says yes. If I don't see you this evening when I get back, I'll see you tomorrow for breakfast. Thanks for the tea, Alice."

With that he grinned broadly, turned and let himself out. Alice remained at the parlour table, listening as the front door closed. Then she heard the throaty roar of the Austin starting up and pulling away from the house.

She sat in silence for a while, trying to analyse what she felt. A sense of impending excitement was gnawing away at her. Even though it was nonsense, she suddenly felt a little bit more alive, a little bit more on edge than she had before Jack's arrival. She caught herself smiling for no apparent reason and forced herself to stop. This was crazy. He was only staying a few nights and would then be gone. He came from another world and would be returning there soon. Alice got up from the table and started to prepare Jed's meal.

That evening when Jed returned home, he was exhausted from repairing a barn roof in the searing thirty degree heat. His face was burned red and his hands were blistered.

"Jed, I got a surprise for you."

"What sort of surprise?"

"Well, you know Mrs. Burns, the one you're not partial to?"

"The old snob who runs the WI?"

"That's her. Well, she came round this afternoon asking if we'd take in a paying guest. Apparently all the accommodation in Cromer is full and there's people looking for rooms over the bank holiday."

"Well, I hope you told her no."

"No, I told her yes."

"You told her what?"

"Look, Jed, it pays us twelve shillings a night. He's staying two nights. That's twenty four shillings. We can't afford to lose that, Jed."

"Who's paying twenty four shillings?" spluttered Jed. "Where is he? Get him out of here immediately."

Over a meal of steak and ale pie which Alice had prepared in anticipation of Jed's objections, Jed slowly calmed down as the implications of earning twenty four shillings began to dawn but he resolutely refused to endorse the idea.

"So he's a rich bugger is he, this guest of yours. Probably looks down his nose at the likes of us then," Jed grumbled as he wiped his plate clean.

"No, he doesn't, not at all. He was ever so complimentary about you building the house. Said he was looking forward to meeting you."

"Well, I ain't looking forward to meeting him. So you make sure we stay apart, Alice, 'cos I ain't going to sit and make idle conversation with 'im."

"Oh, but I thought you might meet over breakfast tomorrow, Jed, before you go out."

"I'm not eating my breakfast with him in the parlour. You serve mister high and mighty in the sitting room. I'm telling you, Alice, I want no part in this. It's all your doing."

They ate in silence for the next few minutes whilst Alice pondered the problem of the next day's outing.

"Jed, I forgot to say but Mr Malikov – Jack – asked if we'd like to go for a ride in his car tomorrow. I told him I thought you'd be working."

"Too right, I'm working. No time for gallivanting round the country in some posh car. Someone's got to earn the money."

"He asked if I could go – to show him the sights."

"Of course, you can't go. What would people round here say if you, a married woman, went off with a single man for the day. Have sense, Alice."

"I said if Flora could go too, you would probably say yes," ventured Alice, trying to disguise a 'wobble' in her voice.

"Oh, Alice, how could you do that? I don't like the idea of another man in my house and I think you should be respecting my wishes, not going off with your fancy man whilst I work all hours to keep up payments on this place. I'll just have to leave it up to you. You do what you think's right."

It was gone ten when Alice heard the growl of the Austin as it coasted to a halt outside the cottage. She heard the sound of a key being turned and the front door opening. Footsteps, light as if someone was trying to tiptoe, made their way up the stairs and into the guest room. She tried to imagine him again, tall, imposing, his mysterious accent, his easy smile.

She heard him using the toilet but strangely it didn't bother her. She waited for the flush and then heard him retrace his footsteps into the bedroom. There was a squeak of old springs as he fell into bed and then silence.

Alice lay in the dark – Jed asleep beside her. Her body tingled in anticipation of the day ahead.

Jed lay with his eyes closed feigning sleep. He wanted to put his arms round Alice and hold her but something was preventing him. He was uneasy. Deep inside a pain had begun to take hold.

The Guest Who Stayed: Chapter 10 – August Bank Holiday 1921

The next day Alice was up at six preparing the breakfast. The sun was streaming in through the parlour windows and the promised fine bank holiday looked set to unfold. Jed wandered into the parlour still rubbing his eyes and sniffed at the smell of sizzling sausage and bacon.

"It's going to be another hot one, Alice. I expect I'll get burnt up same as yesterday."

"Not if you cover up properly. I've packed you plenty of water so make sure you drink that."

"You didn't mean what you said last night about going out with this Jack, did you?" asked Jed as he wiped the last remnants of bacon from his plate with a piece of bread.

"I dunno. Let's just see what happens."

"It don't seem right to me, you going off with some strange bloke and I'm out working."

"Flora will be with me, I told you," replied Alice, more tetchily than she had anticipated.

"Hello, I smelt breakfast cooking."

Alice and Jed turned to see Jack standing in the doorway. He carried a small bag over his shoulder as if he was already prepared to go out.

"Oh, Mr. Malikov – I mean Jack. You're early. I didn't expect you just yet," muttered Alice in a state of confusion. "This is my husband, Jed. Jed, this is Mr. Jack Malikov, our guest."

Jack leant forward and held out his hand to Jed, who responded by wiping his hands on his trousers.

"Got fat on my hands."

"Oh right," replied Jack, withdrawing his hand quickly. "Anyway, it's nice to meet you and I want to thank you for letting me stay these few days."

Alice watched aghast as Jed poured tea into his saucer and slurped the liquid into his mouth. It was an old farming practice and one that Alice had banned.

"Jed, please don't do that, my love – not in front of our guest."

"I'm in a hurry. Can't drink hot tea."

"I had hoped you could join us for a drive in the car today," ventured Jack. "But I understand you're busy with your work. I quite understand that. I was telling Alice yesterday that this is my first break for three years."

"I don't take breaks," replied Jed reproachfully. "And I don't 'ave a posh car either. I have a barrow. Still, it's good enough for me. I best be going now. Goodbye, Alice, my love."

"Wait, Jed. You need your lunch and your drink." Alice rushed forward with Jed's lunch bag and placed it firmly over his shoulder. "You take good care now and I'll see you later."

Jed gave Alice a fleeting glance, his eyes betraying a hidden anxiety. Then he turned and set off for work.

"Jed's not quite himself. He's working hard and to be honest he's not convinced about us having a paying guest. But the truth is, Jack, we needs the extra money, so I'm really glad you're here. And now I'm going to get your breakfast ready."

It was gone nine o'clock before breakfast had been cleared away and they were ready to leave. Shortly before that, Flora arrived and was introduced to Jack. His affable manner made her laugh and all three were soon relaxed in each other's company.

Jack seemed well prepared for the day. He wore white flannel trousers and a light navy jacket. Alice and Flora had no previous experience of day trips to the coast and so they had to improvise from their limited wardrobes. Flora had put on a blue cotton dress secured around the waist with a white sash. The dress had probably fitted when she was in her early teens but now it was tight around the bust and showed off her figure to good effect. Alice wore a white cotton skirt which reached down to her calves and a pink jacket buttoned up to her neck. But having seen how Jack's eyes were drawn to Flora, Alice surreptitiously undid her top buttons to reveal more of her white chest.

Sitting in the Austin Twenty was an intoxicating experience for Alice and Flora. The seats were made from brown leather and the dashboard was veneered in dark oak. When Jack turned the starter handle, the engine roared into life and enveloped them in a throaty, mechanical ambience.

Jack had guided Alice to sit by him on the front bench seat and Flora sat on the back bench seat. As the car navigated Duck Lane and then headed out of Frampton, the wind caught Alice and Flora's hair and whipped it into a frenzy of twisted strands, rendering their meticulous preparation hopelessly redundant.

Once the car was on the A140 to Cromer, they made good time but as they reached the outskirts, traffic began to build up with many other day trippers also on the road. Open top charabancs carrying boisterous groups of people on a day's outing from the towns jostled for position on the narrow road into Cromer.

As they got close to the sea front, they were diverted into a field which had been designated for temporary parking. When the engine was turned off, Jack produced a silver flask from the car's glove compartment.

"Just to get us in the mood, ladies."

"What is it?" asked Alice, viewing the flask suspiciously.

"It's whisky – Glenmorangie – one of the finest single malts. Try some."

"After you. You have some first," Alice replied with scepticism. She had a deep aversion to liquor having seen the effect on her father over the years, yet didn't want to appear prudish. She watched as Jack unscrewed the small silver cap and sipped from the flask. He closed his eyes and threw his head back, allowing the single malt to slide slowly down his throat. It was clearly a treat he had enjoyed before and one that delivered to him a few moments of personal ecstasy. Alice felt uneasy but tried to brush the feeling away.

"Now you and Flora."

Alice sniffed at the flask and recoiled quickly. She was overpowered by the fumes.

Jack laughed. "Try it again."

This time Alice approached the flask slowly, knowing what to expect. She lifted the flask to her lips and let a small amount of whisky slide into her mouth. Her first reaction was to wince in horror but then, as she let the liquid roll around her mouth and slide slowly down her throat, she began to enjoy the experience and the feeling of mild elation she was left with.

Flora's attempts to drink from the flask were less decorous and, having swigged a large amount of whisky, she sprayed most of it over the front seat as she involuntarily choked.

The whisky had the effect of relaxing them even more and with the car properly secured they began to make their way into Cromer. As they left the car park, they soon came upon the sea for the first time, glistening under the intense light of the morning sun. For Flora, it was her first ever sight of the ocean and she was transfixed by its seeming infinity.

"You mean it just goes on and on. It must end somewhere?" she asked incredulously.

They followed the crowds along the coast path towards the resort centre. As they turned a corner, they suddenly caught sight of the pier stretching majestically out into the sparkling waters of the North Sea.

"That's Cromer Pier," announced Jack. "I particularly wanted to see that. It's one of the finest in the country. It was built in 1901."

"What's it for?" asked Flora, not quite understanding why it didn't appear to go anywhere.

"Well, it's for walking along and enjoying the sea air. And it's got lots of amusements and a pavilion where they put on shows and it's even got a restaurant. Let's go and see it."

They followed the crowds along the headland and down to the pier front. The scene was one of noisy, good humoured chaos. Flags flew from the pier head gates and people jostled at the ticket office to get in. Posters above the entrance advertised entertainments and amusements

– dancing to the romantic Blue Viennese Band in the pavilion, traditional Punch and Judy show at the end of the pier, rowing boats for hire from the lower level.

All around, street vendors and entertainers competed for attention. The crowd roared approval as a young man on a unicycle juggled flaming torches. A man selling balloons pressed his wares on Flora and Alice but Jack intervened firmly and guided them away.

"Let's go on the pier," he said. "It'll be less crowded."

"That's a very nice idea," said Flora, turning suddenly bright red and casting her eyes downwards, "but truth is I haven't got much money, Jack, so you and Alice go ahead. I'll just wait here for you."

"That's nonsense, Flora," he replied, leaning forward to touch her lightly on the arm. "Today's on me. You'll pay for nothing. It's my way of saying thank you to both of you."

At Hall Farm, Jed struggled up the ladder with another basket of tiles to where Dan was sitting astride a rafter on the exposed roof. Jed placed the basket on a makeshift platform and wiped beads of sweat from his brow.

"I wonder if she's gone then. She said she hadn't made up her mind. I don't mind telling you, it's playing on my mind."

"I 'spect it's nothing," replied Dan without lifting his eyes from the cement he was mixing. "I mean, she's just showing the fellow around and she's got Flora with her. And don't forget it's the Women's Institute what arranged it and there ain't no more moral and saintly group of people in Frampton than the WI. Anyway, what would you have her do? A young girl don't want to be by herself all day on a sunny bank holiday."

"That's not quite the point is it? I've got to be up on this bleeding roof with you on a sunny bank holiday and it don't seem right that my wife's off with another man havin' the time of her life."

Once through the turnstile, they linked arms again and stepped out along the wooden pier. Devoid now of shelter, they felt the wind from the sea whip around their legs and tug at their clothes. Jack was experiencing a heady mix of elation and contentment. Compared with yesterday when he had been merely an observer, today he felt as if he was at the centre of events. He couldn't help noticing admiring glances in his direction from passers–by, no doubt wondering about the two good looking young women who clung to his arms. Further along the pier they arrived at a cluster of stalls selling snacks and cold drinks. They were drawn to one stall where the vendor was apparently spinning a web made from some sort of fibre in a rotating drum.

"What is that Jack? I never seen the likes of that before," asked Flora, peering into the spinning container.

"I think it's called candy floss," replied Jack. "To tell you the truth, I've never tried it so I can't tell you what it's like."

"Why don't we try some?" suggested Alice, her face animated by the prospect of something new.

Jack ordered three candy floss sticks and they watched as the vendor skilfully built a ball of spun candy on each stick then handed one to each of them. They soon discovered that there was no polite way to eat candy floss. As Alice tried to insert her tongue into the pink ball, her nose seemed to arrive there first and then strands of her hair stuck to the sticky sugary fibres. Jack fared little better and his face was soon covered in specks of pink. They dissolved into laughter at the sight of each other and had to hold onto railings to steady themselves. When the laughter subsided, Jack took a clean handkerchief from his top pocket and offered to wipe the sticky substance from the girls' faces. Holding Alice's shoulder, he wiped slowly around her mouth with a clean edge of the hanky. Alice found herself staring into his blue eyes and trembling slightly at his close physical proximity. But he held her gaze and smiled at her as he worked slowly around the edge of her mouth removing traces of the pink sugar.

Jed handed Dan another tile and waited while it was secured with a nail.

"Don't seem to 'ave made so much progress today. Reckon we've got a full day here an' then another one tomorrow too. I trust you will be 'ere tomorrow, Dan?"

Dan didn't reply immediately, focusing instead on his preparation for the next tile. Once he had secured this he looked Jed squarely in the eyes.

"I been thinking about saying this to you for a while now, Jed."

"Saying what?"

"You got to lighten up, lad. You seem to be takin' the cares of the world on your shoulders and it don't make you an easy person to be with."

"Oh, come on, Dan," said Jed, raising his voice and hurling the next tile back into the basket from which he'd just taken it.

"What do you expect, eh? I'm trying to make this business a success and make us some money. Somebody's got to worry about what we're earning 'cos you surely ain't. To start with you could collect all the money that's owing to us. If we got that we could both take a holiday."

"You don't get it do you?" replied Dan, in a quiet and controlled voice. "We're in business here because people trust us and because we help them when they most need it. If someone's down and you tell 'em you're only going to help if they pay you, I promise you, Jed, you'll have no business within weeks. Come harvest we'll get paid. We always does."

"That's the old fashion way. You can't run a business like that now, not if you want me to be in it with you."

"Oh, so that's it, is it?" said Dan, raising his voice suddenly and moving toward Jed. "If I want to go on working with you it's got to be your way has it? I got to take my orders from you now, have I? Well, let me tell you this ..."

As Dan moved closer to Jed he caught the edge of the platform with his foot, dislodging one of the supports. The platform tipped and ejected its content of tiles and cement onto the concrete floor twenty feet below.

"Oh Christ, Dan, look what you've bloody done now. Can't you watch where you're putting your sodding feet?"

There was silence. Neither knew what to say. Jed turned away and pretended to busy himself. Dan moved slowly to the ladder and climbed down to the ground. Jed searched for words but could find none. He couldn't decide whether he owed Dan an apology or whether he was simply asserting his position as owner in waiting. Perhaps Dan would be impressed that he was being assertive and taking his role seriously. After all, if he was going to take over the reins of the business, he had to demonstrate leadership and maturity. He had to speak his mind.

Jed moved his position so that he could see Dan who was now sitting below on the floor of the barn. His shoulders were hunched and his head was buried in his arms.

"Come on then, Dan, let's get some more tiles up here shall we?"

A band was playing on the pier as Flora, Alice and Jack walked back to the promenade. They stopped by the bandstand as the uniformed musicians struck up a strident rendition of 'I do like to be beside the seaside'. The optimism of the music was infectious. The bleakness of the post war years seemed finally to be lifting and each in their different way felt that perhaps something better lay just beyond the horizon.

For Jack, memories of those dark times still surfaced regularly and could drag him back into a state of acute melancholy but this new friendship with Alice and Flora seemed to offer some hope of redemption after the horrifying death of Yvette and possibly Simone for which he still held himself responsible. His heart ached to think of their loss but for now he must focus on the future and enjoy this opportunity which fate had delivered suddenly into his hands.

"Isn't it kind of weird," ventured Flora, "that all these people have come here just to have fun? I didn't know such places existed."

"It's the new world," said Jack, gesturing expansively. "The war's over and now it's time to move on – time to do new things and put the past behind us. We can't go through that hell again. There'll be no more world wars like that one. The politicians have learnt that you can't just send people to be slaughtered like cattle. People won't let them do it again – you'll see."

They left the pier and walked along the beach. It was crowded with people sitting in hired deck chairs basking in the warm sun. The water's edge was busy with day trippers dipping their toes into the still icy water. Some had changed into bathing costumes and were venturing further into the water shrieking as waves lapped over their white bodies. Alice and Flora had never seen such blatant pleasure seeking before. They had been brought up in the tradition of daily struggle and unrelenting grind. The idea that there were places where the sole purpose was to provide people with pleasure seemed completely alien.

"Ladies, look," said Jack excitedly. "You see over there by the breakwater, there are boats for hire. Let's go for a row. I used to be a bit of a champion oarsman before the war. Maybe I could impress you both with my skill."

Within minutes they were taking their shoes off and being helped by the attendant into one of the boats. Flora sat in the bow looking out to sea whilst Alice sat in the back, directly in Jack's gaze as he positioned himself in the centre of the boat and took command of the oars. With powerful strokes he pulled them away from the beach and away from all the attendant noise and confusion.

Here, there was just the sound of the oars dipping rhythmically into the sea. No one spoke as the vastness of the seascape seemed to make trivial conversation redundant. Alice watched Jack as his powerful shoulders drove the blades into the water. She realised how easy the conversation with him had been. Unlike most men she knew, Jack was easy to talk to and seemed to take seriously what she had to say. His laughter and his enthusiasm were infectious. She was beginning to realise that her experience of the world was very narrow and confined to a small rural community. Here, floating at the edge of a sea that joined with oceans that flowed to the other side of the world, an uneasy sense began to dawn on Alice that she had perhaps raised the drawbridge to her chosen fortress rather early in her short life.

"Alright, Dan, I'm sorry. I didn't mean what I said and I'll be more careful. Now, will you get some more tiles up here, please," said Jed, rather as if he was addressing a petulant five year old.

The idea that Dan had been impressed by Jed's unguarded outburst was now clearly wrong. Jed realised from Dan's demeanour that he was deeply hurt. There was no banter and no retaliatory abuse which Dan would usually deliver with sarcasm and wit. This time, there was just silence and a sense of awkwardness.

"Come on, Dan, I'm waiting."

They had reached the seaward end of the pier and Jack had paused the rowing so that they could look back to the shore and take in the picture postcard scene. The sea was more choppy now and the boat rocked as the waves persistently knocked against the wooden hull.

"I think we should turn back now," said Alice, sensing a shift in the wind direction from on shore to off shore.

"I think you're right," responded Jack, taking hold of the oars and turning the boat back to the shore. A gust of wind chased across the surface, whipping the sea into small white crests. The boat began to pitch forward as the off shore wind sculpted the waves into razor edges that spat angry drops of salty water into their faces.

"Is it alright, Jack?" asked Flora anxiously as she made her way back from the front of the boat. Memories of a similar incident two years earlier flooded into Alice and Flora's minds. But Jack was unflustered. He pulled strongly on the oars and the boat surged forward. Alice screamed as a large wave crashed against the side of the boat and sent a spume of water surging over her dress.

"Hold on! Stay calm!" commanded Jack. We're almost there. We'll be in the shadow of the groin in just a few minutes. We're almost there."

Ten miles inland the gust of wind that had whipped up the sea in Cromer was now swirling and tugging at Jed and Dan as they tried to finish their work. Dan had finally agreed to resume the task of keeping Jed supplied with roof tiles. He filled another hod and made his way to the bottom of the ladder. Usually, he would alert Jed that he was about to begin the climb to the top but this time he chose to remain silent. The roof was high and the ladder was positioned so that it was almost vertical.

Jed took the last tile from his supply and hoped that Dan was on his way up. The rising wind meant that he had to work with his arm wrapped around a rafter to stop himself falling and this slowed him down.

Dan held onto the side of the ladder with one hand and clutched the hod full of tiles to his shoulder with the other hand. To avoid falling off the ladder he had to press his body against the rungs as he changed grip and moved his hand to the next rung.

Jed eased the tile into place and secured it with a nail. There were no more tiles left on the pallet now and he turned round to see why Dan hadn't replenished his store. At this rate they wouldn't be finished by dusk and that would mean another day spent here when they could be earning more money on their next job.

Slowly, Dan reached the top of the ladder and prepared to place the hod on the platform. But as he lifted the tiles, the wind suddenly gusted round the ladder tugging at his work clothes and causing him to lose balance. Struggling to stay in control, he managed to hold onto the hod but was forced to lean back. Immediately, the top of the ladder fell away from its resting point on the platform leaving it balanced precariously without any support.

Panic gripped Dan as he tried to call out to Jed but only a frightened gasp emerged.

Jed shifted his position so that he could see what progress Dan was making. What he saw sent pangs of anxiety racing through his body. Only inches away, Dan was clutching the top of ladder which swayed in small circles, unconnected to any part of the structure.

"Dan, Dan, drop the tiles and reach out to me!" ordered Jed.

Jed lay down on the platform and reached out to Dan. His eyes were only inches away from Dan's eyes and he could see the terror reflected in them. He tried to grab the ladder but his fingers only brushed the side as it swung out of reach.

"Dan, push your body against the ladder. Move your weight."

But Dan seemed consumed with fear and his body was locked into paralysis. The ladder seemed to stay still for a moment. Jed prayed it would tip towards him but with gut wrenching finality it slowly tipped away. The top of the ladder gained in speed as it swung towards the floor. Dan held on till near the end but finally his body parted with the ladder and hit the concrete floor with a dull thud, followed by the ladder which fell across his inert body.

Jed let out a cry and gripped the side of the platform.

"Dan, Dan! Are you alright? Say something, Dan." But there was a profound silence.

Jed felt a surge of panic. He clasped his hands together and screamed out a prayer to a God of whom he had little knowledge. With the ladder gone, there was no easy way down. He hunted for a way to escape. Spotting some rope, he managed to climb down one of the wooden roof supports and get to Dan's side.

"Dan, Dan, speak to me. Tell me you're alright."

He pulled the ladder off and put his ear to Dan's mouth to see if he could detect breathing. Then he saw the pool of sticky red blood emerging from under Dan's head and he knew the truth.

Sitting on the veranda of the magnificently gothic Hotel de Paris, Alice and Flora felt that they had arrived in Utopia. Waitresses dressed in starched white pinafores moved swiftly from table to table carrying trays bearing silver teapots and plates of scones. In front of them the pier reached out into the now placid blue sea and strains of music drifted up to the veranda from the band below. A waiter appeared and with a dramatic flourish presented a bottle of champagne which he uncorked with an explosive 'pop'.

"Jack, what's this?" exclaimed Flora. "You said we was coming up here for a cup of tea – not champagne. I've never drunk champagne before."

"It's my treat to you both," replied Jack as he sampled the champagne and gestured to the waiter to fill the girls' glasses. "This is one of the best days I've had in years. I haven't enjoyed myself so much in ages."

"It don't seem right somehow," persisted Flora, "not for the likes of us."

"There's no reason it shouldn't seem right, Flora. You've got the same right to drink champagne and enjoy yourself as anyone else. After all none of us knows how long we've got so there's no point in waiting is there?"

Jack took a long swig at his champagne to drown the sudden realisation that in his case he knew only too well how long he had to live. He felt suddenly angry and was seized by a determination that in whatever time was left he would take the opportunity to enjoy his life at whatever cost. Life owed him that at least.

They motored back to Frampton in silence, each absorbed in their own private thoughts. Flora felt exhilarated. She'd never before experienced the trappings of wealth, eating for pleasure rather than hunger, spending time idly rather than labouring over some task or simply laughing spontaneously. Her religious upbringing had taught her to despise wealth unless it was directed towards the church. Pleasure was sinful. The sole purpose of life was to serve the Lord and suffer. But today she had experienced joy and generosity. She studied Jack, taking in his easy manner and dishevelled good looks. She felt comfortable with him and felt no need to fear her naivety as she did with most other people. He didn't mock her or despise her. Instead, he took time to explain and in turn he listened with interest to what she had to say. She felt inwardly content as the big sedan made its way through the country lanes of rural Norfolk.

Alice felt strangely detached as she sat engulfed by the large leather seat, listening to the low chortle of the car's engine. She tried to observe Jack without looking at him directly. He wore a more intense look on his face now than she had seen previously. How little she knew about him. But in just a short while he had introduced her to experiences and ideas that she'd not contemplated before. His wealth didn't offend her. He was, after all, a self made man. He had built his business by hard graft and was now, quite reasonably, enjoying the rewards of that endeavour. Not only that but he was generous, sharing his good fortune with Flora and herself.

She thought that on occasions he had been flirting with her and worried that she hadn't known how to respond; a shared laugh, a casual touch of her arm or a whisper that she felt was intended for her ears only. It was like playing a game without knowing the rules. She was exhilarated by his zest for life and his spontaneity. They had eaten candy floss, rowed a boat out to sea and drank champagne, all in one afternoon. She tried to put out of her mind what she was thinking – Jed would never do that. He would have been measured and cautious. She allowed herself to look at Jack briefly, before turning away to ponder the image she had fixed in her mind.

Jack felt at ease for the first time in years. He enjoyed the company of women and the day had been a great success. The shadow of the war years hung heavily over him and he realised that for a few brief hours he'd managed not to think of the past. It was almost as if he was being given a second chance. He had lost Yvette and Simone in terrible circumstances. He couldn't bring them back. Perhaps this was another opportunity but he had such a short time left.

He glanced briefly at Alice. She was staring ahead but he had the impression she had stolen a glance at him too. He felt the same feelings well up inside him that he had once felt for Yvette. But it was so different then. During the war, people took what they wanted without spending time to think. They might be dead the next day.

When he and Yvette had made love, there was no concern for the future, no talk of raising a family or making a life together. They simply took what they needed then without any sense of responsibility for their actions. But now any feelings he had for Alice were out of the question. She was married and committed to another man, a simple man, well meaning but dull. He wondered what they were like in bed. He couldn't imagine Jed being overcome with passion. He tried to imagine how he would be in bed with her.

Flora, on the other hand, was single and attractive, though naive. She reminded him of Simone, obedient and unquestioning. He wondered, though, whether he had misjudged Simone. Was he in danger of misjudging Flora too?

When the car turned into Duck Lane the light was fading fast. As they reached Hope Cottage, Alice expected to see a light in the window indicating that Jed was home. But the house was in darkness. They made their way into the parlour and Alice was just about to turn on the light when she saw a figure slumped over the table.

"Jed, whatever's wrong? Are you alright?"

"It's Dan – he's dead!" sobbed Jed with his head buried in his folded arms. "He's bloody well dead and it's my fault."

The Guest Who Stayed: Chapter 11 – August 1921

Alice rushed to comfort Jed, throwing her arms around him, not believing at first what he had just told her.

"What do you mean he's dead? What's happened Jed? Tell me what's happened to Dan!"

Jed recounted the story in between sobbing and gulping for breath. He explained about their row, how he had accused Dan of not pulling his weight. He admitted to losing his temper and swearing then regretting it terribly when he saw how deeply he had hurt Dan. He told them about the wind that had caught the ladder and blown it away from the platform and how he had stretched out to grab it and how it had brushed past his fingers and fallen to the ground, crushing Dan onto the concrete floor below.

Flora and Alice were crying too as the story unfolded, Alice with her arms wound around Jed and Flora held tight in Jack's arms as he tried to comfort her. Jack suggested that he take Flora home in the car, sensing that Alice and Jed needed time alone.

As the Austin retreated slowly down Duck Lane, Alice and Jed sat in silence, contemplating the enormity of what had happened.

"Jed, my love, terrible as this is, you've got to see it as an opportunity," suggested Alice as her mind began to function again. "With Dan gone, you'll take over the business and be the boss. That's what you wanted, isn't it? It'll be your business now and you can run it as you want."

"How can you be saying that with Dan just dead? We haven't had time to mourn him yet."

"It's a terrible thing, Jed, and I'd never have wished it on poor Dan. But it's happened and it'd be foolish not to see that it gives you an opportunity."

"It ain't that simple," replied Jed, lifting his head from its slumped position on the table. "Without the two of us I doubt I can make the money to pay the rent on Dan's premises. I know that he owed the landlord money and there's people who owed him money who won't pay now he's dead."

"So, we'll move the business back here. We've already discussed it. There's plenty of room outside for a builder's yard and you could make yourself an office. It'd be nice, you working from home, Jed."

"You don't understand, Alice. We may not even have a home. There may not be enough money to pay the loan on this place and then we'd have to sell it. It looks like all our dreams are crumbling, Alice, and there's nothing we can do about it."

They both lay restlessly awake in bed that night with jumbled thoughts preventing the anaesthesia of sleep from numbing their pain.

Jack guided the big Austin through the streets of Frampton with Flora providing peremptory instructions.

"Here, Jack, stop just here, please," she ordered as they came to a small road junction.

"Can't I take you to your home? It'd be no trouble," suggested Jack, softly.

"No, really, it's better here. I'll be alright."

Suddenly Flora was crying again, tears streaming down her cheeks. Jack pulled a crumpled handkerchief from his jacket and wiped the wet trail.

"It was an accident, Flora, no one's fault. Life's like that – just when you think you're up you take a tumble and you're back down again. But you'll get over it, I promise you. I've seen some terrible things in my life and you do manage to carry on living afterwards."

"What sort of things? What terrible things?" enquired Flora, wiping her eyes.

Jack regretted the course that the conversation had inadvertently taken. He didn't like talking about the war years but he had begun to open his heart to Flora and now he had a duty to satisfy her curiosity.

"It was the war. I got captured by the Germans. But so did two young French girls who had hidden us."

"What happened?"

"The Germans found out about us. I think someone may have given us away. Anyway, we were all taken away for interrogation. They treated us very badly. Thought we would all die. On the third day, the Brits organised a raid to get us back. Didn't want us giving away secrets to the Germans. It went badly. Two of my men were killed."

"What happened to the French girls?"

"I think they were both killed too. I know one of them was. I'm not certain about the other. So I carry an awful burden. It was down to me that those people died. I was responsible for recruiting them."

"How about you, Jack – were you injured?"

"The physical scars healed but the mental ones are difficult to deal with; the memories, the regrets, wondering if you could have done it differently."

"Who do you think betrayed you?"

"I'm not sure. I've got my ideas but it's sometimes frightening to confront the truth."

They sat in silence for a few minutes, each gathering comfort from the proximity of the other.

"What brought you here then Jack – why Frampton?"

"Trying to escape. I hated my old life and I wanted something new. I had no idea what that would be. I just set off in the car and fate brought me here."

"Well, I'm glad that fate brought you here, Jack. It's been a wonderful day with a terrible ending. But I'm glad you're here none the less."

Jack gently pulled Flora towards him and she willingly sank into his arms, glad of the reassurance and comfort he was providing. He felt the warmth of her breasts through her thin summer dress and inhaled the sweet odour of her body. Suddenly he was kissing her, her face held in his hands and her lips turned toward his. It was a strong passionate kiss, urgent and demanding.

Flora had not been kissed before and the intensity took her completely by surprise. Her body was wedged into the seat by the car's controls and her head was held in a vice like grip. She succumbed to the kiss and felt the wetness of his lips pressing hard against hers and his tongue exploring her mouth. She expected him to give up at any minute but his position shifted closer to her. Then she felt a new urgency in him as a hand slipped beneath her dress and clutched at her leg. She began to struggle and pull away but his grip tightened. Now he was making noises that frightened her, gasping like an animal as he pulled at her clothes. She wedged her hands against his chest and pushed herself free.

"Jack, Jack, what are you doing? How dare you do that to me! I've got to go," and she leant forward to open the passenger door. Jack seized her arm.

"I'm sorry, Flora, I thought you wouldn't mind. I mean, we've had a great day and I thought you'd be grateful for that."

"Grateful, grateful, is that what you think I should be? And is that how you expect me to pay for my nice day? I'm really disappointed. I thought you were a gentleman and you've spoilt all of that. And Dan being killed today as well. Didn't you think about that?"

"I only thought about you, Flora. I'm sorry but I couldn't help myself. You have that effect on me."

Flora paused for a moment. No one had ever said anything like that to her before. She stared out of the car at the silent streets. This was her drab world of obedience, control, penitence and self deprecation. Now here was a man who had seized hold of her because he desired her, a man who listened to her and spoke to her like an equal.

"Jack," she said in a measured voice, "I am angry because what you did frightened me. It was sudden and you didn't ask. But it's not the kissing I mind. I liked kissing you but it was just the way you went about it. So although I'm cross, I don't want you to think I don't like you because I do. I do like you very much."

There was a silence and he took her hand.

"I'm sorry I frightened you. I'm not very good at this sort of thing. I sometimes seem to lose control. The last thing I want to do is frighten you. Next time I'll be far more gentle – if you'll let there be a next time."

Flora leant forward and kissed him on the lips.

"Of course, there'll be a next time."

With that she got out from the car and walked down the alley that led to her cottage.

Jack sat still in the car looking after her. He'd broken into a sweat. He hadn't meant to lose control and it bothered him. It had happened before. He started to shiver. Old memories surfaced and began to torment his mind. The interrogation room – thick with the stench of fear and the smell of drink and cigarette smoke. In front of him, bound to a table, Yvette, her clothes ripped from her body, shouting, screaming as they abused her. Revulsion gripped him. But had he been excited by what he'd seen? Is that what made him lose control as he'd just done with Flora? The idea haunted him. He opened the car door and retched violently onto the road.

Alice heard the Austin return, its headlights casting ghostly shadows across the room as it pulled up outside the house. She heard the engine being switched off and the sounds of Jack letting himself into the house and coming upstairs. She heard his bedroom door close and the muffled sounds of a coughing fit.

"Are you still awake, Jed?" she whispered, turning her body towards him.

"Yes."

"I suppose we'd better tell him to go tomorrow – Jack, I mean. He won't want to stay around here with all this going on. I mean, there'll be people to see, the funeral to organise, Dan's place to sort out."

"Of course, he'll have to go," muttered Jed, with his face buried deep in a pillow. "We'll tell him first thing."

Alice and Jed were up by six thirty the next morning, having hardly slept. They were both eating frugally in the parlour when Jack appeared.

"Look, I know how terrible this must be for you both," Jack began, "and, of course, I must get out of your way. But if there's anything I can do to help, you must let me know."

Jed scowled at the wooden table leaving Alice to respond.

"That's very kind of you, Jack, but it's just lots of organising we've got to do. Jed's got to get the train to North Walsham to make a statement. 'Cos he's the only witness there's got to be a proper sworn statement. Then I have to go to the coroner's office in Cromer to register Dan's death and then we've got to start sorting out the funeral."

Tears welled in Alice's eyes as the list of tasks began to grow.

"Well, let me help," volunteered Jack. "I could take Jed into North Walsham this morning and then come back and take you into Cromer this afternoon. Then I can take you both to see the vicar after that. Would that be a help?"

"Well, I don't know," replied Alice, with unusual reticence. "What do you say, Jed? It's very kind of you, Jack, but it ain't really your concern."

"It could solve some problems," replied Jed, with unexpected enthusiasm. "Them trains only run once an hour and I'd be lucky to get to North Walsham and back by late afternoon. If Jack runs me in I could be back by lunchtime and start sorting some of Dan's things."

"Well, that's settled then," said Jack. "Jed, I'm ready to go when you are."

Jed looked uncomfortable in the front seat of the Austin. He sat with his back held straight, his hands clutching nervously at the leather padded bench seat.

"Nice machines these Austins, treated myself to one when I sold the business," said Jack, trying to help Jed feel at ease. "What do you think'll happen to your business, Jed, now that Dan's gone?"

"Go bust I expect. Needed two of us to make a go of it."

"But it should be a good business. It's the only one of its kind in Frampton and you've got a captive market."

"Business is runnin' out of money. Dan was a great bloke but he weren't no good with money. If I had time it'd be different but I'm runnin' out of time."

There was a break in the conversation as Jack turned off the main road and took the turn to North Walsham.

"I might be able to help, you know."

"How do you mean?" replied Jed, turning to look at Jack properly for the first time.

"I could invest in your business. I've got the money and I think that you've got the potential. Seems daft to me that you and Alice stand to lose both the business and your house when you haven't even had a chance to get going."

"We don't need charity," rounded Jed indignantly.

"It's not charity, it's an investment. I put a sum of money into your business and you pay me back with profit in the future. It's up to you to run the business and make a go of it. You make the decisions but I'll be there to give you support."

"You serious about this?" asked Jed, his voice softening.

"Never been more serious. You talk it over with Alice."

After Jack had dropped Jed off at the police station in North Walsham, he motored back to Frampton to pick up Alice. When he arrived, she was ready to leave, dressed soberly in a dark blue calf length dress and black jacket. She said very little as he helped her into the car and they began the journey to Cromer.

Once on the main road, Jack was able to relax and cast occasional glances at Alice. She looked composed and in control.

"How are you feeling, Alice? Are you alright?"

There was a pause and Alice remained looking straight ahead.

"Jed says we may lose the business and the house. And you know the terrible truth. That's why I married him. I saw a way out. Not many men of his age run a business and have their own home. I thought that people like me don't get anywhere by waiting to fall in love. We have to seize our opportunities. That's why I talked him into marrying me."

"I don't think you should feel bad about that," replied Jack. "When you're at the bottom of the heap, you don't have choices so you have to seize chances. I know, I've been there. And besides, Jed needs you too. He's a nice man but he's not a strong man. You are strong, Alice, and he needs you to push him."

"But without a business or a home, there's no point."

Jack swung the car off the road onto a grass verge and hauled on the hand brake.

"I didn't want to say this, Alice, because it's really up to Jed to discuss it with you, but when I was driving to North Walsham this morning with Jed, I offered to invest in the business – not charity, a proper investment with proper returns when the business makes a profit. From what I hear, Jed's a good worker and with you behind him I reckon it'll be a sound investment."

"You mean you want to lend us money?"

"It's how a lot of businesses get started – with a backer to get them off the ground. It'll be up to you and Jed to run things day to day. I'll be there to offer advice. Remember, I've learnt a lot about business the hard way. Oh, and you'll have to get used to the fact that you'll be seeing a bit more of me."

Alice studied him, her eyes moist with emotion.

"Jack, you're a good man but we hardly know you. How can we accept such generosity?"

"Alice, I hardly know anybody else in the world. I've got no roots. I know it's a ridiculously short time but you, Jed and Flora feel like friends and it seems like we've been through a lot together in the last forty eight hours. It would make me very happy if you would accept my offer."

Alice leant forward and kissed him on the side of the mouth, lingering just long enough for Jack to feel a surge of excitement.

Jed left the police station in North Walsham just after midday. It had been a bruising encounter with a young police officer who suggested that Jed had failed to take safety seriously and was, therefore, partly to blame for Dan's death. Ultimately though, there was no proof other than Jed's word and he had been allowed to leave after making a sworn statement. Now, he was making his way back to the train station to return to Frampton.

The train swayed hypnotically as it snorted its way through the fields and pastures of rural Norfolk. For the first time in forty eight hours, Jed was able to relax and think. He dwelt on the conversation that he and Jack had in the car that morning. If Jack was indeed serious about his offer of investing in the business, it might not mean the end of all he had worked for. With time and money, Jed felt sure he could turn the business around. He hadn't liked Jack when he had first met him but perhaps he had been too hasty. Maybe he would be their salvation.

Jack waited for Alice in a small tea shop in Cromer whilst she registered Dan's death. Gone was the bright sunshine of the previous day to be replaced by a mantle of grey sea mist which seemed to seep under the door of the sleepy café and wrap itself around the slow moving waitresses who brought pots of weak tea and plates of sugared biscuits.

Jack bit pensively on a broken biscuit and considered the events of the past twenty four hours. Inextricably, he had been drawn deep into the lives of these people. He had found pleasure in the company of the women and was aware that he was playing with the emotions of both.

Flora caused him more concern. She was inviting and attractive in an uncomplicated way but she was vulnerable and liable to be hurt. Alice was different. She was manipulative and ambitious. He understood these qualities and found them exciting. Jed was no match for her and he sensed Alice knew this.

His offer of an investment in Jed's company was partly to provide support and help him get started but, if he was honest, it also bought him a share of their lives. It opened a door which gave him access to Alice and that was an exciting prospect. He needed roots. He wanted to belong somewhere, however briefly, before he died. Why not here in Frampton?

When they returned to Hope Cottage, Jed was still out. Alice assumed he had gone straight to Dan's premises to start the process of clearing and selecting the tools he wanted to keep. She and Jack had not spoken much on the way back and Jack had gone upstairs to his room to begin packing. Alice sat in the parlour, listening to the sounds of Jack moving about on the boards above. She felt alone and she missed his company. Moving across to the stove, she poured freshly made tea into a mug and added a spoonful of sugar. Then with a shake of her hair, she made her way into the hall and up the stairs. She paused and then knocked softly on Jack's door.

"Is that you, Alice?" The door opened revealing Jack, his tie removed and his collarless shirt unbuttoned to his waist.

"I was making tea. I thought you might like a cup."

"That's very kind."

He opened the door and guided her into the room. His clothes and possessions were spread over the bed as he packed in preparation for leaving the next day.

"I'm sorry you're leaving," said Alice, placing the mug of tea on the dresser. "You've only been here a short time but such a lot seems to have happened."

"But I'll be back, Alice. There'll be lots of work to do to get the business running properly. I'll need to look after my investment."

Alice stepped forward and took his hands.

"You didn't have to do this, you know. I just want you to know how grateful I am."

He gazed at her momentarily and then his face was buried in hers, kissing aggressively at her lips and sliding his mouth across her cheeks and neck.

He waited for her to pull away but it didn't happen. She was tugging at his unbuttoned shirt and when he released her from his arms the shirt fell to the floor. Momentarily, they caught each other's eyes and read the same message. Roughly, he tugged her shirt from her body, exposing a flimsy camisole beneath. Pulling the straps from her shoulder, the camisole fell to her waist exposing her breasts. Jack drew her forward and kissed her with a furious passion, forcing her to arch backwards as the pressure of his kisses knocked her off balance. As she collapsed into his arms, he gathered her onto the bed amidst his socks and underwear still waiting to be packed. He stripped off his own shorts. Seizing her once more, he covered her body with kisses.

Alice felt a passion rise within her that she'd not felt before. Her body ached and she heard herself gasping loudly. All thoughts other than the moment vanished from her mind. As Jack's big frame bore down on her, she felt a delicious sense of fulfilment. When he entered her, her body arched in ecstasy and they held onto each other in a frenzy of sensuous pleasure.

Afterwards, they lay in each other's arms, their legs tightly entwined.

"You can't leave, not now," whispered Alice.

"I have to go, there are things I've got to see to. But I'll be back. Jed'll need support with the business so I'll be back to help him. It's OK, Alice. We're going to be OK."

Jed returned later that evening to find a full three course meal awaiting him and a flagon of his favourite ale. As they ate, he told Alice about Jack's offer to finance the business. She expressed cautious surprise and asked Jed what he thought of the offer.

"Well, I don't mind saying I didn't like the fellow at first. I thought he was stuck up and taking too much interest in you and Flora. But now I've had a chance to talk to him proper like, I've changed my mind. I think he's alright. And the point is, my love, it allows us to stay here in our house and rescue the business. What was it old Dan used to say about following your dream or following your star? Well, this fella's our star and we'd better follow 'im."

Jack returned just after eight o'clock, having eaten at the Fox and Hounds. It was an opportunity to discuss some details of the investment before he returned to London the next day.

"I reckon," said Jack as he warmed to a topic he was familiar with, "there are two aspects to this. One, you've got to keep your costs as low as possible and two, you've got to be efficient so you can maximise your income."

"So what does that mean in plain language?" asked Jed.

"Well, costs – I think that having your yard here at home is going to be a big benefit. You get rid of the rent on Dan's place immediately and start afresh with your own office and new equipment."

"New equipment? Where's all that coming from then?"

"I'm just coming to that. You can't grow if you're still trundling that hand cart of yours around the town. It takes you nearly half a day to get anywhere. You need a truck – your own truck with your name on to advertise your business as you go about the town."

"A truck, new tools – are you crazy? Who's going to pay for all that?"

"I am – your financial backer. What's the point in me investing in a company if it's going to fail? I want to invest in success and to be successful you've got to have the right tools."

"Blimey!" retorted Jed as he expelled air through his pursed lip. "This is all too much for me. What do you think, Alice?"

"I think it's very, very exciting, my love, and it gives you a chance to be a big success. But, Jack, we'll need cash to keep the business going and to pay ourselves a wage. What are we going to do about that?"

"You're quite right. I propose to invest an initial sum of five thousand pounds for six months. After that we review progress and I'll invest more if need be."

Jed expelled another blast of air through his lips producing a high pitched whistle.

"You're a good man, Jack. I don't really know how to thank you."

The Guest Who Stayed: Chapter 12 – August 1921

Jack left the following morning to return to London. Alice felt an emptiness invade the house. It seemed that within the last couple of days her life had been turned upside down. All the certainties that gave boundaries to her life had been dismantled and she felt exhausted but also strangely exhilarated. With Jack's investment there was a real chance that the business could prosper. Jed had lost a good friend with Dan's death but he'd gained a business mentor – surely a better prospect given their present circumstances.

And then she had acquired a lover. She had expected to feel guilt but she didn't. She always knew deep inside herself that Jed was a means to an end. She didn't intend this to be hurtful. She loved Jed in a caring, cherishing sort of way and she wanted to help him to prosper. But now that she had experienced the passion of illicit love, she knew that she could never return to Jed's sterile love making in the bedroom.

Dan's Funeral took place on the 15th August, 1921. St. Martin's Church was full and many people were forced to wait outside in the summer sunshine. Alice and Jed chatted to those in the congregation who had memories of Dan's kindness when it was needed most. Jed realised that Dan had been respected and trusted. Maybe he hadn't understood this properly. In his obsession with building the business and taking control, he'd begun to patronise Dan and treat him disrespectfully, forgetting that it was Dan that people came to when they needed help, not him.

During the service, Jed read falteringly from Ecclesiastes, chapter three, which seemed to sum up the contrasts of Dan's life from impoverished child to warrior, to craftsman and sage.

"A time to be born and a time to die,

A time to plant and a time to uproot,

A time to kill and a time to heal,

A time to tear down and a time to build."

The words pricked at Alice's conscience as she sat in the front row with Flora. 'A time to tear down and a time to build'. Was she tearing down something she'd only just started to build with Jed – something that could lead to her ambitions being fulfilled? Was her relationship with Jack putting that future at risk? She felt a shiver run down her spine.

"A time to be silent and a time to speak,

A time to love and a time to hate,

A time for war and a time for peace."

Jed struggled to the end of the reading and rejoined Flora and Alice. Dan's coffin was borne from the church by pall bearers, drawn from amongst his drinking friends. He was laid to rest in the churchyard by the wall facing the pub.

Friends and acquaintances gathered in the Fox and Hounds afterwards. Jed was pleased to discover that many people there had assumed that he would be taking over Dan's business and there was plenty of talk of work that needed doing. Two local farmers approached Jed about repairs to barns and the clerk to the town council enquired whether Jed would be available for general maintenance work.

That night in bed, Alice and Jed lay talking about the day's events.

"You know, Alice, I'm feeling optimistic about this whole business idea. People at Dan's funeral seem to have accepted that I'm the boss now and were treating me right, you know, like I was somebody."

"You are somebody, my love, and you've worked hard for it. You deserve their respect."

There was a pause before Jed spoke again.

"I've been thinking, my love, when we've got that truck, the one that Jack's getting for us, well, I've been thinking about what words it'll have painted on the side."

"It'll have our name, Carter," replied Alice, looking slightly puzzled, "and something like 'builders merchants' – is that what you mean?"

"I was just thinking, sometime in the future I could imagine it saying 'Carter and Sons', you know, like a real family business."

Alice felt herself stiffen. Jed had begun to mention children a few times recently and it rang alarm bells. Their sex life was still virtually non–existent and this sounded like Jed attempting to inject some fresh impetus into it. And besides, with Jack coming into her life she didn't think she would cope with dividing her loyalties in bed.

"I'm not sure now's the right time to be thinking about children. We're both going to be so busy building the business over the next few years. Wouldn't it be better to wait for a while until we're a bit more secure?"

Jed knew that what Alice said was right. Having children now would be a burden but he hoped it would encourage Alice to be more accommodating in bed. Perhaps if there was a good reason to make love she would be less inclined to dismiss his advances towards her.

"I just thought, Alice, that you might want children and maybe we should be doing a bit of practicing."

"There'll be plenty of time for that, my love, in the years ahead. Now, let's go to sleep, we've both got a busy day tomorrow."

Two days later the postman delivered a letter to Hope Cottage after Jed had left in the morning to start a new job. Alice knew immediately from the postmark that it was from London and must be from Jack. She nervously opened the envelope and unfolded the hand written letter.

Dear Jed and Alice,

I hope things are going well for you. I thought about you both on the day of Dan's funeral and, of course, I thought about poor Dan too.

But now for the good news. I have the £5,000 ready to transfer into your business account. But then it occurred to me that you may not have a business account. So, Jed, you need to put on your best suit and get down to see that bank manager and open an account.

"Best suit," thought Alice, "he doesn't even have one suit. We'll have to buy a second hand one."

And now for the really exciting news. I've found a truck. It's an Austin truck built in 1917 for the army but sold at the end of the war to a coal merchant in Dulwich. A friend of mine heard it was for sale so I went to see it. It was pretty dirty but I think it'll clean up OK. I'm hoping to drive it up to Frampton next Thursday and then stay a few days to help Jed sort out a proper business plan.

Alice's heart skipped a beat when she read this. In her mind she hadn't planned for Jack coming back so quickly. She wasn't sure that she was mentally prepared.

I'll finish now but just to say thank you for allowing me to stay with you over the bank holiday and a special thank you to Alice for looking after me so well.

She blushed.

I look forward to seeing you next Thursday.
Yours truly,
Jack P. Malikov

Alice held the letter tight in her hands. Events were moving so quickly that they were taking her breath away. Since Jack P. Malikov walked into her life, nothing was the same.

The next two days were hectic. Alice bought a reasonable suit for Jed in the second hand shop and, with a little strategic trimming and sewing, it looked good enough. On the Wednesday before Jack was due to arrive, they went together for a meeting with the manager of the local bank. It stood in single story premises on the main square. Inside, it was dark and austere. Clerks sat writing at wooden benches and cashiers were incarcerated like criminals behind iron grills.

Alice and Jed were made to wait for twenty minutes before being shown into the bank manager's office. Ignoring Alice, the bank manager, who was corpulent and balding, addressed himself to Jed.

"Now then, young man," he began, in what Alice considered was a most patronising tone, "I don't understand why you want to open a bank account. Having a bank account is a great responsibility and I understand that you building types deal mostly in cash. So are you sure you need a bank account?"

Jed seemed perplexed and lost for words so Alice leapt to his support.

"We have an investor, someone who's going to put money into the business and we need an account for that."

"I was addressing the question to your husband, Mrs. Carter," replied the bank manager. "I assume it is his business?"

"It belongs to both of us," responded Jed, suddenly finding his voice. "We're partners, Alice and me, and we're doing this together."

Alice had never actually discussed with Jed whether she had any formal position in the business but Jed's description of her as a 'partner' pleased her and she realised again how much he needed and depended upon her.

"Our business partner's going to invest £5,000 in the business and that's just to start with," she heard Jed telling the bank manager.

The bank manager looked up causing a bead of sweat to trickle from his balding crown and run down his sagging cheek. Now he was interested. His pen was poised above a sheet of clean paper and Alice could see him write down the figure in bold numerals – £5,000.

When the documents were signed and the account was set up, Alice and Jed walked back through Frampton. Alice looked again at Jed in his freshly pressed suit, carrying a black valise with the bank documents inside. He was no longer the uncoordinated boy she had married. He carried himself with an air of confidence now and she noticed a couple of passers–by look briefly in his direction. Perhaps there really was a chance that he would do well. But then it appeared that Jack was key to that success and, worryingly, she seemed to have a stake in both camps now.

On Thursday afternoon, Jed returned to Hope Cottage with the first batch of tools piled onto his hand cart. These were the tools he would need to build his new office and work shop. Alice was inside the house sewing curtains for the sitting room.

The discordant noise of a horn brought them both running into the front garden. Making its way slowly down Duck Lane was a large motor truck. Its square cabin sat solidly behind a black engine compartment and to the rear was an open wood–panelled goods box painted in bright red. As the truck drew nearer, the gold lettering on the side became visible – *'CARTERS – High Quality Builders and General Repairs'.*

The horn sounded again as the lorry ground to a halt outside Hope Cottage. Jack leapt from the driver's seat, grinning broadly.

"What do you think then? Do you like her? She's an Austin three ton lorry. Ideal for the building trade."

Jed's mouth hung open, a look of stupefaction painted across his face. Alice broke the silence by squealing with delight.

"It's beautiful, Jack, and the name on the side, it suddenly all seems so real." She leant forward and kissed Jack on the cheek, avoiding his eyes as she turned quickly away. Jed by now was running his fingers over the wooden panels, exploring the tail gate and making his way round to the driver's cab.

"How about a run out in her then? What do you say, Jed?" asked Jack with boyish delight.

They all jumped up into the cab with Jack at the wheel and Alice sitting between them. The lorry lurched up Duck Lane with Jack struggling to engage the gears. As they approached the centre of town, Jack hooted enthusiastically at passers–by. People in turn waved back, recognising the occupants of the lorry from the name garishly displayed on the side.

In the town square they drove round three times, drawing a small crowd of admirers. Then on to the Fox and Hounds where a group of afternoon drinkers raised their tankards in salute.

"Let's go out into the country and you can have a go at driving, Jed," suggested Jack as they made their way out of Frampton. "Have you driven one of these before?"

"No."

"It's not difficult, I'll teach you."

Jed's initial attempts were nearly catastrophic with the truck veering towards drainage ditches, only to be rescued by Jack seizing the steering wheel. But slowly Jed got the hang of the steering and the double declutching necessary to change the gears. A broad smile soon replaced the look of studied concern. By the time Jed drove the truck back down Duck Lane in the receding light of the evening, he was in love with the vehicle. Alice had never before seen a look of such joy and fulfilment as he brought the vehicle to a halt outside the house.

That evening the three of them ate together and Jack brought them up to date with plans to transfer the first sum of investment money. Jed was keen to discuss how the business would be run in the future. It was agreed that he would build a workshop and office in the garden at Hope Cottage and move the business home. They also discussed employing additional labour to help with the peaks of demand. Jed suggested that his brother might be able to help out. The farm was doing badly and his father was under threat of eviction.

After the meal they retired to the little used sitting room and drank ale and cider to celebrate their new venture. Alice marvelled at how well they were all getting on and how natural it seemed for the three of them to be together. As a little group they all had something different and unique to offer. If only it could work at this level always. Yet underneath she knew lay the spectre of sex which was so often partnered by jealously and deceit.

The next morning Jed was gone by six thirty to start work on a barn repair close to the centre of Frampton. The Maltings Barn had once been at the hub of a thriving farm but as the town had grown it had become detached from the country it served and had been turned into a municipal store. The town council was debating plans to convert it into a public hall and assembly room and so needed Jed to carry out basic repairs to the structure until the rebuilding was agreed. Jed hoped that his readiness to carry out this work could lead to him being awarded the contract for the full refurbishment.

Alice heard Jack moving around upstairs long after Jed had departed. She busied herself in the parlour, feeling uncomfortable about the prospect of being alone in the house with Jack. She found herself in a strange dilemma. On the one hand, she was still strongly attracted to Jack and wanted nothing more than to be in his physical presence yet, on the other hand, Jed's growing confidence and enthusiasm left her feeling more guilty about the relationship she had begun with Jack. The irony was not lost on her that Jed's improved prospects and sunnier disposition were down entirely to the generosity of Jack. Since he had come into their lives, their fortunes had undergone a complete transformation.

"Am I too late for breakfast?" he said, lingering in the doorway.

"No, of course not," she said, smiling wanly as she indicated a chair at the table.

"Would you like a cooked breakfast?"

"If that's not too much trouble."

"I've got the bacon cooking already."

There was silence, interrupted by the sound of spitting fat.

"I know you think it's peculiar," he said, "but sometimes it's best to let things be. Jed is happy because his business is going to be a success. I'm happy because I'm with you. But what about you, Alice, what are you feeling? What do you want?"

Alice stopped what she was doing and stared out of the window at the garden. The sky was a bright blue interlaced with whispers of white cloud. There was no easy or simple answer to Jack's question. She turned to face him.

"I don't know, Jack, I really don't know. Well, that's not true. I want to be with you. But then I hardly know you so maybe that's illogical. I know I'm scheming and I know I'm hard but I can't bring myself to destroy Jed."

"But you don't love him, not really. You may like him alot and you may be great friends with him but you don't love him."

"He needs me."

"I don't think he does. I think he needs looking after. That's an entirely different thing. I don't think he craves you like I do."

"Don't do this, Jack," she said raising her voice now. "It's not fair. You can't ask me to do this."

"But you're happy for me to finance the business and provide Jed with a new truck. Haven't I at least got a right to discuss this with you?"

"So that's what this is about is it?" she said with her voice rising in anger. "You think you can buy me and Jed, do you? You come knocking at our door one bank holiday, walk into our lives and think you can take us over. Well, sod you, Jack Malikov! You can take your money and your lorry and you can piss off, 'cos no one's buying me."

She threw her apron to the floor and rushed upstairs.

Jack strode purposefully along Duck Lane avoiding the muddy potholes which littered the road. He couldn't decide whether he was hurt, angry or sorry. He was hurt because Alice had suggested he was trying to 'buy' her. Genuinely, he felt that this was a gross misinterpretation of the situation – which led to his next feeling, anger. How could Alice possibly believe that his offer of an investment in the business was anything but honest? He was investing in a good business proposition because he believed that, in time, Jed could become successful. And he was sorry because he had acted stupidly. He had let his guard down and allowed himself to become vulnerable. All his previous experience behind enemy lines during the war and building his business in the East End of London had taught him to present an impregnable front to the outside world.

Alice lay on the bed in the main bedroom, shaking. She hadn't intended the conversation in the parlour to take that turn. She didn't really think that Jack was trying to buy her but she was confused by the conflict of loyalties and by her own realisation that there was a question of morality here that she hadn't previously considered. She knew she didn't love Jed but then she had married him knowing this to be the case and to her knowledge many marriages were based more on pragmatism than love. And without Jack's money and his advice, the business would certainly fail. If this happened, their marriage would surely fail too.

Jed finished securing a new roof beam and lay down his tools. He felt exhausted. The last week had been traumatic and without Dan he was having to cope alone with the workload. He decided that a short break would be in order so he clambered down the ladder to the floor below. The barn was used to store an odd range of municipal requirements from temporary seating to market stalls. But the main incumbent was hay, stored as feed for the many horses which still provided the bulk of transportation within the town. Jed spotted some bales to one side of the barn and settled down behind for a short sleep.

Flora was preparing to leave the dress shop where she worked. She was only required to put in a half day as compensation for having worked on Saturday. It had been a quiet morning with only three customers venturing into the shop. It had given her time to think about Jack. She hadn't seen or heard from him for over a week since he had driven her home after the news of Dan's death. It surprised her. She felt that she had left the door open for Jack to contact her and given what he had said about his feelings for her, she was surprised that she had heard nothing, not even a letter. She took her bag from behind the counter and gathered up two boxes of dress patterns which she had promised to dispose of. Outside, the day was sunny with a slightly chilly breeze blowing in from the coast. She gathered her shawl tightly around her.

Jack turned out of Duck Lane and into the high street. He strode towards Market Square with the idea forming in his mind that he might continue beyond there and find solace in the Fox and Hounds. He knew he would have to return soon and face Alice but a stiff drink first would help to harden his resolve.

In the barn, Jed had fallen into a deep sleep, the stresses of the past days having drained him physically and mentally.

Jack quickened his pace as he entered the square, convinced now that the Fox and Hounds was a good destination. Suddenly, he clashed with a person coming out of a side turning, sending boxes spiralling onto the cobblestones. Apologising profusely, he bent down to pick up the scattered papers and found himself staring into Flora's eyes.

"Flora, it's you. I'm sorry, I didn't mean to crash into you but how lovely to see you again. It's my lucky day."

They were both on their knees on the cobblestones surrounded by papers which were blowing in the breeze.

"I didn't know you were here, Jack. I thought you had gone to back to London."

"I had but only to find Jed a truck and sort out some paperwork. Then I came back yesterday to deliver the truck – and to see you, of course." He was aware that this sounded hollow. Kneeling on the cobblestones seemed an inappropriate place to carry out a conversation and they were beginning to attract attention from passers–by. They quickly gathered up the patterns and Jack helped Flora pack them back into the boxes.

"I was going to contact you again when I got back to Frampton, so no need to do that now. I've thought about you, Flora, I really have."

"I'm sure you've been far too busy to think about me," said Flora, turning her gaze away from him.

"Look, Flora, I was just going to the Fox and Hounds for a spot of lunch. Why not join me?"

Flora had never been in a pub before. It was strictly against the rules of the Brotherhood. But now there was really no reason to stop her accepting Jack's invitation.

"Alright, but not for long mind. I've got to get back to keep a check on my parents."

Alice came down from the bedroom and poured herself a cup of tea. She sat with her mug cupped in her hands, staring out of the parlour window into the unkempt garden beyond. She was starting to think more clearly now. It was critical that Jack's investment remained in place otherwise the business would fail, Jed would have no income and the house would have to go. She would be back to where she was a couple of years ago at the bottom of the pile. It would also be a terrible disservice to Jed if that happened because he was unlikely to find any other employment other than low paid farm work.

The price was deception. She knew that Jack wanted to continue their affair and a big part of her wanted this too. She still tingled at the memory of their love making and knew that marriage to Jed would never provide that degree of fulfilment. Realistically, she believed the affair with Jack would not last. He would return to London and meet someone more eligible. And if the affair didn't last long Jed would never even know. Yet the business and their future would be secure and she would have lingering memories of a passionate affair to sustain her through a lifelong dull marriage. Suddenly, it all seemed clear. It was her duty to protect Jed and their future. If that meant sleeping with Jack it was simply part of the process by which people like her had to fight their way up from the bottom. It was a strange logic but then she had grown up knowing that to succeed there is always a price to pay.

Jack held the door open for Flora and she went nervously into the public house. They were standing in the main bar which contained a handful of men in shabby working clothes drinking from tankards. They looked up as Flora entered and their conversation tailed off.

"Not here, Flora, we'll go into the snug." He took her arm and led her into an adjoining room, closing the door behind them. It was a small room with padded leather chairs arranged around three tables. There were no other customers in the room.

"Look, they don't serve much in the way of food, Flora, but they do quite a good pork sandwich with pickle. Could you manage one? And they do a very good local cider too. I'll order you a glass."

Jack brought the food and drink to the table. The bread was soft and fresh and the cider was still and chilled. Flora suddenly felt very relaxed.

"It's really good to see you again, Flora, I missed you. I'm sorry about my behaviour last time. I hope you won't hold it against me."

Alice's mind began to turn to the practical question of how to tell Jack that she would continue their affair. He was angry at the moment and she didn't want to risk upsetting him further. She decided that a strategy of leaving little clues would be the best course of action. Gathering fresh flowers from the garden, she arranged two large bunches in vases and placed them in his room. She sprinkled rose petals on his pillow and put lavender by the side of the bed. Standing back to observe her handiwork, she felt pleased with her guile.

Flora was happy to be leaving the Fox and Hounds. The second glass of cider had gone to her head and her sight was slightly blurred. Jack had his hand around her waist as they made their way back towards the town square.

"Flora, I'm so happy we've met again. But we can't just leave it like this. Is there somewhere we can go?" asked Jack.

"What do you mean?" asked Flora, struggling to understand.

He whispered into her ear "I'd like to kiss you again properly, not like last time."

"It might have to wait, Jack, people go up on the heath for that sort of thing but it's a bit of a walk from here."

They were passing an old barn on the edge of Market Square. A side door was open and workman's tools and materials were lying outside.

"What's in this place?" asked Jack, pushing at the door.

"It's just an old barn – the Maltings. They store hay in there for the horses."

"Let's go in there quickly. I want to kiss you – now."

"Well, I don't think it's ..."

But he had grabbed her arm and was pulling her in. The inside was cavernous and lit by shafts of light from windows above. Paraphernalia from civic life was stacked around the sides, folding seats, trestle tables, piles of bunting. Against one wall, bales of hay were stacked high.

Jack pulled Flora urgently towards him and began to kiss her. Forewarned this time, she placed her arms between them.

"Slowly, don't be so anxious. Just kiss me nicely like."

From behind the hay bales, Jed was roused from his slumber. He had heard strange noises and momentarily couldn't make out where he was. Quickly his orientation returned and he tried to make sense of the sounds. All he could hear were the occasional muffled cries of a woman urgently saying "No."

Jack was starting to grab at Flora's clothing, pulling at her shirt and trying to untuck it from her waistband.

"No, Jack, you said a kiss, that's all – just a kiss."

Jed wasn't keen to be seen lying behind the hay bales as he had been employed to work, so he decided the best option was to remain hidden and hope that the intruders left. He turned round on to his knees to see if he could get a glimpse of who was making the noise.

Jack pulled Flora sideways onto the scattered hay and pinned her down with his legs. She let out a scream and tried to wrestle him off. He reacted instinctively. He was back in combat. He had to overpower his attacker quickly. Seizing hold of Flora's throat with both his hands, he stifled her cries.

Jed could see now between two hay bales. His heart missed a beat when he recognised the two people. He could just make out Flora underneath Jack, her clothing dishevelled, her legs and thighs exposed. Jack had removed his jacket and was sitting astride Flora, holding her down.

Jed's first reaction was to stand up and shout at Jack to stop. But he held back, unsure of what to do. Then it struck him that if Jack was pursuing Flora, he wouldn't also be pursuing Alice. He had suspected that Jack and Alice were interested in each other but perhaps he had been wrong. Perhaps it was Flora. Perhaps Flora was taking part willingly. He was no expert in these matters. Also, he didn't want to fall out with Jack now that the money had been agreed. He decided to remain out of the way. It would be over soon.

Jack was seized by an urgency he couldn't control. He felt anger gripping his body – anger that he'd suppressed for so long. When he looked down, it wasn't Flora he saw. It was Yvette. He looked for passion in her eyes but all he saw was mockery. He cried out and slapped her face with his hand. But it wasn't Yvette. It was the face at the window – Simone, accusing, knowing, her lips silently rebuking as he bore down on her. He could show no mercy. None had been shown to him. He would be dead soon so nothing mattered. But it wasn't Simone. It was Alice who looked up at him longingly, lovingly, but it was too late now. He had lost her too. He let out a yell and seized hold of Flora.

Jed glanced again from behind the hay bales. Flora had stopped shouting but was whimpering quietly. Jack was on top of her, their bodies nearly naked. Ripped and tangled clothes lay on the straw around them. Jed sunk back behind the hay bales. Perhaps he was wrong. Perhaps he should have intervened. He felt soiled and unworthy. Had he failed Flora when she needed him most?

Jack rolled off Flora and sat beside her. He looked around, half expecting a German guard to lash him with a rifle butt. Then he heard Flora crying quietly by his side. He looked at her – her clothes lying strewn around. Suddenly, he realised where he was and what he had done.

"Flora, I'm so sorry. I got carried away again. You're alright, Flora, I know you are."

Flora turned her back to Jack and the sobbing continued.

"Sorry if I was a bit rough, Flora, but that's how it takes me. I get seized with this fire and I can't stop myself. I'll make it up to you, Flora. I'll buy you something nice."

Jed saw Flora get up and put on her clothes. Jack tried to hold her arm but she brushed him away and rushed from the barn – sobbing and gasping for breath. He saw Jack standing, running his hands through his hair and looking confused. He watched him sit on a hay bale and light a cigarette, drawing on it strongly as he stared into some unseen place.

After five minutes, Jack stubbed out the cigarette on the sole of his shoe and walked morosely from the barn. Jed remained crouched behind the hay bales, a sickening realisation coming over him that he had behaved like a coward.

The Guest Who Stayed: Chapter 13 – August 1921

Alice expected that Jack would return later in the day, once he had taken time to cool off. She had consciously taken a little more care over what she was wearing, having discarded the housecoat that she usually put on for tasks around the home in favour of a loose fitting summer dress with a high hem line. But having changed out of her work clothes, she found it difficult to attend to her usual chores so resorted reluctantly to darning whilst nervously awaiting Jack's return.

Jack headed back to the Fox and Hounds. It was the only place he knew in Frampton other than Hope Cottage. He avoided the snug that he and Flora had occupied earlier and chose instead to sit at the far end of the bar in a dark alcove, clearly indicating to anyone who wanted to engage him in idle talk that he wished to be left alone.

Jack had considered following Flora back home but then he realised that would cause her further distress if there was a confrontation in front of her parents. He downed his ale and tried to focus his thoughts. He knew he had lost control of himself and raped Flora. There was no other word for it. He felt sickened. His hands were shaking as he emptied his glass and signalled to the bar man to bring another. As the drink took effect, images that he had tried to obliterate flooded back into his mind – the lash of a whip biting into his bare skin; the thud of a fist penetrating deep into his stomach; the sound of his own voice emitting a high pitched squeal.

"Wake up, sir, are you alright? Having some sort of turn, are we?" It was the publican who was shaking him by the arm.

Coming out of his trance, Jack tried to regain his composure.

"I'm sorry, George, bad dream that's all. Must be your piss awful ale."

They knew each other well enough.

"Never mind my ale, mate. It's your mind I'm worried about."

Jed packed his tools deeply troubled by what had taken place. Should he tell someone or remain silent? If he confronted Jack or told the police, his whole business venture could collapse. If he told Flora what he had seen it would make him out to be a coward or a voyeur. Then should he confide in Alice? In one respect it would be good to do so because it would show her what a bastard Jack was but, on the other hand, it would make his behaviour seem shameful.

As the truck pulled up outside Hope Cottage, he had resolved to keep quiet. There was little advantage in spreading gossip and plenty to lose. He was sure he hadn't been seen and therefore, as long as he kept quiet, life should go on as before.

When he entered Hope Cottage, he was surprised to see Alice in a summer dress rather than her usual work clothes. He thought how pretty she looked but said instead,

"You got a date then, all dressed up like that?" It wasn't what he had wanted to say but, as usual, it came out wrong.

"Some chance of a date when I'm married to you. More chance of the moon being made of cheese."

Jack weaved his way back from the Fox and Hounds having drunk five pints of ale. He wasn't thinking clearly and was struggling to order his thoughts. If Flora told Alice that he'd forced himself on her then everything would be finished. Perhaps if he told Alice first and tried to explain why it happened, she might listen to him and give him another chance. Whatever happened he wouldn't renege on his promise to fund the business and support Jed. What had passed was his fault and if he had to return to London and support Jed from a distance, then that was a price he would have to pay.

But what if Flora didn't say anything to Alice? Only he and Flora knew what had happened and Flora wouldn't want word to get around. It was more likely that she'd remain quiet. But could he live with that?

Alice and Jed were in the parlour finishing supper when Jack returned. They heard him fumbling with the door key and then letting himself in. Moments later he was standing by the door of the parlour. It was clear from his dishevelled state and his slurred speech that he'd been drinking.

"I think that, I think that I must go back – go back to London tomorrow. Got some things to do, you know. I'll go to the ba– ba– bank first and make sure the money's in. Then I'll write to you, Jed, about the business. Well, better be going to bed now. Goodnight all."

Jed had avoided looking at Jack but he turned now as Jack made to leave the room.

"So you're still going to invest then, Jack. Nothin's changed has it?"

"No, Jed, nothing's changed."

"You need a coffee, Jack, before you go to bed," said Alice, getting up from her seat and moving to the range.

"Just water, if you don't mind. Just a glass of water, please."

Alice poured a large glass of water for Jack and he made his way out of the parlour.

"Jack don't seem right tonight," Alice said to Jed as soon as they were alone. "I wonder if something's happened to him."

"He's alright. Just had a bit too much to drink, that's all. And the investment's alright, you heard him say so. That's the most important thing, the business."

Alice sat by the range thinking after Jed had retired to bed. Was Jack about to walk out of her life? Where would that leave her then? Again, events were moving so fast that she felt out of control. She couldn't let Jack go before she had a chance to challenge him properly.

Jed, as usual, was out early the next morning, keen to make a good impression with the town council as he had been told to expect news about the redevelopment of the Maltings Barn soon. It was gone eight when Jack presented himself for breakfast in the parlour. Alice cooked him a full breakfast and took comfort in the activity which avoided the need for conversation. Then she washed dishes in silence whilst Jack ate his breakfast.

"That was very good," said Jack placing his knife and fork together on a now empty plate.

"So what's this all about?" said Alice, turning finally to face him. "A week ago you were telling me how much I meant to you and if you remember we made love in your bedroom. Had you forgotten?"

"How could I possibly have forgotten, Alice?"

"So when you came back here I thought it was to continue in some way. I know I was angry yesterday but you've got to see it's not easy.

I've got to sort out in my mind how I feel about Jed and where he fits into this. But now you're going again and I don't understand how you feel or what you want. You've bought your way into our lives with this business investment. I'm not complaining about that. It's very generous and it could be the making of Jed. But just tell me, Jack, what's going on between us, surely you owe me that?"

Jack shifted uncomfortably and stared hard at the table before looking up again at Alice.

"Alice, I can't tell you how much you mean to me and how much I want to be with you. But what you said yesterday about 'buying' you made me think. You are married to Jed and I should have thought about that before we made love. I have a problem, Alice, I'm sometimes blinded to reason. I rush into things recklessly. It's since the war. Things happened to me then which I think damaged my mind. Sometimes I hurt people when I don't mean to and I don't want to hurt you and Jed."

Suddenly Alice was crying – tears streaming down her face. Jack got up from the table and held her tightly in his arms.

"I'm just so confused," sobbed Alice. "I know why I married Jed and it was for the wrong reasons. But there was no other way. Then you come along and suddenly I see that there is another way, another way to feel about someone and another way to love someone. Now you're going. Is that it? Do I go back to pretending with Jed for the rest of my life – just living a lie?"

Jack returned to London by train that afternoon. Alice walked with him to the station. They kissed goodbye on the platform and Alice watched the train steam slowly around the bend in the line and out of her life. As she walked back to Hope Cottage she felt heavy with sadness.

In the two weeks that followed, Alice tried to adjust herself to the pretence of married life. Jed required two things from her, food and support. Food was easy. A cooked breakfast, a packed lunch and then a full meat and veg dinner when he came home in the evening. Supporting Jed and listening to his many worries was a more daunting task. What to some people might be an opportunity was to Jed a worry or a problem. Alice would try hard to help him see the positive side of some business or social concern but Jed was not comfortable being happy. He got much more pleasure from seeing himself as a victim.

Even in the bedroom Alice had tried to overcome her inhibitions, hoping that once she restarted sexual relations with Jed, she would find the idea less daunting and slip into an easy routine. On the first occasion, Jed had passed into a deep sleep. On the second occasion, they had both drunk too much cider with their evening meal and agreed to postpone their love making.

Following Jack's departure, he and Jed exchanged a number of letters regarding the business and, as Jed was barely literate, Alice did much of the letter writing and was consequently very involved in the way the business was developing. A cause for great excitement was that Carters had now been formally invited to tender for the refurbishment of the Maltings Barn. Two other companies were also being asked to tender but neither of these were based in Frampton and the town council were keen to have local craftsmen if possible.

However, it had been made clear to Jed that he would have to submit a competitive tender and prove that he was capable of doing the work.

The refurbishment of the Maltings aroused great excitement and controversy in the town. It had been planned before the war to provide a large venue for townsfolk for meetings, concerts and even amateur dramatics. During the war it had been put on hold but was now being rolled out again as the flagship project of the ruling party on the council. Whoever won the contract to refurbish the Maltings would acquire additional prestige and status because it was a cherished municipal project.

Jack sent Jed advice on putting together a tender document and on creating a business plan which the town council had asked to see. Alice spent many hours with Jed in the evenings, laboriously creating the tender document by hand.

In the third week after Jack's departure, Alice first noted some changes to her body. Her breasts seemed a little sore, especially around the nipples and she began feeling slightly sick around lunchtime. Initially, she put this down to an infection brought on by late nights, but as the symptoms persisted and she began to feel some tightness around her stomach, a chilling concern began to grow within her. She knew too well that these were the physical signs of pregnancy yet it was over eight weeks since she had last made love with Jed and even then she wasn't sure they had got it right. The last time she had slept with anyone was with Jack on the day after Dan's death. It was unplanned and spontaneous. She hadn't thought about becoming pregnant because her few love making sessions with Jed had shown no evidence of her conceiving. She had half begun to believe that she might be infertile. The thought now that she might be pregnant from her one afternoon of passion with Jack was too awful to contemplate. Alice could hardly imagine the consequences. It would certainly mean the end of her marriage with Jed and amidst the ensuing recriminations, Jack would probably withdraw his investment and Jed's business would fail. Alternatively, Jack might deny being the father and Alice might end up alone with the baby. Alice had no alternative but to make an appointment to see the doctor.

Dr. Murray ran his hands over her stomach and listened with his stethoscope. His elderly nurse stood guard to one side, making the occasional note when Dr. Murray mumbled incoherently under his breath.

"Well, Mrs. Carter," he said at last. "You and Mr. Carter are to be congratulated. You are expecting a baby and you are about five weeks pregnant. The baby will be due in early May next year."

Alice said nothing. She lay on the couch with her dress pulled up above her exposed stomach. Her mind felt numb.

"You can get up now," she heard him saying. "Nurse, can you help Mrs. Carter get her clothes on, please?"

Alice sat in the parlour of Hope Cottage trying to focus on what she should do but instead her mind kept racing out of control and playing different doomsday scenarios. Supposing both Jed and Jack rejected her? She'd be alone with an unborn baby and have to rely on charity. She'd be carted off to an asylum and probably never see the light of day again. Supposing she tried to get rid of the baby? She'd heard of people doing that but it involved big risks and you needed money. Could she claim the baby was really Jed's? He would know that they hadn't made love for over eight weeks but perhaps she could pretend and then at the end of her term claim that she was overdue. It was a risky strategy. Farming people knew the reproduction process well and Jed might soon smell a rat.

Should she tell Jack? If she did, how would he react? He could deny any knowledge, refuse to accept that they'd made love and leave her a laughing stock. Or maybe this would be the thing that brought them together. In an ideal world she saw herself with Jack, bringing up the baby far from Frampton – a new life.

But could she do that to Jed – take everything from him? He was longing for a baby but she had constantly put him off. Now to tell him that she was going to give birth but that he wasn't the father could destroy him. There was one obvious course of action – she must tell Jack. He was the father and he had a right, in fact, a duty to know. If she wrote to him now she could still catch the afternoon post and the letter would reach him the following day.

My dearest Jack,

I have some alarming news for you. Dr. Murray has told me that I'm expecting a baby and that I'm five weeks pregnant. As I told you confidentially, Jed and I have not made love for over two months so it seems, Jack, that you are the father from that afternoon when we made love. I expect that you will be as surprised as I am.

Trouble is, Jack, I don't know what to do. If I tell Jed he'll be furious and he might even throw me out. He'll also have it in for you and that could wreck the business partnership.

What shall I do, Jack? I need your advice. Please help me.

With much love, Alice

She walked to the post office that afternoon to make sure the letter caught the last post from Frampton. That evening and the following day passed in a daze. Jed asked her on a couple of occasions if she was feeling alright and Alice protested that everything was fine. Jed was so preoccupied with putting together his tender for the Maltings Barn that he let the matter drop without any further probing.

On the third day, the postman called after Jed had left for work. Alice sifted through the half dozen buff envelopes that contained mainly invoices from suppliers until she reached the small brown envelope extravagantly addressed in Jack's handwriting. She ripped open the envelope and unfolded the letter.

My Darling Alice,

I hardly know how to begin. That our one afternoon of passion should lead to a new life seems hardly possible. Have no doubt, my darling, that I will stand by you. There will be many obstacles to overcome but I want to be with you and our baby forever.

We have known each other for only a short while but in that time I have fallen in love with you. You have seen some of my shortcomings and I have no doubt you will see more as you come to know me better. I am no angel but I do love you and will not let you down.

You will receive this letter tomorrow morning, Thursday, and I will be up in the afternoon. Tell Jed that it's to do with the tender, I've some important information to show him. I'll be up about two thirty and we can hopefully have some time alone together to discuss this matter.

With all my love, Jack

Alice clutched the letter to her breast and cried hot tears of relief. At least she wasn't going to be abandoned. Jack would soon be with her and together they would work out something. It was now eleven thirty and she needed to let Jed know that Jack was arriving that afternoon. She had to make it sound convincing.

As Alice entered the Maltings Barn, she was drawn to the site of Jed's work by the sound of heavy hammering. She looked up into the beams that soared high above the ground and saw Jed sitting astride the main centre beam hammering a new section into place.

"Jed, Jed," she called out, "come down a moment, I got some news to tell you."

"Can't come down, Alice, I'd have to work my way along the beam to the ladder at the far end. Can't you just shout the news up to me?"

It didn't seem the sort of news to shout from floor to rafter but Alice was left with little choice.

"It's Jack," she bellowed. "He'll be here this afternoon."

"This afternoon? But he's only just gone."

"I know that, but he needs to see you about the tender. He's got something important to tell you."

"Well, I won't be back till after six, you'll have to entertain him till then."

Alice was taken aback by his choice of words, but assumed they meant nothing.

"Alright, Jed, I expect he'll have things to do. We can talk over supper tonight. Did you hear me, Jed?" But the hammering had already resumed.

As Jack drove the Austin along empty country lanes on his way to Frampton, he churned over in his mind the implications of Alice's news. He realised how stupid he had been to make love to Alice without considering she might get pregnant. But there was no point in dwelling on that now. Although he'd never thought about it, the idea of having a baby had some appeal. He would leave this world having left a new life behind. The child might grow up to be a great success and make up in some way for his own troubled life. But on the down side he had less than three years to live. How could he be a real father to a child knowing that he'd never be there as that child grew up? There was also the question of Jed. Surely a man couldn't be expected to stay with a wife who was bearing another man's child?

Alice heard the sound of Jack's car picking its way through the potholes as she sat nervously waiting. He was early. Alice watched from the front room window as Jack climbed from the car. She was always pleasantly surprised by his appearance. He was broad shouldered and his torso tapered to a trim waist. His body was long in relation to his legs and that gave him a powerful appearance. Although largely dark haired, wisps of grey were beginning to populate his temples, signalling that his youth was now well behind him.

Alice was by the door when he knocked and she opened it immediately. He stepped straight into the hall and clasped her tightly to his body, seeking her lips with his and kissing her hard and long on the mouth.

"Don't worry, Alice, I'm here now. We'll sort it all out."

"I'm so glad you came quickly. You've no idea what this means to me. Let's take your bag upstairs and then we can talk."

She led him up the stairs into his bedroom. The flowers that she had placed in the room as an act of 'guile' were still there though their heads were drooping.

"I'm afraid I haven't had a chance to change the bed since you were last here, you know, what with all that's been happening."

"Never you mind about that, Alice." And with that he dropped his case to the floor and took hold of her again, drawing her body into his."

"You know, there's one advantage of this situation, you can't get pregnant twice."

They made love passionately and without inhibition. He was a skilled lover and Alice allowed him to take her on a sensuous voyage of carnal discovery which left her breathless and weak. This time he was gentle and considerate except when he reached the climax of his love making when again he seemed to be lost briefly in some other place. Afterwards they lay together on the bed naked and breathless. To be naked with Jack seemed natural. Now he ran his hand slowly over her body, kissing her gently and telling her how much he loved her. Lying together, they could look out across the adjacent countryside bathed in the soft light of another summer's day. Alice felt curiously at peace.

"We need to talk, my darling," said Jack softly, breaking an easy silence. "We're made to be together and we're going to have a baby. We could simply go, set up home somewhere else. I've got the money."

"What would happen to Jed if we did that?"

"Well, it's hard but he would have to deal with it. It's happened before to other people."

"I didn't set out to hurt Jed. You do believe me, don't you?"

"What you did was understandable. How did you know that this unpredictable stranger would come knocking on your door one hot bank holiday and fall madly in love with you?"

She pulled him towards her and kissed him hard on the lips then playfully bit at his earlobes. Suddenly she let out a gasp.

"Jack, what's all this on your back?" she asked, leaning around him to get a better look. The last time they had made love in a semi darked room and Alice had failed to see the purple scars and red weals that cut savagely into his skin. "My God! What's happened to you?"

Jack sighed and reluctantly recounted his story. He told her about the spying behind enemy lines, about being discovered by the Germans and about being savagely beaten. He didn't tell her about Yvette and Simone. He had resolved to try to lay this spectre to rest in his mind.

Alice was clutching a fist to her mouth as Jack recounted his story.

"How did you survive, Jack, why didn't they kill you?"

"Oh, they would have done, but word got back to our HQ and they were terrified that we'd give too much away, so they mounted a rescue mission. Twenty specially trained soldiers came in to get the four of us out. In the end, two of my unit were killed in the rescue and five of the lads who'd come to get us out were killed too. But life was cheap, Alice. Thousands dying every day in the trenches, so what were a few more lives?"

Alice turned Jack onto his side and ran her fingers over the scar tissue that covered his back.

"It's why I'm like I am, Alice. I sometimes don't think, I just get driven by the moment. It's why I had to sell the business. As it got bigger, I was making too many wrong decisions, falling out with people and being reckless. I realised I was the wrong person for the job so when the offer came to buy the business I jumped at it."

Alice folded her arms around his muscular torso, pulling him close to her.

"I'm sorry, Jack, I'm so, so sorry. But I had to ask you. You don't have to tell me any more though. It's not your past I'm interested in – it's our future. What about our future, my darling?"

They decided to dress and carry on the conversation downstairs. Alice returned to her own room, her mind still swimming with the heady ecstasy of illicit love making. She selected fresh clothing and lightly powdered her face. She knew that the conversation that she was about to have with Jack would be crucial. One side of her wanted no more than to run off with him and start afresh. Yet alarm bells sounded in her head. Supposing this was just a glorious short interlude which might end as quickly as it had begun. She knew so little about Jack, other than he was unpredictable and had a personality which was scarred by his experiences during the war. If she went off with him she would certainly burn all her bridges. However, if Jack left, she was convinced that Jed would forgive her and she would still have a home.

As they sat at the parlour table later, Alice tried to put an idea to Jack that was slowly taking shape in her mind.

"Leaving Hope Cottage is one option but let's just think about others. What's important for Jed is his home, having two good meals a day and building his business. He needs a wife, not a lover. What if you came to live here, Jack, permanently, as a proper paying guest. We could give Jed the choice. If he wishes, we could leave. But if he wants me to stay, you have to remain too."

"You can't do that to a man, Alice, that's cruel – ask his wife's lover to come and live under the same roof. What'd the locals say? They'd be outraged."

"Round these parts people don't talk about what goes on behind closed doors. It's how you appear on the outside that folks take notice of. So as far as anyone's concerned, Jed is the father and you're the lodger."

"You can't do that, Alice, it's a lie. You can't bring a baby up believing its father is someone else."

"You know, last time you were here, Jack, and all three of us were sitting in the parlour drinking ale and cider and we were discussing the business and how we would make it successful, I thought then what a good team we made – Jed the builder, you the entrepreneur and me the manager. Why can't it be like that? It may be unusual but that doesn't make it wrong."

"Because Jed would never accept it. No man would ever accept that situation, not in his own house."

"Supposing I could persuade him, would you give it a try?"

The Guest Who Stayed: Chapter 14 – August 1921

That night, after Alice and Jed had gone to bed, Jack sat up late reviewing what Alice had said earlier. On one level he was astounded by the audacity of her idea and the deception it involved. Three people pretending to the outside world that they were a harmonious family with a paying guest whilst in reality a pernicious web of deceit was being spun behind their closed doors.

Yet there was a logic to what Alice had proposed, even if she wasn't fully aware of it. Within three years he could be dead and then the child wouldn't have a father. If everyone, including the child, believed that Jed was the father, then the deception could continue after his own death. And at least he would have three years with his son or daughter – some small compensation for dying.

It was agreed that Jack would return to London and allow Alice to speak to Jed on her own. Alice was sure that she could persuade Jed to see the practicality of the proposition if she had time to nurse his inevitable hurt. Before leaving, Jack needed to meet with Jed to discuss the Maltings Barn bid. It was after all the reason for his sudden visit to Hope Cottage. The meeting was convened over breakfast the next morning.

"That town clerk were in again today," garbled Jed as he tried to talk and load his mouth with food at the same time. "He reckons we're in with a good chance. It's what he calls 'a community project' – something that's paid for from local taxes and there's many on the council want to see it go to a local person."

There was a noisy pause as Jed scraped the remaining breakfast from his plate.

"Trouble is, this fellow told me I'm not big enough and I don't have financial security if something goes wrong."

"Well, that's why I'm here to help," replied Jack. "I'm your financial backer and I can provide financial guarantees. I've been working on a draft tender and that's one of the points I'm making. Not only that, but I'm your business advisor. That means you can get on with the building work and I can look after any administration."

"Do you know when they're going to make a decision?"

"Well, bids have got to be in by the end of the month. Then the council engineer has to make a recommendation to the council meeting in November. That's when they'll make their final decision."

"OK then, we've got a couple of weeks to put the finishing touches to the bid. That shouldn't be a problem."

"I gotta say, Jack," said Jed, pushing himself back in his chair, "it's good having you round here. I don't mind tellin' you that when you first came, I wanted to see the back of you quick. But now, with you being a business partner and that, I'm glad to have you around, and I know Alice is too."

Jack hoped that Jed didn't notice the bright red flush that spread across Alice's face as she averted her gaze.

Jack planned to leave after lunch the following day. He and Alice tried to remain at arm's length during the morning to discuss their complex situation rationally but it wasn't long before they were in each other's arms again and making their way urgently up to Jack's room where their clothing was discarded with breathless haste. Their love making was even more intense, as if time in this brief opening chapter of their relationship was running out. Their bodies locked together and their inhibitions were discarded as they hungrily sought satisfaction from each other.

Alice spent the next two days rehearsing her conversation with Jed. He would be devastated when he learnt that she was having Jack's baby and his first reaction would be self pity. Alice would have no alternative but to offer to leave but she felt sure Jed would resist this. When he did, she had to be ready with her counter offer. She would stay if Jack could come to live with them and play a part in bringing up the baby. All four of them would be a family. To the outside world, she and Jed would be mother and father and Jack would be a kind of benevolent uncle who resided as a permanent paying guest. That way she got to stay with Jack and she now realised that there was no compromise available on that issue. But Jed got a lot from the proposal too. She would care for him and cook for him as she had done already. There would be a baby to bring up too and as far as anyone else knew Jed was the proud father. And the business would survive and maybe prosper. Jack's investment would remain and possibly grow. Jed could realise his dream of running a prosperous business.

Weaving his way around slow moving vehicles and horse drawn carts, Jack made his way back to London in the Austin. Events had moved so fast in the past few weeks that he hadn't had time to think rationally. He had never thought of himself as 'father' material and the thought of bringing a baby into the world alarmed him. It wasn't that he disliked children, it was more that he doubted his own ability to act responsibly and consistently. Most of his life he had pleased himself and he found the idea of suddenly becoming responsible for another human being daunting. Also, he knew that his bronchial condition was getting worse. He had uncontrollable coughing spasms and had started to exhale spots of blood. Would he even survive the promised three years?

The more he thought about it, the more Alice's plan for them all to live under the same roof made a crazy sort of sense. But how to deal with Jed. Of course, he was weak and Alice was not in love with him but that didn't make him a bad person. He didn't deserve what was about to happen and, of course, he would hate him and had every reason to do so.

As Jack entered the suburbs of London, he began to look for the first time with disdain at the drab tenements on either side of the road and the piles of rubbish left in the streets. In the distance, the cranes of London docks could be seen above the roof tops, unloading produce and raw materials from distant dominions. Seagulls screamed angrily as they swooped low across the Mile End Road. Suddenly, he longed for the tranquillity of Hope Cottage, the fragrance of the scent from the wild roses in the garden and the warmth of Alice's body next to his.

Jack downed another glass of whisky in his sitting room and stared once again at the row of neat terraced houses opposite. The only card he had to play was to make Jed successful, in the same way that he'd made himself successful. If Jed prospered then he would regain his self respect and Jack would give him back what he was about to take away. And in the long term, he thought Jed would make a better entrepreneur than he would a husband or lover.

Alice's mind poured over the dilemma constantly but, in spite of exploring other possible options, she kept coming back to the same solution. Finally, she resolved to tell Jed the news one evening after supper.

It was a Friday and Jed usually started work a little later on a Saturday. Alice had baked a fish pie and listened as Jed explained the complexities of replacing the rotten roof joists in the barn. He seemed not to be stopping for breath, almost as if he sensed Alice looking for an opportunity to speak.

"Jed, Jed. I'm expecting a baby."

She watched his face freeze and his eyes move slowly to meet hers. Briefly, the beginnings of a smile lit his face but then it was as if a dagger ripped into his heart and pain gripped his body.

"A baby, Alice? But how can ... is it mine?"

"No, Jed, I'm so very sorry but it's not yours."

A look of incomprehension siezed him as he struggled to understand. "It's Jack's baby. Jack is the father, Jed."

Incomprehension turned to dark fury.

"You and Jack, but when? In our bed, was it, when I was out working? How could you? What did I do to you?"

"You did nothing, Jed. It's not your fault. It's just that Jack and I fell in love. A powerful love that neither of us could resist."

"But we were in love. That's why we married – partners, soul mates, best friends."

"We are, Jed, we are partners and best friends and soul mates but we're not lovers – we never have been."

"But you said it would come, Alice. Not to worry because it would come. That's why I didn't want to pester you."

"It wasn't right, Jed. It didn't feel right for either of us. It was more like something we had to do, something mechanical, not full of pleasure and joy."

"Is that what he does then, pleasures you whilst I'm out working? Is that when you done your whoring?"

At this point he broke down, loud anguished sobs seizing his body. Alice rushed to hold him and they both clung together – aching. After a while the sobbing subsided and, as Alice predicted, the self pity set in.

"So what becomes of me then? Are you and Jack going off to set up home somewhere or are you expecting me to leave Hope Cottage?"

"No one's expecting you to leave Hope Cottage. It's your house, Jed. You built it and you'll always live here."

"So are you going? Am I to be left here on my own then?"

"If that's what you want, Jed. Only if that's what you want."

Jed started crying again.

"But I thought you'd always be here for me, Alice. I thought that's what marriage was about. I'm no good by myself, we both know that. It's why I agreed to marry you and why you agreed to marry me – because we make a good partnership. Jed and Alice. Alice and Jed."

"That's exactly it, Jed. We both did it like it was a business contract we were entering into. Look, I admit it. I thought that by marrying you I could escape from all this poverty once and for all. Here was you, a young man with prospects and his own house – unheard of in these parts for the likes of us. And I knew I could offer you something too. You needed caring for. You needed someone to encourage you and help you. You still do, Jed."

"But now you're going. You're going to walk out and leave me."

"Not necessarily."

"What do you mean, 'not necessarily'?"

"Think about it, Jed. We've always been realistic. We've done what's necessary to get on and better ourselves. Maybe this isn't as bad as it seems."

"I can't think of anything worse. A man's business partner pleasures his wife and destroys everything that man holds dear."

"But maybe not everything's destroyed. Look, Jed, we all get on well, you, me and Jack. And soon there'll be a baby too. Just supposing we stayed together as a family, helping each other and being supportive. You want a baby and soon we'll have one. You need Jack to help you with the business. Well, supposing he was here, able to help you every day, making the business a big success?"

"What are you saying? You must be out of your mind. Are you suggesting that bastard actually comes and lives in my house?"

"I know it seems strange, Jed, but take time to think about it. We'd have to say that you were the child's father and it'd take our name – Carter. Jack would be like an uncle."

"What would people say? We'd be laughed out of Frampton."

"No one would know. It'd be our secret. We'd just say that Jack was coming to stay as a permanent paying guest. We'd say his bronchitis had got worse and the doctors had ordered him out of London."

"And you'd get your fancy man into your bed whenever it suited you."

"I'm not going to compromise about Jack. He's the father of my baby and I'm going to live with him. But you have a choice. Either I go or Jack comes here and we live as a family. I'll promise to care for you and Jack will help you make the business into a success. It's your choice, Jed."

They sat up late that night with recriminations and regrets abounding in equal measure. Neither slept, though they shared the same bed and were aware of each sniffle, cough or sigh the other made. In the morning they were drained of conversation and went about their tasks like sleep walkers.

Jed was pleased to leave the house and head off to work. It had become oppressive just being in each other's company and he felt as if his head was about to burst. He went through the motions of working, moving tools around and stacking bricks but all the time his mind pondered the terrible blow that he'd been delivered.

Ideas drifted through his mind. Maybe he should simply expose them – show them up for what they really were – liars and cheats. Tell people about them, have then drummed out of Frampton, jeered at, spat upon, laughed at. But he couldn't do that to Alice. They were still partners, maybe not lovers in the physical sense but he thought of them as one being, two sides of the same coin. And however hard you tried, you couldn't split a coin.

Jack, on the other hand, was a different matter. He'd come into their lives and destroyed everything that Jed had worked for. He was the real enemy, not Alice. He'd probably seduced her, like he had

Flora. Oh God, Flora! With all that happened he'd forgotten about Flora and that bastard Jack raping her. Now, he would tell Alice. That would show her what he was really like. Yes, that was it. He'd go home and tell Alice what he saw – Jack raping Flora.

The car driven by Dr. Murray's dour faced nurse made its way slowly up the long drive. Flora sat alone on the back seat, wrapped in an old army blanket to cover her bulging tummy. Outside, a light drizzle was falling from a grey sky. As the car rounded a bend, Flora saw the asylum for the first time. It was an ugly grey gothic building with tall chimneys reaching up high into the mist. A steep flight of functional steps led up to the main entrance doors. As the car drew to a halt by the steps, Flora felt herself gripped by fear and she began to sob uncontrollably.

Jed sat with his head in his hands on a bag of cement. Maybe Alice's proposal was worth considering. After all, there was no guarantee that this relationship between the two of them would last. It was an infatuation on Alice's part. She was overawed by his ostentatious wealth, the car, meals in Cromer and all of that. But Jack'd soon be bored. Soon he'd be back to London and his fancy women there. Then Jed would be able to take the moral high ground. He'd tell Alice that he'd have her back. He'd even take the baby and rear it as his own. Alice would be so grateful she'd fall back in love with him forever.

It would be nice to have a baby in the house. He'd found himself recently thinking more about it but the more he tried to raise the issue with Alice the more she became silent on the subject. They'd have to keep it secret, mind. If anyone found out the truth, they'd be laughing stocks. And what about telling the child sometime in the future? Well, that was for the future.

More than anything Jed wanted to keep Dan's business going. It was how people knew him now. It was his identity. He knew that people in the town referred to him as 'Jed the Joiner' and it pleased him to be known by his trade. Whatever happened, the business had to survive and if that meant going along with Alice's plan then maybe he could do that in the short term.

But he needed to talk to someone – someone who would listen and hear his pain. His mind wandered immediately to Flora. He had often thought that if Alice hadn't asked him to propose and painted a picture of a rosy life together, he might have asked Flora to marry him. Of course, she lacked the drive and the ambition of Alice, but she was simple and loving in a completely uncomplicated way. He felt a pang of warmth and regret shoot through his body. With the pressure of building the business and the shame that he felt for not having protected Flora, he realised that he'd pushed her to the back of his mind. He wanted to be with her now and the more he thought about it the more obsessed he became with the idea. He would go now and find her. He was sure they needed each other.

It was four o'clock by the time he'd packed up at the Maltings and set off to where Flora lived. The streets were busy with people doing final shopping before the shutters were pulled down for the evening. A surprising number of people greeted him or nodded as he passed by, lifting his spirits slightly as he felt a growing sense of belonging to this small rural community.

He left the centre of Frampton and began retracing his steps along the route he'd taken a year earlier when he had come to rescue Flora from her zealot parents. Turning into the narrow lane that led to the cluster of cottages where the Brotherhood lived, he soon arrived at the small square. Immediately, he noticed that things had changed. Previously, the cottages had been plain but well tended. Now they looked distinctly shabby, with grey curtains hanging drunkenly at broken windows and open doors creaking threateningly in the breeze. Some cottages had clearly been deserted. He turned to face the cottage that he knew to be Flora's home. There was a thin plume of smoke escaping from a broken chimney so Jed assumed someone still lived there.

With some trepidation he approached the peeling front door and banged loudly. There was no sound from inside so he tried again. Still no sound. He backed away from the house, looking for other signs of habitation. Then he heard a bolt being pulled and then another and finally the door opened slowly. Standing there was an old man who Jed just recognised as Flora's father. But he had aged considerably. His white hair now hung in thin strips down his sallow face. His eyes were sunk into their sockets and his mouth was drawn tight across his black stained teeth.

"I know you, don't I? Weren't you here once before?" he enquired gruffly.

"I'm Jed Carter. I'm a friend of Flora. I've come to speak to her."

"I don't know no Flora. There ain't no Flora here."

"Don't be crazy, she's your daughter, Flora Fulton. You must know where she is."

"This humble dwelling ain't no place for sinners. Any sinners have been expelled and sent away. 'Blessed is the man that walketh not in the counsel of the ungodly'," he shouted, his voice rising to a crescendo.

"What have you done with her, where is she?" shouted Jed, rushing towards the old man as he tried to close the door.

"The woman you call Flora was a fornicator, a harlot. She was with child. They've taken her away. You'll not find her." And with that he managed to shut the door and secure it with the bolts.

Jed stood transfixed outside the house, his head spinning. If Flora was expecting a baby, did that mean that Jack was the father? There was no proof but he couldn't imagine Flora sleeping with anyone else. What did this change – anything? Could he use it in some way against Jack? And what of Flora? Where was she? What could he do to help her?

All these thoughts crowded his head and spun round like a nightmare fairground ride as he made his way reluctantly back to Hope Cottage.

The Guest Who Stayed: Chapter 15 – October 1921

It was agreed that Jack would take three weeks to wind up his affairs in London before joining Alice and Jed at Hope Cottage. For Jed, the intervening weeks took on a surprising normality. He and Alice spent many hours talking in the parlour as they had done so often before. By some unspoken consensus, they both avoided talking about the impending change that was about to take place in their lives. Instead, they talked of local people, events that had happened during the day and laughed at simple things. It was almost as if the present was frozen in time.

When Alice started to get early symptoms of morning sickness, it was Jed who was there to fetch her glasses of water. It was Jed who placed a shawl around her shoulders and it was Jed who silently held her. The only reminder of what was about to happen was the almost daily arrival of letters from London. Alice would usually wait until Jed had left for work before reading them and by the time Jed returned in the evening they were nowhere to be seen – except for one day when Alice was feeling particularly sick and had spent most of the time sleeping on the couch in the sitting room. Jed came across one of the opened letters in the parlour. His curiosity got the better of him. He wanted to know how Jack and Alice talked to each other. What was so different to the way he and Alice communicated?

He unfolded the letter and read:

Darling Alice,

I know these times are difficult for you but I will soon be there to hold you in my arms again. I miss you so very much and I long for that wonderful intimacy we shared. How is our baby? Have you felt him wriggling yet? Have you thought of a name for him?

I hope that Jed isn't making you unhappy. He's a good man but not the one for you. I'm not sure how this arrangement is going to work with the three of us sharing the house. It seems to me it may be fraught with problems. But I'm prepared to give it a try for your sake. I think it's very generous of you to maintain your commitment to Jed.

It's less than a week till I join you and I'm counting the hours.

All my love and devotion, Jack

Jed folded the letter and placed it back in the envelope, his hands shaking as he did so. He realised that he had been deluding himself. These past two weeks had lulled him into a false sense of security. In less than a week another man would be living in his house and sleeping with his wife. He felt sickness welling in the pit of his stomach and ran into the garden to retch.

Jed made sure he was out working when Jack arrived five days later and it wasn't till he returned that evening that he knew for certain that Jack had arrived. As the truck drew to a halt outside Hope Cottage, he could see that the yellow Austin was already there. He avoided going in through the front door and made his way instead to the rear of the house and let himself into the parlour. It was empty, though he could hear muted voices coming from upstairs. After a few minutes, footsteps in the hall made it clear that a confrontation was inevitable.

"Jed, we need to talk," said Jack as he led Alice into the room. "Look, old man, I know all this is ghastly for you and I'm really sorry. I know you must hate me. But it's happened and we've got to make the best of it. Alice thinks that we can all live together as one family, you, me, Alice and the baby. Now, I'm not sure it's going to work myself but I'm prepared to give it a try. Are you?"

There was a long pause before Jed replied. When he did, his voice was faltering.

"You came into my life and stole all that was precious to me. You took Alice and you gave her a baby too, something she denied to me. Not only that, you've tied me into a devil's contract. I need your money to make my business work because without my business I'm nothing. So you got me trapped. I can't throw you out and I can't leave. And I can't live without Alice so if that means I've got to live with you too, then I'll have to do it. But don't expect me to like you because I don't and I never will."

For the first time, Jack seemed genuinely shocked. The blood drained from his face leaving a sickly white pallor.

"I understand what you say, Jed, and I respect that. It wasn't meant to happen like this but that's the way it's turned out. I hope in time you'll hate me less and we can be friends. I know that's going to take a while. In the meantime, the best I can do is help you make a success of this business and I hope you'll not let this domestic situation get in the way of us working together."

"Like I said, the business is all I have left so if the price for making that succeed is working with you then that's what I'll have to do. But don't think that makes everything alright. Inside me, it's like my soul's been ripped out. That's what you done to me, Jack. You've taken my soul."

Domestic arrangements were organised so that they each had their own room. Alice remained in the main bedroom and Jed moved into the second guest room. Jed was glad that when he built the house he'd taken a little extra trouble to install sinks in the guest rooms as it would reduce the chance of encountering Jack as they competed for the bathroom.

Eating arrangements were also clearly set out. As Jed was an early starter and often away from the house by seven thirty, Alice would provide a cooked breakfast for him each morning at half past six. In the evenings, there would be a hot meal when he finished work. She and Jack would eat together later.

The new regime began its fragile existence. After breakfast, Jed would leave the house before Jack had risen and spend the day attending to his work. When Jed returned in the evening, Jack would usually be drinking at the Fox and Hounds. This at least enabled Jed to spend some time with Alice on his own. Sometimes little was said but simply being in her presence provided Jed with some degree of comfort.

Around about eight o'clock, Jed would hear the front door opening as Jack returned unsteadily from the pub. Unless there was business to discuss, Jed would take this as his cue to leave and seek refuge in his workshop outside. Jed had constructed the workshop in the garden to replace Dan's premises. It looked like a small stable, with two windows set either side of a double barn door. Inside, the walls were covered with shelves which contained Jed's tools. They were neatly arranged in racks, with the smallest at one end and the largest at the other. Jed had also installed an ancient wood burning stove on which he could heat a mug of tea and close by the stove was a large wooden rocking chair.

Jed took to sitting here in the evening after he'd eaten his meal. From the rocking chair, he could see the back of the house quite clearly, though the interior gloom of the workshop made it difficult for Jed to be seen from the house. He would witness Jack's return home, see Alice kiss him hungrily on the lips and watch the easy way in which Jack touched her. As twilight encroached, the sound of laughter would drift from the house and increase Jed's growing sense of melancholy and isolation. Gradually, the pain of this nightly performance began to grow and obsess Jed. He became sulky with Alice and their earlier conversations at meal times were replaced with grudging and monosyllabic communication.

One night, the pain became so bad as Jed sat in the workshop after his dinner that he reached for a bottle of whisky. Jed was not a drinker, especially spirits, but he found that the fiery liquid helped to relieve the pain and lull him into a restless sleep. He took to drinking regularly from the bottle and when that was empty, replaced it with another. Night after night, the ritual would be repeated as if he was watching a recurrent nightmare and night after night he would fall asleep in his chair, waking when it was dark to stagger into the house and discover oblivion in his own bed.

As late summer turned into autumn and Alice's pregnancy progressed, Jed found his mood beginning to change. Misery and self pity slowly began to turn to jealousy and rage. He began to spend less time thinking how unfortunate he was and found himself instead turning to ideas of revenge. These were ill conceived and impractical notions but they nevertheless marked a critical change in Jed's persona.

One evening, Jed returned from work early. He had been mending a roof locally and had not used the motor truck because parking in the narrow street was difficult. Instead, he used his old hand cart to transport the building materials that he needed. Now, trundling his cart slowly through Frampton, he stopped briefly to acknowledge clients and answer questions about the state of Alice's pregnancy.

When he arrived home he left the cart in the front yard, distracted by the fact that the front door was wide open. He had hoped to spend some time alone with Alice in an attempt to repair the fragile atmosphere but as he made his way down the corridor to the parlour he was dismayed to see that Jack was already there. Jack had his back to him and was facing the work surface. Two legs appeared to be sticking out either side of his thighs. Jed thought it was a trick – some puppet perhaps. Then he noticed that Jack's trousers were unbuttoned, hanging loose around his buttocks. As he saw the rhythmic moving of two bodies locked together, the truth hit him with the full force of a sledge hammer.

He let out a roar like that of a wounded animal and ran from the house to his workshop where he threw himself inside and barricaded the door. Seizing the whisky bottle, he gulped at the contents and immediately vomited.

He sat for hours in a state of semi trance. At some point he had heard Alice's voice outside but he remained silent and the voice went away. Somehow the reality of this situation had evaded him. He had been seduced by clever talk and brainwashing and hadn't comprehended the degrading, gut wrenching truth of having another man having sex with his wife in the house he had built for them both to spend the rest of their lives in.

He sat in the gloom cradling his shot gun in his arms. Normally, the gun was locked in a secure cabinet but now, resting on his lap, it helped to feed the fantasies that were flooding his mind. The shaft felt cool to the touch of his sweating palms. It was dark outside with only the light from a waning moon casting weak shadows across the garden. He lifted the gun and aimed it at Alice's bedroom window. The curtains were open but he could see no movement. His finger gripped the trigger and he slowly pulled it, squinting through the sight at the mid point of the window. The trigger clicked and Jed quietly mimicked a shot, imagining the effect of a loaded gun.

The whisky slid down his throat more easily now, relieving the pressure in his head and filling his mind with a false confidence. A box of cartridges lay open by his side. He lifted one out, slid the cartridge into the gun and clicked the barrel shut. Taking aim at the window again, he slowly squeezed the trigger almost to the point of firing.

He continued to stare down the gun sight at the dimly lit window. He could see movement now, just shadows projected against the drawn curtains. He felt his anger rising and his jealousy taking hold. His head began to throb and he felt warm tears trickle down his cheek. He clutched the gun and kicked away the improvised barricade. Pushing open the door, he was hit by the coolness of the evening air. There was dampness around him and a light mist hovered over the ground.

Jed made his way slowly to the back door. It had been left open as usual for him to go to bed. There was a single light on in the kitchen. He noticed evidence of a meal – pans stacked on the drainer and a candle which had toppled over in its tray.

As he made his way into the hall, he began to experience a sense of nervous excitement. He was locked now into a course of action from which he could see no return. The stairs were in near darkness as he made his way slowly up. He knew every recess and bend. He had built them. He could see light escaping from under Alice's door and thought he heard sounds.

Now he stood outside the door. He felt totally rational. He had to show them that he had control. He couldn't be walked over. He wasn't always going to be the victim.

He kicked at the door and lunged forward. The light momentarily blinded him. He swung the gun to the left where he knew the bed was positioned. There was a scream – a woman's voice. He briefly glimpsed Alice leaping from the bed. She was naked, reaching towards him with her arm outstretched. He was struck momentarily by her beauty.

An arm grasped him round the neck from behind. It was strong and covered in black hair. Jed was spun round roughly. He found himself facing Jack as his body continued to spin towards the floor.

Alice came into sight once more, her hands reaching for the barrel of the gun, her breasts brushing Jed's face as she stretched across him. The force of the gun being wrenched away caused Jed's finger to pull on the trigger. There was a blinding flash and a deafening roar followed by screams. Jed couldn't tell who was screaming – perhaps it was him.

As Jed spun further towards the floor, Jack again came into vision. He was naked too and his face was contorted. His fist was accelerating towards Jed's chin and made splintering contact throwing him headlong onto the wooden floor.

Only half conscious, Jed was aware of being pinned down. Alice was lying on top of him, her sweet scent invading his nightmare, her limbs entangled with his in a way he might only have dreamt of before.

In a distant dream, snow fell from the sky and covered their bodies as they lay together.

A final blow from Jack to the back of Jed's head dispatched him to oblivion. Alice and Jack were both gasping as they extricated themselves from the tangle of limbs and brushed away the white plaster that was still falling from the shot–ridden ceiling.

Jed awoke to a throbbing pain in the back of his head slowly penetrating his consciousness. He kept his eyes tightly shut and tried to order his memories. His mouth felt rancid and stale. A lingering taste of whisky clung to his pallet. Bits of dirt and hair had lodged between his teeth.

Slowly his eyes flickered open. He didn't immediately recognise where he was. It was dark but fingers of light creeping in from beneath a closed door penetrated the blackness. As his eyes began to focus, he saw familiar objects around him. His bike was propped against one wall. Coal was stacked at one end of the room and logs piled against another wall.

He was in the coal house. His hands were bound but his legs were free. He pushed himself up onto his knees but the pain in his head exploded, knocking him back onto the floor.

They must have put him here – dragged him unconscious from the bedroom.

Jed remembered very little about the previous night's events. He recalled being in the workshop cradling his shot gun but after that events were blurred. However, he had an overwhelming foreboding that something was dreadfully wrong.

Strange images of Alice started to appear, naked and bearing down from above. He assumed the blow to his head had caused delirium. But he also recalled the smell of male body odour and the feel of rough skin pressed against his own. He remembered the searing pain as his head splintered against the wooden floor.

Slowly, his recollections began to slot into place – his slow progress up the stairs, his stumbling towards the light that crept from beneath her door. He had felt in control. He hadn't wanted to hurt anybody, just to be heard – not always to be the victim.

Now, as he sat huddled on the floor of the coal house with his head clasped between his hands, he didn't know if he'd killed anyone. What if he'd shot Alice? She'd been lying on top of him and could easily have been wounded by the shot. If she was dead he could not live either. She had wronged him badly but she was the only person he could talk to, the only person who had any sense at all of the world as he saw it. Without her he was nothing.

If he had killed Jack, then perhaps there was justice after all but people would call him a murderer. He would be locked up for a long time, perhaps even hanged. He tried to remember something that he had heard about crimes of passion and mitigating circumstances. Surely these were mitigating circumstances.

Someone was turning the door handle. He knew he was about to be faced with the consequences of his actions. The door opened tentatively to reveal Jack standing there. In the dim light he appeared pale and haggard. Jed slowly turned his head to meet Jack's gaze.

"We have to talk," said Jack in an urgent but hushed tone. "That was a terrible thing you did last night. You could have killed us both. We've got to sort something out. How are you feeling? Is your head alright? I'm sorry I hit you but I had no alternative."

There was a pause whilst Jed cleared his mouth to talk.

"How's Alice? Is she hurt? Did I shoot her?"

"Alice is OK. She's very shocked that's all. Didn't think you were capable of that sort of thing. She's frightened. Doesn't know what's going to happen next. That's why we have to talk, the three of us, to sort something out. Let me look at your head."

Jack made his way over to where Jed was still sitting on the floor. He leant over him to look at the wound on the back of his head. Jed involuntarily pulled away.

"Can you get up?" asked Jack, holding out a hand. "Let me remove that binding. I had to do it, Jed. You were out of control."

Jack removed the cord from around Jed's wrists and helped him to his feet. Jed winced as the pain in his head returned with renewed ferocity.

"I'll ask Alice to bathe that for you," said Jack as he guided Jed out of the coal house and into the damp greyness of the early morning. "We've got things to say to you that you won't like but they've got to be said."

Jed followed Jack timidly as they entered the house and made their way to the parlour. As Jed entered the room he saw that Alice was already there, her head turned deliberately away from him. He felt his stomach clench with anxiety and he felt tears welling in his eyes. He still loved her so much and to be confronting her in this way made no sense to him at all.

Jack indicated a chair to Jed and he obediently sat down. Alice now turned to face him, joining Jack on the other side of the parlour table. Jed studied her face, searching for some sign of sympathy or pity. But her face was full of anger. Her eyes were cold and accusing. He wanted to say something, to justify his actions but the bravado of the previous night had deserted him and the comfort of the whisky bottle was a distant memory.

"You disgust me. You could have killed us both. How stupid you must be to think that a gun would solve anything," she barked in a hoarse voice suggesting lack of sleep.

Jack placed a restraining hand on Alice's shoulder and quickly attempted to change the tone of the attack.

"You see, Jed, what you did last night was wrong. We thought we had an agreement with you. OK, it may be tough but that's what you said you wanted – Alice to stay and the child to be brought up as yours. Christ, man! Don't you think that's difficult for me too, knowing I'm the father and seeing another man getting all the credit?

It's tough for all of us, Jed, but that's the way it is and for you to take a bloody gun and try to blow our brains out is just too stupid for words."

"You keep saying you love me," interrupted Alice as she pushed Jack's hand away from her shoulder, "but what you really mean is you need me, like a child needs its mother. And last night you behaved like a child and you made me hate you."

Alice dissolved into tears and Jack placed an arm round her shoulders.

"You see, Jed, Alice is just too frightened to stay here now, what with the baby due and all that. I mean, you might do it again and next time you might succeed. So I think we've got to go, Jed. We've talked about it and we think that's going to be for the best."

Jed felt himself begin to shake. This was the one outcome he dreaded at all costs. Once Alice went he feared he could never get her back. As long as they still lived together he would be able to exploit any weakness in her relationship with Jack and eventually win her back.

"No, don't do that," he began to argue earnestly. "What I did last night won't happen again."

"But how do we know that?" persisted Jack. "Alice doesn't feel safe with you in the house."

"Then perhaps I can move out of the house, just for the time being, until things are right between us again."

"Where will you live?" asked Alice, knowing how important the house was to Jed.

"I could live in the workshop. It's OK in there. I could fit a bed in and the stove'll keep me warm. Maybe it's for the best."

And so, as the winter approached, Jed took up residence in his workshop in the garden. Alice still cooked him meals but after supper he would make his way back to the workshop and the doors of the house would be locked. Sitting close to his stove and looking out onto the house that he had built, he spent long hours reflecting on the events that had brought him to this wretched state of misery.

It was a Saturday morning in early November. A light frost was coating the ground and Jed was stoking his stove to encourage more heat from its ancient innards. He had no work on today and he worried that his usual supply of odd jobs seemed to have dried up.

Suddenly he heard Alice calling from the house. He opened the barn door to see what she wanted.

"Jed, come here. There's a letter for you. It's come by special courier."

Jed rushed up to the house and took the brown envelope from Alice. He studied the wax seal which secured the flap and recognised it as the seal of Frampton Town Council. With his hand shaking, he broke the seal and pulled out the enclosed document. Jed read the contents out loud as Alice held her breath.

It was addressed to Mr. Jed Carter, Manager, Carters Builders and Contractors, Frampton.

Dear Mr. Carter,

I am instructed by Frampton Town Council to inform you that Carters Builders and Contractors has been selected by the aforesaid Council to undertake the refurbishment of the building known as the

Maltings in accordance with the details set out in the procurement document.

May I offer you my warmest congratulations and suggest that you contact me at your earliest convenience to arrange a meeting.

Yours sincerely,

R. J. Turret (Town Engineer)

Jed whooped with delight. Alice threw her arms around him and kissed him firmly on the cheek.

The Guest Who Stayed: Chapter 16 – Winter 1921 – Autumn 1922

The awarding of the Maltings contract to 'Carters Builders and Contractors' had an immediate effect on all of their lives. The contract was worth fifty thousand pounds, far bigger than anything Jed had tackled before. Almost immediately, he was required to attend meetings with the town planners and quickly learnt that he needed Jack with him to lend an air of confidence and professionalism. Sitting with council officials, Jed felt a sense of resentment that he couldn't negotiate and parry questions in the way that Jack could. Jack was quick and good with numbers. Jed always took his time to think and this was mistakenly construed as being slow witted.

Of particular concern to the planners was Carters' ability to meet the proposed schedule. The town council had already planned a grand opening ceremony in September of the following year.

"Mr. Carter, I have some concerns to raise with you," began the chief engineer at one particularly tetchy meeting. "We were all sorry to learn of the death of your colleague, Daniel, in that terrible accident, but you seem to have made little progress in replacing him. What are you going to do about this and did you take the costs for additional labour into account when you provided us with your quote?"

"Well, I haven't exactly put my mind to that," began Jed, addressing a point on the table in front of him. "I expect we're going to need extra help though there's no one can say that I don't put in the hours myself and when it comes to ..."

At this point Jack hastily interrupted and took control.

"What Mr. Carter is saying is that at this stage of the contract we would be adding unnecessary cost by employing more people. But as soon as construction begins we will, of course, be recruiting. In fact, we have already started conducting preliminary interviews."

Jed's jaw noticeably dropped as he digested this news.

"And if you look at our cost schedules you will see that labour charges progressively rise in months two, three and four as additional labour is employed."

"Thank you, Mr. Malikov, I am reassured," mumbled the chief engineer rather grudgingly.

Although Jed still held a great dislike for Jack for obvious personal reasons, he had to admit to himself that on the business front things seemed to be going well. Jack was a slick business operator but he always allowed Jed to make the decisions when it came to matters of construction. Their enthusiasm for the project even began to spill over into their home life. Following a site visit, both Jack and Jed arrived home at Hope Cottage together and, rather than eat separately, they decided to break the rule and eat together so that they could continue their conversation over a meal.

"Seems to me, Jack, we need to start recruiting now. All that baloney you gave the council about a plan is just rubbish. What plan 'ave you got in mind?"

"We'll make a plan. We'll do it now," replied Jack as he tucked in to a portion of suet pudding.

"You must know people who need work, Jed," added Alice, "good people that we can trust. What about your brother, Tom?"

"Tom's OK but he knows nothing about building. I'll have to train him."

"And what about your father, Alice?" suggested Jack." I know he has a drink problem but maybe this would give him back some self respect."

"My drunken slob of a pa!"

"He's strong as a carthorse, your pa," replied Jed. "May not be such a daft idea as it sounds."

On these occasions, as the banter flowed easily round the table, Alice began to feel that the plan was working far beyond her expectations. The idea that the three of them could live in harmony as a family was clearly preposterous, especially given the circumstances of her seduction by Jack. But against all the odds, here they were, sitting together and making plans like any normal family. Alice supposed it worked because they all needed something and each had something to offer to the other. Jack needed to belong. He needed roots and he needed her. What he had to offer was money. Jed needed that investment to give him the success he craved. But he also needed Alice to care for him and motivate him. What did Jed have to offer? There was the house that had somehow come to symbolise their unique relationship. It was at the centre of their unorthodox life and was the setting in which this drama would unfold. He was also a part of her life that she didn't want to let go of. She couldn't be his lover but she could still be his friend. Then what about her – Alice? What did she need and what did she have to give? All her life she had wanted to climb out of poverty. Jed had been her pathway out of the mire and she owed him so much for that. But she didn't love him and never would.

She loved Jack and she needed the passion and physical reassurance that he gave her in bed. Their love making had to remain covert so that Jed would not be goaded into aggression again. So long as Jed was shielded from the truth, he was able to shut out those things that he found unpalatable. The question now was whether Alice could maintain this delicate balance with both men, especially with the imminent arrival of a baby. She realised that the route ahead was strewn with obstacles but it was the only one open to her now and she would have to venture along its perilous way with her eyes fully open.

Work started on the Maltings in the middle of November. An unusually mild autumn meant that they made good progress. Tom was recruited first and proved he was a quick learner. Freed from the controlling influence of his father, he soon became brighter and more sociable. For the first time in his life, Jed found himself actually liking his brother.

Alice's father joined the business in December. He had initially refused the offer of work, not believing that anyone would want to employ him. But after Jack had spoken to him and persuaded him that the offer was genuine he had accepted with the promise to cut down on his drinking. He took on the role of labourer and uncomplainingly moved bricks and slates around the site to keep Jed and Tom supplied. Occasional lapses led to unscheduled days off but he would soon return and carry on as before.

May 1922

The worst of the winter was over and warm spring sunshine streamed in through the parlour windows. Alice shuffled uneasily round the kitchen preparing Jed's breakfast. Her stomach had ballooned in the past few weeks with the birth of the baby due in less than a month. Jed was silently focused on his plate of food and communicating with Alice only by means of the occasional grunt. Work on the Maltings was now in full swing and Jed spent most of his time preoccupied with keeping the project on schedule. He was now employing five men and a number of sub contractors. All the exterior work was complete and they were working hard on the interior fittings which included tiered seating for two hundred and fifty people.

Jed was roused from his preoccupations by a shout from Alice. She was clutching at her side and looking down anxiously at a pool of water that was growing beneath her. Jed got to his feet, awkwardly offering to help but not knowing how.

"Jed, get Jack. My water's have broke and I need Jack."

Jed felt irritated that it was Jack that Alice wanted at this time of need but the urgency in her voice left no room for doubt. He raced up the stairs calling out Jack's name. Jack emerged from Alice's room pulling on his trousers.

"Jack, Alice says to come quick. Her water's broke."

Jack pushed past Jed, nearly falling down the stairs. He took Alice in his arms and held her tightly. Jed felt confused and looked away.

"I'll take you upstairs, my darling, and lie you down. Then we'll get help. Everything is going to be fine," cooed Jack softly.

He went to lift Alice up into his arms but a coughing spasm suddenly seized him. Jed had noticed recently that the attacks were becoming more frequent.

"Well, come on then, man, help me," demanded Jack.

They took hold of an arm and a leg each, then with difficulty manoeuvred Alice up the stairs and laid her on the bed in her room.

"You need to fetch the midwife quick," gasped Alice.

Both Jack and Jed had been well rehearsed for just such an eventuality. The town midwife was Mrs. Burns, a plump fifty year old widow who had delivered half the population in Frampton.

"I'll go," volunteered Jack.

"No, I need you to be here with me. Besides, it might look odd if you go. It's better if the father goes. Well, you know what I mean. Jed, will you go and fetch Mrs. Burns?"

It took Jed ten minutes to sprint into the centre of town and make contact with Mrs. Burns who lived in a small labourer's cottage just off the market square. Within minutes of Jed's arrival, Mrs. Burns had mounted her bicycle and was making her unsteady way back to Hope Cottage. Jed jogged behind, his heart pounding.

Mrs. Burns took over with well practised military efficiency. Both men were banned from the bedroom and banished to the parlour. If Mrs. Burns wondered about the presence of the lodger in the 'mother–to–be's' bedroom she said nothing. She had been witness to many strange carryings on at birth and had reconciled herself to the idiosyncrasies of family life.

Jed and Jack stood in the parlour drinking strong coffee and saying little. Jack smoked a cigarette and wheezed after each drag.

"I'm feeling nervous," volunteered Jed. "Like I'm the real father."

"You are the real father. Remember that. As far as anyone's concerned, you're the father and I'm the lodger. That's what Alice wants."

"Is that what you want, Jack?" asked Jed.

"If that's what Alice wants then that's what I want."

There was a pause. Upstairs, the strident but indistinct voice of Mrs. Burns could be heard dispensing orders.

"Don't you think it's wrong – both of us loving the same woman?" said Jed after a while.

"I can't say that it's wrong. In some ways it seems perfectly obvious. If a woman attracts one man then she's just as likely to attract another. In some cultures it's the other way round. A man can have more than one wife. So I don't see why a woman can't have more than one husband. It's just convention."

This line of reasoning was rudely interrupted by a piercing shriek followed by a fusillade of commands from Mrs. Burns. Jed and Jack were stunned into silence. There followed another shriek, longer than the first and then sobbing. More commands from Mrs. Burns and then a scream that gave way to the sound of a baby crying. Jed and Jack awkwardly shook each other's hands and then raced up the stairs to Alice's room.

They both burst into the bedroom to be confronted by Mrs. Burns holding a baby wrapped in blankets.

"Only the father, please. Other visitors later," commanded Mrs. Burns.

There was an embarrassed pause as no one knew how to react to the instruction.

"Mr. Malikov is a very close friend," replied Jed quietly. "It'll be alright."

A look of understanding mixed with disapproval spread across Mrs. Burns face.

"It's a girl," she said as she handed the baby to Jed.

Jack pushed past Mrs. Burns and clasped Alice's hands, speaking softly to her out of earshot. Jed cradled the baby in his arms, a broad smile spread across his face. She looked beautiful. She had small, neat features and striking blue eyes. Short wisps of blond hair covered her head with the faintest hint of auburn. For a moment Jed felt ecstatic – holding his daughter and gazing into her eyes.

"Let me see her, Jed. Bring her to me," he heard Alice say.

He carried the baby over to the bed and placed her in Alice's arms. Jack was sitting by her side on the bed. Together they embraced the baby and wrapped their arms around each other.

Jed plunged from ecstasy to despair. A moment ago he was staring into the eyes of his daughter. Within seconds he had handed her over to her real father, yet he would continue to act out the pretence of being her father. What devil's pact had he signed up to?

"I'll be going now," announced Mrs. Burns. "The doctor will be calling by tomorrow morning. Congratulations, Mrs.Carter. And, er, to the father too."

Jed followed her out of the room and tried to sound like a grateful and overjoyed new father. But his voice betrayed him. As she was about to leave by the front door, Mrs. Burns looked Jed squarely in the eyes.

"Do your duty, lad, as best you can and one day it'll come right. Good luck, lad."

The days after the birth were very hectic as the new family took stock. Jed couldn't imagine how a normal family of two parents could possibly cope as it seemed hard enough with three. Although Jed was at work all day, he found himself literally holding the baby as soon as he walked in through the door. In fact, so keen was Alice to involve Jed that she suggested that he give up his residence in the workshop and move back into the house. Jed was reluctant to do this as he'd become fond of his humble shed and valued the peace it provided when he needed it most. However, keen to demonstrate his commitment to the baby, he was left with no choice.

For the first few days after the birth, the new arrival was referred to simply as 'Baby', which seemed to satisfy everyone. However, by the fourth day Jed was beginning to feel that the child deserved a name and so he raised the question with Alice one evening as she was placing 'Baby' into his care.

"Don't you think we should give the little child a name, Alice? I've been thinking about something simple but local like Joan or Ethel or Sarah."

"Those are very old fashioned names, Jed. I don't want my daughter to sound like some milking maid."

"There's nothing wrong with them names. They've been in my family for generations. They're good solid farming names."

"Well, I'll discuss it with Jack. He needs to be in on it too. I'll tell him what you've said."

"But I think we all need to be involved in this, Alice, not just you and Jack."

Later than night when Jack had returned from the pub and slipped into bed beside Alice, she broached he same subject.

"Jed thinks it should be something traditional like Joan or Ethel. But I'm not so sure. I don't want our baby to be chained to the past. I want her to be modern and independent."

"What have you got in mind?"

"I'm not really sure. Something like Julia or Hazel."

Jack didn't reply immediately. An idea had been taking shape in his mind over the past two days which he couldn't share with Alice. For a while he had wanted to create some lasting memorial to Yvette. It troubled him that she had been blown into oblivion by one of his own side's grenades and that for all anyone knew she might never have existed. He felt that she deserved to live on in some way and, as he had been instrumental in her death, he felt obliged to do something. Here was an opportunity for her to live on through his child – a child that might have been her own in different circumstances.

"There is a name I've been thinking of, Alice. I've always liked it."

"What is it, Jack, tell me then?" demanded Alice, turning to face him in bed.

"It's Eve. What do you think?"

"Eve. I would never have thought of that myself. But I like it. It's pretty. Tell me why you chose it?"

He hesitated.

"It's simple yet it means so much. Eve was the first woman – if you like, the mother of us all. She was the essence of humanity. She gave meaning to life."

"Didn't she tempt Adam in the Garden of Eden? Didn't she invent sin?"

"I don't see it that way. For me she was a realist – she wanted knowledge and she wanted progress. She knew they couldn't live forever in the Garden of Eden. She was a modern woman."

"Well, I want our daughter to be a realist. We've just come through one terrible war and there's no knowing what's next. I think Eve is a great name."

'Baby' was eventually christened Eve Sarah Danielle Carter at a simple service in St. Martin's Church. Mother, father and lodger stood together around the font as the Reverend Bowman conducted the short service.

"Parents and godparents, the Church receives this child with joy. Today we are trusting God for her growth in faith."

Alice had insisted that Jack was one of the godparents along with two of her friends from the bakers shop. Jack wasn't sure he was equipped to be entrusted with the moral upbringing of a new baby but there was no backing out now.

"Will you pray for her, draw her by your example into the community of faith and walk with her in the way of Christ?"

"With the help of God we will."

July 1922

The intervening weeks had been relentless and tiring. Alice found being a mother was difficult and had developed what the doctor called 'post natal depression'. She spent much of her time in bed with Jack looking after her. In the first few weeks after the birth, Jed had taken considerable time off work to care for 'Evie' (as she was now called) and had bonded closely with her. But then things started to go wrong at work. Supplies weren't ordered on time and the schedule began to fall behind. The chief engineer paid more regular visits to the site and grumbled increasingly about short comings. Eventually, Jed had to return to full time work and a live in nurse from Norwich was hired to care for Evie. This, of course, meant that Jed had to give up his room again and was relegated back to the workshop.

Miss Cavendish, the nurse, was a substantial lady in her late fifties. She was undoubtedly capable but had about her the aura of a hospital matron. She had a tendency to issue orders and offend. Her wardrobe consisted entirely of brown clothes – brown smock, brown cardigan and brown stockings. Under her regime, life at Hope Cottage took on a distinctly subdued quality.

The arrival of Miss Cavendish meant that Jed was able to focus full time on the Maltings restoration. The inside was now taking visible shape with a concert stage erected at one end of the hall and a foyer under construction facing onto the town square. Annoyingly for Jed, a different type of visitor had now started to turn up. He had just about got used to the gruff interventions of the chief engineer and his team but the new arrivals were here to plan the grand opening ceremony. A date had been fixed for September 23rd and the town's newly formed cultural committee was busy inviting local groups to participate. Jed, therefore, had to deal with a trail of aspiring artists picking their way through the building rubble as he strove to catch up with the agreed schedule. There was the leader of the town's wind band, the head of the WI's regional choir, a newly formed girls dance troupe and someone who claimed he had once performed in front of the cameras in Hollywood.

But in spite of all this activity and the expansion of his business, Jed felt an emptiness in his life. Alice's illness meant that she spent much of her time in bed and there had for long been an unspoken agreement that her bedroom was out of bounds to Jed. Regular hot meals were a thing of the past and Jed had got used to catering for himself now. He missed the opportunity to talk to Alice and was jealous of the time she spent shut away with Jack.

His thoughts turned once more to Flora. He had tried to put her out of his mind following the angry confrontation with her father. There seemed little he could do if she was pregnant. He couldn't prove that Jack was the father and didn't know for certain that he was. He couldn't offer Flora a home and couldn't let her into the terrible secret about the paternity of his own child. But still he felt a horrible sense of guilt, witnessing the rape yet doing nothing about it.

He had found out that pregnant unmarried mothers were often taken to the asylum which lay in the countryside between Norwich and North Walsham. The vast house, known as Manston Hall, had once been the country residence of an aristrocratic family but with their demise in the 1880s it had been taken over as a refuge for the mentally ill and others that society wished to be kept out of sight.

One Friday afternoon he allowed himself to take a half day off work and drive out in the Austin truck to find Manston Hall. It was a fresh late July day with sunny spells giving way to short sharp showers. After turning off the main A149 at Thorpe Market, he found himself driving along narrow leafy lanes that were difficult for the truck to navigate. Its height caused it to frequently dislodge overhanging branches and to leave a trail of broken debris behind. Jed almost missed the sign to the Hall. It was nothing more than a small wooden plaque attached to a stone wall. A covering of moss made it difficult to read.

He swung the truck into the drive, past two ancient brick posts with rusting gates that had long since ceased to close. The drive wound through rough pasture on either side with little evidence of any serious farming. Finally, Manston Hall came into sight, an enormous stone edifice with tall chimneys reaching into the summer sky. Two cars were parked outside the front but otherwise there was no sign of life. Jed felt the presence of the truck there might seem out of place so he parked it to the side of the building.

The entrance was up a sweeping flight of stone steps that had perhaps once been grand. Now, flagstones were loose and missing in places. The balustrades were grimy and cracked.

Jed made his way up the steps and into a large foyer. It was sparsely furnished and offered no signs of welcome. Noises and shouting echoed from distant parts of the building. Jed stood awkwardly, wondering what to do next. Then a nurse appeared, heading with determination for another door. She was dressed in a starched blue uniform with a white apron.

"Excuse me," said Jed, trying to attract her attention.

She didn't respond so he moved rapidly towards her and placed his hand on her arm.

"Get off me at once!" she retorted. "I'll call for help if you touch me again."

"I only wanted to know who I could speak to. There's nobody here to ask."

"We don't allow visitors, not without prior approval. Who are you?"

"My name's Jed, Jed Carter. I've come here to find a friend. Her name's Flora Fulton. Is she here?"

"We're not allowed to give out information, not unless you're family. You're not family are you?"

"I'm her friend. I just want to find her and help her."

"Stay there," retorted the nurse abruptly and then disappeared through a nearby door.

Jed remained in the unwelcoming hall, staring up at what had once been a grand staircase leading to the upper floors of the house. He wondered when the walls had last vibrated to the sound of laughter and merriment – distant echoes in a building that was now cloaked in melancholy.

He waited for what seemed like ages before another door opened and an older uniformed woman appeared. She carried with her the aura of authority.

"What do you want?"

"I've come to enquire after Flora Fulton. She's a friend."

"What makes you think she's here?"

"I think she might have been expecting a baby. She wasn't married. I've been told that girls in that situation are brought here."

"Are you the father?"

"No, no, I'm not."

"Do you know who is?"

"I can't really say. I mean, I don't know."

"Young women who come here when they are pregnant come here because no one else will have them. There's no father to take responsibility and no family to take care of them. No friends to help them. They come here because society wants them out of the way. Forget about your friend. You must pretend she doesn't exist – has never existed."

"How dare you! Flora does exist. She's as real as you and me and I'm going to find her."

But the uniformed woman turned and disappeared back through the door. Jed rushed to prevent her leaving but the door had closed and was locked from the far side. He kicked at the door and shouted, his protestations echoing round the great hall like disembodied voices. Eventually, he left the gloom of the hall and made his way out into the sunshine. He felt angry and guilty – angry at the way he had been treated and guilty because he knew that what she said was true. Flora had been abandoned by her friends, all of them too intent on building their own lives to get involved.

As he rounded the corner of the house and headed towards the truck, a small side door opened revealing a girl, possibly in her early twenties, dressed in white overalls. It wasn't the uniform of a nurse but she may have been a kitchen maid or a servant of some kind. Jed stopped and looked at her. She was standing in the shadow of the doorway with her eyes cast down.

"I knew Flora," said the girl in a weak voice. "She was here. She was very nice."

"How did you know her? Were you her friend? Are you a patient here too?"

"It doesn't matter who I am."

"Then do you know where she is now?" pleaded Jed.

"I only know that she was sent away after she had the baby – a baby girl. That's what they do here – send them into service."

"How was she? Was she well?"

"She was happy to have the baby but I knew she was sad. I think she'd just sort of given in."

"And you don't know where they sent her?"

"No. You won't find her. They give them a new identity. I must go now. I've said too much."

"Wait!"

But she had already slipped back through the door – engulfed by the morbidity of the building.

Saturday, 23rd September

It was a day that Jed would never forget. The whole town had taken on a carnival atmosphere to celebrate the opening of the Maltings. Jack, Alice and Jed were in the town square by two o'clock and had prime positions to watch the carnival procession that would lead the mayor and his entourage to the opening ceremony. Evie was with them too, cooing happily in her perambulator which was a present from Jack to celebrate her birth.

Jed was brimming with pride as people who knew him came to offer their congratulations. From the outside, the Maltings had been transformed from a derelict barn into an impressive public venue, complete with theatre style foyer. To one side was a new tea room which doubled as a bar when productions were being staged.

Alice stood close to Jed, basking in the reflected glory of the occasion. It felt to Jed as if Alice and he belonged together again. What he had achieved in two years would have been unimaginable when they got married. He knew that Alice was proud to be by his side and he felt things were finally beginning to go his way. A shout from Jack drew his attention.

Standing by his side, Alice felt that she shared in Jed's success. She had been the power behind him, urging him to raise his prospects with Dan and to take on the business when he died. She had been responsible for introducing Jack to Jed. Without Jack's investment and business know how, none of this would have happened. Certainly their family arrangement was unusual but, if it worked, who cared? The call from Jack sounded urgent.

"Have you got Evie? I can't see the pram. Is she with you?"

Alice's blood turned cold. She had left Evie with Jack.

The crowd erupted into applause as the brass band approached, followed by the mayor and councillors dressed in their gowns of office.

Jed pushed his way to the back of the crowd. "Evie was with you, Jack. Alice asked you to keep an eye on the pram."

"I did. I just left her for a moment to watch the band. When I turned back she'd gone."

Alice reached them and screamed. Jack caught her as she began to fall. Jed looked up and down the street. Everyone was straining to see the band and procession. The noise of the cheering crowd was deafening. He took a chance and raced towards one end of the square. There were only a few people here, mostly latecomers hurrying towards the parade. There was no sign of Evie. He was seized with panic wondering which way to go. Then he realised he was standing by the entrance to Threshers Cut, the narrow alley that led to the yard where Dan's workshop had been. He prayed his hunch was right and headed off as fast as he could down the alley. He soon found himself in the yard, empty save for a tethered horse and a stray dog. The yard was a dead end, except for a hole in the fence which was used as a short cut to a street of derelict cottages. Jed raced to the hole and stared at the street beyond. At one end, he thought he saw a figure turning a corner into the next road. Gathering his strength, he forced himself to run faster than ever before. At the next turning, he saw the figure clearly now about a hundred yards ahead. He ran forward yelling, trying to attract their attention. The fugitive turned and saw him then started running with the pram. Jed picked up a stone from the gutter. Praying that he could repeat his triumph at the fairground, he hurled the stone. It hit the person squarely between the shoulders and brought them tumbling to the ground. Jed raced up to where they were lying and saw it was a young woman, wrapped in a shawl, almost certainly one of the gypsies camped on the common.

"God damn you, woman! That's my baby."

His attention was suddenly caught by the pram which was gathering speed as it continued to run down the steeply cobbled street. He had no time to stop and raced at breakneck speed to catch the pram. Pain began to seize his chest and his legs felt like pulp. He heard himself shouting as he raced after the pram.

"Evie, Evie, I'm coming! Papa's coming!"

His lungs felt as if they were about to burst. He was at the end of his endurance. With a final sprint he almost caught the pram but his hand just failed to make contact. In desperation, he dived at the pram, jamming his fingers into the wheels. He screamed with pain as the spokes cut into his fingers and bent them against the pram's chassis. The pram ground to a halt and toppled onto its side throwing Evie onto the cobbles. With one hand still caught in the pram's wheel, he managed to pull himself round and grab her. She was yelling but seemed unhurt. Jed buried his face in her warm blanket, inhaling the sweetness of her smell.

"Evie, my baby! Thank God, you're safe! I love you so much."

Then there was the sound of shouting from the top of the street. People were running down the road towards him. Alice arrived first, grabbing Evie from Jed's arms and smothering her in tears. The local policeman was there and Jack arrived minutes later, wheezing heavily and clutching at his chest.

"I'm sorry, so sorry," he kept repeating. Then he put his arms around Alice and Evie and they held each other in that locked embrace for what seemed an eternity to Jed as he looked on, with his hand still mangled in the pram wheels.

Jed went to the gala dinner by himself that night with a heavily bandaged hand. Fortunately, his fingers weren't broken, just severely bruised. He was sad that Alice wasn't there to hear the mayor congratulate Carters on their craftsmanship and professionalism. He wished Alice could have seen the show put on by locals and heard the rafters ringing with applause. He wished she had heard the conversation with the chief engineer who confided that there were other major building projects on the council's agenda which he felt sure would be of interest to Carters. He was bursting with pride. The seemingly impossible had happened. And yet he felt suddenly miserable. He was jealous – jealous of Alice, Jack and Evie back home together. He had believed at times today that Evie was his own child, yet each time this happened he was quickly reminded that it was a lie – a lie on which the success of his business was now built and one that he would have to keep on living perhaps for the rest of his life.

The Guest Who Stayed: Chapter 17 – Christmas 1927

The sitting room looked magical. A tree stood in one corner decorated with real candles. As this was Christmas Eve, Alice had allowed the candles to be lit for the first time. The room was hung with holly and mistletoe. In another corner was a nativity scene which Jed had painstakingly cut out and painted for Evie. Mary sat on a straw bale holding baby Jesus whilst a bearded and two dimensional Joseph looked on, his hands clasped in humility. A donkey and a sheep completed the tableau. Jed hadn't had time to make the shepherds. Outside a fierce wind whipped flurries of snow around Hope Cottage but inside the roaring log fire made the house seem warm and friendly.

Evie had finished her tea and was bouncing around excitedly on Jack's knees. He was pretending to let her fall back but catching her just in time, accompanied by peals of laughter.

"Careful, Evie. Mind you don't bang your head on the floor when you do that," warned Jed from his chair on the opposite side of the room.

"Don't be silly, Daddy. Uncle Jack's strong. He won't let me fall. You're always being silly."

"She's alright, Jed," snapped Alice. "Just let her be."

It was increasingly like this. Evie saw Jack as the kind uncle, fun to be with, seldom cross, always ready with a game. Jed, however, had been designated the role of disciplinarian. Alice was always telling him to "stop Evie doing this," or "warn her about doing that." As a consequence, Evie increasingly argued with Jed, encouraged sometimes by Alice. It hurt Jed. He loved Evie but he wanted to bring her up properly. Already she was showing signs of becoming precocious.

Jack was suddenly convulsed with a coughing fit and Alice pulled Evie from his lap.

"Now, go and see your daddy. Tell him it's time to take you to bed. If you're good he'll read you a story."

"I don't want him to read a story. I want Uncle Jack to read a story. Daddy can't read properly."

Jed felt humiliated. He knew it was true. He had always been a slow reader and he struggled with long words.

"Evie, go upstairs with your daddy or Santa Claus won't come tomorrow morning," warned Alice as she tried to help Jack, who was still choking.

"Come on, Evie, let's go upstairs then," said Jed, getting up from his chair and lifting Evie from the floor.

"No, no. Let me go! Let me go!" shouted Evie, kicking and screaming. It was like this most nights. Jed would try to read her a story but she would refuse to listen, screaming and hitting out at him. Eventually, Jack would go upstairs to see her and Evie would dissolve into fits of giggles before slipping into sleep. It hurt Jed dreadfully that he couldn't bond with Evie in the same way as Jack and matters were made worse by the fact that Alice seemed almost to condone her behaviour towards him.

The next morning Evie was up early, keen to ensure that Santa had left the promised presents under the tree. Alice brought her downstairs and together they admired the pile of gifts wrapped in coloured paper and tied with bows. In spite of Evie's impatience, she was made to wait until after breakfast before beginning to attack the pile. There were numerous small presents and two larger ones which Alice insisted must be left until last. After an assortment of crayons, chocolates, cuddly toys and jigsaws had been unwrapped, Evie could contain herself no longer and selected the bigger of the two boxes to open next. Alice helped her remove the wrapping paper to reveal a beautifully detailed dolls' house – a replica of Hope Cottage. Jed had spent many months building the dolls' house in his workshop and had been longing for the day that Evie would be allowed to play with it.

"See here, Evie," he said as he got down onto his knees, "see how the front opens up."

He undid a catch and opened up the front wall of the house to reveal a fully furnished interior, complete with miniature dolls representing Alice, Jack, Jed and Evie.

"And see just here, Evie. Put your hand on this switch."

He guided her hand to a small switch at the back of the house and flicked it down. Immediately, the whole house was lit by small electric light bulbs.

"That's wonderful, Jed. You must have spent so much time on that," said Alice.

"True craftsmanship that," added Jack. "It'll be worth a fortune one day."

"Mummy, can I open the next one now?" demanded Evie.

"Don't you want to play with this first?" suggested Jed, rearranging the little people in the parlour so that they were all sitting around the table.

"No, I want to open that one," cried Evie, pointing to the remaining gift.

"Don't spoil her fun, Jed, it is Christmas Day," said Alice, pulling the parcel from under the tree.

"It says 'To our darling Evie, from Mummy and Uncle Jack'. Shall we see what's inside?"

Alice helped Evie tear the paper off to reveal a miniature baby carriage, a replica of the pram that Alice had used for Evie. Inside was a baby rag doll. Evie grabbed the doll and held her tightly.

"My baby. Evie's baby."

For the rest of Christmas Day, Evie couldn't be parted from the rag doll and the pram. Jed watched disconsolately as the dolls' house remained untouched. By the end of the day its doors had been closed and it was put out of reach like an exhibit in a museum and a constant reminder to Jed of the chasm which separated him from Evie.

New Years day was bitterly cold. Jed had no work on but still rose early to light a fire in the parlour for Evie when she got up. She appeared at seven thirty, clutching her rag doll and demanding warm milk from Jed. He complied without a murmur, having learnt it was best to reserve his lessons in behaviour for more serious issues. As there was no sign of Alice and Jack, he got Evie her breakfast and then cooked himself some scrambled egg on toast. Evie sang happily, a burbling concoction of different rhymes that had become muddled in her head.

"Three blind mice. They all fell off the wall. Cut off their tail with a kitchen knife. Three blind mice."

Jed loved to watch her. She would play for hours engrossed in some game that only she could understand. He was amazed at her capacity to be self sufficient, only calling for help when she was hungry or stuck.

By ten o'clock, Alice and Jack had still not appeared. Jed began to get a little concerned. It was unusual for Alice not to be up and supervising Evie and Jack would normally be preparing Alice's breakfast. He thought of calling upstairs but there was still an unspoken rule that they didn't get involved in each other's private affairs.

Just after ten thirty Jack appeared, still in his dressing gown. Evie rushed up to him, begging to be picked up and swung around. But, unusually for Jack, he refused.

"Sorry, Evie darling. I must speak to your daddy. Go and put your dolly in the pram and take her for a walk."

Mistaking this for the beginning of a new game, Evie rushed off to find the pram.

"What's the matter, Jack – something wrong?" Jack paused.

"There's a bit of a problem, Jed. It's Alice – a bit personal. She's found a lump."

"What do you mean? What sort of lump?"

"She's worried it's the same thing her mother had. She was only five then but remembers whispered conversations about a lump."

"Where is this lump?"

"In her breast."

Jed was stunned. Breast cancer was one of those illnesses that people didn't talk about. He knew of women, usually older women, who had taken to their beds with the disease and not recovered. He knew very little about it other than it struck fear into those who were diagnosed with it.

"What are you going to do?"

"I'm going to drive Alice to the hospital in Norwich. There's no point in going to see Dr. Murray. He wouldn't have a clue. There are specialists in Norwich. You can pay to see them privately. If necessary, we'll go to London. I'm not going to let anything happen to her, Jed."

Alice and Jack started out for Norwich later that morning, leaving Evie in Jed's hands. He found it difficult to concentrate on playing with her as his mind kept dwelling on that morning's news.

"Come on, Daddy, your turn to push the pram now. Let's pretend I'm the mummy and we're going to the shop. Suzie is our baby and we're taking her in the pram." Suzie, the rag doll, was bundled into the pram and an imaginary journey to the shops followed with Jed being frequently admonished for not being a proper daddy.

It was ten o'clock that evening before Jed heard the sound of the returning car. Evie had long since been settled into bed after a tiring and rancorous story telling session. When the front door opened, Jed was surprised to see that it was only Jack.

"Where's Alice? What's happened?"

Jack looked pale and older as he removed his coat and threw it over a chair.

"They've kept her in. They've got to do more tests. The news isn't good, Jed."

With that, Jack buried his head in his hands to stifle his anguish. Jed awkwardly placed a hand on his shoulder and waited for him to continue.

"It's cancer, Jed, they're sure of that."

Jed couldn't speak. He was breathless and weak. He sunk to into a chair and struggled to find words.

"But what about those private doctors? You said you would pay."

"I spoke to the top man in Norwich. He said there's little they can do. They could try operating but it'd be nasty. They seem to think these cancers may spread to other parts of the body. If it has spread, it's only a matter of time."

"How long?"

"It could be a matter of months."

The following week, the diagnosis was confirmed – an aggressive form of breast cancer, The prognosis was six months, maybe as little as four months.

The house that Alice returned to was very different to the one she had left. All the Christmas decorations had been taken down and the mood was sombre. Alice seemed to be in a dream, slightly removed from reality. On the surface she was calm but underneath Jed and Jack knew that she was in anguish. It was decided to try and keep things as normal as possible for Evie. She wouldn't understand that her mummy was going to die and it would be cruel to try and explain. Alice said that she would think of ways to leave messages for Evie to help her understand as she got older.

The first night that she returned from hospital in Norwich, Jack and Alice lay together on the bed in Alice's room. The crying had been exhausted and they simply lay together in each other's arms.

"It's Evie I'm most worried about, Jack. You and Jed will have to try and find a way to make up for me not being here. It'll be hard for a little girl without her mummy. You must help her, Jack, promise me you will."

"Of course, I'll help her darling. I'll devote my life to her. I promise you that I will."

Jack held Alice tight and wondered whether this was the time to tell her what was on his mind. He had lived longer than the London doctor had predicted. It was now seven years since he had left his former life. Perhaps it was the country air, perhaps it was being in love with Alice. Whatever it was, he had stolen another two years but he knew his condition was getting worse. The bronchitis caused regular coughing spasms and he knew that was putting a strain on his heart. He couldn't promise Alice that he would always be there for Evie. Rather than lie to her, he had to tell her the truth.

"Jack, I've thought of how I'm going to stay alive in Evie's mind. I'm going to write her a letter for each birthday until she's twenty five. I'm going to talk to her about the things that I think will matter to her at each age – making friends at school, becoming a young woman, meeting young men – all the things that a mum would normally be there to talk about to her daughter – except I won't be there."

Alice sobbed violently and Jack cried too as they held each other.

"I want you to make sure she reads them on each birthday. When she's small you'll have to read them to her. But when she's older, let her read them herself. Some things will be private, just between a mum and her daughter. Will you do that for me?"

It was the wrong time to tell Alice about his own death sentence so he simply whispered that he would do exactly as she asked.

It was difficult for Jed carrying on with the business whilst Alice was ill at home. He couldn't take his mind off her illness and still hadn't properly come to terms with the prognosis. Fortunately, he was helped now by his brother, Tom, who had changed out of all recognition since starting to work for Jed. Instead of the shy and surly youth who had left the farm when financial ruin forced his father to sell, Tom had now turned into a confident and hard working employee who was able to take much of the day to day administration from Jed's shoulders. This left time for Jed to pursue other projects and continue to build the business.

In late January, Jed got a message from the chief engineer that he wanted to meet him at a site to the west of the town to discuss a possible development. Jed would ideally have taken Jack with him to discuss the financial issues but Jack seldom left Alice's side at the moment.

He took the truck and followed the directions. The area he was entering contained a number of small businesses, shoe makers, wood turners, wash houses and a forge with black smoke billowing from a hole in the roof. It was the way he had come many years before when he had attempted to rescue Flora from the clutches of her parents. Then it had seemed vibrant and busy. Now it had an air of decay about it. Many buildings were deserted and the few people who were on the street looked dishevelled and poor. He saw a car up ahead which he recognised as belonging to the chief engineer and pulled the truck to a halt beside it.

"Good morning, Mr. Carter," grunted the chief engineer as he came forward to greet Jed. "I bet you didn't even know this place existed."

"I did once know someone who lived here but that was a while ago."

"Well, they're all condemned, the whole lot of them. We're going to knock them down and start all over again. There's going to be a new centre down here. Follow me and I'll show you."

The chief engineer led Jed along a track that was strewn with debris and human excrement. He recognised it as the track he'd taken to Flora's house before. It led them to the small square where the Brotherhood community had once been based. Now, the cottages were abandoned and derelict. Most had lost their thatched roofs and some had saplings sprouting up from the foundations.

"What happened to all the people?" asked Jed, his mind flooding with memories of Flora and the occasions he had argued futilely with her father.

"We've been evicting them slowly then knocking down the houses. They were mostly vagabonds, prostitutes, thieves – that sort of thing – vermin, not the sort of people we want in Frampton. And that's where you come in, Mr. Carter. We want to redevelop the area and provide model housing for the working people. Simple but honest homes for people who aren't frightened of a day's work. They'll be arranged in groups of four around a courtyard. Each house will have its own outside toilet and running water. Very modern. It's a big job, probably too big for you, but I've respect for that business advisor of yours. What's his name – Mallet or something? You've done us proud on the Maltings so I think it's only fair you have a chance. What do you say, Mr. Carter?"

Alice tried to get up most days and spend time with Evie, even though she was beginning to experience some pain. The medication she had been prescribed to ease the suffering left her feeling lethargic by the middle of the afternoon so Jack would take charge of Evie allowing Alice time to write her letters. On the first two occasions she had simply dissolved into tears and not written a word but now, at the third attempt, she was determined to begin.

My darling Evie,

Today you are six and you're getting to be a big girl. It isn't long since Mummy left you and I expect you're still sad and a little angry. It's perfectly alright to feel like that, my sweet girl. When bad things happen it's natural to feel angry but I promise you that you'll feel better with time.

Remember, my darling, that I will always love you and will always be thinking of you. Be good for Uncle Jack and for Daddy. They will look after you and keep you safe.

I hope you have some nice friends, Evie. It's good to have friends and to treat them well. They will be important to you in the future.

Enjoy your special day, darling, and I'll be watching over you always.

All my love, Mummy XXXXXX

That evening in bed, Jack decided to broach the question of his health.

"Alice, there's something I need to tell you. I've been meaning to do it for a long time but could never find the right words."

"Tell me then," said Alice without expression.

"It's about my health – my bronchitis. Well, it's more than bronchitis, it's actually my lungs. You see, in the war those bad things that happened to me – well, they did a lot of damage. The truth is that before I came down here to Frampton I was only given three years to live."

"Three years," gasped Alice. "Why didn't you tell me?"

"Well, I was going to but everything happened so fast. Suddenly, you were expecting Evie and you wanted me to be with you to bring her up. I didn't want to frighten you. It's why I agreed to us living with Jed. I thought that if I died then at least you'd have him. And it's also why I put money into the business. I wanted you to have a means of support and I knew Jed would look after you when I died. But then I didn't die. It's been seven years now. But I don't know when it might happen, Alice. I just don't know."

Alice was silent – her face ashen, her heart pounding.

"Say something, Alice," implored Jack.

"If you die, Jed couldn't look after Evie. He's a lovely man but he's not capable of bringing up our daughter by himself. She might end up in an institution and I couldn't bear that."

"Maybe we should begin to think about foster parents or sending her to a boarding school," suggested Jack.

"No, not that. Jed must find a wife. He needs a wife, someone who will care for Evie too."

"But who?"

"Flora. If it hadn't been for me using him for my own ends, he would probably have married Flora rather than me."

Jack looked startled. He had pushed the incident with Flora to the back of his mind. He had heard rumours that she had a baby but had no idea where she was now.

"They're better suited," continued Alice. "Flora's easygoing and grateful for what she has. She would have made Jed a much better wife."

"But Jed would never be where he is now without you. If he'd married Flora he would still be an odd job man or a farm labourer. It was your ambition and your determination that got Jed to build his business. Don't think badly of yourself, Alice."

"What's done is done. But, Jack, I want you to find Flora. Let Jed know where she is. But don't let him know where the information came from."

"How do I do that?"

"It's what you do, Jack. It's what you did in the war. It's time to do it one last time."

Dearest Evie,

Happy birthday, darling. Today you are twelve and starting to be quite grown up. Soon you will be a young lady. I expect by now you are reading this alone without Daddy to help you so I can begin to share some secrets with you so that you can feel you know me a little better.

When I was twelve, darling, I had no mother either. She died when I was five. I only had my daddy who was an unhappy man and was sometimes cruel to me. I also had to look after my little sister, Polly, and protect her too. I am telling you these things because I want you to know that I understand how you may be feeling. It's likely that Uncle Jack has died now because the war years made him very ill. So you might feel quite alone. I found great support and comfort from my friends and I hope you have good friends too. I learnt that it is important to trust your friends and always be loyal. I fear, my darling, that I used my friends a little and that is a lesson I learnt. Let them be what they want to be and support them. Then they will always be there for you too.

Enjoy being twelve my darling – you are coming towards the end of your childhood and soon you must begin to deal with the challenges of being a young adult. Try to laugh and try to be happy. These are years you will look back on in the future and draw strength from.

Remember that I am with you always and that I love you.

Your ever loving Mummy XXX

Jack shut the toilet cubicle door and hung his bag from a hook so that it couldn't be seen from outside. The toilet smelt of urine and carbolic. It put him off the idea of eating the sandwiches which he had packed into his bag to while away the hours. He checked his watch. It was six o'clock. Most people would be leaving the council offices now. It would get dark about eight o'clock and he felt sure that the night watchman would do his rounds about then. He would have to wait for another two hours before it was safe to leave his cubicle. He practised drawing his legs up under his chin so they wouldn't be seen when the night watchman came in to check the toilet. His stomach rumbled and he reluctantly delved into his bag for the sandwiches.

It was a struggle for Jed getting Evie ready for bed that night. He still couldn't understand why Jack was away. Alice had said it was something to do with urgent business. Jed needed to talk to him about the housing redevelopment. They would need to expand. They would have to employ more people and acquire more vehicles and equipment. They would probably need a bigger yard as Jed's garden office was surrounded now by a growing assortment of tools and equipment, provoking Alice to remark that the house looked more like a building site than a home.

"Daddy, wake up. You're falling asleep again. Tell me that story about the princess with long hair."

"Once upon a time, a princess was locked in a tower by an evil witch."

"No, not that one – silly. The one where the forest grows up all around her."

"That's Sleeping Beauty and she doesn't have long hair."

"Yes, she does. You're stupid. You know she does."

And with that, Evie buried her face in the blanket and screamed, kicking her feet furiously on the end of the bed.

Jack checked his watch. It was eight thirty. The night watchman should have made his rounds by now. He listened out for some sound, doors opening or the shuffle of feet in the corridor, but all he could hear was the slow drip of a tap in the washroom. He felt a cough developing in his lungs and tried to control it by breathing heavily and slowly. It emerged as a splutter developing into a series of gasps which he tried hard to suppress.

Suddenly, Jack detected movement. Instantly, he was transported back to his wartime persona. His hand reached for the knife which he kept strapped to his shin and he braced himself for the attack. But this was a lavatory cubicle in 1928, not a rendezvous in war torn France. And he was about to encounter the night watchman not a German commando unit. He relaxed slightly.

The door to the toilet opened and he heard feet shuffle in. A thin beam of light from a hand torch shone around the room and searched beneath the closed cubicle doors. There was a pause and Jack expected the feet to retreat. But instead, they moved into the room and he heard a cubicle door being pushed open. Jack braced himself. He couldn't afford to be discovered. If necessary, he would quickly overpower the night watchman, knock him to the floor and make his escape. He pulled his feet up to his chin and sat perched on the toilet seat. The cubicle door next to his was kicked open. Feet shuffled in. There was a grunt followed by incomprehensible mumbling and then the sound of urine flowing into the toilet in a slow and intermittent stream. Another grunt was followed by the rasping sound of wind being passed. Jack struggled to control his breathing as an acrid odour invaded his cubicle. Then he heard the feet retreating from the toilet and the door slam shut.

Hello, my darling,

Today you are eighteen and you are quite a grown woman. It will seem a long time since I left you now. I wonder what your world is like. I expect it's very different from the one I knew. It's strange writing to you knowing that you will be eighteen when you read this. As I write this letter you are five and you are playing at the foot of my bed with your rag doll. You're a very pretty little girl but you're strong willed and impetuous. How will you manage these qualities when you're older? I want to say something to you that matters, something that will give you strength, something that maintains the bond between us. But I struggle to find the right words.

There are still things I want to tell you so that you understand more about me and more about yourself. But the time is not yet right. I want to prepare you, though. Let me just say this. At eighteen you may have experienced, or you may be about to experience, a relationship with a man. This will present you with many different powerful emotions – love, loyalty, desire and possibly despair. But the strongest of all emotions is passion. It's powerful because it comes not from the mind but from the heart, deep inside of you. It lacks the logic of the other emotions yet is has the power to drive your destiny forward in unexpected ways. You can't avoid passion if it comes your way but be ready for the chaos it brings with it. Passion is difficult to identify until it has engulfed you. It can cause you to destroy those things that you hold dear whilst at the same seducing your entire being with sublime joy. Passion has many faces, my darling, and I urge you to beware. But I believe you are strong and whilst you will face many dilemmas, as I have done, you will eventually rise above the turmoil.

Your ever loving mother, Alice

The hypnotic drip, drip of the tap had lulled Jack into a stupor from which he awoke with a start. He stretched his cramped limbs and looked at his watch. It was nine thirty and he could tell from the gloom that it was getting dark outside.

Slowly, he eased himself off the toilet seat and cautiously opened the cubicle door. The washroom was empty. He splashed cold water from one of the basins onto his face and tried to bring himself to a state of alertness. The door creaked as he let himself out into the corridor beyond. It was painted in grey, interspersed with green doors at intervals along its length. Each door announced the municipal functions of the people who worked within – engineering, drainage, highways, rural affairs. Jack made his way with stealth along the row of doors until he recognised the one that his informant had told him would provide the answer he needed. It said simply 'Parish Needy'. Jack turned the handle but the door was locked. He reached into his pocket for a small screwdriver and with the skill of a seasoned saboteur, he turned the lock.

Inside the room was a large table with four seats arranged around it. Behind the table were rows of polished wood filing cabinets. Jack made his way to the first of these and shone his torch cautiously over it. The label stated simply 'Parish Paupers'. He moved along the line of cabinets passing 'Cripples and War Wounded', 'Foundlings', 'Work

House', 'Destitute Widows', 'House of Correction' – a sad litany of Frampton's rejected and ostracised. His eyes were suddenly caught by a label on the next cabinet 'Lunatics and the Insane'. Under this were drawers labelled 'Certified Lunatics', 'Simpletons and Idiots', 'Short Term Care' and 'Illegitimate Births'.

Jack pulled open this bottom drawer to reveal a row of hand written cards. The first one read:

Adams, Mary. Baby 273. Born 4th December, 1917. Mother died in asylum 16th July, 1918. Father believed killed in action. Baby sent for adoption.

Jack wondered at the sad destiny of Baby 273. Did he or she survive? Did anybody ever love or care about Baby 273?

He flicked through the cards until he got to the 'F's and searched for 'Fulton'.

Fulton, Beatrice. Baby boy 357. Born 7th July, 1919. No known father. Mother and baby placed into service 21st July, 1919.

Fulton, Catherine. No known family. Baby girl 382. Born in asylum 25th December, 1920. Mother and baby died December 27th.

'Fulton, Flora'. His heart skipped a beat. He pulled out the card.

Fulton, Flora. Unmarried pregnant woman aged twenty years. Disowned by parents and placed into Parish care 12th February, 1922. Baby 372. Born 14th May, 1922. And there was a scribbled note in the margin next to the baby's number which said simply 'Emma'.

Further down was the information Jack needed.

Recommendation that mother and baby be placed in service. It was dated 22nd July, 1922. But there was no mention of where Flora had been sent. Jack turned the card over but the other side was blank. The idea that his night spent in a toilet cubicle had been in vain caused him intense anger. He tried to think what he would have done in the war if he was trying to decipher a captured enemy document. The card had been filled in with a heavy hand. Splodges of ink testified to this. It gave him an idea. He shone his torch from underneath the card, searching for any impressions that may have been left whilst someone was pressing down on another piece of paper. At the top right hand corner of the card he could just make out the faint lines of some other writing. He focused the torch beam on this area. They seemed to be part of an address. He was certain he could see 'Norwich' but the road name was more difficult to make out. It looked like All Saints, but it could have been Old Souls. It was near enough. He could check the details later. And there was a name. It looked like Hunt or Gunt. Jack wrote the details quickly into his notebook but not before the shuffling of feet could be heard rapidly approaching down the corridor. Instantly, his war time skills kicked in. He grabbed an ornamental letter opener from the desk and crouched behind the office door, his sinews tensed like coiled springs, ready to strike.

Darling Evie,

This is the last letter that I will write to you. I am growing tired now and I sense the end may not be far away. Writing these letters has been such a comfort to me. They have helped me to feel that the end is not so final, that through these words you and I have kept our love alive over these past twenty years. I have spoken to you about thoughts and ideas that seemed important to me and that I hope have meant something to you too. But in a sense, all that I have been telling you has been preparing you for this final letter. Because, Evie, my darling, there is something that I have kept from you and that I must tell you now because it's your right to know. As a result of this you may hate me but that is a risk that I must take. I hope that in time you can come to understand what led me to do as I did and to forgive me ...

Jed poured himself a large whisky. He was relying more on drink these days. The bedtime routine with Evie had been more demanding than usual. She had wanted to see Alice but Jack was with her, helping her to cope with a new intensity of pain that was beginning to rack her body. Evie had accused Jed of preventing her from seeing her mummy. She told him that she hated him and that he was the most horrible daddy in the world. Jed tried to remain sanguine but inside the hurt penetrated to the core of his sole. Not only was he a bad husband but he was also a terrible father. He gulped at the whisky and sat down disconsolately at the parlour table. He pulled a copy of the weekly Frampton Gazette towards him. The front page was full of the latest gossip to hit the sleepy town – the break in and subsequent assault of a night watchman at the town hall the previous week. The town was alive with theories and motives. The night watchman, who had suffered a bruise to the back of the head, had asserted that he was attacked and beaten by a band of at least five men dressed in military-style uniforms. He had fought bravely to defend the interests of the town but his wounded leg and the clear imbalance in terms of numbers led to him suffering the indignity of being bound, gagged and strapped to an office chair where he remained until discovered by cleaners the following morning. Given the severity of the crime, police support from nearby North Walsham was called in to help the local police constable. However, the mystery was compounded by the fact that nothing appeared to have been stolen and there was no evidence of forced entry. The supervising police officer from North Walsham claimed that the break in showed signs of a military operation. The cord binding the night watchman's limbs had been applied with military precision and was out of all proportion to the restraints needed for the lame victim. Rumours abounded in the town of a renegade group of German prisoners of war who had been roaming the Norfolk countryside since the end of hostilities, unaware that the war was over. Others argued that the night watchman was clearly complicit in the operation as he had fallen asleep after having been bound and made no attempt to call for help.

Jed cast his eyes over the headlines with mild amusement. Then he turned his attention to a small pile of unopened letters that had arrived that morning. He recognised most as bills. These would be handed to Jack who still managed the business finances. There was one letter, however, that he didn't recognise – a small white envelope of the type people used for sending invitations. It was addressed to him. He opened it and unfolded a small sheet of white paper. He was transfixed by what he saw. The blood drained from his face leaving a deathly white pallor. The note said simply:

'Flora Fulton, The Larches, All Saints Avenue, Norwich'. Jed stared at the piece of paper for nearly ten minutes. He tried to think who might have wanted to tell him this. Of course, it might be a joke, some misplaced prank. But maybe it was genuine. He knew for certain that he would need to find out.

The Guest Who Stayed: Chapter 18 – Spring 1928

Alice died on May 27th, 1928. It was a warm spring day and the garden was ablaze with new blooms and ripening blossom. The cherry trees cast a pink mantle over the house that had symbolised Alice and Jed's shared hope when they married.

Jack held Alice in his arms in her last moments. The medication had induced a state of semi consciousness in which it was impossible to know whether Alice understood what was being said. Jack's final words were whispered and barely audible.

"I'll never let you go. You're inside my heart and my soul. I love you."

Her eyes were closed. There was a fleeting smile, then a deep breath. Then she had gone.

Jed was downstairs attempting to amuse Evie. He had opened the dolls' house and was trying to get her to arrange the furniture but she was more intent on sitting inside the box that the house was kept in. A desperate shout from upstairs brought Jed to his feet. Evie rushed to Jed and he swept her up into his arms. She clung to his neck, sensing that something was wrong. There was another shout followed by a long anguished sob. Slowly, Jed went upstairs, clutching Evie tightly. As they entered Alice's room, Jack was on his knees by the side of the bed with tears streaming down his face. Jed placed his hand on Jack's shoulder and then held Evie up to look one last time at Alice. To Evie, she looked beautiful – at peace, with her auburn hair spread across the white linen pillow – like Sleeping Beauty. It was an image that would stay with her for the rest of her life.

In the weeks leading up to Alice's death, both men had spent time alone with her. Each knew that the other had his own private thoughts and memories to share. For Jack, there was the anguish of losing a lover, someone with whom he had shared passion and created new life. Knowing too that his own life would soon be at an end, he and Alice spent many hours discussing death. For Alice, the notion of being switched off like a light bulb, with all the finality that implied, was irrational. Watching the changing seasons through her bedroom window and seeing the continuous cycle of birth and death, made her want a better explanation. Though neither Jack nor she were particularly religious, they found it hard to discount the idea that there was some further dimension in which the essence of themselves – their souls – might continue. Although Jack normally took a cynical view of such things he had found himself questioning his own disbelief. On a number of occasions recently he thought he had felt the presence of Yvette. It wasn't that he could see her, just a sense of her being present and still being a part of him. It was enough to open his mind to the possibility of a continued existence – a feeling which he found strangely exhilarating.

Jed spent long hours with Alice, many of them in silent reflection. Understanding his hurt, Alice talked to Jed about his strength and courage and how these would support him in the future. She begged him to look after Evie and told him that she was as much his child as she was Jack's. And she told Jed that he must find another wife, a better wife than she had been.

The funeral was held at St. Martin's Church a week after Alice's death. Jack and Jed stood together at the graveside, both visibly moved. If bystanders wondered about the relationship that these two men had shared with the same woman, nothing was said. What happened behind closed doors was not their business.

In the weeks after Alice's death, Jed and Jack tried to cope and create an atmosphere of normality for Evie's sake. Jed was out for much of the day working, leaving Jack to cope with the domestic chores. When Jed returned exhausted in the evening, he would take over the role of caring for Evie and cope with her increasingly aggressive tantrums. When Evie was finally in bed, both men would slump into chairs in the sitting room and the conversation would soon turn to Alice. They had a need to keep her alive in their minds and in the process to understand the relationship which had bound them together.

"What I'll never know, Jack, is what would have happened if you'd never come into our lives. Would it have worked for Alice and me? You robbed me of that chance to find out. Alice always said it would take time and I was prepared for that. She said that love grows. In time, things would have been alright between Alice and me. You just need to let things take their time."

"Alice wasn't that sort of person, Jed. Alice was impetuous, she wanted to seize the moment, she wanted to live dangerously. I don't think she had the patience to wait. I'm not saying what I did was right but I provided something that Alice needed. I opened her eyes."

"And you took her to bed. You had sex with my wife."

"And I'm sorry but we didn't think about the consequences. Our bodies took over. Sometimes it happens like that. Call it what you like, passion, lust, greed. These are powerful emotions and sometimes you can't control them."

"Well, that's where you and I disagree. I think if a man can't control his emotions he's no right to call himself civilised. You think it's right just to take what you want regardless of what it does to others?"

Jack paused and studied the flat horizon just visible through the sitting room windows. The sun was setting and casting heavy shadows across the garden.

"I'm dying, Jed, that's why I did it."

"What do you mean, you're dying?"

"When I came here, they'd given me three years. It focuses your mind, Jed. You don't have time to wait. It's a powerful emotion knowing you're going to die. Just like falling in love's a powerful emotion. You don't have a choice. That's what it was like with Alice. I didn't have a choice."

It was Jed's turn to sit in silence and digest this latest information. In some ways it was a comfort to him to learn that Jack 'had no choice'. It somehow made the betrayal less painful. His mind turned to Jack's other news.

"When you goin' to die then, Jack?"

"They gave me three years, five at the most. It's eight years now, Jed."

"Well, it ain't the right time for you to go dying now, Jack. We've got Evie to bring up and the business is takin' off. I need you around,

Jack. It pains me to say it but, with Alice gone, you and me have got to make a go of it together. I don't want you dying just yet."

It soon became clear to Jack and Jed that they couldn't manage to care for Evie by themselves and they needed help. With painful memories of Miss Cavendish still alive in their minds, they decided this time to seek the help of a local girl. Amy was nineteen. She came from a family of eleven. Surviving in a family that size with a meagre income from a land labouring father, she had learnt skills and wiles that she put to good effect in her management of Evie.

With Amy established in the house, routine began to return. Jed was able to concentrate more on his work and resume cordial business relations with Jack whilst making it clear that on a personal level they remained at arm's length. Jack, who was increasingly housebound due to his attacks of bronchitis, tried to entertain Evie when he could, though often it was the younger company of Amy that she sought out to take part in her wildly imaginative and energetic games. Jed took over the evening role and slowly developed a working truce with Evie. First, Uncle Jack was allowed to read her a story that she had chosen, after which Jed would read a story of his choice until Evie fell into a stupor, induced by Jed's sonorous story telling voice.

The chief engineer arranged to meet Jed on the site of the new building project in the middle of June.

"We've had a number of quotes now, Mr. Carter," he announced as they surveyed the wasteland that had previously been home to a thriving community. "We've whittled it down to three and you're one of those three."

"That's great news," enthused Jed. "It would be an honour for us to be awarded this contract. And we really appreciate your support."

Jed hoped he didn't sound too ingratiating but had learnt now that a degree of obsequiousness made for good business practice.

"This would be a great challenge for us and we'd not let you down."

"Yes, yes, I know that," mumbled the chief engineer, shuffling his feet in the dried earth and seeming unimpressed. "But if you're going to compete with the big boys, you've got to play by their rules."

"I don't follow you."

"I'll be blunt with you, Carter, and I'll deny I ever said this. Payback."

"I don't follow."

"I make sure you get awarded the contract and you pay me one percent of the contract value. You build the additional cost into the bid."

There was a pause whilst Jed tried to take in what he had just heard.

"You mean I pay you for awarding the contract to Carters?"

"If you want the contract – yes. If you won't do it, one of the other companies on my list will. I suggest you discuss it with that finance man of yours – what's his name, Millet, or something? Strikes me as a man of the world."

The scullery was dingy, lit by a single electric bulb. The only daylight entered though a small window set high in the outside wall.

Flora adjusted the white cap that she was required to wear and fixed it to her short dark hair with a clip.

"Mummy," called Emma softly, "can you play with me now?"

Flora knelt down beside Emma who was sitting on a blanket on the stone floor.

"Not just yet, my little girl. I have some more jobs to do. Wait a while longer and then I'll tell you a story."

Flora returned to the scullery sink and resumed scrubbing the pans that had been employed in preparing the Blunts' evening meal. On the table to the side of the sink lay the leftovers, mostly untouched and untried. The Blunts would insist on being served a three course meal for which they would dress in full evening costume and would then leave most of what Flora had prepared for them. One of the servant's bells rang in the scullery. Flora knew it was summoning her to the drawing room. The routine was the same every evening.

"Wait there awhile, Emma, my love. Mother won't be long."

Flora climbed the narrow spiral stairs which led into the entrance hall and from there she made her way into the drawing room, straightening her white apron as she did so. The drawing room was cold and inhospitable. Bare wooden boards were covered only by a meagre rug placed by the lifeless fireplace. The only decoration in the room was a single large painting of Mr. Blunt's father, an arch deacon, posing with a melancholy stare in a gloomy ecclesiastic setting.

"Flora, stand by the rug will you!" commanded Mrs. Blunt. She was a thin lady with a pinched face in her early seventies. She wore wire rimmed spectacles and supported herself with a cane stick.

"You will have noticed that we didn't eat much of the food you served us tonight. To be honest with you, it was disgusting. The soup had too much salt and was inedible."

"And the lamb," continued Mr. Blunt, "was like eating leather." He should know. He had made his money in the shoe trade but as the only son was despised by his family for not following in his father's footsteps. "And the dessert," he continued, "was indescribable. What was it?"

"It was rhubarb pie, Mr. Blunt, sir."

"Full of lumps and sharp as lemon peel," added Mrs. Blunt.

"You see, Flora," continued Mr. Blunt, "we'll have to consider sending you back to the asylum if this continues. You know this is an act of charity, providing you and your 'bastard' daughter with a home." His face quivered as he said the word.

Flora knew the rest of the sermon by heart. It was delivered to her at least twice a week. She was a sinner, a fornicator and was cast out by the Lord. It was only through the likes of Mr. and Mrs. Blunt that she would find salvation. Her ingratitude and indiscipline would lead to her being sent back to the asylum and she would be separated from her daughter and never see her again.

"Do you understand what I am saying, Flora?" continued Mr. Blunt.

"Yes, I do, sir, and I'm truly sorry. I will try to do better."

She wanted to run. She wanted to scream at them and tell them that they were sick and perverted. But where would she go. Her parents had disowned her. She would end up in the poor house and Emma would have to be fostered. She couldn't bear that.

"Leave us now, Flora, and think hard about what we've told you. There won't be a second chance."

Later that night, Flora lay awake in her cot bed. Emma was asleep in a box beside her. A movement outside the door caused Flora to freeze and nausea to grip her body. A dim light moved slowly towards her open door. Flora knew what to expect and she had no means to avoid it. Clutching a candle and dressed in a night shirt, he made his way to the bed and lay down beside her. Then without any words he placed his hands under the blanket and ran his bony fingers across her body, breathing heavily and stinking of whisky as he abused her. After he had gone, Flora sobbed silently late into the night.

"What do I do then, Jack?" asked Jed as they finished supper. It's bribery and it's corrupt. Do I report him?"

"There's no point in that, Jed," replied Jack. "They're all corrupt up there. If they're not taking bribes they're stealing pencils. They wouldn't understand what you were going on about."

"So, do I just do as the rest? Does that make it right? Because that's the way it's done I have to follow suit?"

"If you want the contract, Jed, you've probably got no choice. It's a big one and you're going to give employment to a lot of people in the town. If it goes to somebody else they'll employ their own people. It's all very well having principles, Jed, but sometimes principles cost jobs."

"I've always tried to be straight with people. That's the way I've done business. It's what I learnt from Dan – be honest with people and they'll be loyal to you. Once I start going against my principles I'm left with no standards. All of a sudden anything goes – if the price is right."

"Well, I can't make up your mind for you, Jed, but sometimes you've got to balance principles with reality. It doesn't mean you're any the worse for it, just that life is full of compromise. If you don't compromise some things, you'll die virtuous but poor."

After Jack had retired to bed, Jed got out the ageing map book that he had taken from Dan's premises. It had last been revised in 1910. He pulled out the now crumpled piece of paper which he had been carrying round with him for the last fortnight and examined the address 'The Larches, All Saints Avenue, Norwich'. The book was open at the Norwich street map. Jed thought 'All Saints' might be near a church but then Norwich was full of churches so that didn't help. He spotted the cathedral, close to the city centre and traced his finger along the route of Bishopsgate which led out to the west of the city. Round an area of parkland, he noticed a cluster of roads – Priory Lane, Chapel Street – and there it was, All Saints Avenue. Jed realised that his heart was beating fast. He stared at the page for what seemed like a long while, unable to tear himself away. Somewhere in that road he would find Flora. What would he say to her? What would she think of him? She might despise him for not having rescued her sooner. Perhaps she was happy, living with a prosperous family and bringing up her daughter in posh surroundings. And how did he feel about her? Once, he had thought he wanted to marry her. That was before Alice had laid claim to him. He had always thought her pretty in a natural sort of way. She didn't spend time on her looks but had a simple, easy charm. He stayed deep in thought into the early hours of the morning.

As the business had grown, Jed was less able to borrow the truck for personal use when he needed it. So he had purchased his own car, a small Austin 7 of which he was immensely proud. Dwarfed in size by Jack's Austin Tourer, it had none of the status or kudos of that vehicle, but it fitted completely with Jed's self image and aspiration.

Racing along the A140 on his way to Norwich, Jed felt elation mixed with misgiving. At sixty five miles an hour the red and black Austin 7 bounced drunkenly on the pot holed road. Clinging to the steering wheel, Jed realised he had no plan. Would he walk up to the front door, knock and ask to see Flora or should he resort to more covert tactics?

Having found the cathedral, Jed took a number of wrong turnings until he found himself driving along Bishopsgate, a road of mixed dwellings. Small terraced cottages were interspersed with shops and rundown work premises. Once he had crossed the river, the houses appeared larger and were set in their own grounds. Side roads intersected with the main road and at the third intersection, Jed saw the name 'All Saints Avenue'. He turned the Austin onto the unmade gravel surface. The houses were set back from the street and were partly obscured by large oak and sycamore trees.

Jed noted the names of the houses as he passed – Park House, The Cedars, The Mount and Faversham Lodge. Just as he appeared to be coming to the end, he spotted the name he was looking for – The Larches. He stopped the car on the opposite side of the road and tried to catch a glimpse of the house.

The front consisted of two bay windows either side of a large wooden door with a stained glass window. It was detached and built of weathered brick – probably dating from the 1850s. It had two main floors but also appeared to have a basement scullery and attic rooms. There was no sign of movement and no sign of habitation except for a wisp of white smoke that escaped from one of the tall chimneys. Jed sat in the car for over half an hour, churning over in his mind what he should do. He wished he had the daring and courage of Jack or the guile of Alice.

His thoughts were interrupted by the sound of another car coming down the road. A large grey sedan, possibly a Bentley, drove slowly into sight. Jed could see that a uniformed driver was at the wheel. The car drove right up to where he was parked and then turned into The Larches. Jed watched as it crawled around the circular drive and stopped outside the front porch. A chauffer got out of the car and knocked on the door. He removed his cap as it was opened by an elderly couple. The woman leant on a stick and was helped by the man into the car. Fleetingly, Jed thought he saw another person behind the door, a thin woman in a white apron and cap but the door was quickly closed and she disappeared from sight.

Jed ducked down below the dashboard as the sedan made its way down the drive and into the road. When it had gone he sat up and resolved to take action now.

To avoid making a noise he stepped across the lawn, bypassing the gravelled drive. Rather than approach the main door, he made his way to the side of the house. A heavy wrought iron gate barred his way. Having failed to shift the lock, he resorted to climbing over the gate and dropping down onto the other side. He found himself looking at an overgrown garden. Large trees cast heavy shadows over the uncut lawn. Ornamental statues covered in moss suggested that the garden had once known better times.

Making his way slowly round the side of the house, he spotted a small open window a few feet above the paving stones. He bent down and peered into the gloomy room which appeared to have no other source of light. It was like a cell with a wooden table and two chairs pulled up beside. There was a small cot bed against one wall and a large wooden box by the side of the bed. His eyes gradually acclimatised to the gloom and he suddenly made out the silhouette of a small child sitting on the floor. She was staring into the darkness, making no movement and making no sound. He thought that perhaps she was deaf or mute.

Suddenly, she turned and looked in the direction of the open door. A woman walked in wearing white overalls and a white cap. She looked pale and thin. She scooped up the small child.

"It's OK, my sweet. They've gone now. We'll be by ourselves all evening, just you and me," he heard her saying. She sat down on one of the chairs and held the child on her lap. He heard her sobbing quietly. Then she pulled off her cap. Jed gasped. It was Flora, but not the Flora he had known. Her face was thin and her long black hair had been cut short. She was pale and tears trickled down her cheek.

"Let me tell you a story, Emma, my love. What will it be about?"

Jed picked up a stone and tapped gently on the window. He saw her stop and look anxiously around.

"It's alright, Flora, it's only me – Jed."

"Who's there? Who's that?" Flora shouted, panic now seizing her. She stood up and clasped the child to her body.

"It's me, Jed. Do you remember?"

She gasped and looked uncomprehendingly at the window. Jed tried to lower his face to the open pane.

"It's me – Jed," he managed to say in a louder voice.

Flora screamed and thrust a fist into her mouth.

"I'm sorry, Flora. I didn't mean to frighten you. I've come to get you. I'm here to help you."

It was a ridiculous position from which to carry out a conversation. His head was on the ground and his rear was pointing to the sky.

"Look, can I come in, Flora. I know they've gone out. I saw them go. I need to talk to you."

Flora slowly removed her fist from her mouth, still looking dazed.

"There's a scullery door down some steps just ahead of you," she stammered.

Jed found the steps and made his way to the door. Through the frosted glass he could see a light coming towards him. He heard bolts being drawn back and then the door was opened. For a moment they stared at each other in disbelief and then he pulled her into his arms.

"Flora, Flora. I'm so sorry. I should have come earlier, much earlier."

She buried her face into his shoulder and cried uncontrollably. In the dark scullery he met Emma for the first time. He bent down to speak to her but she hid behind Flora's skirt.

"She's frightened of people, Jed. You see, we don't get out much."

"Why's that?"

"I can only go out when they give me permission and that's not often. They say they provide me with all I want and I don't have a need to go out."

"Why don't you run away, Flora? You could just walk out."

"Where would I go? My parents threw me out when I got pregnant. Anyhow, they're not there now. They were evicted by the council – them and all their neighbours. I don't know where they've gone or even if they're alive."

Jed felt himself redden at the thought of his involvement in redeveloping the site where Flora's parents had lived.

"Come with me, Flora," said Jed, urgently. "Come with me now, you and Emma. I'll look after you both."

"You can't. You're married to Alice. How can you look after me too?"

There was a pause. Jed searched for words.

"You don't know then?"

"Know what?"

"Alice is dead. She died six weeks ago. It was cancer."

Flora turned deathly white and Jed helped her to sit in one of the chairs. He took her hands in his and knelt beside her.

"I'm sorry, Flora. I know that you and Alice were good friends. If we'd known where you were ... So don't you see, it's different now. I can look after you and Emma too."

"That's not possible, Jed," Flora said softly, staring at her hands.

"Why ever not? I always thought we were made for each other, Flora. Now there's nothing stopping us."

"Yes, there is."

"What?"

"You know who fathered my baby, Jed. You were there."

Jed froze. Panic gripped his body.

"You were there, Jed, that afternoon and you did nothing to help me. How can you live with that, Jed? That's why we can't be together."

Jed looked at her in disbelief. It was no use denying the truth.

"I had no idea you knew."

"Why do you think I came into the barn that afternoon? Jack was becoming demanding. He's sophisticated and gets his own way. I didn't know how to handle him. I'd seen your tools outside the barn when we were on our way to the pub. I knew you were in there and so I thought that if I took Jack inside we'd meet you and that'd be an end of it. But you weren't there and Jack starts getting out of control, pulling at my clothes and kissing me hard so I couldn't shout out. I tried to call but he put his hand over my mouth. Then as he pushed me down, I saw this head, looking straight at me from behind some hay bales. When I thought back over it, as I have done every day since, I remembered that face. It was you, Jed. You were there and you did nothing. You see, what made it worse was that I was in love with you. I always have been. And when you got engaged to Alice it broke my heart. But I had to carry on. Alice was my friend and I admired her. I admired you too, Jed. So, to see you watching and doing nothing just destroyed me. I think I had a breakdown. My parents couldn't cope so I ended up in the asylum."

Tears streamed down Jed's cheeks as he heard Flora's account. There was no point denying anything or trying to explain. However much he tried to justify his actions it would always look as if he let Flora down. They sat in silence for a while, trying to understand.

"I accept I let you down, Flora, and I won't try to justify what I did," said Jed. "But that doesn't mean I can't help you now. You've got to get out of here. You're a prisoner, you and Emma."

"But I've nowhere to go and no money. I'd need a job."

"I'll give you a job, Flora, in my business. It's doing well now and I need someone to help me with the organisation, ordering things, making appointments, keeping the books."

"I can't do that, Jed. I've had no proper schooling. I'm only fit for domestic work."

"That's not true, Flora. You just haven't had the chance. I'm going to give you the chance."

"But I've got to live somewhere too."

"Don't worry. I've got a plan. I'll find you and Emma somewhere to live."

"How can you do that?"

"I know someone. I can pull some strings."

"I don't know, Jed. I thought I'd left all that behind. And I'm not sure I could face Jack again."

"Why didn't you tell Jack about the baby?"

"I couldn't prove it and men like him don't own up. He'd just make me out to be a liar. Anyway, I didn't love him."

"Will you tell Emma?"

"You mean, tell her that Jack's her father?"

"Yes."

"Eventually, I suppose I'll have to. I don't like living a lie. But it can wait. I'm in no hurry."

"Let me tell you something, Flora, that I've never told anyone else. This is going to be very difficult for me."

There was a pause whilst Jed swallowed hard. "Our Evie, our little girl, well, I'm not her father."

"What do you mean, Jed? She's yours and Alice's daughter."

"Everyone thinks I'm her father but I'm not. Jack is."

Flora gasped and clasped her hands to her mouth again.

Jed continued in a faltering voice. "That time that Jack came to stay with us on that August bank holiday in 1921, he and Alice had an affair. He made her pregnant."

"Oh God, Jed! I'm sorry. I didn't know."

"They were going to go off together and leave me alone in the house. But I begged them not to. I thought if only I could get Alice to stay, she'd realise her mistake and come back to me."

"But how could you live with that man under the same roof, Jed? I'd have wanted to kill him."

"I tried."

"What – you tried to kill him?"

"I tried to kill them both. I took to drinking. One night I got the shot gun and went after them. Fortunately, I was too drunk to do anything."

"Oh, Jed, I'm so sorry. But you could have thrown him out of the house."

"I couldn't, Flora. It gets worse. I was forced into a devil's pact."

"Devil's pact – what sort of pact?"

"Making a success of the business was really important to me. It was for Alice too. After Dan died I really wanted to make a go of it but it just wasn't working. We were in danger of losing the house. Then when Jack turned up he offered to invest in the business and help me build it. It was like a life line. But then I found out he was sleeping with Alice and she was pregnant with his child. I was devastated, Flora – destroyed. And to make it worse, if I threw them out I'd lose the business too. So we agreed that Jack would stay but I'd pretend to be the father. That way things would be respectable. So, you see what I mean about a devil's pact? My life's one big lie too and I can't get out of it. It's too late."

They both sat in silence for a while, absorbing the implications.

"So, what are you saying, Jed?" asked Flora. "That we both continue living this lie?"

"I don't see how we can get out of it now. I can't tell Evie the truth and suddenly turn her world upside down. It wouldn't be fair. If I lost Jack as a partner, the business could collapse and we'd have nothing. As for you and Emma, you're right. Jack could just deny it happened. I always thought I was a man of principles, Flora, but it's strange how life conspires to make you do things differently."

"My parents were people with strong principles too," replied Flora, "but it blinded them to reality. They got cheated on by the very people they looked to for leadership."

"So, what do you say, Flora. Will you come away with me – now? There's nothing to stop you. Come now."

"No, not now, Jed. I've got to think first. It's not just me, it's Emma too. I've got to do what's best for her. Give me some time to think."

"How long?"

"A week. Come back in a week. They always go out on a Thursday night, regular as clockwork. Don't come in. Just wait outside. If I've made up my mind to leave, I'll be out a few minutes after they've gone. If I don't come out, you must go and not come back. Do you promise me that?"

"If you want me to."

"I do."

Jed waited in the snug of the Fox and Hounds. It was lunchtime and there was nobody else in there. He ordered a single malt whisky and relished its smooth clinging taste. The door opened and the chief engineer walked in.

"So what's this all about, Carter," he asked in an exaggerated whisper. "Never done business with you before in The Fox, though I'm not complaining. Are you buying?"

"What do you want?"

"Same as you. Make it a double."

Jed waited whilst two more malt whiskys were served.

"About the western redevelopment," Jed began. "Last time we met you asked me for a payback to secure the job."

"OK, Carter, keep your voice down. We don't want the whole bloody pub to know. Like I said, it's the way things are done and if you want to play in the same league as the big boys you play by the rules."

"I've thought about it. I'll do it."

"Glad you've seen sense. Thought you would."

"But I want something else in return."

"You're getting the bloody job, that's what you're getting. What else do you want?"

"I want one of the houses set aside for a friend of mine. There'll be over one hundred houses built up there and I want her to have one of them."

"That's difficult. There's a long waiting list and I don't control that. Who is she? Some floozy you're having a bit on the side with."

"It's nothing like that. She's a friend, an unmarried mother. I'm sworn to help her."

"Well, like I said, I can get her name on the list but there's hundreds of families waiting for public housing."

"That's not good enough," replied Jed, aware that he was now entering uncharted waters. "I want her to be allocated a house. That's the deal. Your one percent in return for that."

Jed was gambling on the notion that no other builder had yet agreed the one percent payback and if the chief engineer saw the prize within his grasp, he would do all he could to seal the deal.

"I've told you, Carter," he said, downing the last dregs of the whisky, "I can't do that. I don't control that department. You're speaking to the wrong person."

"I think you can do it," replied Jed, with a threatening edge to his voice. "I think you can do what you want. And if you want that payback you'll find a way. That's the deal."

A week later, Jed parked the Austin 7 in All Saints Avenue, slightly further away from The Larches than before so as not to be conspicuous. He settled down to wait for the chauffeured sedan to arrive and take the Blunts out. It was a quiet summer evening. The sun was setting and the encroaching dusk was making it difficult to see detail.

On time, he saw two large headlights making their way down the avenue and turn into drive. He could just make out the Blunts being helped into the car by the chauffeur and, as before, he ducked out of sight as the car edged down the drive and onto the road.

Once the lights had disappeared, he sat up and looked out expectantly for Flora and Emma. The house was in darkness and there was no sign of movement. He waited for fifteen minutes, becoming increasingly anxious. Eventually, he got out of the car and walked up to the house, peering into the gloom for some sign of activity. He recalled Flora's words that he was to go if she didn't appear and never come back. But he'd come too far now. He wanted Flora with an urgency he'd not felt before. He couldn't believe that staying here was right for her. At least he needed her to tell him to his face that he must go.

He climbed over the locked gate again, ripping a wide gash in his trousers as he did so. There was light coming from the small casement window and he knelt down on the hard stone to peer in. He saw Flora, hunched on a chair, her head down. She was clutching Emma to her lap. Grabbing a large stone, he hit the pane harder than he had intended and broke the glass. Flora leapt from her chair in panic.

"Why didn't you come, Flora? Please think. You can't remain a prisoner here," he pleaded.

Flora rushed to the broken casement window.

"They've locked me in. They found out someone had been here. One of the neighbours saw you. They've threatened to have Emma taken away and to send me back to the asylum. You've got to get me out, Jed. Please."

"Wait there, Flora, I'll be back."

Jed sprinted into the overgrown garden and searched anxiously. Stacked by a rotting shed was a pile of logs. He seized the largest of these and returned to the back door. Using all his strength, he battered the door. The log splintered and sent fragments of debris flying over the ground. He hit the door again. The log was firmer now and a crack appeared round the lock of the door. He used all his might to hit it one more time and the door burst open. Once inside, he made his way down the unlit corridor to the scullery. There was no room to swing the log so he dived at the door, hitting it with his left shoulder. He felt an agonising pain shoot up his arm but the door opened. Flora was crouching in a corner and Emma was sobbing uncontrollably.

"Come now. Just get out immediately!"

They made their way into the front hall and unlocked the main door from the inside. Once outside, they crossed the lawn, keeping well within the shadows to avoid being seen. Flora climbed into the front of the Austin, still clutching Emma. Jed looked at Flora and saw the anxiety on her face. He leant forward and kissed her then put the Austin into gear and raced off down the road and away from Norwich.

The Guest Who Stayed: Chapter 19 – July 1940

Evie cycled cautiously along Duck Lane, concentrating hard on avoiding the growing number of potholes. As she worked for the council, she had tried on numerous occasions to get something done about the state of the road but the war had put a halt to all highway expenditure unless it had a military benefit.

Nearing Hope Cottage, her attention was caught by the sound of an aircraft somewhere overhead. She stopped pedalling and scanned the skyline. Large white clouds billowed up into a blue sky, making it difficult to identify the plane. Suddenly, the noise intensified and the plane swooped low from behind the house, skimming the roof of Hope Cottage and nearly causing Evie to tumble from her bike.

She watched the small plane, clearly a fighter of some sort, soar up into the sky and disappear behind a towering cloud. Moments later it reappeared and seemed to be preparing to dive bomb the cottage. Evie assumed it must be a German attack – possibly the beginning of the feared invasion. She threw herself from the bike, taking refuge in a wet ditch by the side of the road. Muddy water rose up her stockings as the plane dived low and then roared above her head. She waited for the explosion but none came. When she looked again, the plane appeared to roll in the sky and then disappear to the west.

She crawled out of the ditch, squirming as the cold muddy water ran down her legs. She picked up the bike and walked with it the last hundred yards to the cottage. Leaning the bike against a tree in the front garden, she made her way into the parlour where Jack was sitting in his wheelchair.

"Did you see that bloody stupid pilot, Uncle Jack? He dive bombed our house and made me jump into a ditch. I thought he was going to bomb us. Just my luck the ditch was full of water. Look at me now. Can we write to somebody and complain? He should be court martialed."

"I think that might have been Peter," Jack replied sheepishly.

"Peter? Who's bloody Peter?"

"Peter's my nephew."

"Your nephew? I didn't know you had a nephew. In fact, I didn't think you had any relatives."

Evie was removing her wet stockings as she spoke, revealing two shapely and athletic legs.

"I thought your brother was dead – killed in the war."

"He was. But before he signed up he'd got a local girl into trouble. I'm sure it was his intention to marry her after the war but, of course, he never came back."

"So what happened to the baby?"

"The girl's parents put him up for adoption. There was nothing my parents could do. They couldn't look after a baby at their age."

"So how did you make contact again – with Peter – after so many years?"

"A letter – out of the blue. Seems Peter had been adopted by an older couple in Birmingham. He'd been brought up well but then they'd died. Peter decided that he wanted to find his real family. He did a bit of research, tracked me down and we started writing. A week ago he told me he'd been posted to that new aerodrome at Coltishall. He's in the RAF – a pilot. He had to deliver a new Hurricane and said he'd fly over the house as he passed. Didn't say anything about dive bombing."

The arrival of a new man on the scene was worthy of attention. Evie spent most of her time bemoaning the fact that Frampton was such a sleepy and lifeless place. At eighteen, she had developed a keen and sometimes precocious interest in men and was distraught that the few she felt worthy of her attention had signed up for military service. She desperately wanted to join the armed forces too but her father had made it clear that she had duties at home. Jack's health was failing fast and she was required to provide care for him, something she found unpleasant and stifling.

"So, where's he staying?"

"I suppose he'll be staying on the base eventually but the accommodation isn't ready yet. He's asked if he could spend a week with us first. It appears he's got some leave to take now that he's finished his training."

"Well, it's a bit inconvenient isn't it, Uncle Jack?" Evie never liked to show enthusiasm in case it compromised her later. "I mean, this isn't a hotel. If he thinks I'm going to look after him and cook his meals and wash his clothes, he's got another thing coming."

"I'm sure he'll be happy to muck in, Evie. And your father's said it'll be OK."

"Oh well, that is alright then, isn't it?" she said with over dramatic irony.

"Perhaps you can introduce him to Emma."

"Why the hell should I introduce him to Emma?" Evie thought to herself as she made her way upstairs to change and brush the tangles out of her long auburn hair, inherited, she was told, from her mother. Emma was Evie's best friend. They had met years ago at school and teamed up because they were both bullied by other children. They discovered that they were stronger when they acted together and soon acquired a fearsome reputation for retribution if they were picked on.

Over the years their friendship had grown strong and they had supported each other through many trials. Emma's mother, Flora, worked for Jed in the construction business. Evie knew that they had been friends for many years but Flora never visited their house and Evie was seldom invited to theirs. Jed, however, seemed to spend long hours in Flora's company at work and would even go back to her house sometimes to continue working in the evening.

"Evie, Evie, I need you. Can you come down please?"

Evie tensed as she heard Jack calling her. She detested playing the role of nurse and found it degrading to have to help Jack go to the toilet.

"Coming, Uncle Jack."

Jack was now confined to his wheelchair, unable to walk more than a few paces without assistance. It was nearly twenty years since he had been told by the doctor in London that he would be dead within three to five years. But his condition had stabilised and in the first ten years new medications, improved diet and the country air had enabled him to play a full role with Jed in bringing up Evie. The last ten years, however, had seen a faster decline as his lungs slowly gave up. Now, his presence in the house and his constant demands were a source of irritation to Evie who had acquired a reputation for her short temper and restless moods. Over the years that Jack and Jed had struggled to raise Evie together, there had been plenty of confrontations and acrimony, but slowly the two men had built a trusting relationship which both felt owed much to their separate memories of Alice and their promises made to her in the days before she died.

It was six o'clock and the summer sun was still high in the sky. Jed stood at the office window watching the activity in the yard. He employed over twenty men now and most were busy tidying away equipment and preparing tools for the next day's work. He ran his eyes along the line of parked vehicles, open trucks, tractors, diggers and bulldozers. At the far end was his first truck, the old Austin. It seldom left the yard these days but Jed liked to keep it. It reminded him of the early days when he was struggling to build the business and it reminded him too of Alice. He'd come to terms with her death now and filtered out the bad memories. And he only had to look at Evie with her slim build and flowing auburn hair to be reminded of her each day.

"Jed, I think you should sign this before we go."

He turned to see that Flora had come into his office brandishing some papers. Her appearance brought a warm smile to his face. This was where his life was focused now. All these years Flora had refused to marry him but they had become close. She had turned out to be an excellent office manager and Jed relied heavily upon her.

"What is it, Flora? Can it wait till tomorrow?"

"It's the work schedule for the new military buildings up at the hall. They want them by tomorrow morning."

With the coming of the war, work had escalated dramatically. New aerodromes were being built, port installations constructed and military bases carved out of virgin country. The work schedule was for new office and residential accommodation at the local manor, acquired by the Ministry of War for a highly secretive project. Jed had no idea what was going on up there but the level of security entailed all of his men being put through weeks of screening before being allowed onto the site.

"OK, you'd better let me read it first. What shall we do after? Can I come back to your place?"

He saw a knowing smile pass briefly over her face. She knew what he meant. They had been lovers for over five years. It had taken time. After Jed had rescued Flora and Emma from the slavery into which they had been incarcerated, Flora had suffered a breakdown. Knowing who the father of her child was and living close to him yet not being able to tell her child the truth was a very great burden for Flora. Slowly though, and with patient support from Jed, she recovered and came to terms with her situation. As she began to work for Jed, her confidence increased and eventually they slept together, though she made it plain she wouldn't marry Jed whilst Jack was alive.

"I'll cook you a meal but you can't stay. Emma will be home."

Jed watched Flora as she prepared the documents for signing. She had lost some of her youthful freshness but had acquired a comfortable and mature look which Jed found very reassuring. In bed, he had found with Flora a freedom and exhilaration that Alice had denied him.

There were no targets or goals. They simply rejoiced in the intimacy of their love making and the enjoyment it gave to them both.

The following Friday, Evie left work at four in the afternoon. She and Emma planned to go to a dance at a nearby military base where there was bound to be a good selection of soldiers newly posted to the region and keen to meet the local female population. They normally spent the weekends together and Emma would often stay over at Hope Cottage.

As Evie negotiated the last of the pot holes in Duck Lane, she looked up and saw an unfamiliar blue sports car parked outside the cottage. On closer inspection, she saw that it had the MG mark on the front grill. She guessed it must belong to Peter. Momentarily, she toyed with the idea of creeping round the back of the house to avoid him. She had been looking forward to soaking in a bath before going out for the evening. But the idea of being forced to act furtively in her own home by this new interloper was unappealing and so, having propped the bike against the usual tree, she braced herself for introductions.

She heard voices from the sitting room and made her way there. Jack was in his wheelchair and sitting opposite him was a very young fresh faced man in an RAF uniform. His dark hair flopped over his forehead and he sported a small clipped moustache on his upper lip. "To make him look older," thought Evie to herself. He was about five foot eleven and had a slim build.

"Ah, Evie, my dear," spluttered Jack, coughing mucus into a large white handkerchief. "I'm glad you're back. Come in and meet Peter."

Evie extended her hand as she moved into the room. It was taken enthusiastically and shaken like a puppy playing with a slipper.

"I'm so pleased to meet you," he announced. "Uncle Jack has been telling me all about you. I understand that you look after him very well."

"I'm not his nurse, you know," replied Evie defensively.

"Oh, I know you're not. But I'm sure Uncle Jack appreciates everything you do for him."

There was a short embarrassed silence as Evie sought to change the conversation.

"You're just out of training then?"

"That's right. I was sent down from Manchester to deliver a Hurricane. Then I'm going to join my new squadron – 242 Squadron. They're based at Coltishall now."

"So you haven't seen any action yet?"

"Not yet – but I think we will soon. Hitler's amassing an invasion army on the French coast and we're going to knock the hell out of them."

"I hear the German Luftwaffe have got more planes than the RAF. You may have quite a battle on your hands."

"Oh, we'll take whatever they throw at us and whip their backsides too. Once the RAF gets to work on them I reckon the war will only last a few more months."

"Well, I admire your enthusiasm, Peter, unrealistic as it may be. But you must excuse me, I'm going to take the dance floor by storm tonight so I must go and put my battle dress on."

With that, Evie turned and left the room.

"What's wrong, Uncle Jack – something I said?" asked Peter.

"Oh, our Evie's quite a feisty young lady, Peter. Got a mind of her own she has. To be honest with you, she's a bit of a handful for me and Jed. When she gets together with that Emma, they're a force to be reckoned with."

"Who's Emma?" asked Peter.

"She's the daughter of Jed's office manager. Mother and daughter live together on the other side of town."

"No father then?"

"No, no father. Can you help me to the toilet, Peter? Better not disturb Evie now."

"Have you worked out what they're doing up at Manston Hall yet, Jed?" called Flora from the kitchenette.

"I think it's to do with some special warfare unit. There's a lot of young navy types up there and they're often bussed up to the coast. Rumours are that it's to do with landing soldiers from submarines."

Jed finished clearing the table and joined Flora in the kitchenette. The house was small but cosy. By normal standards it was modern with a small cooking range and a coke boiler to heat the water. It had its own individual lavatory outside the back door and two small bedrooms upstairs. Jed was proud of the development. It was one of the first public housing projects in this part of the country and enabled many families from rural slums to be rehoused. Flora had been one of the first tenants to move in. The chief engineer had little difficulty persuading the appropriate official.

"You're not going to kick me out tonight then," said Jed as he placed his hands around Flora's waist.

"Emma's at your place, I think, so we've got the house to ourselves. But if you snore again, you're going to sleep in Emma's room."

"It's not sleep I'm thinking about. Get up those stairs!"

Emma's arrival at Hope Cottage was, as usual, like a typhoon hitting land.

Her coat never quite reached the hook in the hall and her shoes parted company with her feet seconds after entering the house. On meeting Peter, her verbal rhetoric knew no limits.

"Oh, are you Peter? You must be. I mean you look like a pilot. That funny little moustache. Not that yours is funny, just that I've seen pictures of pilots with funny little moustaches. So what do you fly? Oh, I know it's aeroplanes. But what sort of aeroplanes? Are they bombers and have you dropped any on Germany yet because ..."

"You must be Emma," Peter eventually managed to say. "You're Evie's friend."

"Yes, that's right. We're off out. Do you want to come?"

"Where are you going?"

"There's a dance at this new base just outside Cromer. There's an open invitation for local girls."

"Well, I guess that excludes me then."

"Oh God, yes," replied Emma. "I suppose it does."

"But I can take you two girls in my car, if you'd like."

"Would you really do that?"

"It'd be my pleasure."

"Oh Evie," shouted Emma rushing from the room and bounding up the stairs. "I've fixed us a lift – with the pilot."

Flora's bed was small and soft – rather like a nest. Jed loved the intimate contact it provided as their bodies wrapped around each other's contours. They made love in the same way they always did. There was no need to prove anything to each other. Afterwards, they lay close together, limbs wrapped in a contented tangle.

"Will you marry me?" asked Jed.

"You always ask me that and the answer's always the same. Not whilst we're both living a lie. I can't do it, Jed. Could you imagine me coming to live in your house with Jack? It'd be insane. Two girls, both fathered by him but neither of them knowing he's their father."

"I'm not sure he's got long to live, he can hardly get out of his chair now."

"You've been saying that for years. Anyway, it's not about Jack dying, it's about the truth getting out, because one day it will and then we'll both have a lot of explaining to do. Have you thought about that?"

It was early evening and Peter accelerated the blue MG 18/80 through the country lanes en route to Cromer. He said little, concentrating on holding the car to the road as he raced it round tight bends. Evie sat by his side, occasionally stealing a glance at his preoccupied face. Emma was on the bench seat at the back, holding down her clothes to prevent the wind ripping them from her body. Talking was almost impossible because of the noise.

"She's got a lovely ..., don't you think?"

"What?" yelled Evie.

"It's a two point five cc in line ..."

"What's in line?"

"The cylinders. Six in line."

"Wow, that's great!"

To Evie he seemed immature. She hadn't much experience of boyfriends but she'd had a few dates, usually with men in their mid twenties, often farm hands or labourers. They were usually silent types, serious and with little conversation. She hadn't met anyone like Peter before with his boyish enthusiasm and boundless optimism.

They found the base easily on the outskirts of Cromer. It was a newly constructed site for an infantry regiment. Nissan huts stood in long rows behind barbed wire. Two armed guards stood at the entrance. Peter pulled the car into the side of the road some distance from the gate to let the girls out.

"I expect they'd let you in, Peter," Emma called out as she jumped from the back of the car. "We could have a word with the sentries."

"No, Emma, thanks. This is their dance and they won't want intruders. If you like, I'll pick you both up later."

"Don't worry," replied Evie. "We'll get the last train back."

"It's no problem."

"Oh, why not, Evie?" said Emma, rushing to join in the conversation. "It's a twenty minute walk from here to the station.

We'll have to leave about eleven thirty. I don't expect Peter would mind if he picked us up at, say, twelve thirty – would you, Peter?"

"Well, I suppose not."

"That's it then. See you here at twelve thirty, Peter. Come on, Evie, the band's already playing."

The recent arrival in the area of thousands of extra soldiers and airmen had dramatically improved the social opportunities for young women like Evie and Emma. With no shortage of men, they danced away the night to the sounds of a big band from London and drank copious amounts of martini. By the end of the evening, both had teamed up with young soldiers and when the lights in the mess went on at midnight, they drifted out with many other couples to say their goodbyes beyond the perimeter fence.

The war and impending action had already induced a sense of reckless disregard for conventional behaviour and values. Lined up along the outside of the fence were more than twenty couples locked into passionate embraces. Evie's 'Tom', a former plasterer from London and a 'whiz' on the dance floor, was getting carried away. His hands were sliding up Evie's legs and she was beginning to push away from him, desperate to disengage her lips from his. Smudges of bright red lipstick were smeared across their faces as the struggle intensified.

"Hey, you – soldier. Leave that woman alone!"

Tom released his hold and stared uncomprehendingly in the direction of the voice. Evie did the same. Over the road, standing by the blue MG, was Peter.

"Just keep your hands off that woman. That's not on, doing that sort of thing in public."

"Peter, what are you doing?" exclaimed Evie. "Go away. I can look after myself."

"You heard what the lady said," echoed Tom, moving across the road to where Peter was standing. "Move your scrawny RAF body out of my sight before I move it for you."

Evie didn't like what was happening. Peter looked as if he'd never thrown a punch whereas Tom was brought up in the East End of London and had been fighting for most of his life.

"Just mind your manners, that's all," said Peter, backing away towards the car.

Evie noticed that other soldiers were breaking away from their embraces and moving towards the scene of the confrontation.

"Manners. I'll teach you some fucking manners!" And with that, Tom threw a punch that landed heavily on Peter's face and knocked him into the car. All hell was let loose after that. Soldiers were running from all directions. Suddenly, Emma was by Evie's side.

"Get in the car. We must go. Quick!"

Tom, surprised by Peter's fall into the car, was squaring up for another punch but was knocked off balance by Evie and Emma jumping into the MG.

"Get going, Peter!" yelled Emma.

Tom delivered a glancing blow into the car, hitting Evie on the shoulder and knocking her to the floor. With a roar and a screech of tyres, the car exploded into life and shot forward towards the line of advancing soldiers. Peter managed to take control of the wheel and executed a hand brake turn. More soldiers were advancing from the opposite direction so he aimed the car for a small gap in their lines.

Driving up onto the embankment and using the hill to his advantage, he slipped through the gap and sped off in the opposite direction.

Once they were well away from the camp, Peter pulled onto the verge to help Evie off the floor.

"What was that all about then?" she demanded angrily.

"He was groping you. He had his hands up your skirt."

"That's none of your business and you had no right to interfere. He was ten times the size of you and could have killed you."

"I felt responsible for you," protested Peter. "I brought you both here and I was taking you back. How could I have looked Uncle Jack in the eye if I'd just left you to it?"

"You're not my keeper. In fact, you're nothing to me, Peter. Just drive us home."

The rest of the journey took place in awkward silence, save for the roar of the wind gusting over the open roof of the MG. When they got to Hope Cottage, Emma, who was suffering the after effects of the martini, made her way straight to bed, leaving Evie and Peter alone in the parlour. Peter broke the silence.

"Look, I really am sorry if I acted a bit out of place. I suppose I just didn't like what he was doing to you."

"It was none of your business what he was doing to me. I can't stand people trying to control me," Evie replied petulantly.

"I admire your spirit. I think it's important to be a free thinker."

"Don't patronise me."

Peter paused and looked uncomfortably at the floor.

"Evie, I would really like to have a conversation with you but we don't seem to have any point of contact. It's a shame. I really like you."

"Then try harder," she replied in a challenging tone.

"Erm, tell me about yourself," Peter stammered awkwardly. "What sort of person are you?" Evie sighed and replied in a monosyllabic voice.

"I'm eighteen. Got no mother, brought up by two men – probably damaged me for life. Boring job, part time nurse – dull, dull, dull."

"What about boyfriends?"

"I find most men boring too. They just want to grope me."

"Do you find me boring?"

"Well, so far I have to admit you haven't been boring, what with dive bombing our house and taking on the entire British infantry single handed. No, you're not boring – just stupid."

"Oh," replied Peter disconsolately, searching for something to say that didn't sound stupid.

"Don't take it personally," added Evie with an artificial brightness to her voice. "I'm just screwed up."

"Well, in that case you need someone to talk to. What about Emma, she's your friend?"

"Emma's screwed up as well. She doesn't know who her father is. Mother won't tell her. Sometimes we feel like sisters – almost think alike. But I couldn't talk to her about things."

"Why not?"

"I don't understand them myself. I don't know why I'm like I am."

There was a pause whilst Evie poured tea from a pot on the stove.

"What do you remember about your mother?" asked Peter.

"A bit. I can remember playing by her bed when she was ill. I can remember looking at her just after she had died. I thought how beautiful she looked – like Sleeping Beauty."

"Were you happy?"

"I think I was happy. I had a mother, a father and a doting uncle. But I have this strange feeling that all wasn't well. I remember Daddy often looking sad. And I remember Mummy and Uncle Jack laughing together a lot. It didn't mean anything to me then but in recent years ..."

Evie's voice tailed off.

"Go on. Tell me what you've been thinking."

"I've just started to wonder about Uncle Jack being in the house all that time. I mean, it's a bit strange having a permanent lodger living in the house. I know it was because he was ill and Mum and Dad needed the money. But I've started to get this feeling that there's a lot I don't know."

"You could be just imagining it," replied Peter thoughtfully.

"I'll tell you something that almost no one else knows," continued Evie. "Before my mother died, she wrote me a letter to open on each birthday until I'm twenty five. She gives me a little bit of advice, the sort of things a mother might say if she was here. And in these letters I think she's hinting at something. It's almost as if she's preparing me."

"Why don't you open them all and see?"

"No, I won't do that. In the very first letter she makes me promise to only open each letter on the birthday it's meant for. If she was preparing me for something I've got to wait until the right time."

There was another pause whilst they both sipped tea.

"Have you told anybody else these things?" asked Peter.

"No, only you. And I don't know why I've done that. I feel embarrassed now. I'd better go to bed."

"Don't feel embarrassed. I'm pleased you told me. I'm pleased you trusted me."

Evie smiled and finished her tea.

"It's late. I'll see you in the morning." She kissed him lightly on the cheek and brushed past him on her way to the stairs. A shiver of anticipation ran through his body.

Alone in her room, Evie felt disturbed by the night's events. Whilst Peter had been reckless at the military camp, he had an inner maturity which she had only just recognised. He was the first person she had spoken to about these issues and she couldn't understand what had led her to open up in this way. She hoped he hadn't been too hurt by her earlier feckless comments. Her mind dwelt on the things she had discussed with Peter.

Evie reached across to the silver trinket box that Jed had bought her to keep the letters in. This was her most treasured possession, her one link to the person who could help her understand. She took the key from its hiding place in a small vase and opened the lock. Inside was a neat row of folded letters. At the end of the row were seven remaining unopened envelopes. Evie took the last opened letter and read it once more.

Hello, my darling,

Today you are eighteen and you are quite a grown woman. It will seem a long time since I left you now. I wonder what your world is like. I expect it's very different from the one I knew. It's strange writing to you knowing that you will be eighteen when you read this. As I write this letter you are five and you are playing at the foot of my bed with your rag doll. You're a very pretty little girl but you're strong willed and impetuous. How will you manage these qualities when you're older?

Evie wiped tears from her eyes. She knew she was strong willed and impetuous. It was her way of surviving, her way of keeping control when life seemed to overwhelm her. Without a mother there were whole areas of her life she hadn't been able to discuss. Jed and Jack were loving and caring but they couldn't understand the turbulent emotions of a teenage girl.

There are still things I want to tell you so that you understand more about me and more about yourself. But the time is not yet right. I want to prepare you, though. Let me just say this. At eighteen you may have experienced, or you may be about to experience, a relationship with a man. This will present you with many different powerful emotions – love, loyalty, desire and possibly despair. But the strongest of all emotions is passion. It's powerful because it comes not from the mind but from the heart, deep inside of you. It lacks the logic of the other emotions yet is has the power to drive your destiny forward in unexpected ways. You can't avoid passion if it comes your way but be ready for the chaos it brings with it. Passion is difficult to identify until it has engulfed you. It can cause you to destroy those things that you hold dear whilst at the same seducing your entire being with sublime joy. Passion has many faces, my darling, and I urge you to beware.

But I believe you are strong and whilst you will face many dilemmas, as I have done, you will eventually rise above the turmoil.

Your ever loving mother, Alice

Evie tried to imagine what her mother was telling her. Her relationships so far had involved few of the emotions her mother spoke of. She craved attention. She wanted to be liked, to be asked out and to be seen on the arm of a man. But none of this was to do with love or desire. And passion – this was a word that meant nothing to Evie. She had kissed men hard with her mouth open and their tongues interlocking – but was this passion? Evie hoped not. So what had caused this introspection? What had happened that had made her want to connect again with her mother? There was something about Peter that had struck a chord but she didn't yet know what. She hoped she hadn't burnt her boats.

Evie got up late the next morning to discover that the car had gone. She was puzzled. She thought Peter was staying until Sunday before returning to his base.

"What's happened to Peter?" she asked Jack, as she was brewing tea in the parlour.

"He left early, about six o'clock. There was a telegram waiting here for him when he got back last night. He's being recalled early to Coltishall. There's some sort of emergency. Seems the Germans are trying to bomb the airfields and obliterate the RAF before they try to invade us. I think it's serious, Evie."

The reason for Peter's early recall soon became clear. From mid July, the BBC was announcing a series of German raids on shipping convoys in the channel. British and other Allied fighters were engaged in heavy dog fights with German Stukas to keep shipping flowing freely. Jack had received a brief letter from Peter thanking the family for their hospitality. One line stood out for Evie.

Please tell Evie how much I enjoyed talking to her and I'm looking forward to many more thought provoking chats in the future.

In mid August, the focus of the German attacks changed to bombing British airfields in the lead up to the anticipated invasion. Like many people, Jack, Jed and Evie remained glued to the radio, listening to the progress of the battle. August 15th was an especially bad day. The news was sombre.

Here is the news, and this is Alvar Lidell reading it. Today, August 15th, has seen the greatest number of raids so far by the German Luftwaffe on British airbases and coastal defences. British and other Allied fighters have been relentless in their pursuit and destruction of enemy aircraft. Out of 115 bombers and 35 fighters sent, 16 bombers and 7 fighters were destroyed.

The battles continued over the south of England for the next few days, reaching a climax on August 18th when losses on both sides were at their greatest.

This is the six o'clock news. Today has seen intense fighting in the skies over the south of Britain. Allied Spitfires and Hurricanes repeatedly repulsed wave after wave of attacking German bombers.

Evie listened with mounting concern as casualties rose, not knowing whether Peter had become one of those statistics. Then after the 18th, the raids suddenly seemed to subside, caused partly by the poor weather and partly by the exhaustion of pilots on both sides. It was enough for the British Prime Minister, Winston Churchill, to address the nation and talk of the 'tide turning'.

The gratitude of every home in our island, in our Empire, and indeed throughout the world, except in the abodes of the guilty, goes out to the British airmen who, undaunted by odds, unwearied in their constant challenge and mortal danger, are turning the tide of the world war by their prowess and by their devotion. Never in the field of human conflict was so much owed by so many to so few.

During this period of intense fighting, nothing was heard from Peter. Jed knew from his military contacts that the Hurricanes and Spitfires from Coltishall were flying every day and that the pilots were near to exhaustion. He also knew that many new pilots were being shot down within days of entering service. On August 22nd, a letter arrived.

Dear Uncle Jack, Jed and Evie,

I was shot down last Thursday. I'm in hospital but don't worry. I'm going to be alright but it will take a little time. I was hit over Kent by a Messerschmitt. The engine lost power and I had to come down in a field. Unfortunately, the field had been ploughed so the plane didn't land very well. In fact, it crashed. I now have two fractured legs. They say I'll be in here for four weeks and then I'll be fit to fly again. I'll try to visit you briefly before I'm redeployed.

With best wishes to you all,

Peter

Everyone felt tremendous relief. Evie was surprised by the degree to which she was elated. For the first time since Peter had departed, she felt ready to write him a letter.

Dearest Peter,

We've all been following the battles, listening to our little radio in the parlour. It's terrible that you've been shot down but I'm so happy you're alive.

I feel that we didn't get off to a very good start when you visited us recently. I think I was a bit too opinionated and, to be honest with you, I thought you were a bit smug. Anyhow, I did enjoy our conversations and hope we can have more of them.

I hope you can visit us again when you're better.

With much affection,

Evie

Four weeks later, on her way back from work, Evie spied a Spitfire swoop low again over Hope Cottage and perform a victory roll. This time she didn't fall off her bike, but whoopeed with joy instead and waved frantically at the plane.

Later that same evening, Evie heard the sound of the MG revving outside the house. Pulling off her apron, she rushed outside to greet Peter. He was already out of the car and walking towards her. Without thinking, she rushed forward to throw her arms around him, only realising at the last minute that this was probably presumptuous of her. As a result, she tripped prompting Peter to reach out and catch her, causing them both to fall and end up in a tangled heap.

"This is some greeting, Evie!" exclaimed Peter from underneath his cap which had fallen over his face. "A peck on the cheek would have been fine."

"I'm so sorry, Peter. I was just glad to see you're safe. I didn't mean to ... I mean, I didn't want to ..." stammered Evie.

"Hold on, hold on," replied Peter. "I've had your greeting, now it's time for mine." And with that he removed his cap and kissed Evie firmly on the lips. "You see, when you're being chased by German dive bombers and you think your time's up, you promise yourself that if you get out of this mess you're not going to hang around being timid. You've just got to get on and do what you want to do quickly, before it's too late. So, I resolved to come here and kiss you, Evie. And, by God, I'm glad I've done it."

"I don't know what to say," replied Evie, breathlessly. "I just know that I'm so pleased to see you safe. How long are you staying?"

"I tell you what. I'll answer that when we get up off the ground and go inside. Is that a deal?"

Jack was sleeping when they got inside so Evie and Peter had time to talk. Evie felt that she detected a change in Peter – less arrogance and more introspection.

"We were glued to the radio every day, Peter, listening to the news. We'd cheer every time they announced more German losses."

"It wasn't just German losses though, Evie. We lost hundreds of young British lads too, killed or maimed. I count myself lucky to have been shot down early and survived. If I'd gone another week I'm sure I'd have died. It was statistically inevitable."

"How do you cope with the fear up there, the thought that each minute might be your last?"

"A lot of the time you don't think. You just do what you've been trained to do. But it's strange up there in a Spitfire. When you're not being shot at or chasing Heinkels, you can feel quite detached from the world below. You're kind of in between the real world and whatever else there may be afterwards. It gets you thinking about what matters and what is just vanity."

"And what does matter?"

"People matter. You matter, Evie." He took her in his arms and kissed her, pulling her body close to his.

"This is happening so fast, Peter. I'm confused."

"It must happen fast, Evie. I've only got two days. I've got to report back to Coltishall on Sunday. I'm being posted abroad."

"Why, where are you going?" asked Evie anxiously. "I thought you were needed to defend Britain."

"They reckon the threat of an invasion's gone now. Hitler failed to get control of the skies so an invasion is too dangerous. The war's taking place on lots of different fronts, Evie. They're sending me to Singapore."

That night, they dined quietly at Hope Cottage. The celebration they had all anticipated to welcome Peter home was overshadowed by the news of his imminent departure. After the meal, Peter and Evie walked in the receding light of the setting sun, down Duck Lane and into the pastures beyond. It was a quiet evening save for the gentle lowing of cattle in the distance. The harvest had been gathered and the countryside looked verdant in the orange glow cast by the last of the sun's rays. They stopped by a large oak tree and kissed again, this time longer and with passion.

"Do you want to make love to me, Peter?" asked Evie, looking hesitantly into his eyes. "I mean, with you going away and not knowing what's in store. I just didn't want you to feel that you couldn't ask."

Peter looked at her without smiling and ran his hand through the wisps of auburn hair that hung over her face.

"I do want to make love to you, Evie, but I'm not going to. I do want to very much but if I die you will have a different future and I won't be part of it. I don't want you to allow me into your life now and then have to find ways of cutting me out again later. If I return, Evie, I will seek you out and pursue you relentlessly. But if I don't return you must be free to pursue another life."

Peter was due to return to Coltishall the next afternoon. In the morning, he and Evie took a final walk together out towards Offa's Mount. From the top of the escarpment, they gazed in silence at the green pastures bathed in warm sunlight that were spread out below.

"This is how I want to remember England, Evie, and this is how I want to remember you – just you and me, alone together, looking down on this piece of England."

They promised to write when they could but both understood that they might be apart for a long time. After he had gone, Evie felt a great void developing inside her and a simmering anger that her life was once more outside of her control.

Peter sent a letter before he departed for Singapore in September and then again when he arrived in early January 1942 having spent weeks waiting in Gibraltar for a passage. Evie detected a note of reticence and caution in his words, maybe mindful of the fact that letters were heavily censored.

I arrived at ▇▇g airport on Tuesday where I joined ▇▇ Squadron. There are 42 of us new recruits. The island seems to be full of ▇▇▇▇ and ▇▇▇▇ as well as Brits. An invasion by the ▇▇▇▇ is expected soon. ▇▇▇▇ has already fallen to them and large numbers of British soldiers taken prisoner.

I'll try to write again soon.

All my love,

Peter

Again Evie spent much of her time listening to the radio in the parlour as news of the Japanese invasion of Malaya was relayed back home.

Yesterday, 31st January, Allied forces in the Far East were forced to hand over control of Malaya to the Imperial Japanese Army. As a final act of defiance, the causeway linking Malaya with Singapore was blown up by British engineers.

In early February came the news that Evie dreaded.

Reports from Singapore suggest that the Japanese invasion of the island has begun. A first wave of 4,000 troops landed in the Australian sector at first light yesterday. Their advance is being fiercely resisted by heroic action from Allied airmen who are attacking Japanese lines around the clock.

Throughout February, reports of Japanese advances were broadcast most days. It seemed that the end was inevitable. On February 15th normal programmes were interrupted with the following broadcast:

It has just been reported that the Allied garrison in Singapore has surrendered to the Imperial Japanese Army. The garrison's commander, Lieutenant–General Arthur Percival, formally surrendered to the Japanese Commander–in–Chief at a quarter past five local time yesterday.

Evie was stunned. She hadn't heard a word from Peter since his arrival in Singapore. She knew there had been heavy losses amongst Allied air crew and it was now clear that many thousands of Allied soldiers would been taken prisoner by the Japanese. She knew there were international rules on the treatment of prisoners of war and hoped that Peter would be placed somewhere safe away from hostilities.

February 1942 was bleak. It had rained constantly since early January. Jed had to put much of his building work on hold as the ground was too waterlogged to take vehicles. Friday, 27th was particularly bleak. Gales howled inland from the North Sea and rain lashed at the windows of Hope Cottage. Jed returned home at lunch time from the office and sat in the sitting room staring desolately at building plans. He heard the sound of an engine stopping outside and looked to see who had ventured out in this weather. His body froze. A young man in a peaked cap with a brown cape was getting off his motor bike. A khaki bag hung by his side. Jed's mind immediately flashed back to a similar scene twenty five years ago – a scene that had changed his life.

The harsh rap at the door jolted him back to the present. He opened the door and looked vacantly at the young courier.

"Telegram for you, sir," he said, knowing full well what the contents were. He saluted, turned on his heels and walked quickly back to his bike.

Jed stared at the damp envelope. It was addressed to Jack Malikov Esquire. He closed the door and walked slowly up the stairs to Jack's room. Jack was lying on his bed, breathing in long rasping gasps.

"I've got a telegram, Jack. It's just come. It's addressed to you."

"You open it, Jed. I know what it is. We both know."

Jed tore open the envelope and took out the telegram.

"You read it, Jed. My eyes aren't so good."

"It's from the Air Ministry.

Deeply regret to inform that your nephew, Flying Officer Peter Malikov, is reported as missing, presumed dead. His aircraft is believed to have been shot down off the coast of Singapore. The Air Council professes its extreme sympathy."

Jed sat on the bed by the side of Jack and held him whilst he wept. Tragedy seemed finally to have brought them to a point of reconciliation that neither could have anticipated in happier times.

"How do we tell Evie?" Jack whispered. "This'll destroy her, Jed."

The Guest Who Stayed: Chapter 20 – Summer 1942

After Peter's reported loss, Evie was plunged into despair. In spite of her relationship with Peter being so short, it had changed her in fundamental ways. She had enjoyed their intimate conversations and the feeling that nothing between them was barred. In their short time together they had discussed everything and nothing. But it wasn't what they had discussed that mattered. It was the fact that for the first time Evie found the confidence to reveal her own inner thoughts and fears to another person. She hadn't thought she could ever fall in love with a type like Peter with his affected RAF ways but she knew now that this was wrong.

After six weeks of reclusive living and much self pity, Evie woke up one morning having buried the hurt deep within herself. She announced to Jed that she would be supporting the war effort from now on and that he would have to employ a nurse for Jack. Her days of tending to his increasingly demanding needs were over.

Evie had planned to join the WAAF or the ATS but a local advertisement recruiting civilian secretaries for a new airbase not far from Frampton made her decide to explore that option first. She made the journey in Peter's blue MG. As his executor, Jack had decided that Evie should have the car, a generous act but one which left Evie feeling the loss of Peter every time she ventured out in it.

RAF Oulton was a small airfield with a grass landing strip. It had been constructed as hostilities began in 1939 and was home to a squadron of Blenheims of Bomber Command. Evie provided secretarial and administrative services to the station's commander, a quiet but daunting man with a short temper. She was soon fully absorbed in the life of the base and a succession of relationships with airmen followed. But most were short lived. In bombing raids over Germany, losses were heavy and there were many occasions when Evie waited in vain at the airfield for an airman to return, only to find out later that he had been shot down or ditched in the sea.

The effect on Evie was to make her feel that the old world she had known before the war had disappeared. Now, nothing was as it seemed. What was worthwhile and good one day was a mere memory the next. Life was for living one day at a time. The future and the past became irrelevant.

In 1943 concrete runways were laid down at RAF Oulton and the US Air Force arrived to share the base. The 803rd Bombardment Squadron was stationed at the airfield. The drone of their massive Flying Fortresses and Liberators became a common sound across the flat Norfolk countryside. The influx of airmen and technicians from across the Atlantic became a great source of interest for Evie and for Emma, who had also secured a job at the base. These American airmen spoke differently, were usually gregarious and outgoing. They chewed gum, swore loudly and dated with fervour. There was a succession of men, each with a different story.

Rick was from Saskatchewan. He was a navigator. At home he lived on a ranch and rode horses. His family had lived on their piece of land since arriving as settlers in the 1850s.

"You know, Evie, when I'm out on them prairies, just me and my horse, that's when I feel truly alive. Galloping full out across them grasslands, whooping and shrieking like the devil himself were behind me. Then at night, I'll lay me by a stream and stare up at that inky black sky full of sparkling jewels just glinting down at me. And then I know that I know nothing. But you know, it don't bother me. I just feel so happy being there, being part of something so beautiful and so incredible."

Rick died in early 1944 when his Liberator was shot down over Bremen.

Luke was black. Evie thought him the most handsome man she'd ever met. He was tall and broad shouldered with a deep baritone voice and he would occasionally sing to her – songs from his homeland in Alabama. Evie didn't understand at first why other airmen seemed to be avoiding her, sniggering when she was in his company or calling out names.

"It's different where I come from, Evie. If you's black then you can't do the same things as white folks."

"What can't you do?"

"Well, you can't sit on a bus with a white person. If you's black you gotta sit at the back. Front is reserved for white folks. And you can't stand in the same queue as a white person. They got their own queues and they gets served first."

"But why, I don't understand why? What's wrong with being black?"

"White people just don't think we're as good as them. They call us monkeys and niggers. But I think it's goin' to change with this war. We're fighting and dying alongside white soldiers. When I go back to my home in Alabama, I just know it's going to be different. People is goin' to respect us blacks."

Luke was transferred to an infantry regiment in March 1944 and moved to the south of England in preparation for the D–Day landings. Evie never saw or heard from him again.

Warren was a pilot. He flew the giant B17 Flying Fortress bombers. He reminded Evie of Peter – floppy hair and easy manner. His home was in New England and his father was a banker. Warren had had a good childhood, brought up in a big house in Connecticut and sent to an expensive school. After the war, he would go to college and become a banker like his father. Warren excelled at everything. He was good at baseball. He could drink a pint faster than anyone else and he could make love with consummate skill.

"How was that, baby, eh? Bet you enjoyed that," he enquired, after a night in a hotel by the coast. "I read some of that stuff in a book. Really works, eh?"

He never made the senior echelons of the bank or the pretty whitewashed house in the Hamptons with the stunning wife and the two children and the labrador on the front lawn. He left it too late to eject when his Fortress was shot down over the Channel in December 1943. But due to his efforts, his crew did escape and were taken prisoner.

Evie developed a hard and impervious personality to cope with these losses. At home, Jed and Jack were increasingly at a loss to know how to handle her mood swings. She would not talk to them for days on end and then suddenly she would reappear, full of enthusiasm and zest for life – until the next airman was shot down. The 'live in' nurse often bore the brunt of Evie's sharp tongue, laced with some of the new American expletives that she had picked up at the airfield.

In the spring of 1944, it was clear that the war was moving into a new phase. Infantry regiments were moved south and bombing raids across France and Germany were stepped up. Jitterbugging to the sounds of American big bands in aircraft hangars that had been turned into party venues was now a thing of the past.

On 6th June, 1944 the Allied invasion of Europe began – D–Day, as it was known.

This is the BBC Home Service. Here is a special bulletin read by John Snagg.

D–Day has come. Early this morning, the Allies began the assault on the north western face of Hitler's European Fortress. The first official news came just after half past nine when Supreme Headquarters of the Allied Expeditionary Force issued communiqué no. 1. This said 'Under the command of General Eisenhower, Allied naval forces, supported by strong air forces, began landing Allied troops from this morning on the north coast of France'.

There was a palpable tension amongst people in the wet summer and autumn of 1944 as the Allied invasion progressed towards Germany. Victories reported on the radio were greeted with subdued excitement and setbacks with grim resignation. Evie worked long hours at the airbase as saturation bombing of German cities paved the way for Allied advances. Photographic records of the bombing showed whole cities alight like giant infernos. Amongst the air crews and the support staff at the base, the mood was sombre. Everyone realised that a terrible price was being paid by the German civilians caught up in the Armageddon. The bombing reached its peak between February

13th and 15th, 1945 when the city of Dresden was destroyed by Allied carpet bombing.

Through the spring of 1945 the mood of optimism began to increase as people dared to believe that an end to the war might be in sight. In February and March, Allied forces crossed the Rhine into Germany and Russian forces advanced rapidly from the east. On May 7th German forces on the western front finally surrendered unconditionally to Allied commanders.

Jed, Evie and Jack gathered round the small radio in the parlour to listen to the BBC's war correspondent, Thomas Cadett, report on the surrender proceedings from Rheims in north eastern France.

In the small hours of this morning, May 7th, 1945, I saw the formal acknowledgement by Germany's present leaders of their country's complete and utter defeat by land, in the air and at sea. The whole ceremony was carried out in a cold and business–like basis. If the sense of drama was there – and it was – it was because we carried it in our own hearts, remembering that this meant liberation, freedom from suffering and spared lives for countless thousands in tortured Europe.

That night, Evie and Emma joined an ecstatic throng of revellers in Frampton's market square. Young and old alike celebrated, hardly daring to believe that six years of war and hardship were finally over. An American military band played swing music and couples cavorted energetically late into the night.

Evie threw herself into the celebrations with exaggerated enthusiasm. Soldiers and airmen queued to kiss her, keen to feel the comfort of a woman again. She drank copiously and ended the night with Frank, an airman from Dakota. And that was all she could remember about him.

When she woke late the next morning, she felt herself in the grip of despair and desolation. Whilst the rest of Britain continued to party, Evie spent the day in bed, crying and nursing the scratches to her arms and thighs that she had somehow acquired the previous night.

After two days of celebration, Britain slowly recovered from its hangover and work resumed. Evie reported back to the airbase and submerged herself in duties. On her second day back she received a call from Emma.

"Evie, I need to talk to you. It's urgent. Can we meet off the base at lunchtime? How about that pub in Carlton? I'll see you at one."

Carlton was a small village with one pub about a mile from the airbase. It was a favourite haunt for air crew. Evie and Emma met in the snug, a small room usually frequented by courting couples.

"What's all this urgency, Emma?" demanded Evie.

"You know I've been seeing Samuel for some weeks now. We've been getting on really well and he's asked me to go back to America with him – to get married."

Evie had met Samuel a few times. He was a tall black airman who worked as an aircraft mechanic on the base. She had found him a little reserved and hadn't immediately taken to him.

"Emma, this is all so fast. You hardly know him. And have you thought about the problems?"

"What problems? I can't see any problems. It's such an opportunity, Evie. You've seen what the Americans are like. They've got big ideas, big personalities and big ambitions. America's a place of opportunities. I feel stifled here, Evie, I've got to go."

"But it's difficult for black people in America. They're discriminated against. If you marry a black man the same will happen to you too."

"No, it's alright. I've talked to Samuel about that. He says it'll all be different after the war. In Mississippi, where he comes from, Samuel says there's going to be good jobs and houses for the returning heroes. And there's lots of girls going from here, Evie. They're organising special GI bride ships to take us. I'm so excited."

Emma's announcement and imminent departure caused Evie to feel even more isolated. With American forces beginning to withdraw from their bases and return home, this corner of England that for a short period had seemed like a part of the United States, now began to return to its sleepy pre war ways. Gone were the swing bands, the raucous accents and the droning overhead of giant bombers – echoes now of a seemingly wild intrusion into the unhurried lives of this rural community.

When the end of the war in the Far East was announced on September 2nd, Evie stayed away from the giant street party being held in the market square. Instead, she walked the same route that she and Peter had taken the day before he had been posted to Singapore. She thought about their conversations, about their laughter and about the future they might have built together had Peter been joining the thousands of prisoners of war now starting on their long journey back home to the UK. Standing at the same place where she and Peter had kissed, she wished that she too could somehow die and put an end to the pointlessness of her life.

In mid October, Evie was told that her job at Oulton airbase would be finishing soon. Most Americans had left and RAF flights had been curtailed. It was planned to close the base within months. Sensing her loss of direction, Jed persuaded Evie to come and work for him at the construction company. Flora wanted to spend as much time as she could with Emma before she departed for America and so was more than happy to teach Evie the complexities of running the company.

Evie settled in well to the new job, quickly taking on additional site responsibilities and earning respect from the men who worked for Jed. She felt more at home in overalls and boots than she did wearing her pencil skirt and blouse on the airbase. At home, they were once again reduced to three as Jack's nurse had left for better paid work in Frampton.

The Christmas of 1945 at Hope Cottage was strangely quiet, as if it had somehow missed out on the tumultuous years that had reshaped the rest of the world. Jed and Jack spent time in the kitchen preparing the Christmas dinner. Their friendship in recent years had become close, with past animosities being set aside. Jack was no longer able to leave the house so Jed spent time with him talking or playing cards.

Evie slowly resigned herself to the new reality. She tried to dull down her expectations and accept what fate had delivered to her. If she lived each day as it came, not planning or thinking ahead, she found that she could cope.

After Christmas dinner, Jack, Jed and Evie turned on the radio to listen to the King's speech. In his clipped voice, he spoke about unity and family.

Wherever you are, serving in our wide, free Commonwealth of Nations, you will always feel at home. Though severed by the long sea miles of distance, you are still in the family circle.

As Jed and Jack dozed by the fire, Evie sat in the gathering gloom, silently sipping tea and wondering if she would ever be part of a family circle of her own.

Suddenly, a bell sounded from the hall. Evie nearly spilt her tea from shock before realising that it was the sound of their new phone ringing. Because Jed's work was considered essential to the war effort, he had been allocated a shared party line though it had only been installed weeks before after nearly two years of waiting.

"It's the phone," announced Jed, suddenly roused from his sleep. "Who'd be calling now? There's nobody working today."

"Hadn't you better answer it and find out then?" suggested Evie.

Jed went into the hall and picked up the receiver. "Hello. Mr. Carter speaking."

"Jed, is that you?" asked an anxious voice he recognised as that of the post mistress.

"What are you doing working today, Margaret? It's Christmas Day."

"Jed, we've had an urgent call. Someone wants to talk to Jack. Shall I put them on?"

"Who is it? Jack's asleep."

"It's somebody from the Air Ministry. Captain somebody. Sounds very posh."

"You'd better put him on to me then," suggested Jed. There was a pause and the sound of 'clicks' as a new connection was established. Jed couldn't understand why the Air Ministry would be calling Jack, especially on Christmas Day. Then it struck him. Perhaps they had found Peter's body or his grave and they wanted to let the family know.

Another click was followed by the hollow sound of a new line. "Hello, who am I speaking to?" asked the cultured sounding voice at the other end.

"I'm Mr. Jed Carter, a friend of Mr. Malikov." replied Jed in his formal 'telephone answering voice'. "Mr. Malikov lives with us but he's not very well and has difficulty getting to the phone. Can I help?"

"I suppose so. I'm Captain Johnson, acting head of POW repatriation at the Air Ministry. It's about Mr. Malikov's nephew, Flying Officer Peter Malikov. He's been found alive."

Evie heard a gasp followed by a deep groan coming from the hall. She rushed to see what the problem was and found Jed bent over clutching at his chest.

"Daddy, Daddy. What's the matter?"

"Mr. Carter, are you there? Is everything alright?" came an anxious voice from the receiver.

Evie grabbed the phone from Jed. "I'm Mr. Carter's daughter. He's been taken ill. Tell me why you're calling."

"It's Peter Malikov, Flying Officer Peter Malikov. He's been found alive. It seems that when he was shot down in the sea off Singapore, he managed to swim ashore and hide. But he was caught by a group of collaborators who kept him in an unofficial camp deep in the Malayan jungle. He was never reported to the Red Cross so we assumed he was dead. Anyway, at the end of September they were released and it took them nearly eight weeks to find their way out of the jungle."

By now, Evie too had crumpled to the floor and was sobbing uncontrollably. Jed regained his composure and took control of the remaining conversation. It seemed that Peter was now back in Singapore recuperating. He would begin his return journey to the UK next week via the United States. The last leg of his journey would be by ship from New York. He was expected home in approximately six weeks but the Ministry would call again as soon as his passage had been confirmed.

After the phone call, Jed and Evie sat on the hall floor clutching each other. Although Jed had said nothing to Evie, he had realised the closeness of their relationship and held her tightly now as she gasped and sobbed with emotion. Once they had both recovered, they had to break the news to Jack, taking care that the shock didn't bring on one of his bronchial attacks.

In the days after Christmas, Evie felt that she was living in a dream. She fluctuated from wild elation to inexplicable crying. The news had created a strange vacuum, the knowledge that Peter was alive yet nothing at the moment confirmed this – not even a word from him. On 2nd January, a letter arrived from the Air Ministry confirming the news and providing more detail. Addressed to Jack, it informed him that Peter was physically unharmed though had been subject to psychological mistreatment. It explained that POWs returning from camps in the Far East were receiving rest and support before embarking on the long journey home. An arrival date would be sent as soon as it was known.

On 6th January a telegraph arrived. It was from Peter and was short.

I am alive. Will be back in five weeks. Peter.

Evie began to wonder what it would be like when she met Peter again. Would the war have changed him very much? Stories were now rife in the press about terrible conditions in the Japanese POW camps and about inhumane treatment. She began to wonder if her memories of their short time together were perhaps inaccurate. Maybe she had built it up in her mind to be bigger than it really was.

Emma left for America at the end of January. Evie joined a small group at Frampton station saying goodbye to three local girls, all to be GI brides. They were due to travel to Liverpool and board a specially chartered ship that would take them to New York from where they would disperse to their new homes and new lives. Flora tried to hold back her tears but there was an unmistakable atmosphere of sadness and loss. Emma told her that she would soon be able to visit them in their new home in Mississippi but everyone knew that this was most unlikely. This was possibly the last time that any of them would see her.

A few days after Emma's departure, another letter arrived from the Air Ministry. It stated that Peter was expected to dock at Southampton early on the morning of February 16th aboard the liner, Queen Mary.

Jed immediately agreed that he and Evie would drive down to Southampton overnight to be there when the ship arrived. Evie spent the next fortnight working all her spare hours to prepare the house for Peter's return. She made a banner to hang outside the front door proclaiming 'Welcome home Peter – Our hero'. She also acquired over a dozen Union Jacks which she planned to hang out of windows and tie to the branches of trees.

As dusk was falling on the evening of 15th, Jed and Evie set off on the long journey to Southampton. They had both slept during the preceding day and hoped this would be sufficient to keep them awake through the night and the day to come. They arrived in Southampton at six in the morning. It was still dark and a heavy frost cloaked the ground in white. They found their way to the docks and parked the car on a cleared bomb site close to the Ocean Terminal. Small groups of people were making their way to the quay, wrapped in heavy coats and scarves. Evie was taken aback to see a long line of ambulances parked by the dock gates. The line extended as far as she could see. It occurred to her for the first time that many of those returning would be wounded and damaged in different ways. As they reached the dock gates, the crowd thickened and slowed as sentries checked their passes. Evie studied the faces of people in the crowd. There were elderly couples, possibly parents, supporting each other as they came to greet a son they hadn't seen in four or five years. Their faces looked anxious and drawn. There were mothers with young children coming to greet a father they probably couldn't remember. And there were young women, anxiously touching their hair or adjusting their clothing, coming to meet a sweetheart who had been a cherished memory for so many dark years. How would these lives be changed when their loved ones walked down the gang plank? How long would the joy of reunion last before the realities of adjusting to life in post war Britain took their toll?

As they reached the dock side, they were held back from the water's edge by barriers. Peering into the gloom that was Southampton Water, Evie could see nothing as a heavy mist hung over the sea. The sound of marching boots drew her attention and she watched as a marine band passed by to take up position on a raised platform. As dawn slowly broke, she noticed for the first time that Union Jacks hung limply from dock buildings and warehouses.

Somewhere out in the mist which still clung to the water, a deep blast from a ship's horn resonated across the dock. A ripple of expectation passed through the crowd. Evie noticed the band begin to take their instruments from their cases.

Above them, the sky was brightening to reveal a clear day but still the sea mist hung persistently over the water, obscuring their view. Then the blasts from the ship's horn came again, this time much closer. Three short sharp blasts. People began to cheer and clap, peering into the gloom for some sign of activity. Suddenly, the sun lifted above the horizon and bathed the terminal in light. Almost immediately, the sea mist lifted with a theatrical flourish to reveal the majestic form of the Queen Mary, not fifty yards from the dock side. Painted in war time grey, the great liner towered above the buildings lining the quay. A rousing cheer went up from the crowd as three tugs nudged the liner slowly into her berth. The decks were lined with soldiers, cheering and waving back at the crowds. Some of them were propped up on crutches. Some had bandages wrapped around their heads and others were being held up by comrades. The band struck up 'Land of Hope and Glory'. The crowd joined in and tears flowed freely down the cheeks of the most hardened faces.

It took another thirty minutes before the liner was docked and gang planks were lowered. First off the ship were injured stretcher cases, carried by volunteers who took them away to the waiting ambulances. Evie watched with fascination and sadness as stretcher after stretcher bearing an injured soldier was carried down the gang planks. Some of the injured tried to lift themselves up and wave. Others were motionless. Some were simply covered in bandages. Occasionally, a cry would go up from the crowd as a son or a husband or a father was recognised and the crowd parted to let the anxious relations get to them.

After more than an hour of stretcher cases leaving the ship, the remaining POWs started to disembark. Evie noticed how thin many of them seemed to be. Their coats hung off their shoulders giving a stooped and haunting appearance. Some were smiling but many looked vacant. Waiting relations eagerly threw their arms around some men but others were left looking lost and isolated as they blinked in the cold morning sun trying to make sense of their new situation. It was difficult to tell one man from the next as they disembarked in a long slow line.

"Is that him, Evie?" asked Jed urgently. "Look, the second gangway along. Just leaving the ship now."

Evie strained her eyes to see. A thin man in an RAF greatcoat was on the top of the gangway. He was clutching a kit bag. His hair was cropped short and seemed more grey than black. But the more she looked, the more convinced she was that it was Peter. She pushed her way through the crowd.

"Peter, is that you? Peter, it's Evie."

The queue seemed to have halted and he remained at the top of the gangway, not looking up.

"Peter. It's me, Evie. Hello." She waved her arms wildly.

Then he looked up, peering anxiously into the crowd. It was Peter – she was sure. He looked thin and gaunt – different to how she had last seen him.

"Peter, I'm over here. Over here, Peter."

Now their eyes met. She saw the look of relief on his face. He tried to push his way down but others held him back. They looked at each other, Evie waving and Peter looking intently at her. Finally, the disembarkation resumed and he was at the bottom of the gangway. She threw her arms around him and held him tightly. They kissed but it was an awkward kiss. Not like the last time they had kissed. His body felt taught and awkward – devoid of passion. Evie let go and looked into his eyes. They were not the eyes that she had known before – bright, sparkling and full of humour. Now they looked dull, haunted and distant.

"Peter, it's so good to have you home. How are you? Have you been treated well?"

He looked at her uncomprehendingly.

"I mean, are you injured?"

He seemed to pull himself together. A smile briefly crossed his lips.

"I'm alright, Evie. It's so wonderful to see you."

By now, Jed had caught up with them. He clasped Peter and held him.

"You know Jack can't be here, Peter. But he's desperate to see you again."

"How is Uncle Jack?"

"Not so good. The bronchitis has taken a real hold."

They made their way through the crowds of returning POWs and relatives to Jed's car and began the long journey home. Evie sat in the back seat with Peter trying to coax him into conversation. He wouldn't talk about the war. His eyes went blank if Evie raised the subject. Instead, they talked about mundane things, the winter weather, the amount of traffic on the road and about Jed's business. It felt so wrong to Evie to be here with her returning hero yet all they could do was make polite conversation.

After a while, Peter fell into a deep sleep accompanied by occasional grunts and sighs. Evie began to doze too whilst Jed concentrated on the driving. Suddenly, there was a blood curdling scream and Evie felt hands gripping her throat. She tried to scream but no sound could escape. Through bulging eyes she saw Peter, his face inches from hers. He was contorted with fear and panic. His eyes stared wildly, not seeing her but seeing some other terrible vision that was locked into his mind.

Evie felt the car screech to a halt and heard Jed shrieking at Peter.

"Get off, man! For God's sake, let go of her. Are you out of your mind?"

Evie felt another pair of hands round her neck – pulling. Then Peter was off her, sitting panting in the seat beside her. Jed was holding his arms and pinning him to his seat.

"Peter, what's the matter? Why did you do that to me?" cried Evie, still clutching her neck. He didn't reply. He looked straight ahead, breathless and tense. Then suddenly he lowered his head and began to sob – deep, inconsolable tears, expressions of an experience so terrible that he had no words to describe what had happened to him.

The Guest Who Stayed: Chapter 21 – February 1946

Life at Hope Cottage was strained and tense in the days following Peter's return. It was clear that he was no longer the confident and optimistic young man who had set sail for Singapore in 1941. Before, he moved energetically and enthusiastically. Now, he moved slowly and deliberately, his head often bowed. Conversations at meal times were polite but not illuminating. Any attempt to talk about the war was met with a wall of silence.

Evie found the whole experience very unsettling. For five years she had been nursing the memory of a man she had loved, knowing that he would never return from war. She had allowed her memories to soften and mellow, shutting out anything that deflected from the comfort of those private thoughts. Now she was confronted with a new reality and her private paradise was being shattered. There seemed to be no spark of romantic interest, no endearing words and no close physical contact.

Each morning after breakfast, Peter would leave the house to walk and not return until early evening. Evie asked him where he went and what he was thinking about but he simply replied,

"I need time, Evie. I need time. I'm so sorry."

One evening after Peter had retired to bed early as usual, Evie lay on her own bed trying to make sense of her feelings. She knew now that Peter had suffered and had locked away terrible memories inside his mind. Somehow, she had to help him deal with these.

She caught sight of the silver box on her dresser. She opened the lid and rifled through the letters until she came to one addressed to her on her tenth birthday. There was something her mother had told her about Jack which she needed to read again.

Dearest Evie,

Happy birthday, darling, on your tenth birthday. I expect you're very beautiful now. You've inherited my auburn hair and I'm sure it makes you look very distinctive. How is your life? I hope it's full of love. I know that Daddy cares for you very much and will always love you, whatever the future may bring. Is Uncle Jack still with you? If he is, I expect he's still spoiling you.

I want to tell you a little bit about Uncle Jack. In the future, you may find that he becomes important in your life. Uncle Jack needs to be loved. I think that's why he found his way into our lives. In the war he was badly hurt. He worked behind enemy lines and was caught. He was badly beaten and tortured. He also blames himself for the death of two French agents who worked closely with him. I'm telling you this because I want you to know that he's a very special man, not just the kind old uncle who gives you too many sweets. People who have been through what he's been through seldom want to talk about their experiences but they need to be understood. Please remember this if you ever find yourself harbouring anger in your heart for Uncle Jack.

Evie stopped reading and put the letter down. She had forgotten about Jack's war service but reading the letter again gave her an idea.

The next day she took Jack's breakfast tray to him at eight in the morning. They made polite conversation about the weather as Evie drew back the curtains and put cushions behind Jack's back to help him sit upright.

"Uncle Jack, I know you know what's going on," began Evie.

"There's lots of goings on in this house, Evie, what do you mean?"

"Peter and me. That's what I'm talking about. We were close – before he went away. We made promises to each other. But now it's all different. He's not the same man any more. I want to know why. I want to know what I can do to bring him back – the old Peter who left here in '41. Mum told me in one of her letters that you'd been badly treated in the war. Can you help me to understand? What can I do to help Peter?"

There was a long pause whilst Jack sipped at his tea and gazed intently at the bedspread.

"What did your mother tell you?"

"Just that you were caught behind enemy lines and tortured. Oh and that two French agents were killed too."

"Yvette and Simone," whispered Jack under his breath.

"Did you say Yvette? That's strange. It's so similar to my own name. Who was Yvette?"

"She was a very special and very brave woman."

"How did she die?"

"It's difficult for me to tell you much, Evie. If you experience those things you spend a lifetime trying to forget them. But before you can do that, you need to talk to someone first. That's where your mother helped me. She coaxed me to talk about what happened – to face up to the truth. You see, in that situation no one's brave. In the end, everyone talks. It's just a matter of time. It's not just your own pain – it's seeing pain being inflicted on others, maybe people you love. You're humiliated. They do things to you that I can't bring myself to describe. You say anything in the end – just to make it stop. But, of course, even then it doesn't stop – it just goes on and on. And somewhere in all of that you lose faith. What can you possibly believe in that allows all this to happen? And if you lose faith – you lose the will to live. You might just as well be dead. And then you begin to want to die. Each time you come round from the last beating you curse your luck for being alive."

"I'm sorry, Uncle Jack. I didn't want to intrude. I just wanted to ..."

"You wanted to know how you can help Peter. Do as your mother did with me, Evie. Be there to listen. Don't ask too many questions. Don't make judgements. Just be there when he wants to start talking. And he will want to start talking. Sometime soon he'll need to start talking."

The next morning as Peter was preparing to leave the house, he encountered Evie in the hall putting on her outdoor clothes and boots.

"You're not going to work in those, are you?"

"No, Peter. I'm coming with you."

Peter's face dropped. "But I need to be alone. I thought you understood. I just need time."

"You don't need to worry. I won't talk to you. I just want to be with you. Now, put your coat on and we'll go."

Peter looked confused and a little crestfallen but he did as he was bid. They set off down Duck Lane, away from the town towards the meadows where Evie and Emma had played as children and where in earlier years Alice, Jed and Flora had planned their futures, brimming with optimism and idealism.

They walked in silence along footpaths and climbed styles over walls onto rough farm tracks. Peter walked with his hands in his pockets and his head lowered. Every so often he would stop and look, not at the scene in front of him, but at some other image in a distant place. His face would contort and sometimes fill with fear. Evie said nothing but occasionally took his hand, feeling his damp clammy palm against hers.

The next day was the same. The sky was overcast so they put on waterproof jackets. After an hour of silent walking, Peter stopped and looked at Evie. He reached out to hold her hands and for the first time since his return he looked her straight in the eyes. Evie remained silent, determined that she would ask no questions. Peter seemed to be struggling with words or perhaps with the ideas that would give meaning to his words. But there seemed to be a barrier that he just couldn't overcome. He turned away from Evie unable to bear looking at her.

Twice more on that same day, Peter tried to get his words out but was beaten by the demons that had taken control of his mind. Evie wondered how long she could keep this up. She was needed back at the construction company as Jed was beginning to get anxious about her absence. The third day dawned bright and crisp. A hint of an early spring hung in the air. Wild daffodils formed a yellow ribbon along the embankments and hedgerows.

"Let's go a different way today, Peter," said Evie as they arrived at the first meadow. "Let's go to Offa's Mount. It'll be beautiful up there today. You'll be able to see for miles."

Without saying anything, Peter followed her along the track which led away from Frampton to higher ground to the west of the town. It took just over an hour to trudge the three miles to Offa's Mount. Evie noticed that Peter's walk was getting more steady and confident. He was also beginning to look around him rather than keeping his eyes focused on the ground.

The top of the Mount was sparse, boasting only a stone mound on which was placed a roughly cast metal plate indicating the four points of the compass. Evie and Peter stopped by the mound and looked out over the flat East Anglian countryside. An early mist still hung over the fields giving the appearance of an undulating ethereal ocean. The sun overhead was bright with just the faintest hint of warmth registering on exposed flesh. They both stood in silence, mesmerised by the simple beauty of the scene which lay before them.

When Evie looked at Peter, she was astonished to see tears rolling down his cheeks. She threw her arms around him and held him tightly.

"What is it, Peter, my darling? What is it?"

"When you're in those God forsaken camps, this is what you think about," he replied shakily. "When they tie you up in a cage and leave you to roast in the jungle heat, you try to make your mind go somewhere else. You try to detach it from your body. And this is where I came. You remember, we came here the day before I left. This was my last memory of peace and happiness. I made it my special memory. And when they hit me, or pretended they were about to shoot me or beat my best friend to pulp in front of me, I always tried to come here. To stand at this place and look out over this beautiful country."

Evie held him but said nothing. Jack had told her just to listen.

"It's not so much the pain or dying. The mind has a funny way of dealing with those. It's fear. There's always fear. You learn to live with it, learn to expect it all the time. Fear of being betrayed, fear of letting down a comrade, fear of being weak, fear of just waking up. And that's what it's like now, Evie. I'm consumed with fear. People tell us we're heroes but they didn't see us crying out for mercy or begging for food or begging to die. I've got to live with these memories, Evie, and I don't know how to."

There was a long silence as they held on to each other.

"I can't begin to understand what you've been through, Peter, and I can't say anything that will help. But I can always be here to listen and to help share some of the pain. I know you're not the same young airman who came to visit us in 1941, but I don't know who you are now. I want to find out. I want to be a part of your future – not your past. And I know it's early days but you must begin to think about the future. It's the only way to lay the past to rest."

They sat down by the base of the stone mound and words began to tumble out. Peter talked of being shot down off the coast of Singapore in the days before the Japanese invaded the island. He told Evie how he had managed to swim to the coast of Malaya and hide in the jungle from Japanese patrols. How eventually he'd given himself up to villagers, hoping that they would hide him but how, in fact, he was traded to the Japanese for a couple of bags of rice. Rather than being taken to a main camp, he was held in the jungle in a makeshift prison run by Malayan collaborators, brutal people who exacted terrible punishments for minor infringements of rules. He was there for three years, half starved and often suffering from dysentery. Death seemed like a blessed relief – always just out of reach.

Evie told Peter about her war years. She didn't hide from him the fact that she had relationships with a number of men. She needed him to understand that she too had known despair and desolation – that the old pre war values of chastity and monogamy were irrelevant in a world where relationships might last only a few days before a soldier would be gunned down or an airman shot out of the skies. Whatever remained of their relationship, Evie was determined that it could only be built on honesty, that no dark shadows should remain harbouring demons that might one day endanger their future.

They returned to Hope Cottage by mid afternoon as the sun was losing its warmth. Jack was asleep in his chair by the fire. Peter took Evie silently by the hand and led her through the parlour to his room. He shut the door and pulled Evie to him. Their lips made light inquisitive contact. Then he was kissing her wildly, passionately, out of control.

"Stop, Peter," she whispered breathlessly. "Not this way."

He sat down on the bed, confused. Then Evie began to undress. Peter watched her in silence. When she was naked, she began to unbutton Peter's shirt and remove the rest of his clothes. Then she pulled him down onto the bed.

They made love selfishly and greedily, each seeking atonement for the years they had been forced to spend apart. When they climaxed together, their bodies fused and they clasped each other until they both cried out with pain.

Afterwards, they lay for over an hour in each other's arms. Evie began to talk to Peter about a future, a shared future, perhaps with children. Peter talked about his boyhood dreams to travel and work abroad. Now all that seemed so irrelevant. He had travelled and made it back home. He yearned to belong somewhere and to belong with someone.

That evening, Peter and Evie announced that they were going out and would probably find somewhere to eat in Cromer. Evie had prepared a meal for the two men which Jed put the finishing touches to when he arrived home from work. Jed was glad that he had the opportunity to speak to Jack alone about an issue that was causing him growing concern.

"They seem to be getting on well, them two," suggested Jed as he was ladling out the stew.

"Peter and Evie? I saw it coming," remarked Jack. "It doesn't surprise me. Spent the last three days together they have. Spent a lot of time in Peter's room this afternoon too and I don't expect they were playing cards either."

Jed dished out the vegetables in silence and pushed Jack's wheelchair up to the table.

"You see, Jack, there's a bit of a problem. Suppose they decide to get married?"

"Well, that's alright isn't it? Peter's a good lad. Had a difficult time of it, obviously, but there's no one better placed than Evie to help him sort himself out."

"That's not the point," persisted Jed. "They can't get married."

"Why ever not?"

"Because Evie's your child," said Jed with a sudden edge to his voice, "and Peter's your nephew. Don't you see? That makes them first cousins."

"Well, it's not illegal for first cousins to get married is it?"

"It's not illegal but there can be problems. If they have children there may be, well, health issues. Sometimes they can be deformed. Sometimes they can be a bit ... simple."

"How do you know all about this?" asked Jack, laying down his knife and fork as the conversation became more tense.

"It's been a big issue in these parts, especially in some of the isolated villages round here. 'In breeding' they call it. You've heard of people talking about village idiots. Well, that's what they mean, simple people, often with a deformity and it's usually from in breeding."

"Well, you can't stop them getting married," replied Jack. "If it's legal, you can't get in their way."

"No, but we can tell them the truth and let them decide. You can't let them go into this not knowing."

"You can't tell Evie the truth, not now, not after all this time," replied Jack, becoming visibly agitated. "It would kill her. And what would she think of us? She'd turn against us. She'd know we'd lied to her all these years. You can't do that, Jed."

"But we can't let Evie and Peter marry without knowing the truth. That would be immoral. I always knew this lie would have to end one day and I think that day has arrived."

"It was meant to protect us all. Don't you remember, Jed? You agreed with it. Alice wanted it and we all agreed. You'd be letting Alice down if you told Evie now."

"I'm not sure Alice ever intended it to go on this long and I'm sure if she'd lived she would have told Evie herself. And there's another thing, Jack."

Jed paused and looked away out through the parlour windows to the wintry night beyond.

"It's not just this lie – it's the other one too. I want that out in the open."

Jack looked coldly at Jed, his face hardening. "What other lie?"

"You know, the one about Flora and her girl Emma."

"You better watch what you're saying, Jed. You know nothing about me and Flora."

Jed turned back from the window and faced Jack directly. "I was there, Jack. I saw it. I saw what you did to Flora. You took her forcefully, against her will. You raped her. And it's to my everlasting shame I did nothing about it."

Jack erupted into a violent coughing fit, wheezing and struggling to get his breath. It took over ten minutes before they were able to resume talking.

"You were there like a bloody peeping Tom and you watched. What does that make you?" demanded Jack, with as much venom as his aching body could muster.

"It makes me a coward and I'm ashamed. But it doesn't stop me doing what's right now. If we're going to tell Evie the truth – and we are, I promise you – let's tell Emma the truth too. Let her know that you're her father. Do what's right, Jack, before you die. You were brave in them war years. Prove you're brave now. Prove you haven't lost it."

There were tears beginning to trickle down Jack's cheeks now. He looked his age. His body was thin and bent. He coughed mucus from his congested chest and struggled for breath.

"Jed, I'm begging you," he gasped. "Do you really hate me that much? Is this your final revenge? Is this what you've been planning all these years – to let me go to my grave alone, with everyone against me. I'm begging you, Jed, don't do it. No good'll come of it."

Evie was glad she'd taken a little trouble to dress up. She thought Peter had probably intended that they stop at a small pub on the way to Cromer but here they were, mounting the wide sweeping stairs up to the doors of the elegant Hotel de Paris. Peter had booked a table in the restaurant away from the dance band, making conversation less difficult. The restaurant was busy with couples and a few families. There was still a good smattering of uniformed military personnel, with returning English soldiers slowly reasserting their presence in the vacuum left by the departed GIs. Evie and Peter chatted easily over their main course, avoiding subjects that might evoke pain or regret.

"I asked you here for a reason," Peter announced when their plates had been cleared from the table. "I've thought about it a lot."

"Peter, it's alright. You don't have to …"

"Evie, let me just say this my way. It won't be stylish but it comes from my heart. I can't live without you, Evie. I know that now. The way you've been with me and listened to me with all my worries about the war years, well, there's nobody else I could tell all that to – nobody else I would trust. You've shown such loyalty and love to me that I want to return it. The trouble is, if you accept my proposal I can't tell you what sort of man you're going to marry. I don't know myself anymore. I know I'm not that man who kissed you under the oak tree before going to Singapore. That man's gone, Evie. He died in some hell hole in the Malayan jungle. But I don't know what's left. Only you can help me find out. Will you take that risk?"

The next day was a Saturday and Jed returned from work about two o'clock. He was surprised to find Peter alone in the parlour.

"Oh, Jack's in the sitting room having a snooze and Evie's writing some letters upstairs," explained Peter nonchalantly.

They exchanged pleasantries for a short while – about Jed's current building contracts and about the state of recovery after the war.

"Jed, there's something I need to ask you."

"What's on your mind?" replied Jed a little uneasily.

"Well, it's about Evie and me. Jed, I've asked Evie if she'll marry me. Do you mind? Will you give us your blessing?"

There was a pause as Jed gulped at a mug of coffee and turned to face Peter.

"I saw this coming, Peter. I saw that you and Evie were getting on well. Peter, I can't give you my blessing – not yet."

Peter looked bewildered and crestfallen.

"Why ever not?"

"Oh, it's nothing to do you with you. I think you'd make a good husband for Evie. She needs someone who understands her and listens to her and, of course, loves her. You score high marks there. No, it's not about you, well, not directly that is. But there is something that I have to tell Evie – about her past – something that might change how you're both thinking about the future."

"I don't understand. Surely it's down to Evie and me. How can her past affect how we both feel about each other now?" replied Peter, trying to restrain his anger.

"All I'm saying is that Jack and I need to talk to Evie, to tell her a certain truth and it won't be easy. In fact, I'd like you to be here when we tell her – not in the same room but nearby. She may need you afterwards."

It was agreed that they would speak to Evie that evening. Jed had asked her if she would join them both in the parlour at five because there were domestic issues they wanted to discuss with her. Evie assumed this was something to do with Jack's care and resolved not to give way on the principle that she wouldn't revert to being Jack's nurse. Peter was briefed to stay in his room until he was needed.

Jack and Jed were in the parlour well before five. Jack looked frightened and frail. Jed stood by the fireplace trying to assume an air of authority. Five minutes late, Evie breezed into the room.

"Can we make this quick?" she suggested. "We're going to motor into Norwich this evening – might see a show."

"Evie, my dear," began Jed, "your Uncle Jack and I have something to tell you – something that may distress you deeply. But you must remember at all times that what we did was in your best interests. We did it because we love you."

Upstairs, Peter lay on his bed turning over in his mind what sort of issue was about to be revealed to Evie and how it could affect their plans to marry. Was she ill in some way? Was there some inherited disease or maybe lunacy that was passed down the family line? Maybe he shouldn't have asked Jed's permission. But Evie had wanted it. She had told him that Jed would be so honoured to be asked.

His thoughts were interrupted by a piercing scream. He leapt to his feet, unsure whether to race downstairs or to respect Jed's wishes. Then he heard another scream, the sound of agitated men's voices and a door banging violently. He rushed downstairs to find Jed by the front door and Jack holding his hands over his face by the entrance to the parlour.

"What's happened? Where's Evie gone?"

"It upset her. She couldn't cope with it. She's gone off."

"What couldn't she cope with?" shouted Peter, grabbing Jed roughly by the lapels of his jacket. Tell me, Jed. What have you just said to her?"

"I've told her she's not my daughter. She's Jack's daughter," spluttered Jed, his words constricted by Peter's hold. "And that makes you cousins. So now do you see? You and Evie are first cousins. She had to be told. I couldn't let the lie live on into another generation. Now you know the truth."

Peter looked aghast. He said nothing. Simply looking at Jed and Jack told him that this was the truth. He released his hold on Jed and swung the front door open. Running to the gate he stared up and down Duck Lane. There was no sign of Evie. He decided to turn left towards the meadows. He was certain that was the route she'd take.

Evie reached the end of the made up road and stumbled onto the grass path. It had rained and the ground was soggy. Mud splashed over her legs as she ran. Her head was spinning. Her whole world had been shattered. How could her father, the man she had been brought up to trust and obey, turn out not be her father at all? And how could the loving uncle, who was always there to comfort her, turn out to be the one who had slept with her mother and brought her into this world? What did this make her? She wasn't who she thought she was at all. She was somebody else.

She half stumbled, half ran along the path towards Offa's Mount. She was crying out loud, pain welling up from inside. And what of Peter? What would he think now? Jed had explained that they were first cousins and that they needed to think carefully about the risks. Why would he take the risk of having damaged children? He would leave her and find somebody else.

Worst of all was her mother's betrayal, allowing her all these years to believe that Jed was her father. Through her letters, Evie felt she had come to know her mother. She had let her into her life. She had become her best friend and confidant. But now she felt that she didn't know her at all. Like the others, she had lied to her. She didn't know any of them anymore. She felt completely isolated.

Peter arrived at the meadows, breathless and confused. Had she gone right towards the oak tree or left towards Offa's Mount? He guessed the Mount and set off in that direction. He could hardly comprehend the enormity of the lie, to bring up a child not knowing that her father lived as a member of the same household. How could Jack have done that, allowing another man to bring up his child? And how could Jed, always so righteous and honourable, have subscribed to this deception? No wonder Evie had run from the house. She'd been betrayed – betrayed by those who professed to love her most.

"I told you that'd happen," hissed Jack. "She won't see it like we do. To her, we've lied, cheated on her, made her life a complete parody. And it's down to you, Jed, you and your bloody self righteous streak. Why didn't you just leave things as they were?"

She had twisted her foot and was out of breath. She could go no further. She crawled over to an embankment by a swiftly running stream. She lay on the grass, listening to the burbling water as it tumbled over rocks.

Suddenly, she felt so sorry for Jed. All these years she had treated him with indifference and scorn, reserving her affection for Jack. Jack laughed with her, spoilt her, gave her treats and stuck up for her when Jed was angry. Now she could see why. He was protecting his own daughter whilst refusing to acknowledge her as his own. Yet Jed had unselfishly taken on that responsibility. It was he who dealt with her tantrums, he who chastised her and he who set out the clear boundaries which had guided her upbringing. Even though she wasn't his own child, Jed had willingly taken responsibility and raised her as his own.

"Evie, are you there? Where are you, Evie?" She recognised Peter's voice not far from the embankment. She felt like remaining silent. She needed time to think and plan, like Peter had done when he returned from the Far East. But then she remembered how she had been frustrated by his silence and by being locked out of his life.

"I'm over here by the brook."

His head appeared over the embankment, sweaty and out of breath.

"Oh, thank God you're safe. I thought you might have fallen into one of these streams."

He slithered down the embankment and put his arms around her.

"Jed told me," he said. "He told me about the lie. It must be a terrible shock."

"Of course, it's a shock!" Evie retorted, sounding more aggressive than she had intended. "I've been lied to for twenty four years. I don't know who I am anymore."

"Well, that makes two of us then," said Peter with a wry smile on his face. "Perhaps we'll make a good team, both in search of our identity."

"You know why Jed decided to tell me now, don't you?" asked Evie.

"I can guess. I asked Jed this afternoon for his blessing. He said he couldn't give it – not at the moment, not until he'd spoken to you first. He wouldn't say what was on his mind, just that the time had come for the truth to be told."

"So, it turns out we're first cousins, you and me. They say it's not a good idea for first cousins to marry."

"I don't care what people say or think, Evie. I've told you I want to marry you and I'm not going back on that. Look, we've both come through an ugly war and survived. I'm not sacrificing our future now to some bit of rural folklore."

Peter arrived back at Hope Cottage as dusk was falling. He was carrying Evie in his arms. He took her straight to her room and they both stayed there that night. The following day, Evie remained in her room and declined requests from Jed and Jack to be allowed to talk to her. Peter was with her for much of the day, helping her to make sense of the new situation. What particularly worried Evie was the right or wrong of getting married to Peter. She loved him wholeheartedly but was it immoral to enter into a relationship knowing that their children were at risk?

Later in the afternoon, Peter went for a walk leaving Evie alone. She lay on the bed trying to digest some of the conversations that she'd had with Peter that morning. Her eyes alighted once more on the silver box containing her mother's letters. A thought suddenly occurred. She took the box and opened the lid. One letter remained unopened. It was intended for her twenty-fifth birthday next May. She was honour bound not to open each letter until the appropriate birthday but everything had changed now. She no longer held her mother in the same esteem that she had before learning the truth about her father and she felt she was no longer bound by promises made under false pretences.

Nervously, she slit open the envelope and began to read.

Darling Evie,

This is the last letter that I will write to you. I am growing tired now and I sense the end may not be far away. Writing these letters has been such a comfort to me. They have helped me to feel that the end is not so final, that through these words you and I have kept our love alive over these past twenty years. I have spoken to you about thoughts and ideas that seemed important to me and that I hope have meant something to you too. But in a sense, all that I have been telling you has been preparing you for this final letter. Because, Evie, my darling, there is something that I have kept from you and that I must tell you now because it's your right to know. As a result of this, you may hate me but that is a risk that I must take. I hope that in time you can come to understand what led me to do as I did and to forgive me.

There is no easy way to tell you this. Daddy, my Jed, is not your father. Your real father is Uncle Jack. Maybe you already know this and have come to terms with the news. Maybe this comes to you as a terrible shock and is hurting you now terribly. Maybe you are crying and hating me. I am so, so sorry.

It's a long story and I'm too tired to go into detail. Jed is a wonderful man. I married him because he offered me hope and a way out of the life I despised. But I didn't love him in the way I needed to. Then Jack came into my life and filled it with passion. My plans were all lost. I gave myself to this man because he opened my eyes to a side of me that had lain undiscovered up to that point. Once my soul had been awakened, there was no going back. And you, my darling, are the result. Imagine the hurt to poor Jed. Imagine the rejection of all the plans we'd made together. And so it was decided that we would try to remain a family. To the outside world, Jed would be your father and Jack would be your uncle. I think, my darling, that I thought the affair with Jack would end quickly and then Jed and I could go back to leading a simple life. But then I became ill and it was clear that your future would lie in the hands of two men who had been brought to the brink of hatred through their love for me. It was a terrible situation to wish on both men and a terrible start for you, my dear, in life. I don't know what happened. I pray it turned out for the best.

What can I say to you? Sorry seems irrelevant. I did what I had to do and you were conceived in love. Be impetuous, darling, be yourself but remember that you have the capacity to hurt as well as to love. How you balance these two impostors is the greatest challenge you will face.

Good bye, my love, and may God bless you always.

Your loving mother, Alice XX

Evie wept as she read the letter. Her mother had fallen off the pedestal that she had placed her on but suddenly she had become a real person, someone who made mistakes but lived with them. Her mother was not a quitter. She had lived life fully and given herself to others with energy and commitment. Could she do the same? What would Alice have advised her to do? Surely Alice would go with the man she loved, regardless of obstacles. She would seize the opportunity and live with the consequences. Evie felt the bond with her mother renewing – not as some unapproachable idol, but as a real person, vulnerable, ambitious and loving.

The following day, Evie agreed to see Jed and Jack separately. She felt able now to talk to them without the anger that had gripped her in the previous days. Jed came to see her first. He told her again how sorry he was but that he felt the truth had to come out. She told him that he had been a good father to her and she would always go on thinking of him as her father. She asked him about Alice and about the affair with Jack. He told her that he always thought it would end, that one day Alice would return to him. For that reason he accepted the humiliation of having another man living in his house with his wife. Evie hugged him and told him that there was never a better father than he had been to her.

She met Jack in the sitting room. He was in his wheelchair by the fire, nervously fingering a handkerchief.

"So, you're my father then?" she said in a matter-of-fact voice.

"Yes, I am, Evie, and I have so missed being a real father to you."

"I have a real father – Jed. And that hasn't changed."

Jack lowered his eyes.

"Why did you do it – give up your daughter?"

"Because I loved your mother so very much. At the time it seemed the only way out. She wouldn't leave Jed and I couldn't live without her. I didn't expect to live long. They'd only given me three years. I thought that after I'd gone Alice would get back with Jed and everything would be OK. By then I would've helped Jed build his business and he'd be able to look after you both. I'd just be a memory in the churchyard. That's why I went along with it, Evie, but I've regretted it many times since."

"Why, Uncle Jack?"

"Because I couldn't have that intimacy and bond with you that a real father has with his daughter. Oh, I played the role of doting uncle alright and gave you sweets and toys, but we've never had a proper conversation. You've never let me into your heart, Evie."

The next day, Evie insisted that she and Peter take a walk. It was blustery but not cold. The landscape was still firmly rooted in winter, milky white skies looking down on leafless trees and dormant fields.

"Where are we going?" demanded Peter.

"You'll see," she replied.

It soon became clear that they were heading for Offa's Mount. Peter immediately realised that there was purpose in Evie's walk and braced himself for whatever was about to happen.

They reached the top of Offa's Mount and looked silently over the view that had already played an important part in their lives. Heavy rain clouds racing in from the east cast shadows across the landscape, interspersed with shafts of bright sunlight which lit the scene like a stage. In the distance, they could just make out the sparkling reflection of the sea. To the south and west, pastures and ploughed fields stretched as far as the eye could see.

"There's something about this place," said Evie. "It's where we come when we need strength or when we need to begin again. It seems to have the power to create new energy."

"Why have you brought me here, Evie?"

"Because I want to accept your invitation of marriage. I do want to marry you, Peter, with all of my heart and all of my soul. But I want you to ask me properly, here, now on Offa's Mount. Because it's special to us."

Peter dropped onto one knee and took both of Evie's hands in his. Wind gusted round the Mount and a break in the clouds allowed sunlight to percolate through. He had to shout against the rising wind.

"Evie Carter, I love you with all of my heart and all of my soul. I want to be with you forever. Will you marry me?"

The wind tugged at their clothes and drops of rain started to lash at their faces.

"Of course, I will, Peter. Of course, I'll marry you."

She dropped to her knees and they kissed, alone on Offa's Mount with only the elements to witness their commitment.

The Guest Who Stayed: Chapter 22 – 1947

Evie and Peter married in March 1947 – nothing ostentatious, just a simple ceremony at St. Martin's followed by a buffet lunch at Hope Cottage. Jack was unable to attend the church as he was now confined to bed, struggling to get his breath as his damaged lungs finally gave up. With Peter's help, Evie had come to terms with the events of the past twenty five years and was fully reconciled with both Jack and Jed. The two men had buried their differences, becoming firm friends in what would be Jack's final days. Jed spent many hours by Jack's bedside helping him make peace with some of the memories which still haunted him and holding his hand when the spectre of death looked him straight in the eyes.

Something that concerned Evie and Jed were letters that had started arriving for Jack some weeks earlier. They were postmarked 'London' and were addressed in small neat handwriting. Jack refused to say who had sent them but after each letter he seemed visibly shaken.

Peter and Evie honeymooned for a week near Sheringham on the east coast. It was six days of bracing walks along deserted windswept beaches and lingering meals by wood burning fires followed by leisurely nights of love making. They decided whilst on honeymoon that they wouldn't delay starting a family. They both felt that a baby would help with their new beginning and provide a focus for their life together after the horrors of the war.

The other important decision taken on that holiday was that Peter would accept Jed's invitation to join him in the business, now a thriving construction company with branches in three local towns.

Peter had already spent time in the business and had proved himself very capable. As an engineer by training, he was quickly able to learn the mechanics of construction. But he was also an able businessman, good with figures, calm under pressure and liked by clients. Jed had found himself increasingly relying on Peter as Jack's health deteriorated.

On April 7th, Jack passed away in the early hours of the morning. Jed was by his bedside and Evie was preparing a pot of tea downstairs in the parlour. Jed dozed, lulled into semi sleep by the deep sonorous gasps emitting from Jack's diaphragm. Suddenly, they simply stopped. The silence brought Jed to a swift consciousness. He checked Jack's pulse and felt nothing. For a few moments he simply stared at Jack – this man who had brought so much turmoil yet so much reward into his life. Because of him he now ran a successful business and was highly respected in the community. Because of him he had a daughter. Evie had told him that she would always think of him as her father. Yet for these two important gifts he had sacrificed his wife. He stood up and looked at Jack. Even in death he looked troubled. Jed bent over and kissed his forehead. Then he called for Evie.

Less than a week later, they were all gathered again at St. Martin's Church for the funeral. There were over thirty people present. Jack's former drinking pals were loyal to the end and turned out in force to salute the passing of a former diehard.

As they gathered round the grave and the Reverend Bowman committed Jack's body to the soil – *"Earth to earth, ashes to ashes, dust to dust"* – Evie thought she spotted an elderly woman dressed in a smart black suit waiting just beyond the churchyard wall watching the proceedings intently. After the committal was finished and people drifted away from the graveside, Evie watched as the woman in black walked up to the grave and stood there with her head bowed for several minutes, before turning and walking quickly away. Excusing herself, Evie ran after the woman, drawn by some deep curiosity to find out more. She reached her as she was passing through the gate and turning into the High Street.

"Excuse me, excuse me," gasped Evie, breathless after her dash across the churchyard. "I'm sorry, I don't mean to be nosy. But I'm Jack's, er, Jack's – I'm Jack's daughter. He was my father."

"You must be Evie then," replied the woman in a thick foreign accent.

"How did you know?"

"He told me. He named you after my sister, Yvette. She died in the first war – killed by your soldiers."

"So, you must be ..."

"I'm Simone, her sister."

"But I thought you were dead too. Uncle Jack said – I mean, my father said you were both killed in a raid. They were trying to rescue you."

"Not us – they wanted Jack. We were better dead."

"Look, I'm sorry. We can't talk here. There's a tea shop in the High Street. Can I buy you some tea?"

"I've only got an hour. I've got to be on the five o'clock to Norwich so that I can get my connection back to London."

"There's so much I need to ask you," exclaimed Evie as a pot of tea and two cups were placed in front of them by a waitress. "But why are you here? How did you know Uncle Jack was dead? Have you come from France?"

"Drink your tea and I will explain," instructed Simone, her French accent softening the command. "I am here working in London. I have been working in the office of General de Gaulle who is leader of our Free French Forces. I arrived here in June 1940 after the fall of Paris. You see, after the first war, I did not wish to marry. I knew I could never have a family, so I devoted myself to my country. I worked for the government in the Foreign Affairs Ministry, first as a secretary. But I was good and I was quickly promoted.

When the second war came, we were divided. Some wanted to join with Marshall Petain and his collaborators to set up a new government in Vichy. Others, like me, hated the idea of collaboration with the Germans and wanted to get out. I had worked for Brigadier de Gaulle, as he then was, before the war started. So when I heard that he was going to London to set up a government in exile, I decided I must go too and join him. I got out from St. Malo on a ferry two weeks before the terrible evacuation from Dunkirk and helped the General set up his office. Now the war is over, I must return and help him again. There is important work for me to do. France has been ravished. I am leaving on Thursday."

"Did Uncle Jack know you were here? Had you been in touch before?" asked Evie.

"Only at the end – about six weeks ago. Before that I hadn't seen him since 1917."

"What made you contact him again?"

"Curiosity. And unfinished business."

"What do you mean?"

"You said you wanted to know what happened to Jack – your real father. What do you already know?"

Evie drained the tea from her cup and tried to order her thoughts.

"Well, I know he fought in the war and was involved in espionage. I know he was caught and badly tortured. He believed he was responsible for your deaths too, you and Yvette. I think he was in love with Yvette."

"You are right but also wrong. You see Jack was in love with Yvette but she wasn't in love with him. She despised him. When Jack met Yvette in a bar in 1916 and tried to recruit her for espionage work, she saw it as an opportunity for revenge."

"Why revenge? What had Jack done to her?"

"Jack had done nothing. It wasn't Jack – it was the English. First, you need to understand Yvette. She was pretty, she was charming and everyone loved her. Unlike me – I was plain, not very clever and people ignored me. My parents made it clear who they preferred. But Yvette was scheming, always using people to get what she wanted. Two years before the war she met a young Englishman who had come to stay in a nearby chateau to improve his French. Robert, I think his name was. They were both young – she was eighteen and he was nineteen. Yvette fell for him. He was handsome, he came from a wealthy family and she wanted to marry him. So she used all her wiles to trap him. For a young man it was impossible to resist. Whatever my sister did, she did well. And that included sex. The poor boy didn't stand a chance. Soon Yvette was pregnant and she thought she had him. But she hadn't reckoned with his parents – aristocrats I think you call them. Well, they arrived all posh and arrogant and said there was no chance of their son marrying Yvette. It would ruin their plans for him. So they paid my parents – I don't know how much but it was a lot – to bring up the baby. Then they left with Robert."

"What happened to the baby?"

"She was born later that year. But she died within a matter of days. Apparently, she suffocated in my sister's bed."

There was a pause.

"Do you think she just died in the bed?" asked Evie cautiously.

"Who knows?" replied Simone with a brusque flick of her wrist. "It happened. It was probably for the best. Soon after that my parents became ill and died within months of each other. They wouldn't have been around to look after the baby and Yvette certainly wasn't going to look after her."

"But how does all this affect Jack? Why did she want to take revenge on him?"

"Because she hated all English men. That's how she was. She was all or nothing. She saw it as an opportunity to get back at them all."

"But she had an affair with Jack. They made love. How could she do that?"

"Oh, that was no problem for Yvette. Sex and love were not the same thing for her. She knew how to use her body to make a man completely dependent on her and then she would use him."

"But she was still working with Jack, running the network, supplying information – you both were."

"I thought I was but that was all a sham. Yvie was working with the Germans. They knew all along what was going on and they were using us to supply false information to the English. Jack had begun to suspect that there was a leak somewhere down the line and thought it might be me. He'd always been suspicious of me and he knew that Yvette and I didn't get on. Maybe Yvette had poisoned his mind against me."

Evie felt drained by the news. She suddenly felt desperately sad for Jack, believing all along that he and his men were saving lives and shortening the war but, in fact, he was simply leading them straight into a trap. And she felt sickened by Yvette in whose memory she was named. But one question still puzzled her.

"If Yvette was collaborating with the Germans, why did they capture you both and torture you? Surely you should have been rewarded?"

"She had served her purpose. And the Germans feared there were other groups of partisans doing the same thing. So they wanted to make an example of us. They wanted to show others what would happen to them if they collaborated with the English. So they beat us and tortured us horribly – as they did to Jack and his men. We were forced to watch as they did things to each of us. It's something you can never forget. It wakes you in the night and you still scream in fear – just as we did then."

"But how did you survive, Simone? How did you escape?"

"You heard the English organised a raiding party. Not for us – we were expendable. They wanted to get Jack and his men out before they gave away too much information. Well, just before they arrived, I had broken. Everybody has a breaking point and I had reached mine. I started telling them the names of all our agents – people we'd kept secret from them. So they dragged me off to an office in another part of the building so they could type the list. That's like the Germans – always methodical. Then when the attack happened, I was left tied to a chair whilst my guards went to join the fight. But then the English threw their grenades into the building and brought the roof down. Yvette was killed outright and most of the Germans too. I was buried under rubble but survived. Some of our partisans got me out the next day. I was unconscious for weeks and took months to recover. But I knew I had been badly damaged inside and I knew a normal life was out of the question."

"So you traced Uncle Jack – my father – and you told him all of this?"

"I had to. I didn't know he was dying but I felt he should know the truth. I needed Jack to know that I hadn't betrayed him. I wanted him to know that the love of his life was no sweet angel. She was scheming and self centred. I wanted him to go to his grave knowing that."

Evie could still sense the venom in her voice.

"I can't begin to understand what you've been through," she began, "I just know that war is responsible for so many terrible things and for damaging so many lives. I'm married now to a man who was captured by the Japanese and badly beaten. He's very troubled."

"Then you are very brave and I wish you well – both of you. Now I must go. I have told you all there is to tell."

"Wait! Wait a minute. How did you know that I was Jack's daughter? Did he tell you about all the years of lying and deceit?"

"He told me recently in a letter, yes. He was very worried that you would be furious – refuse to see him. I told him he was stupid. No girl can shut out her father – not for long. When she looks at her father she sees her husband in thirty years. Anyway, in France it is not so bad to have a lover. Many people do that."

"But they don't all live in the same house together."

"We do what we have to do. You didn't suffer. You had two men who loved you in different ways. Why is to be normal so good? I have to leave now to get to the station."

"But there's so much still to talk about. Can I take your address?"

"No, I don't want to be a part of your life and it's better for you that we don't meet again. I've answered some questions for you but don't linger in the past. Live only for the present. Let the past die with the people who made it."

With that she walked smartly out of the tea shop and disappeared from view.

After Jack's death, Flora finally agreed to marry Jed, but they decided to make their home in Flora's house so that she wouldn't be confronted on a daily basis with spectres from the past. Evie and Peter set about modernising Hope Cottage and preparing it for the family they hoped to raise there. The cottage was greatly improved, with a new kitchen and living area. An extension was built to the side of the house with a modern bathroom and an extra bedroom. Jed's old work shop was demolished and a double garage erected to house Peter's pride and joy, an Alvis Speed 25, which he kept in mint condition and only took out onto the open country lanes of Norfolk in the height of summer. As Hope Cottage grew and regenerated, Evie and Peter looked forward with great contentment to their future.

When Evie found out that she was pregnant in late November 1947, friends and family alike were delighted. Only in the inner family, where the secret of Evie and Peter's kinship was a closely guarded secret, were there unspoken worries.

Michael was born in August 1948. As she lay exhausted in the delivery suite at the cottage hospital, Evie sensed something was wrong. She had heard the baby cry but still the doctor and midwife hadn't brought the baby to her. They were huddled around the bundled infant talking in hushed voices. Then suddenly Peter was in the room, drawn into the huddle.

"Peter, Peter, what's going on? Somebody tell me." Evie called out in anguish.

Peter turned and came straight to her side. He took hold of her hand.

"It's a little boy. He's beautiful. But he's got an impediment. One of his legs isn't formed properly. I'm so sorry, darling."

In the days that followed, with countless visits by specialists and consultations with doctors, they learned that with time the deformity could be corrected. It would take many years and countless operations but by the time he was in his mid teens, the doctors had confidence that he would be walking.

After the initial grief, Evie and Peter came to terms with the situation and determined that they would do all they could to give their son a full and happy life. And so began a period which, in many ways, were golden years. Evie and Peter decided that they had better not have any more children and so all their attention was devoted to Michael. Soon, every conceivable place of interest in Norfolk had been visited and the three of them ventured further to seek out new adventures and interesting places to explore.

Flora and Jed happily settled into the role of grandparents and provided back up and child care as it was needed. Flora had lost touch with Emma. The rift came soon after Jed had written to Emma in Mississippi telling her that Jack was her father. He felt that this was the right thing to do when Evie learnt the truth about her own paternity. But whilst it had been possible to help Evie come to terms with the news and adapt to her new identity, Emma was far away in an alien culture and there was no way to support her and help her through the emotional turmoil and anger which would result from the news.

Autumn 1952

It was a normal morning. Peter was preparing to go to the office and Michael was playing with his cars on the floor of his bedroom. Evie shouted to Peter from the bathroom.

"Peter, come here quickly. I want you."

She was standing by the bathroom mirror with her skirt on but no top.

"Peter, I think I've found a lump. Look, here in my right breast. See what you think." Peter felt a damp perspiration form over his forehead as he placed his fingers gently on Evie's right breast. This is what they had always feared but seldom spoken about. Alice had died of breast cancer and probably her mother before her.

"I can feel something but it's probably nothing. I'm sure I've read that most breast lumps are just fatty tissue – nothing to be worried about. Perhaps you should pop down to see Dr. Morgan, though."

"No, Peter. I want you to take me to the hospital. I don't want to take any chances. Will you take me this morning?"

It was a week before the tests were completed and then the terrible news from the consultant.

"I'm afraid the news isn't good. The tumour is malignant and we fear it may be an aggressive strain of cancer. I'm so sorry."

Their world once more was plunged into turmoil and despair.

"How much pain can one family take?" cried Peter one night as he stood outside the house venting his anger on the vast black void above him.

Slowly the need to plan and prepare took over from the anguish. Evie was offered treatment but decided she wasn't prepared to suffer for what would probably be only a few months added onto her life.

Evie was nursed at home and she and Peter spent precious hours together in her final days.

"Talk about me to Michael will you, please, Peter? Keep me alive in his mind. I'd rather I lived through your lips than through letters. Tell him how much I loved him and tell him how much I loved you too. I want him to know that we really were in love."

The Guest Who Stayed: Chapter 23 – August 1960

The swell from the grey sea rocked the liner slowly from side to side as she ploughed through the featureless ocean. Emma stood on the small third class promenade deck. The cold seeped through her coat but it was better than the claustrophobic quarters in which she was forced to make this return trip across the Atlantic.

She thought back to her previous crossing, a 'bride ship' they'd called it, with hundreds of other girls like her going to the United States to join their GI husbands and sweethearts. How full of hope and excitement she'd been. How happy to leave a dismal and gloomy Britain at the end of six years of war.

Of course, people had warned her about the dangers of marrying a black GI. But Samuel had said that it would be different after the war. They had fought alongside each other, black and white together – as comrades. People would treat them as equals now – as heroes maybe.

But she was unprepared for the squalor and poverty of the township in Mississippi that was Samuel's home. A wooden shack shared with three other members of his family. No running water. A filthy shed for a toilet and no privacy. Their relationship never stood a chance.

And people were wary of her – both black and white. The blacks felt that she was an intruder, scornful of their way of life. The whites didn't know how to treat her – with the disdain they reserved for blacks or with the hatred intended for a turncoat.

Samuel couldn't find regular work and took to drug dealing. Emma and he drifted further apart. Finally, he was shot by rival dealers and died in Emma's arms.

Emma couldn't stay in the township – that was made clear to her. She managed to get work as a maid and it had taken her a year to save up for this return trip. She had thought about it endlessly. She didn't belong in America. She had no roots. When Evie's letter arrived, her mind was made up.

She pulled the crumpled letter from her pocket and read the last few lines again.

... but if fate does ever bring you back to these shores, please visit Peter and Michael to make sure they are well.

You are a strong person Emma and I believe you have a bright future. If you could share a little of that strength with Peter and Michael, it would bring me great comfort.

I wish you every happiness.

Yours forever,

Evie

Emma pushed the letter back into her pocket and pulled her coat tight. She had come to realise that her destiny lay not in America but back in the small town in England from which she had fled. But she would not be a victim – not like her mother. Her past and her future were intricately bound up with this family and she would find her roots there.

She remembered what Alice had told Evie in her letters, that when she married Jed, it was not for love but for ambition. It was a way out of the poverty and abuse she had known as a child. There was nothing wrong with ambition. It was what created success.

Spray from the cold ocean burst over the ship forcing Emma back into the cramped quarters which she would have to endure for another five days.

Peter stood in the front garden of Hope Cottage some distance from the house. Around him were the long abandoned vegetable plots that Alice and Jed had begun to cultivate and that he and Evie had inherited. It was a sunny day but a chill wind was blowing in from the North Sea.

His thoughts drifted back to the time when Jed was building the house, full of hope and ambition for Alice and himself. Within those walls, fate had dealt an uncompromising hand, one that had brought with it anger, recrimination and loss.

The machine's engine started up and Peter felt a shiver run down his spine. There was a deafening roar as the driver accelerated and the crane came slowly into view round the side of the house, a large demolition ball hanging from its boom. The crane positioned itself close to the front door and, with a deft swing of the boom, sent the wrecking ball thundering into the wall of the front bedroom. Glass from the windows shattered and masonry tumbled into a dusty pile on the front porch.

It seemed to Peter that within those crumbling walls ambition and passion had created a toxic energy that had bred deceit and betrayal, contaminating each new generation with its venomous tentacles.

Destroying the house, symbolically, put an end to the physical embodiment of this evil, though the psychological scars remained.

The wrecking ball came crashing into the roof, sending splinters of wood and tile cascading to the ground.

"Daddy, I can't see from here. What's happening?"

"I'm sorry, Michael. I got carried away with my own thoughts. Let me bring you over here," replied Peter as he took hold of Michael's wheelchair and brought him closer to where he was standing.

"Do you want to stand up? You can use your sticks if you want."

"Can you hold me up, Daddy?"

"I'll be beside you in case you fall," replied Peter, taking care as he helped Michael to his feet.

"Is this where I used to live, Daddy, when I was first born?"

And here was Michael, tangible evidence of that inherited curse.

A shattering explosion brought him back to the present. The steel wrecking ball had delivered a terminal blow to the end gable which had now crashed to the ground leaving a gaping hole in what had once been Evie's room.

"Daddy, how old was I when Mummy died? Daddy, you're not listening to me. How old was I when Mummy died?"

"I'm sorry, Michael. It was seven years ago. You were just five. Mummy was there for your fifth birthday."

"I think I can remember. Didn't you give me a car that I could sit in and pedal? Was that my fifth birthday?"

"Yes, I think you're right. I remember now, Mummy came downstairs and sat with us in the sitting room. Do you remember that, Michael?"

"Did she have reddish hair, long, down her back."

"That's right. We called it auburn. But it was sort of reddish."

The immediate months after Evie's death had been a dark time. Peter and Michael retreated into an isolated world, relying on each other for company and rejecting offers of help. People would say that Michael was wise beyond his young years. Together, Peter and Michael would visit exhibitions, museums and even art galleries, never tiring of being together. Jed and Flora would often be called upon to lend support, especially as Carters Construction was growing at a rapid pace. Post war reconstruction was well under way and Carters was involved in projects across the whole east of England. Jed had now relinquished control of the business to Peter so that he could spend more time with Flora.

But at home, behind closed doors, Peter and Michael became self sufficient, liking nothing better than to shut out the external world and bury themselves in a fantasy land of Meccano or model trains, cars and planes. People soon came to know that unannounced visits were received with cold disdain.

"Daddy, can we come and join you and Michael? We're fed up in the car. You said just to wait a few minutes."

Peter turned to see the twins, Robert and Julia, standing by the gate.

"Come on then, over here. But don't go any nearer. It's dangerous."

The twins ran over to where Peter and Michael were standing, prompting a broad grin from Michael. Peter smiled to see how they gathered round him, part protecting him and part looking up to him. The twins were five – bright, mischievous and brimming with energy.

"Daddy, what's that ball thing?" asked Julia, pointing excitedly at the wrecking ball.

"It's for knocking down the house. The crane swings the ball and it bashes down the walls."

"Why are you knocking the house down, Daddy?" demanded Robert.

"Because we're going to build something else there."

There was a resounding crash as the remaining roof plunged into the gaping void below. Demolishing the house had not been an easy decision. Jed had decided not to witness the final ignominy of his beloved house being brutally destroyed but for Peter it represented the end of a sequence of events that were now buried in the past. There were too many ghosts in the house – too many memories. It was 1960 now. There was a sense of a new age beginning, new music, new fashions and new wealth. It was time to look forward.

"Daddy, Mummy wants to come and look too. Tell her to join us."

It had been a cold and wet Sunday night seven years ago in November 1953. Peter and Michael were sitting by a roaring fire in the sitting room at Hope Cottage. The remnants of tea were spread across the table and light music drifted from a radio on the sideboard. Rain lashed at the windows and Peter pulled the curtains tight to shut out the elements. There was a knock at the door. Peter and Michael looked at each other in disbelief. No one was expected. The knock came again, this time a bit louder.

Reluctantly, Peter rose from his chair and went to the front door. He opened it to reveal a rain soaked woman standing on the porch.

"Hello. I'm Emma. You don't remember me, do you? Evie's friend. Well, actually I'm your cousin too. Can I come in and talk?"

Peter brought her into the sitting room and helped her remove her soaking outer clothes. He sat her by the fire with a fresh cup of tea.

"What do you mean, you're my cousin?"

"I thought you knew. I'm Flora's daughter. Jack was my father although I didn't know that till I was much older. I've been in America. I married a GI after the war."

Peter had known that Jack had also fathered Flora's child but in the emotional turmoil of discovering Evie's true parentage, this matter had been pushed to a remote corner of his mind.

"So why are you here? What's brought you back?" enquired Peter.

"It didn't work out. He was black. I was naive. We went to live in Mississippi. He said it would be fine after the war. He said that blacks would be treated like heroes and be given houses and jobs. Were they, like hell? They were given nothing. Same old discrimination as before. And it was the same for me. A white woman being married to a black man – well it didn't go down well over there. Then my Samuel, well he got involved in some drugs to help make ends meet and he ends up getting shot. He died in my arms in the free hospital. Well, there's nothing to keep me there in America so I worked for a year to buy a passage home. I got back to Tilbury early this morning."

"Why not go straight to your mother's?"

"First, I don't know where she lives. We kinda fell out after I learnt about my father. Second, I know she's married to Jed now and I wasn't sure how popular I'd be just turning up out of the blue. And third, I heard about Evie. She was my friend remember. We had a lot in common – even shared the same father. I felt I wanted to come here and talk to you – find out a bit about what happened – meet Michael. Evie wrote to me before she died. Will you let me read you what she said?"

"Yes, of course," said Peter.

Dear Emma,

I've got some tragic news. I'm going to die. Like my mother before me, I've been diagnosed with breast cancer and I've only got a few more months left. I know I won't see you again because you're living in America but I just wanted to thank you for your friendship when we were younger. You were always there when I needed you and I want you to know how much that meant to me.

Of course, we have something else very special in common. We share the same father. I only learned that Jack was my father a few years ago and, as you can imagine, it caused me great unhappiness knowing that I had been lied to for all those years. I understand that you learned the truth after you'd gone to America. It makes us half sisters and explains why we always felt so close.

My biggest regret is not for me, it's for Peter and Michael. I think it's going to be a struggle for them, especially having to cope with Mike's disability and the operations he's going to need. I know there's not much you can do about that in America but if fate does ever bring you back to these shores, please visit Peter and Michael to make sure they are well.

You are a strong person, Emma, and I believe you have a bright future. If you could share a little of that strength with Peter and Michael, it would bring me great comfort.

I wish you every happiness.

Yours forever,

Evie

"As I couldn't go to my mother's, I came here. I hope you don't mind."

"No, of course I don't mind," replied Peter, trying to disguise his annoyance. You'd better stay the night. You can't go anywhere in this weather."

"Mummy, over here." shouted Julia.

Peter turned to see Emma standing by the gate – no longer the drowned soul who had turned up at Hope Cottage that stormy night seven years ago but now an elegant woman, slim, dark haired and striking. She had stayed the night. The next morning she helped Peter cook breakfast and then played with Michael. Then she stayed the following night and after that she never really left. They married in late spring of 1954 and the twins were born in early 1955 – strong healthy children who brought laughter and joy into their lives. There were difficult times with Michael, innumerable operations and long stays in hospital. But in the summer of 1959 he stood for the first time and took his first steps.

"Is it safe over there?" called out Emma.

"As long as we go no nearer than here we'll be OK," shouted back Peter.

Emma joined them, putting her arms around Michael to steady him and fending off a tirade of questions from the twins. Peter put his arms around her shoulders and pulled her close.

"Are you sad?" she said to Peter. "Seeing the house demolished like this?"

"No, not really. This is the past. I'd rather live in the future. You and the children are the future. I want to let the past die in the rubble."

As they spoke, a large bulldozer rumbled onto the site. Emblazoned across the yellow paintwork in bright red lettering was the name 'CARTERS'.

"Is that one of yours, Daddy?" exclaimed Michael excitedly.

"It is, Mike. We've got four of those now. We use them for clearing sites."

"What are you going to build here, Daddy, when the house has gone?"

"It's going to be a very large shop called a supermarket – all part of the redevelopment."

"What's a supermarket?" demanded Julia.

"They've got them in America," answered Emma. "They're very large shops where you can buy all your food and all the things you need for your house. You just take what you want and put them into a large basket on wheels."

"Don't you even have to pay for them?" asked Robert incredulously.

"Yes, you've got to pay," laughed Emma, "but you don't pay till you've filled your basket. Then you pay for everything together at what they call 'the check out'."

Further conversation was drowned out by the sound of the bulldozer caving in the ground floor walls. They fell like matchsticks to join the pile of rubble that had formed in what had once been the parlour. Nothing was recognisable now of what had once been Hope Cottage.

"Come on, you lot," said Peter. That's all for now. Granny Flora and Grandpa Jed have got tea waiting for us. Let's be on our way."

Michael and the twins made their way back to the road, leaving Peter and Emma to take one last look at the remains of Hope Cottage.

"There's a lot of demons buried under that rubble," remarked Peter.

"Then leave them there," replied Emma "Let's go and explore that future you were on about." They kissed and ran to join the children. As Peter's Alvis pulled away from the place that had once been Hope Cottage, the radio was broadcasting the number one hit for that week, 20th October, 1960 – Roy Orbinson's 'Only the Lonely'.

About the author:

Roger Penfound runs his own video and media company. Before that he worked for the BBC for twenty five years in various radio and TV production jobs.

He is married with children and grandchildren and gains inspiration walking in the woods with his white retriever, Diggory.

The Guest Who Stayed is his debut novel and is based on a true story.

A note from the author:

Thank you very much for reading the Guest Who Stayed. I hope that you found it an enjoyable and rewarding experience.

You can find out more about the book and the background to the story at:

www.theguestwhostayed.com

Finally, as a self–published author, I would be very grateful if you would consider placing a review on my Amazon book page. Self–publishing places a great responsibility on the author to publicise his or her work and your help would be greatly appreciated. You can either go direct to Amazon Kindle and type in 'The Guest Who Stayed' or you can use the following link and click on the appropriate national flag.

http://authl.it/172

Kind regards

Roger Penfound

Lightning Source UK Ltd.
Milton Keynes UK
UKOW05f0613260617
304104UK00001B/261/P